Guilt's Echo

GUILT'S ECHO

A NOVEL BY

BOB PERRY

Guilt's Echo

Copyright © 2010 by William R. Perry

All rights reserved. No part of this book may be used or reproduced by any means, graphic, electronic, or mechanical, including photocopying, recording, taping, or by any information storage retrieval system without the written permission of the publisher except in the case of brief quotations embodied in critical articles and reviews.

CreateSpace
100 Enterprise Way, Suite A200
Scotts Valley, CA 95066
USA

Certain characters in this work are historical figures, and certain events portrayed did take place. However, this is a work of fiction. All other characters, names, incidents, organizations, and dialogue in this novel are either products of the author's imagination or used fictitiously.

www.bobp.biz

The sins of some men are conspicuous, pointing to judgment, but the sins of others appear later. So also good deeds are conspicuous; and even when they are not, they cannot remain hidden.

Paul's First Letter to Timothy

PART 1

THAT HARVEY GIRL

Chapter 1

"Sun's up," Samantha Harvey's elderly father coaxed. "The cow won't milk herself."

Samantha cuddled in a soft quilt made by her mother, as a cool breeze drifted through the small house. The colorful blanket created strong emotions in the young woman each morning — a reminder her loving mother was gone.

The past year had been difficult. Besides losing her mother, Samantha struggled adjusting to her new home. The drowsy girl wanted to sink into the soft feather bed and forget her troubles, but she knew her feeble father needed help with the daily chores.

"Samantha!" her father patiently called again. "Are you up, yet?"

Pretending to be alert, Samantha replied in a chipper voice, "Yes, Papa."

Samantha dressed quickly and stepped into the small kitchen to kiss her father on the cheek, as he sat at a small table.

"Good morning, Papa," she greeted cheerfully.

"The cow's already bawling," Mr. Harvey replied.

"I'm on my way," Samantha smiled.

Samantha grabbed the milk pail and headed to the barn while her old dog Blue trailed close behind. Their cow was not much of an animal but produced enough milk for Samantha to sell in town.

Samantha looked at her worn shoes and sighed audibly as she milked. Stiff cardboard coated in candle wax patched the soles, but a small hole worn on the top of the left shoe exposed her pinky toe. Samantha hoped the shoes would last until summer when she could roam barefooted and delay buying a new pair until fall. Moving the left foot under her right shoe hid the hole and Samantha knew that would have to do. After milking, she fed the chickens before heading inside for breakfast.

Mr. Harvey sat at the table finishing his oatmeal when Samantha returned. He was old enough to be her grandfather and many made that assumption. Samantha's mother had been only twenty-five when she married Mr. Harvey, a fifty-eight year old widower at the time. Mr. Harvey came to central Oklahoma during the land runs, and he had been the principal at the school where Samantha's mother taught. Most of Samantha's life, her father farmed rented land subsidized by a small pension. Mr. Harvey was now an ailing seventy-six years old with an eighteen-year-old daughter preparing to graduate with the class of 1916.

"You're a good girl, Sammie," Mr. Harvey smiled. "Better have some oatmeal."

Mr. Harvey called his daughter Sammie, and it always caused her to smile. Samantha called her father Papa, and the greeting generated a similar reaction.

"Are you ready for your special day?" Mr. Harvey asked with a gleam in his eye.

"What do you mean?" Samantha asked coyly.

"Graduation, you silly girl," Mr. Harvey reminded. "You graduate today."

Without looking up from her breakfast Samantha replied, "It's just another day."

"Another day!" her father roared. "It's the start of a new day — there's nothing as exciting as a graduation, an end and a beginning at the same time."

"I suppose," Samantha shrugged.

Studying his daughter for a few moments, Mr. Harvey said, "There's more to school than books and lessons, Sammie."

"I know."

"You know," Mr. Harvey huffed. "Won't there be some grand parties and shenanigans with your friends tonight?"

"Probably," Samantha sighed, "but I—"

"Surely there's at least one young man that's caught your eye," Mr. Harvey interrupted. "I'm sure more than one young lad has noticed you."

"I doubt that, and I really need to go," Samantha defended. "I'll have to walk fast as it is now."

"Nonsense," Mr. Harvey smiled. "The last day for a senior is practically a day off."

"Not for me," Samantha assured.

Samantha's father meant well, but she was uncomfortable with his prying questions. She was no closer to finding a husband than when they moved to Chandler, which she knew concerned her father. Returning to her room, Samantha quickly brushed her sandy-brown hair and tried to straighten her faded flannel dress. She frowned again as she noticed her worn shoe, but made herself smile as she left the room, knowing her smile made her father happy. Grabbing a scarf for her shoulder-length hair, Samantha headed out the door hoping to avoid further conversation about her social life.

From his chair, Mr. Harvey shouted, "I'll see you at graduation tonight!"

Samantha stopped at the door a moment before saying, "I wasn't planning on going to the ceremony. The school will mail my diploma."

Mr. Harvey struggled to pull himself up from his chair as he stepped toward Samantha to say firmly, "I'll be there. Surely you don't want to break an old man's heart."

Shamed into submission, Samantha said, "I'll see you this evening at graduation."

"Bye, Sammie," her father smiled.

With a reactive grin, Samantha walked quickly toward school. The warm, muggy air foreshadowed the approaching summer. Bright, morning sunshine behind her contrasted with dark clouds on the western horizon, and she wondered if she would get wet on her walk back from school. Samantha crossed a small footbridge over the trickle of a creek called Indian Springs east of Chandler and noticed her worn left shoe again. The unsightly shoe reminded Samantha how much she did not want to go to graduation. Samantha did not have the time or money to buy new footwear today, so she would have to camouflage the old shoe as best she could.

The town of Chandler sat on a high point in the center of Lincoln County on two hills with a small valley between where the railroad tracks ran from south to north. In the distance, Samantha saw the towering courthouse in the heart of town. The school was on the other side of the courthouse, and she had to hurry as she picked up the hem of her skirt to walk more quickly.

Samantha had no time for distractions this morning, but as she walked by the train depot on the eastern edge of town, she saw a tall, slender young man she had noticed several times since moving to town. He appeared to be in his early twenties and was somewhat handsome in an awkward sort of way, but something about him always made her uneasy.

She tried to walk by unnoticed, but the young man said smugly, "Good morning."

As he nodded to acknowledge her, his eyes fixated on the hole in her left shoe. The young man stared long enough to be conspicuous, before looking back at Samantha. He said nothing, but words could not have been as insulting as his condescending look. The humiliated Samantha found the composure to smile at the stunned young man. With a slight tilt of her head, she marched away and left him standing alone. When he was out of sight, she frowned to herself and walked quickly, eager to hide the worn shoes under her desk at school.

Samantha's past year had been challenging. She was new to Chandler and thought the town possessed an unmerited self-importance. Students, merchants, and citizens had a community pride she did not understand. She wanted to belong, but her classmates had attended school together for many years, and it seemed difficult to be included. The isolation reminded Samantha how much she missed her mother.

Samantha Harvey lived on the outskirts of town and felt as if she existed on the fringe of everything else. She often heard whispers of "that Harvey girl" from strangers she had never met. The uncomfortable tone of familiarity and awkward glances were impossible to ignore. She did not know what the unwanted notoriety meant, but something about her was different, and she had felt it ever since moving to town.

Samantha walked past the courthouse taking a moment to look down Eighth Street at the homes on Silk Stocking Row — Chandler's most prestigious neighborhood, located on the edge of the hill looking across a valley west of town. She stopped most mornings to look at the fine houses, wondering what life was like in the part of town where whispers would not matter. She did not have time to daydream about Silk Stocking Row this morning, however, and scampered down the hill to the high school. Samantha moved quickly to her classroom and slipped behind the safety of her desk, hoping no one would notice her tattered shoes.

One more day, she thought to herself. I can make it one more day.

CHAPTER 2

"CAROLINE!" WOODY CARLSON WHISPERED loudly trying to attract the short girl's attention.

Caroline Kendall looked up from her desk in the stuffy classroom to smile sweetly, and replied, "Hey, Woody."

Class would start soon, and Woody Carlson desperately wanted to speak discreetly with Caroline, hoping to avoid attention that would lead to inevitable teasing from his classmates. The chaotic shuffle of feet and chairs sliding on the wood floor made it impossible for his whispers to be heard, so he moved quickly to a seat next to Caroline.

Caroline Kendall had known Woody for as long as she could remember. Their families lived on top of a high ridge known as Silk Stocking Row located close to the stately courthouse. The neighborhood featured fine homes housing some of Chandler's most prominent citizens. Caroline's sweet disposition caused her to make friends easily. She was a small girl with delicate features and refined manners. Two deep dimples framed a restrained smile, and tufts of silky brown hair were usually tucked under a bonnet. Woody and Caroline started school together twelve years earlier and would graduate this evening.

"You got a minute?" Woody asked nervously.

Woody was a skinny boy with wavy auburn hair and large ears that seemed to overwhelm his face. Always a pleasant young man, he displayed a calm demeanor and was rarely as rattled as he seemed today. Caroline thought he might want to ask her to the senior social, but she knew that invitation would be awkward.

"Sure," Caroline replied with a slight tone of concern, "but class is about to start."

"It'll only take a minute," Woody assured, as he quickly looked around to see if any classmates were close enough to hear their conversation.

Caroline listened with some angst as Woody asked, "How well do you know Samantha Harvey?"

Breathing an unnoticed sigh of relief, Caroline smiled slyly and said, "About as well as anyone, I guess."

Caroline's answer was an overstatement. Samantha Harvey came to Chandler High School for her senior year from somewhere in the country. The girl was an enigma to her classmates. No one knew much about her or from where she came. Samantha was a pleasant girl who got along with almost everyone without anyone really knowing her. After twelve years of school, most of the students of Chandler High School had developed friendships that did not include Samantha Harvey.

Caroline sat by Samantha in several classes and felt guilty she did not know her better. Socially, Samantha kept to herself, but in the classroom, she was smart, outspoken, and candid—especially for a girl.

"Why do you ask?" Caroline grinned, already suspecting the answer.

Samantha Harvey kept to herself but had a special quality that made people, particularly boys, notice. She was an unremarkable-looking young woman, if her features were evaluated separately. Her lightly freckled face, sandy-brown hair, and plain, unadorned eyes contrasted with an infectious smile and demeanor, which radiated unmistakable poise. Samantha was tall and almost lanky, but she carried herself as if she did not care what others thought. Her clothes sometimes bordered on silly, and she often wore trousers under her dresses because she had a long walk to school. Any other young woman might have been embarrassed at the appearance of poverty, but Samantha Harvey seemed comfortable with herself and her natural beauty, which added to her intrigue.

"Do you want to ask Samantha to the social?" Caroline teased as Woody hesitated to answer directly.

Woody's noticeable blush at Caroline's deduction of his interest in their pretty classmate answered her question.

"I was just wondering," Woody finally whispered back in a tone indicating his desire to keep their conversation private. "You know...if she was planning to go to the social."

Not wanting to let Woody off the hook so easily, Caroline feigned pouting and said, "I should be offended. I thought you were going to ask me to go."

Woody was not distracted by Caroline's playful mockery as he said, "I would, but David Simpson will always be your guy. Samantha seems interesting, and I thought she might like some company and...maybe she'd be desperate enough to sit with me."

Caroline regretted teasing Woody and said seriously, "Any girl would be proud to be with you. If David doesn't come see me soon, I may claim you myself."

The commanding voice of Mr. Fleming boomed from the front of the classroom interrupting their conversation, as he said, "You think this is the last day and that all of the exams are finished, but we still have work to do."

Mr. Fleming liked to lecture about life, responsibility, and citizenship for the seniors at the end of the term. The students had enough fear of their teacher that they would not challenge him, as they turned to listen.

With a quick look over her shoulder and a demure smile, Caroline said to Woody, "Don't worry about Samantha...I'll talk to her during the picnic."

CHAPTER 3

JONATHAN KENDALL ARRIVED at the train depot with some anxiety. David Simpson returned to town this morning. He was eager to see his old friend, but Jonathan suspected the homecoming might renew old tensions, since David had been a special friend to Jonathan's sister Caroline.

Jonathan was tall and slender with a serious demeanor and reserved smile. He looked to be in deep thought often and measured his words carefully. David had been his friend since Jonathan's father moved to Chandler in 1903 with big dreams and sound business sense. Jonathan's father, John Kendall, came to Oklahoma from western Michigan soon after the land runs and began shrewdly buying and leasing land in Lincoln County. By 1916, John Kendall had achieved financial and social success, and his family lived on Silk Stocking Row in a stately home perched on the ridge on the west of town. The twenty-two-year-old Jonathan was the eldest of three Kendall children and worked under the tutelage of his father in the family's cotton gin.

The train depot was almost vacant as Jonathan looked at his dusty brown shoes and wished he had taken the time to polish them the night before. He had wanted to match his friend's dapper dress and knew David Simpson would never arrive in town with shoes looking so shabby. As Jonathan tormented himself at his fashion failure, he glanced up in time to see the pretty Harvey girl walking up from Indian Springs. The girl was a classmate of his sister Caroline. Jonathan had seen her around town, but he had never been introduced.

"Good morning," he had greeted clumsily, as he attempted to be overly cheerful.

Naturally shy, Jonathan instinctively looked at the ground to avoid eye contact. He once again lamented his dusty footwear before noticing the young woman's shoes, which were splattered with the morning dew. Her tattered shoes made him feel apologetic for worrying about his own footwear. Before he could think of anything to say, the attractive young woman smiled critically and walked away without breaking stride.

The distant whistle of the approaching train interrupted Jonathan's angst about his awkward encounter with the girl and a smile eased on his face at the thought of seeing David Simpson again.

"Over here!" Jonathan shouted, as David Simpson stepped off the train.

Jonathan Kendall had waited that morning with conflicting emotions. The two young men had been the best of friends as boys. David moved to Oklahoma City to work in the law office of James Robertson as a clerk the past year. Jonathan, always outdone by his more charismatic friend, enjoyed being out from under David's shadow more than he would have thought.

"Jonathan!" David shouted back.

Dropping his bag, David greeted his friend with a vigorous handshake that evolved into a hug. David Simpson was slightly shorter than average with trim, blonde hair and sharp inquisitive eyes. Although short in stature, he was tall with confidence and presented a commanding presence. Dressed in a light-colored linen suit and wearing a finely woven straw hat, he looked as if the train platform was his stage. Jonathan could not help noticing David's shoes were flawlessly polished.

"It's great to see you," David smiled, as he stepped back to look at his childhood friend.

"Good to see you," Jonathan said with a nod. "How was your trip?"

"Stuffy," David replied. "A lady in a big hat sat in front of me and refused to lower the window."

"Caroline'll be glad to see you," Jonathan said timidly.

Jonathan watched carefully for a reaction. David Simpson had been his sister Caroline's beau for several years, and the Kendall family expected an engagement before David left for Oklahoma City. When David went away the year before, however, he had left things with Caroline unclear.

David Simpson sighed, "It'll be great to see Caroline."

After a hesitation David asked, "How is she?"

"Busy," Jonathan answered, still looking intently at David. "All the senior stuff is happening this week."

With a broad smile, David said, "Remember our senior week?"

"Sure," Jonathan replied with a grin, recalling his graduation.

"We were the kings of this place," David stated. "I came back for the alumni banquet."

"Is that all?" Jonathan asked.

Taking a moment to size up his old friend, David answered, "No, I'm moving back to Chandler."

"That's great!" Jonathan smiled. "Did you get tired of the city?"

"I needed a change—needed to get back home," David stated.

"What are you going to do?" Jonathan asked, although he really wanted to ask if David had come back for Caroline.

David looked slyly at Jonathan as if he knew what his friend really wanted to know and answered, "I've got an opportunity."

"Chandler's full of opportunity," Jonathan shrugged. "What are you going to do?"

"We'll have time to discuss that later," David assured. "Let's get to town."

"Looks like it might rain," Jonathan said, as he watched thunderheads build in the west.

Looking at the billowing clouds, David confidently replied, "It won't rain—not on my homecoming."

CHAPTER 4

CAROLINE KENDALL LISTENED TO Mr. Fleming's lecture, but her mind wandered nostalgically. Today would be her last time in class with the friends she had become so comfortable being around the past twelve years. Mr. Fleming's class would be the only thing resembling academic work this last day. The afternoon would be filled with the senior picnic and graduation activities. There would be an alumni banquet, and the senior social afterwards, but this would be her last time in the classroom. Graduation was exciting, but part of her wished she were back in grammar school.

Mr. Fleming addressed the class passionately about personal responsibility, citizenship, and principles of success. Caroline looked intently at her instructor but thought about Samantha Harvey. Of all the girls at Chandler High School, Samantha was the most intelligent and outspoken. Some would have said she was one of the prettiest girls, but Samantha did not seem the type of girl to worry about her appearance. Caroline decided to use Woody Carlson's inquiry as an opportunity to get to know her better.

"Remember students," Mr. Fleming preached. "Doing the right thing's not always easy, but it's always the right thing to do. Congratulations on your graduation. I wish all of you the best."

Mr. Fleming's remarks were heartfelt, but as soon as he concluded, the classroom roared with noise as students clamored for the door. Caroline spotted Samantha Harvey exiting the room and moved quickly to catch her before she escaped.

"Samantha!" Caroline greeted above the confusion.

For a moment, it seemed as if she had not heard Caroline, but after one more tentative step, Samantha stopped and replied, "Hello, Caroline."

Moving close enough to cause Samantha to take a step back, Caroline asked, "Are you going to the social tonight?"

Samantha had not expected the question and awkwardly answered, "No."

A disappointed Caroline squealed, "You have to!"

"Why?" a blunt Samantha answered back.

Samantha, aggravated for not being more diplomatic, frowned and wished her response had sounded less argumentative.

Caroline was not discouraged, however, and eagerly replied, "The social is…well, the social is something that we've been looking forward to all year. You simply must come."

Samantha instinctively thought of an explanation to avoid the social and said, "I don't have anything to wear and my father needs me at home."

Samantha hoped this excuse would end the matter, but she could see the disappointment in Caroline's face. Although Samantha had limited interaction with the short, spunky girl, she did not like telling a half-truth. Samantha's father would want her to attend the party, and there were certainly others in the class without a fancy party dress.

Samantha quickly added to her justification by saying, "I was going to skip the picnic and try to find some shoes for graduation."

Caroline's head began gently shaking before she pleasantly said, "You can't miss the picnic. That's when we get to torture the poor juniors. We get to dress them any way we like. It's great fun."

Seeing Samantha was not convinced Caroline sincerely added, "I know you're new here...and...well...I guess some of our traditions seem silly. The year's gone by so fast, and I hate that I haven't got to know you better. We can remedy that at the picnic. You don't want to come back in thirty years for a reunion and not know anybody."

Caroline's thoughtful manner was an irresistible force, and Samantha could barely believe she was hearing herself say, "I guess a picnic would be fun."

Caroline squealed with delight at her persuasion and replied, "Of course it will, and the social will be even more fun —"

"I really don't have anything to wear to a party," Samantha interrupted.

"I have plenty of clothes," Caroline chirped. "We'll make you the belle of the ball."

Samantha looked suspiciously at Caroline and could not help smirking.

"What?" Caroline innocently asked.

"I appreciate the offer, but I'm nearly a head taller than you, and you're...well you're more filled out," Samantha explained. "I'll look even sillier in your clothes than in my old flannel dress."

Caroline laughed kindly and replied, "I wasn't thinking of you wearing one of my dresses. That would cause a scandal with your knees showing. My little sister Augusta is about your height, and I think we can make one of her outfits look stunning."

"I don't know," Samantha muttered, desperately trying to think of another excuse.

"I know something that might change your mind," Caroline grinned. "There's a boy that would give anything to sit with you tonight."

Samantha tended to be candid and outspoken in her conversations, but this revelation by Caroline Kendall left her speechless. Her mind quickly thought of boys in the school that might be interested in her.

Samantha tried to contain her curiosity, not wanting to sound like one of the senseless girls she had secretly scoffed at the past year.

"Who is it?" Samantha finally asked, as she hoped her facial gestures did not betray to Caroline how silly she felt asking such a juvenile question.

Caroline did not notice any of Samantha's angst as she blurted out, "Woody Carlson!"

Samantha did not know what to think. She had never had any conversations with Woody and had never really thought about him.

"Woody?" Samantha whispered, almost to herself.

"Woody!" Caroline excitedly whispered back, trying to keep their now juicy conversation more private.

Samantha did not say anything more, and after a few seconds Caroline said, "Woody's a very nice boy. I've known him for years."

Samantha regained some composure and replied, "Yes, he always seems very polite."

"Very polite," Caroline confirmed in a tone of voice that reminded Samantha of a salesman in a store, "and funny...at least after you get to know him a little better."

"I don't know," Samantha lamented.

"It'll be so much fun," Caroline pleaded. "There'll be a band and great food. I helped with the decorations myself. Woody really is a nice boy."

Samantha did not respond.

"It would mean a lot if you'd just sit with him," Caroline pleaded. "It's not like your marrying him or anything, but...a girl could do much worse."

Samantha was not convinced until Caroline begged one more time and said, "It'll be fun. We can go together to the picnic and get to know each other better. Later we can go to my house and work on a dress for you. My sister Augusta is almost exactly your size. Mother will fix a big supper. Then we'll be ready for graduation and the social."

Caroline lived in one of the houses on Silk Stocking Row. Samantha was an unpretentious girl, but she had wanted to glimpse inside one of the extravagant homes since moving to Chandler. Caroline had been considerate to include her in the class activities, and there was an authentic kindness to the small girl that Samantha admired.

"Thank you, Caroline," Samantha finally replied. "It sounds like great fun. Do I need to bring anything for the picnic?"

"Nothing but yourself," Caroline giggled in glee. "We'll go to my house after the picnic and start getting ready for tonight. I have a feeling it's going to be special, and we may be starting a great friendship."

CHAPTER 5

As JONATHAN KENDALL AND David Simpson walked from the train depot toward town, the dark clouds from the morning drifted north. With the bright sun to their back, Jonathan smiled at David's bold prediction that it could not rain on his homecoming. The city of Chandler sat on a hill, making it easily visible from miles around, but the train depot was located in a low valley dividing the city from south to north. The two young men were halfway up the hill before they saw the courthouse with its clock tower rising above the other buildings.

"The town's changed a little since you left," Jonathan suggested.

"A little, but not much," David assessed. "It's one of the things I missed. The more things change the more this place seems to stay the same."

"I guess," Jonathan replied. "You want to drop these bags at you mother's house?"

"Sure," David said, "and then I have an appointment."

David Simpson's parents lived in a modest house a few blocks from the train depot. David hugged his mother but seemed distracted. Jonathan excused himself from the homecoming and started walking back to his office at the cotton gin.

"Wait up!" David yelled when Jonathan had only taken a few steps. "I'll walk with you."

"Where to?" Jonathan asked.

"Just to town," David smiled. "Maybe you can show me where you work."

"Sure," Jonathan shrugged.

The city streets surrounding the courthouse were paved with brick from the old brick factory that operated in town before statehood. The brick-paved streets were about the only thing surviving a tornado in 1897. Almost all of the buildings were constructed after the storm, including the fine homes adorning Eighth Street on Silk Stocking Row.

The main street called Manvel ran through town north and south, parallel to the train tracks. The numbered streets were laid out east to west. Most homes were down the hill or across the tracks to the east, but the finest homes in town, including the Kendall home, were on Eighth Street close to the courthouse.

David and Jonathan walked past stores on Manvel including McAleer's Drug Store, Hood's Jewelry Store, and Hellman's Department Store, where employees busily prepared a front window display. The buildings across from the courthouse included Hoyt Abstracting, Dr. Adams' Clinic, and several law offices. The First National Bank and the Union Bank were on opposite corners to each other with several offices upstairs, including a dentist office. The Downing Lumber Company was located across the street across from the St. Cloud Hotel and The Kendall Cotton Gin was down the hill, close to the southern edge of town.

As the two young men approached the Kendall Cotton Gin, David said, "Here's my appointment."

"Here?" Jonathan questioned. "With my father?"

David nodded slyly, as he opened the door to let Jonathan enter first. The customer area to the Kendall Cotton Gin was utilitarian, but neat. Freddy Fletcher, a man Mr. Kendall hired to collect rents, sell seed, and help with the ginning of cotton during harvest time, sat at a small desk in the corner chomping on the stub of a cigar.

"Hello, Mr. Fletcher," Jonathan greeted.

"Hey," Mr. Fletcher grunted back.

Freddy Fletcher was a short German man with a gruff disposition, but a shrewd mind. He had worked for Mr. Kendall for several years. He had a broad round face, a pot-belly, and thick, strong forearms, which indicated he had not been a stranger to hard work before becoming Mr. Kendall's right hand man. Jonathan headed past the surly Mr. Fletcher to his father's office in the back.

"There you are," Mr. Kendall barked at hearing Jonathan enter the office. "Work around here won't get done any sooner just because you get here later."

Mr. Kendall was a distinguished-looking man with graying temples, a thick mustache, and an air of purpose to him. Cordial and friendly, he still had an authoritarian tone to his voice, which dared anyone to challenge him — especially his only son, Jonathan.

Continuing to study his ledgers without looking up, Mr. Kendall asked, "Where have you been? We still open at eight o'clock, don't we?"

"Yes, sir," Jonathan apologized. "I went to the train station to meet David."

"David's a capable young man," Mr. Kendall asserted. "I'm sure he can manage without you holding his hand."

"I probably could have," David Simpson interjected, "but it was nice to have Jonathan's soft hands to guide me here."

"David!" Mr. Kendall exploded, as he quickly rose from his desk to greet the young man.

Jonathan had studied his father for years and believed he understood him very well. Mr. Kendall was a calculating man with little time for nonsense. He provided well for his family, served on the business committee at the Presbyterian Church, and had turned down several requests to run for mayor of the city. Everyone Jonathan knew, including himself, treated Mr. Kendall with respect bordering on fear. The one exception seemed to be David Simpson and to a lesser extent, Jonathan's two sisters. Mr. Kendall had long been partial to David Simpson, who once courted Caroline and was the only person Jonathan knew that seemed to have permission or the courage to tease his father.

"Why didn't you tell me you brought David here?" Mr. Kendall scolded his son.

Without giving Jonathan a chance to explain, Mr. Kendall grabbed David affectionately by both shoulders and said, "It's good to see you, David."

"Good to see you too, sir," David replied while grasping Mr. Kendall's hand to shake it vigorously.

Looking at his son, Mr. Kendall said, "Now this is how you shake hands, Jonathan — like you got the world by the horns."

Jonathan smiled and nodded slightly. He had grown accustomed to having his father compare him to David Simpson over the years.

"I'm glad you took my offer," Mr. Kendall gleamed.

"Sounded like a good opportunity," David replied.

"Opportunity indeed," Mr. Kendall affirmed, "and I bet the chance to see Caroline more often sweetened the deal a little."

Jonathan cringed at this statement. He knew David had been lukewarm at the idea of a romance with his sister from time to time.

"A little," David smiled. "How is Caroline?"

"She'll be doing great when she knows you're back in town," Mr. Kendall boasted.

"You haven't told her I'm coming back?" David asked.

"No," Mr. Kendall answered. "I thought it would be a great surprise for her graduation."

"I can't wait to see Caroline again," David affirmed with more enthusiasm than he showed earlier at the train station.

"Are you ready to get to work?" Mr. Kendall asked. "I've cleared the office by mine for you."

"That would be great," David replied, "but I thought maybe I'd get unpacked today and get settled back into the old house. I'll start tomorrow, if that's okay?"

"See what a go-getter he is?" Mr. Kendall said to his son. "Tomorrow's a Saturday, and he's eager to start."

Jonathan nearly burst into laughter when his father turned back to David Simpson and said, "Jonathan and I were going to take Saturday off, but we'll come in to help get you started."

Jonathan knew his old friend David Simpson well enough to know Saturday work had not been his plan, but without blinking David said, "That would be wonderful. I'll see you then."

"You'll see us before then," Mr. Kendall stated. "You're coming to the house for supper tonight before Caroline's graduation. I insist."

"No need to insist," David smiled. "I wouldn't miss a supper fixed by Mrs. Kendall for anything."

CHAPTER 6

"I TOLD YOU THE picnic would be fun," Caroline giggled, as she skipped back to the shade of the tree where Samantha sat in the cool grass with her worn shoes hidden under her skirt.

"Did you win?" Samantha asked, as she had watched classmates playing a game.

"Heavens no," Caroline confessed. "I just tried to stay out of the way of the ball, but it's fun watching the boys show off. You should've played."

"Wouldn't want to show up any of our fearless young men," Samantha sarcastically replied.

"Did you just make a joke?" Caroline smiled.

Samantha blushed without replying for a moment and then said, "Thank you, Caroline."

"What for?" Caroline asked.

"For inviting me to the picnic," Samantha explained.

"Everyone's invited," Caroline said, "juniors and seniors."

"Thank you for making me feel welcomed," Samantha added. "This has been one of the best days I've had in a while."

"I'm just glad you came," Caroline grinned. "I would have hated to miss this chance to know you better. I feel somewhat selfish for not making the effort sooner."

"I'm not the easiest person to get to know," Samantha sighed. "It's been a hard year."

"Your mother?"

Samantha nodded, "We lived in the country in this perfect little house with a green meadow and wild flowers like a painting you'd hang on the wall. Mother got sick, and Papa sold the place to try to take care of her. We couldn't have taken care of the place anyway, but a part of me wishes to go back."

"I admire you, Samantha," Caroline said.

"Why?"

"You're smart and you don't mind speaking your mind, even to the boys," Caroline explained. "I remember when you spoke up in class about needing a suffrage amendment. You must have known that wasn't going to be popular with everyone, but I thought it brave."

"I don't ever feel brave," Samantha said.

"That makes you even more brave," Caroline reasoned. "You're willing to take a stand even when it's uncomfortable. I could never do it."

"Sure you can," Samantha encouraged. "I've sat by you in class enough to know you're as smart as anyone. You just need to be more assertive."

Shaking her head Caroline said, "You're like my sister, Augusta. Believe me, she doesn't hesitate speaking her mind. I like to get along with everyone and not cause any disruptions. I doubt I would stand up against anything. That's my weakness."

"I wish that was my weakness," Samantha lamented.

"What are you going to do after graduation?" Caroline asked.

Samantha laughed sarcastically and said, "You're talking about me being brave, and I've been too much of a coward to tell anyone what I really want to do."

"Oh, please tell," Caroline coaxed.

After a slight hesitation, Samantha removed a crumpled brochure from her pocket.

"I would like to become a pharmacist," Samantha timidly revealed. "Look at the brochure it says, 'the work is clean, pleasant, and agreeable: and women are particularly adapted to it.'"

Caroline studied the brochure before skeptically saying, "I've never heard of a woman pharmacist."

"There's got to be a first," Samantha said in a tone seeking some affirmation.

"Maybe," Caroline admitted. "What does your father think?"

Samantha sighed audibly and replied, "I haven't told him, and I know it's not what he wants."

"What does he want?"

"He would like to see me married, of course. Papa never says anything, but he's—well my father is older than most. I think he worries about me. My mother was a teacher, and we've talked a little about me going to the Normal School to become a teacher, but I really don't see how I could afford to do either. I think it's been a strain on my father just putting me through high school."

Samantha wished to change the subject so she asked, "How about you?"

"I've thought about teaching, but—" Caroline hesitated a second before saying. "I hope to be married soon."

"To who?" Samantha asked. "I haven't seen you with anyone special."

"My David," Caroline revealed wistfully. "He moved to Oklahoma City, but I keep in touch with letters, although I write ten for every one he sends back."

"What's he like?" Samantha asked.

Caroline glowed as she said, "David's perfect...in every way. He's handsome, bold, witty...my father loves him."

"Are you going to play Red Rover?" Woody Carlson interrupted.

"Sure," Caroline quickly replied.

"Hurry," Woody encouraged, as he looked anxiously at Samantha. "We're choosing teams now."

"Let's go," Caroline said, as she stood up.

"Play without me," Samantha replied.

With her hands on her hips, Caroline stubbornly said, "You haven't moved from this shade all afternoon."

"Isn't Red Rover a child's game?" Samantha asked.

"You'll see," Caroline winked coyly. "I won't take no for an answer."

Samantha slowly rose from her grassy seat and followed Caroline. She did not know the attraction of Red Rover, but she quickly learned her petite friend with china doll features had a quiet stubbornness that was hard to resist.

CHAPTER 7

"When did you decide to hire David?" Jonathan asked after his friend had left the office.

Without looking up from his ledgers, Mr. Kendall said, "A month ago."

"You didn't think to tell me?" Jonathan questioned.

"It didn't concern you," Mr. Kendall answered, as he stopped to look at his son.

Jonathan stared at his father without saying a word.

"Look, Jonathan," Mr. Kendall said in an instructing voice. "You're doing well enough, but you still have a lot to learn about this business. David Simpson has—gumption. He's got a certain audacity that frankly you're lacking."

Sensing he had offended his son, Mr. Kendall added, "You have your strengths, Jonathan. You're level headed, mostly responsible, but I can't see you collecting accounts on some of these people that have been riding us for months. This business is a lot more than ginning the cotton at harvest. We have an inventory of land to manage. We have seed and supplies to sell the farmers. We have to maximize our assets. That's our business. We're building something here, and David can help."

"Caroline has nothing to do with this?" Jonathan asked.

Agitated at his son's questioning, Mr. Kendall replied, "Caroline has everything to do with it. I had business in Oklahoma City a few months ago and ran into David. I invited him to lunch. The conversation led to Caroline and David's desire to get back to Chandler and take a wife."

"David said he wanted to marry Caroline?" Jonathan quizzed.

"It was implied in our conversation," Mr. Kendall continued. "David isn't making enough as a clerk to support a wife, so I decided we needed some help in our business."

Jonathan stepped closer to his father and said in lower tone, "Have you talked to Caroline?"

Confused, Mr. Kendall said, "I don't know what that has to do with anything. Caroline's made it plain she's fond of David."

"When David left town, it hurt Caroline," Jonathan observed. "She may not have the same feelings—"

"What do feelings have to do with anything?" Mr. Kendall roared. "It's a good match. I approve."

"We're living in the twentieth century, Father!" Jonathan exclaimed. "You can't make business deals involving your daughter without her knowledge!"

"Don't use that tone with me," Mr. Kendall warned. "It's my business and my daughter. I can manage things just fine. Besides, you're not one to give advice on romance. Have you found a girl, I'd approve of? No! Do you have any prospects? Again no! If I could hire a woman to fit your fancy, I'd have to expand the business even more!"

Mr. Kendall's frustration at his oldest son's delay in starting a family had existed since Jonathan returned from college, but this was the first time the conflict had been verbalized. Jonathan knew a continuation of this argument with his father would have no good end.

With a cynical smile, Jonathan stepped away from his father and headed to the door.

"Where are you going?" Mr. Kendall asked in a more diplomatic tone.

"Looks like I'm working tomorrow," Jonathan said. "I'm taking my leisure time today. I'll see you at supper."

Jonathan left his father in the office with Freddy Fletcher and headed up the street still confused about David Simpson's role in the family's business.

CHAPTER 8

"RED ROVER, RED ROVER send Lou Berta on over!" the seniors of Chandler High School chanted across the grassy field.

Tiny Lou Berta Cassidy took the challenge and ran toward the line of classmates, who were grasping hands to catch her. Lou Berta could have been Caroline Kendall's sister. Both girls were short in stature with pleasant dispositions and doll-like faces, which were creamy white with rose-colored cheeks and delicate, refined lips.

The game Red Rover was a simple children's game that involved two lines of people holding hands and challenging players from the opposite side to run into the line trying to break through. Samantha soon understood why her classmates liked playing the game. Many of the students maneuvered to hold hands with a sweetheart without the chaperons complaining. Lou Berta looked like she might lunge between two of the boys, but at the last moment she veered toward Samantha and Caroline. The slightly built girl would have had no chance of breaking through the athletic boys, and Samantha was surprised how light Lou Berta was as she glided into the grasp of Samantha and Caroline.

"Got'cha!" Caroline squealed as Lou Berta fell into her outstretched arm with little force.

Lou Berta smiled and took her place in the line between Samantha and Caroline.

"That wasn't much of an effort," Caroline teased.

"Oh well," Lou Berta replied pleasantly. "I thought I would like this side better anyway."

Small girls like Lou Berta and Caroline had made many trips between the two lines of classmates because they were slightly built and amiable.

"I thought you'd let the boys catch you," Caroline whispered.

"I've already been caught twice," Lou Berta giggled. "I wanted to talk to you."

"How did you know you wouldn't break through Samantha and me?" Caroline asked.

"I didn't try very hard," Lou Berta grinned. "My mother told me David Simpson was back in town."

"What?" Caroline exclaimed. "Are you sure?"

Lou Berta nodded mischievously while Caroline looked back toward town strangely.

"You don't seem too excited," Lou Berta noted. "I thought you'd be delighted."

"I am," Caroline assured. "I'm just surprised David didn't tell me was coming. I hoped he would come back for the alumni celebration, but I'd about given up on that."

"Have patience," Lou Berta encouraged. "That's what my mother always preaches."

Smiling politely, Caroline said, "It'll be wonderful to see David again…it'll be worth the wait."

"Red rover, red rover…send Samantha on over!" two boys yelled from across the field.

"Huh?" Samantha muttered as Caroline and Lou Berta smiled playfully.

"They want you to try to break through," Caroline giggled.

Only two boys were left on the opposite side: Nathan McCarthy, an excitable boy who was one of the youngest members of the class, and Woodrow Carlson. The two boys waited eagerly for Samantha to run into their arms.

Letting go of Caroline's hand, Samantha said, "I don't want to do that."

"You have to," Caroline explained. "It's how the game's played."

Samantha did not look convinced as the always-positive Lou Berta added, "You can do it Samantha. If you break through, we win and the game is over."

Samantha sighed slightly as she studied the two boys grinning impishly less than twenty yards away.

"It'll be a thrill for them," Caroline teased. "It might be their only chance of touching a girl today!"

With a coy smile at Caroline's assessment, Samantha began trotting effortlessly toward the two anxious boys. The two boys were not the most athletic students in the class, but both were taller than Samantha and looked capable of preventing her from breaking through especially at the easy trot with which she approached. Both boys grinned with confidence until Samantha quickly accelerated when she was within two steps causing Nathan to lose his grip. A more resolute Woody grabbed Samantha by the waist to hold her, but the girl's sudden burst of speed caused him to lose balance. The determined Woody continued to hold on as the two tumbled to the soft grass.

An explosion of laughter erupted from the whole class. Samantha believed she could not be more embarrassed until she looked over to see the humiliated Woody awkwardly sprawled on the ground.

Samantha's embarrassment quickly turned to empathy, as she rose to her knees and asked, "Are you all right?"

A stunned Woody could only mumble, "Uh-huh."

"That's how you win the game!" a gleeful Caroline greeted playfully, as she ran to Samantha. "That will show the boys who the bosses are around here."

The class tired of playing the game and quickly diverted their attention to other activities. Samantha jumped to her feet and unintentionally embarrassed Woody further by offering to help him up.

By that time, Caroline was by Samantha's side to say, "You better take her hand Woody."

Woody still lying on the ground was looking at the open toe of Samantha's torn shoe. Noticing him staring at the shoe, Samantha quickly moved the foot gracefully behind her ankle. The polite boy did not say anything, but he was further worried that he had accidentally offended the girl he had wanted so much to meet. Flustered, he quickly rose to his feet and stood awkwardly.

"You better ask now," Caroline coaxed.

"Huh?" Woody stammered.

"Remember," Caroline replied. "What we talked about."

"Oh, right," Woody finally said as he sheepishly looked at Samantha and desperately attempted to regain some level of poise. "Could you...I mean would you be...what I'm trying to say is —"

"Woody wants to know if you'll go to the party with him tonight," Caroline explained.

Samantha had not expected the question and looked unsure for a moment before saying, "That would be nice."

"Really?" a surprised Woody gasped.

"Really," Samantha assured.

"That's...that's just swell," Woody beamed. "I'll...well, I guess I'll see you then...at the social tonight."

"I'll see you," Samantha affirmed.

Woody looked as if he would have liked to say more, but his better instincts took over, and he retreated with the victory of having secured an escort for the evening's activities.

"What was that all about?" Lou Berta asked, as she joined Samantha and Caroline.

"Woody Carlson just asked Samantha to the social tonight," Caroline beamed.

"Really?" Lou Berta frowned. "That's...great."

"I guess," an unsure Samantha replied, as she studied Lou Berta.

"Oh, it is," Lou Berta assured, "Woody's a wonderful person."

"Girls, we have a party to get ready for," Caroline stated boldly. "Let's get to the house and get ready."

"I have to run some errands," Lou Berta said, "but I'll see you at graduation."

"Can you give me about an hour?" Samantha asked.

"Of course," Caroline replied.

"I need to tell Papa I'm going to a party," Samantha explained.

"See you at the house," Caroline smiled. "The address is —"

"I know the house," Samantha assured. "I'll see you there."

CHAPTER 9

WALKING OUT OF THE office early had been an impetuous decision Jonathan Kendall already regretted. After stopping for lunch, Jonathan wandered the streets trying to determine how to use the leisure time he had demanded from his father. He would have gone back to the office, but his pride would not let him return until the next day. Jonathan already dreaded the evening supper and inevitable encounter with his father.

Jonathan's shoes shuffled along the sidewalk, as he headed toward the western edge of town to see preparations for the Oklahoma National Guard's upcoming encampment. Soldiers used the low-lying field down the hill from Silk Stocking Row for training. In a few weeks, hundreds of men would camp among the pecan trees and wild flowers for training. A long concrete retaining wall stood one thousand yards away for target practice. As a lieutenant in Company B, Jonathan decided visiting headquarters would be a good way to spend his afternoon.

Jonathan remembered the excitement the previous year when hundreds of soldiers arrived in town. Neighbors, including Bill Tilghman the famous lawman from Indian Territory, crowded on the back porch of the Kendall home watching the boys march and shoot

Springfield rifles. Sheriff Tilghman was asked to critique the soldiers, and the men eventually coaxed him into retelling some of the daring deeds of the outlaw days, while the women listened in shocked disbelief at the violent tales. The thrill of the encampment would disappear after a couple of days, as the sporadic gunfire upset animals and the peace of the community. The trampled field would become a mud hole, and flies would feast on the scraps left by the soldiers.

As Jonathan thought about the upcoming camp, he quickly rounded the corner and felt a nudge against his arm before colliding into someone. Looking down, Jonathan noticed the worn shoe of the young girl he had awkwardly encountered earlier at the train station. Samantha Harvey sprawled on the sidewalk after the larger Jonathan had knocked her ungraciously to the ground. Her embarrassment turned to anger as she watched him staring at her tattered shoes.

"Are you—are you hurt?" the stunned Jonathan stammered, as he unconsciously looked at her feet.

Quickly pulling herself up, a terse Samantha replied, "I'm fine, and you should watch where you're going!"

"I was watching," Jonathan defended clumsily. "I just—I just became distracted—my mind was somewhere else."

Samantha already regained her feet before a bewildered Jonathan thought to extend his hand to help her from the ground.

"You need to get your mind back on your shoulders," Samantha scolded, "and watch where you're going!"

Before Jonathan had an opportunity to apologize, Samantha stormed away down Eighth Street. After a moment, Jonathan recouped his composure and decided to catch the girl to offer an apology. Jonathan had never been introduced to the girl, but he had offended her twice in the same day.

"Miss!" he called to the girl walking away. "Miss!"

Samantha did not break stride and walked at a faster pace. She continued down Eighth Street, as Jonathan followed.

"Miss!" he called again.

Samantha looked back long enough to see the man rushing toward her.

"Leave me alone!" she demanded, as she began walking even faster.

It was two blocks to Caroline's house, and Samantha was determined to keep her distance from her tormenter, who was now interrupting her leisurely stroll down Silk Stocking Row.

"Could you wait up?" she heard the man plead from behind her.

Samantha maintained her distance, but walked so fast that she was somewhat out of breath. More agitated than afraid, Samantha resented the young man spoiling her invitation to Silk Stocking Row. Walking quickly, she noticed a large two-story house on the corner with white trimmed lace gables. She wanted to admire the colorful flowers planted in front, but the man still chased her.

Across the street, Samantha saw the largest house on Silk Stocking Row. The home was a three-story house with a porch wrapping all the way around the first floor and a second story porch across the front of the house. Ivory painted trim and impressive columns around the porch accented the creamy-yellow house. A small observation deck on top of the third floor added to the grandeur of the home.

On her side of the street, Samantha approached a two-story brick home with a second floor tapered with decorative wood shingling. A natural rock fence separated it from the street, and a second-story porch looked across the street to other impressive homes. Looking behind her, Samantha was about thirty paces in front of the man who had knocked her to the ground, but he now seemed to be walking with more determination.

In front of the two-story house with the decorative wood shingles, a short, barrel-chested man stood in the front yard. The man's eyes squinted from years of living outdoors. He looked to be in his early fifties and had a demeanor of complete control.

Although Samantha felt she was trespassing in this man's neighborhood, he had an air of authority that compelled her to ask in an anxious tone, "Sir, could you help me?"

Looking at her, the man calmly asked, "What can I do for you?"

"There's a man following me," she frantically replied.

He calmly looked back at her pursuer and said, "That man? Has he threatened you?"

"He knocked me to the ground," Samantha exaggerated.

"That doesn't seem very gentlemanly," the man replied.

Jonathan Kendall quickly approached Samantha, when the short man put out his hand to the young man as if to order him to stop. Samantha instinctively moved to where the man could shield her.

"I'll get to you in a moment," the older man barked to the younger man. "You're that Harvey girl, aren't you?"

A surprised Samantha timidly replied, "Yes, sir."

"Your father taught school over Warwick way?" he asked.

"He used to," Samantha nodded.

"Stay back," he warned the anxious Jonathan.

"Where are you headed?" the man asked Samantha.

Pointing to the next block, Samantha said, "To Caroline Kendall's house."

"Really?" the man muttered.

Samantha's answer caught the man off guard, and she sensed he was not accustomed to being surprised.

"You a friend of Caroline's, I'm deducing?" he said.

"Yes," Samantha confirmed.

"Can you make it all right on your own, if I keep this character here 'til you're inside?" he asked

"Yes," Samantha smiled. "Thank you."

Samantha gloated at the young man who had been following her before scampering away to the safety of Caroline Kendall's house.

"Young Jonathan," the man asked in a tone of familiarity. "What did you do to torment that poor girl?"

Walking up to his neighbor, Jonathan said, "I have no idea, Mr. Bowles."

Grinning, Sam Bowles said, "She sure seemed anxious to get away from you."

Sam Bowles was once a deputy for Sheriff Bill Tilghman and still served as a bailiff at the courthouse. He lived in a cottage behind the Tilghman home. Sheriff Tilghman had moved to Oklahoma City a few years earlier, and Sam watched his place. The short and slightly bow-legged deputy was a common fixture on Silk Stocking Row where he eagerly told anyone who would listen about the exploits of Sheriff Tilghman and himself.

"I ran into her and accidently knocked her down," Jonathan explained. "I was trying to apologize, but she ran away."

"Smart girl," the deputy teased.

"What's she doing?" a confused Jonathan asked, as he watched Samantha Harvey enter his home in the next block.

"Look's like she's going to your house," Sam stoically replied. "You know who that is, don't you?"

"Not really," Jonathan confessed. "We've never been introduced."

"She's the Harvey girl," Sam stated. "Your daddy had land dealings with her family a few years back and did good off the deal."

"Sounds like Dad," Jonathan sighed. "So that's why she hates me."

With a sly grin Sam said, "I doubt it. She'd have to know you better to truly hate you. I imagine your smooth ways with women have only allowed her to develop a deep dislike of you — the real hate will come later."

Sensing the old deputy was having fun at his expense, Jonathan said, "Thanks for the advice."

Laughing at his young friend, Sam Bowles said, "You're a good sport, Jonathan, and a good kid—don't see any future for you in business."

"My dad'd agree with you," Jonathan frowned.

"Your dad's a hard man," Sam admitted, as he spit some chew out of his mouth. "He wants the best for you. He's been successful, but you got to be your own man—find your own way. You can't be like him."

"I guess so," Jonathan replied.

"When are you soldier boys coming to play war?" Sam asked.

"Two weeks," Jonathan answered.

"Two weeks 'til my afternoon naps get interrupted by you yahoos missing the target half the time," Sam fumed.

"Practice makes perfect," Jonathan said.

"No," the old deputy corrected. "Perfect practice makes you a little better. With a gun in your hand, you hope you're just a little better than the other fellow. Sheriff Tilghman taught me that. You boys better hope you don't have to use those guns for real."

"If we're called on, we'll be ready," Jonathan confidently proclaimed.

Looking warily at his young neighbor Sam Bowles said, "Let's hope that call never comes."

Putting his hand on Jonathan's shoulder, Sam continued, "War's a terrible thing. You don't ever want to see a man die, but war puts you in the place where that's your best outcome—to see another man dead. Believe me, it ain't a pretty sight. You goin' to see that girl now that she's trapped in your house?"

"I'm headed to find Captain Gilstrap," Jonathan revealed. "I think I've had enough humiliation for the day. She must be a friend of Caroline."

"She's pretty," Sam sighed, as he looked down the empty street as if the girl was still there.

"Caroline?" a confused Jonathan asked.

Smiling at the awkward young man, Sam said, "Both of 'em...if you hadn't noticed."

Jonathan smiled at Sam's teasing and slowly walked away. He strolled past his house and continued to a set of steps that went down the hill toward the field where the soldiers would soon camp. The old deputy rubbed his chin and looked at the Kendall house on the far end of Silk Stocking Row, as Jonathan disappeared from sight. The cagey lawman knew the importance of details. He also knew things about the Harvey girl and was puzzled as to why she would be at the Kendall home. Sam Bowles sighed heavily, as any good explanation eluded him. The afternoon sun beat down on the sidewalk, so the deputy retired to the shaded porch and sipped iced tea.

As he sat on the porch, he looked one more time to the end of Silk Stocking Row where the Kendall house perched on the high bluff overlooking the field below and whispered to himself, "What's that Harvey girl doing in the Kendall house?"

CHAPTER 10

SAMANTHA HARVEY'S ANXIETY ABOUT visiting the Kendall house vanished after a cordial greeting from Caroline's mother. A plain woman, Mrs. Kendall wore a simple gray dress with a white apron hiding a protruding waistline. Mrs. Kendall was pleasant but reserved, with a sadness that defied her affable character. The sweet aroma of fresh-baked bread permeated the immaculately neat house, as Mrs. Kendall led Samantha to a spacious bedroom Caroline shared with her sister, Augusta.

"There you are," Caroline greeted as she rose from the floor where she had been trimming ribbons.

The large upstairs bedroom featured two beds with a dressing mirror in between and a privacy screen in the corner. The room was painted eggshell white with turquoise patterns stenciled on the walls. Lace curtains decorated a large window that looked out to the other fine homes on Silk Stocking Row.

Mrs. Kendall quietly retreated from the room as Caroline cheerfully announced, "This is my sister, Augusta. I told you she was about your size."

Augusta stood up from the spot where she had been sitting. Taller than her older sister, Augusta was a thin, gawky-looking girl with long legs. She had quick, inquisitive green eyes and a mouth that seemed to frown and smirk at the same time.

Looking at Samantha carefully, the brash young Augusta turned to Caroline and said, "She's about my height, but she'll fill the dress up a might more than me."

"Oh, Augusta," Caroline scolded. "You'll have to get used to my sister. She has a tendency to speak without thinking."

"I can't complain about someone speaking their mind," Samantha smiled. "I've been accused of that myself. It's good to meet you, Augusta. I hope you don't mind —"

"Mind you wearing my old Easter dress?" Augusta interrupted in a pouting tone. "It's not like I'm going to any parties soon."

Samantha could not help grinning at Augusta's bluntness.

"We don't have time to hear you complain about being too young for parties," Caroline replied. "When I was fifteen, Daddy never let me out of the house."

"He let you go see David," Augusta corrected.

"That was different," Caroline defended. "He was Jonathan's friend."

Turning to Samantha, Augusta stated flatly, "David and Caroline are lovers."

"Augusta!" Caroline shrieked. "You don't know what you're saying."

"I stand corrected," Augusta shrugged. "He's just a boy Caroline loves."

Caroline glared at her sister without saying a word.

"What?" Augusta finally said, as if she needed to clarify herself. "I've read your diaries."

"Augusta Kendall!" Caroline scolded in a voice that was as loud as she dared without attracting the attention of her mother. "David and I are good friends...and you don't have any right reading my personal thoughts!"

"Sorry," Augusta replied. "I didn't think you would mind. It's not like you wrote anything I didn't know."

Caroline knew any further conversation with her sister would be senseless, so she turned to Samantha and said, "Do you have sisters?"

"I'm an only child," Samantha answered.

Looking at Augusta, Caroline said, "You're lucky."

Augusta looked baffled, unaware that she might have embarrassed her sister in front of her friend.

"It's okay, Augusta," Caroline finally said. "You're still my favorite sister."

"I'm your only sister," Augusta said.

"I know," Caroline smiled. "And I love you. We don't have much time, though. Get the dress so we can see how it fits."

Augusta shrugged her shoulders and trudged out of the room.

Caroline smiled at Samantha and said, "I think you'll love this dress."

In a moment, Augusta returned with a white linen dress trimmed with blue embroidery across the shoulders and down the sides. The sleeves were sheer with lace cuffs.

"It's beautiful," Samantha sighed. "You're sure you don't mind?"

"No," Augusta said while shaking her head. "I'm not wearing it tonight, and it'll look great on you."

"Thank you, Augusta," Samantha replied.

An eager Caroline added, "Try it on."

Samantha stepped behind the screen in the corner of the room and quickly slipped out of her old clothes and into Augusta's starched linen dress.

Hesitantly, Samantha walked out from behind the screen and timidly asked, "What do you think?"

Caroline looked at Augusta as if to get an approving nod before saying, "It looks wonderful on you."

The two sisters immediately began circling Samantha looking at the dress more carefully, examining every pleat and seam.

"We can take it in at the waist, just a touch don't you think?" Caroline asked.

Augusta nodded in agreement and added, "I told you it would fit her better."

All three girls were giddy as Samantha took off the dress, and they began making their careful alterations. It was nearly time for supper, and there was little time to spare. Samantha enjoyed the banter between the two sisters and soon felt at home with her new friends.

"Oh!" Augusta abruptly gasped. "I almost forgot."

Augusta quickly stepped to the closet and rummaged inside for a moment before bringing a box out to the room.

"You'll need these," Augusta said as she handed Samantha the box.

Samantha carefully opened the box and saw a lovely pair of white shoes with heels. She sighed softly, knowing her own worn shoes would have distracted from the attractive dress.

"Thank you," Samantha said softly.

"You better try them on," the practical Augusta suggested.

Samantha slipped on the shoes and was dismayed to learn that Augusta's feet were larger than her own.

"Try this," Caroline said, as she stuffed paper into the toe of the shoe. "See how that feels now."

Samantha teetered slightly as she stood in the shoes with a slightly higher heel than she was accustomed to wearing. She was relieved to find Caroline's remedy worked, and she was soon walking with ease.

"One more thing," Caroline said, as she hastily looked through her dresser. "That dress will show a little ankle, so you'll need these."

Caroline handed her new friend a pair of delicate silk stockings. Samantha had only worn wool stockings in the past, and she gingerly held the white stockings Caroline had given her.

"Really?" Samantha asked.

"Of course," Caroline smiled. "They'll make the outfit."

The excitement of preparing for the senior social allowed Samantha to forget the troubles and uncertainty of her future. Her worn shoes that caused embarrassment earlier in the day would not spoil her senior party thanks to Caroline's kindness. Caroline and Samantha had bonded quickly that afternoon, and both girls believed they had made a friendship that would last for years. Neither girl, however, could have known how their acquaintance would shape their lives for years to come.

CHAPTER 11

"Somethin' smells good," David Simpson teased, as he walked into Mrs. Kendall's kitchen while she diligently prepared supper.

"David!" Mrs. Kendall greeted. "When did you get into town?"

"This morning," David replied.

"Did you come for the alumni banquet?" Mrs. Kendall quizzed.

With a sly smile, David said, "I'm back for more than that."

"What?" Mrs. Kendall asked with a perplexed look on her round face.

David, surprised by her puzzlement, said, "I'm going to work at the Kendall Cotton Gin...for Mr. Kendall."

"Oh David!" Mrs. Kendall exclaimed. "That's wonderful news."

"Mr. Kendall hadn't told you?" David asked.

"No," Mrs. Kendall shrugged. "Mr. Kendall doesn't tell me everything, but it's a wonderful surprise. Have you seen Jonathan?"

"He met me at the train this morning."

"I suppose he's excited to have you working with him?"

"I think he was as surprised as you were," David answered.

"Mr. Kendall likes his secrets," Mrs. Kendall reasoned.

"I guess," David acknowledged.

"Have you seen Caroline?" Mrs. Kendall timidly, but hopefully asked.

"Not yet," David smiled. "I thought I'd surprise her for supper. I'm guessing Mr. Kendall hasn't told you he invited me."

"Of course not," Mrs. Kendall pouted. "But there's always enough, and you're always welcome."

"I've looked forward to one of your meals all day," David said.

"Caroline will be so thrilled," Mrs. Kendall sighed. "She's upstairs now."

A slight creak from the bottom step on the staircase alerted Mrs. Kendall and David to the approach of someone from upstairs.

"That'll be Caroline now," Mrs. Kendall gleamed.

Samantha Harvey stepped into the kitchen instead and Mrs. Kendall squealed, "Oh!"

Samantha stood awkwardly wearing the white linen dress, Augusta's shoes, and Caroline's silk stockings. The first thing she noticed about David Simpson was his confident and unmistakable charm. David was only slightly taller than Samantha, but he seemed much larger. Samantha stared at the dapper young man longer than she would have liked, but there was something about him she found irresistible.

David Simpson smirked slyly and said, "She's too tall to be Caroline and although she looks a little like Augusta, she's a bit too...mature. Have you been hiding another daughter from me, Mrs. Kendall?"

Mrs. Kendall giggled at David's teasing and said, "No, she's a friend of Caroline's. They're getting ready for the party tonight."

"You look like you're ready to go," David complemented.

Mrs. Kendall remembered she had not introduced the two when she said, "David Simpson, this is Samantha—"

Mrs. Kendall hesitated a moment before saying, "I'm sorry, dear, I don't know your last name."

Continuing to look at David, Samantha said, "Harvey — Samantha Harvey."

A loud crash interrupted the introductions as Mrs. Kendall dropped the spatula.

"Oh my," an ashen Mrs. Kendall muttered, "how clumsy of me."

David quickly bent down to retrieve the spatula and asked, "Are you okay?"

"Yes," Mrs. Kendall tried to assure. "I've just got butter fingers today."

Regaining her composure, Mrs. Kendall continued, "David, this is Samantha Harvey. She's one of Caroline's classmates."

"You must be new to town," David Simpson confidently stated.

"How did you know that?" Samantha asked. "It's true, but I'm sure we've never met."

Looking at Mrs. Kendall, David said, "I used to make a habit of keeping track of all the pretty girls in Chandler, and I'm sure I would have remembered you."

Samantha blushed at the flirting complement.

Mrs. Kendall looked uncomfortable and asked Samantha, "Is Caroline upstairs?"

"Yes," Samantha answered. "She said you had a blue bonnet that matched this dress."

"Yes," Mrs. Kendall said, as she mentally checked off all of the possible locations for the bonnet. "Tell Caroline it's in the front closet in a box on the top shelf."

"Thank you," Samantha smiled.

"That's a beautiful dress," David admired.

"I borrowed it from Augusta," a suddenly bashful Samantha replied.

With a mischievous twinkle in his eye, David Simpson said, "Something old, something new, something borrowed, something blue — don't tell me you're looking for a six-pence in your shoe?"

"Oh no," Samantha immediately replied, as David laughed at her embarrassment.

"David!" Caroline interrupted with a shriek.

David turned and said, "Hey, Caroline."

"When did you get into town?" Caroline quizzed.

"This morning," David answered, as he stepped close to Caroline. "I thought I would surprise you."

"It's a great surprise, David," Caroline beamed, as she hugged David. "Are you staying for supper?"

"I've already been invited," David replied.

Looking at the still blushing Samantha, Caroline said, "Excuse my rudeness. Samantha, this is David."

Looking at David, Samantha said, "We've met."

"Are you going to the banquet?" Caroline asked anxiously.

"I wouldn't miss it," David assured.

Caroline struggled to hide her disappointment. The Alumni banquet was scheduled at the same time as the senior party. Although David had been a popular boy with his class, Caroline hoped he might skip the banquet to escort her to the party.

"Samantha and I have been getting her dress ready," Caroline interjected. "She's going to the senior party with Woody Carlson."

"Woody Carlson?" David replied skeptically. "The skinny boy from next door?"

"Woody's just lean," Caroline tactfully corrected.

"He was awfully lean last time I saw him," David added. "So lean I'd call him...skinny. I may have to go to the senior party and see for myself."

Caroline smiled broadly, "Does that mean you'll take me to the senior party?"

"The senior party's still for seniors and their escorts, isn't it?" David asked.

Caroline nodded enthusiastically.

"If you'll let me escort you, I'll get to see how Woody has filled out since I've been gone," David said. "That is, if you'll let me escort you."

An exuberant Caroline said, "It's the best graduation present I can imagine!"

CHAPTER 12

CAROLINE AND SAMANTHA RETREATED upstairs to prepare for the party, while David Simpson helped Mrs. Kendall with supper. Samantha intended to go home before graduation, but Caroline convinced her to stay for supper by reminding her David would be at the table.

"Come to dinner, girls!" Mrs. Kendall shouted, as the front door slammed at the arrival of Caroline's father.

Caroline scampered down the steps with Augusta close behind while a more timid Samantha followed. Halfway down the stairs, Samantha stopped. Mr. Kendall was a tall, foreboding man with a stern demeanor. His temples were graying, but he looked young compared to Samantha's older father. Mr. Kendall appeared vibrant and forceful, which caused Samantha to linger on the stairway and out of sight.

"Where's Jonathan?" Mr. Kendall roared.

"I thought he was with you," Mrs. Kendall answered factually.

"He took off this morning in a huff, and I haven't seen him since," Mr. Kendall complained.

"Whatever for?" Mrs. Kendall asked.

Mr. Kendall was in the process of muttering a response under his breath when he noticed David standing in the kitchen.

"David, my boy!" Mr. Kendall greeted in a tone of voice more cordial than the one he had used with his family. "I see you've made it."

"Wouldn't miss it, sir," a chipper David responded.

"Here's a man that knows the value of a good meal," Mr. Kendall bantered back.

Looking at Caroline, Mr. Kendall asked, "Have you even noticed David's back home?"

A glowing Caroline said, "Of course. David told us all about the new job, and he's taking me to the senior party tonight."

David looked at Mr. Kendall sheepishly as Caroline's father bellowed, "Imagine that...just like old times! I'd have to say, I'm not surprised."

"Not much surprises you, does it father?" Jonathan Kendall asked, as he slipped in behind his father.

Samantha gasped, as she recognized the condescending young man who had tormented her earlier. Stepping back, Samantha tried to hide her face from those below and wished she could vanish from the house.

"Don't use that tone with me," Mr. Kendall warned. "Where have you been all afternoon?"

"With Captain Gilstrap," Jonathan Kendall replied.

As Mr. Kendall glared at his son, David Simpson tried to ease the friction between them by asking, "Is Harry Gilstrap still in charge?"

Jonathan nodded.

Captain Harry Gilstrap commanded the local National Guard and was a close friend with General Roy Hoffman who rode with Roosevelt during the Spanish American war. General Hoffman was responsible for the Oklahoma Guard encampment being held in Chandler each year.

"National Guard foolishness," Mr. Kendall fumed. "It distracts you from your business."

Trying to be diplomatic, David interjected, "When is the encampment?"

"In two weeks," Jonathan replied.

"Surely, you're not going to get involved with this nonsense?" Mr. Kendall asked David.

"I don't think I'll have time," David tactfully replied.

"Of course, you won't have time," Mr. Kendall assured. "Jonathan doesn't have time either, but he fancies himself a hero or something."

An exasperated Jonathan sighed, "It's not about being a hero. It's about duty and being prepared."

"For what?" Mr. Kendall asked. "The war in Europe will end before Wilson gets us involved. What business do we have in Europe anyway?"

"Hopefully none," Jonathan sighed.

"Then these exercises *are* just a distraction to your work," Mr. Kendall proclaimed.

"Supper's getting cold," Mrs. Kendall advised meekly.

A flustered Mr. Kendall refrained from saying more and took his seat at the head of the table, as Mrs. Kendall began shuttling food to the large dining table.

"Caroline and Augusta help me," the calm Mrs. Kendall ordered. "David, sit at the right hand of Mr. Kendall—by Caroline. Jonathan, you sit by me. Samantha you can sit across from Jonathan."

Samantha had managed to retreat up the stairs far enough to hide her face and stay out of view. Silence permeated the room, as

Mr. Kendall and Jonathan looked at their visitor from the waist down.

"Come down, dear," Mrs. Kendall coaxed, as she went to the kitchen to direct Caroline and Augusta.

Left alone with the men, Samantha slowly walked down the stairs.

"Who's this?" Mr. Kendall shouted to his wife who was now in the kitchen with the other girls.

"Samantha," David informed.

Mr. Kendall became silent while Jonathan strained to get a glimpse of the attractive young woman descending the stairs.

"Good evening," Samantha greeted.

"Samantha's a friend of Caroline," David explained.

"You know my daughter?" Mr. Kendall quizzed.

"Only, barely," Samantha replied. "We're classmates, and Caroline helped me with this dress today."

Samantha glanced at the tall, young man who had knocked her down earlier. Jonathan looked as if he wanted to say something, but retreated to his side of the table instead.

"You're eighteen then?" Mr. Kendall asked Samantha.

"Yes, sir," Samantha replied.

"Married, engaged?" he continued to question.

"No," an uncomfortable Samantha replied.

"Jonathan," Mr. Kendall began to lecture in a blunt tone. "You're always telling me there are no eligible girls in this town, and it seems as if your sister has found one without any difficulty."

"Father!" Jonathan replied in a hushed shout. "That's not appropriate…you're embarrassing her."

Mr. Kendall appeared oblivious that he might have insulted the young woman by talking so plainly about her availability to marry.

Unfazed by Jonathan's frantic attempts to quiet him, Mr. Kendall continued explaining, "I'm just saying she's an attractive young lady and you're unattached. I thought maybe you could escort her sometime—aren't there parties this evening?"

Samantha now felt sorry for the young man who had embarrassed her earlier, as he now seemed equally humiliated by his father.

She was about to respond to Mr. Kendall when David Simpson cleared his throat and interjected, "I think, Mr. Kendall, you've underestimated the young lady. You see she already has an escort for the evening."

Mr. Kendall raised his eyebrow slightly, as David continued, "She's being taken to the senior party by Woody Carlson."

Turning to Jonathan, Mr. Kendall said, "See what I mean. A bean pole like Woodrow Carlson can find a girl to spend a Friday night with while you sit here alone."

"What's this chattering?" Mrs. Kendall asked, as she and her daughters paraded in from the kitchen with ample servings of food.

David Simpson smiled slyly and said, "We were just discussing Jonathan's social life."

"Oh dear," Mrs. Kendall groaned. "Let's all have our seats...supper's ready."

Samantha watched, as David pulled out a chair and gracefully assisted Caroline to her place. Turning around, she noticed Jonathan Kendall staring awkwardly at her from across the table.

"I'm sorry about this afternoon, Miss Harvey," Jonathan said in a low tone.

"What did you say?" Mr. Kendall bellowed.

Jonathan saw that his father's question had everyone's attention before replying, "I was apologizing for something that happened earlier today."

"What did you do?" a concerned Caroline asked.

"Never mind that," the domineering Mr. Kendall instructed. "What did you call her?"

Jonathan was accustomed to cross-examinations by his father, but was puzzled about this question, as he replied, "Miss Harvey."

Mr. Kendall's countenance deflated, as he seemed to be at a loss for words.

After a few seconds, Samantha said, "We ran into each other earlier. It was just a misunderstanding."

Looking across the table at Jonathan, she said, "There's really no need to apologize, I—"

Samantha stopped talking to think for a second before asking, "How did you know my name?"

A sheepish Jonathan looked at his father before turning to Samantha to say, "Deputy Bowles told me this afternoon."

Seeing she still did not understand, Jonathan explained, "The short man you talked to down the street…Deputy Bowles is what we call him, although I'm not sure he's technically a deputy now. He told me your last name."

"What else did he say?" a desperate Mr. Kendall asked.

A confused Jonathan said, "Nothing."

Mrs. Kendall cleared her voice and said, "That's enough talk. David, would you say our blessing?"

The family and their guests enjoyed Mrs. Kendall's meal without further interrogations. The evening's conversation was polite, but not about anything of consequence. Samantha's earlier resentment of Jonathan Kendall faded slightly at the harassment he endured from his blunt father. Jonathan seemed intelligent but reserved, and his withdrawn demeanor made him as interesting as Mrs. Kendall's hominy to Samantha. David Simpson, however, had charisma that made everyone take notice. Samantha listened with fascination to his clever anecdotes and entertaining, sometimes boisterous stories.

Jonathan watched Samantha discreetly, as she listened to David Simpson entertain the table with exaggerated tales. Jonathan admired the pretty girl's self-assured poise and the way she graciously laughed at David's silly stories. Although he could not think of anything clever to say himself, he studied her throughout the evening and was intrigued about the conversation he had earlier with Sam Bowles. What truly fascinated him about Samantha Harvey was the humbling effect she seemed to have on his father. Mr. Kendall typically dominated dinner conversation taking every opportunity to instruct and correct his children. Tonight, however, Mr. Kendall sat in stoic silence sneaking glances at Caroline's young guest. Mr. Kendall's sudden change in disposition made Jonathan wonder why.

CHAPTER 13

CAROLINE AND AUGUSTA CLEARED the dinner table while Mrs. Kendall brought out a steaming apple pie. Mrs. Kendall asked Samantha to slice the perfectly baked golden-brown pie. The men watched, as Samantha nervously cut the flaky crust, hoping not to mangle it.

"I'm going to get some air," Mr. Kendall announced in a subdued tone.

"Before having your pie?" a concerned Mrs. Kendall asked, as she brought dessert plates for the pie.

Mr. Kendall was nearly outside when he said, "I just want to smoke a pipe and get some air."

Without further explanation, the patriarch of the Kendall home stepped outside leaving the rest to enjoy Mrs. Kendall's pie. Mrs. Kendall stepped to the window to watch her husband walk down the street with his pipe in hand.

Turning back to her guest, Mrs. Kendall said, "I wish we had made some ice cream."

As Samantha handed David Simpson the first piece of pie, he joked, "Ice cream with this pie would make my belt bust."

Mrs. Kendall smiled graciously and returned to the table taking pleasure in the group enjoying her pie.

"You girls better hurry," Mrs. Kendall encouraged. "You're supposed to be at school in half an hour."

"We have time, Mother," Caroline assured.

"When's the party, David?" Mrs. Kendall asked, as the girls began eating their pie.

David's mouth was full so Jonathan answered, "The alumni banquet's at seven."

Caroline giggled, as David looked at Jonathan in awkward silence.

"What?" Jonathan asked.

"David's taking me to the senior party after graduation," Caroline cheerfully explained.

"You're going to miss alumni?" Jonathan asked.

"I'm taking Caroline to the party," David answered, as he wiped his mouth after a bite of pie.

Sensing Jonathan's disappointment, David added, "I'll try to stop by for a few minutes to see the fellows. Besides, we'll have all summer to catch up."

"It'll be fine," Jonathan assured. "I wasn't really looking forward to going out tonight."

"You're not going?" David quizzed.

Jonathan shook his head and said, "I think I'll stay in."

"Jonathan," Mrs. Kendall said. "Why don't you go to the party with David and Caroline?"

"The party's for the seniors," Jonathan explained.

"David's going," Mrs. Kendall shrugged.

"He's Caroline's escort," Jonathan replied.

"Then find you a nice girl to escort," Mrs. Kendall suggested.

Jonathan unintentionally looked across the room at Samantha who listened passively to the conversation.

Upon making eye contact with Jonathan Kendall, Samantha frantically said, "I've already got an escort."

"Oh I—I wasn't suggesting," Jonathan stammered.

"Samantha's meeting someone at the party, but no one would mind if you tagged along and escorted her to the party," Caroline explained.

A bewildered Samantha looked at an embarrassed Jonathan before both turned to address Caroline.

Before Jonathan or Samantha had a chance to speak, Mrs. Kendall sternly, but kindly said, "Caroline, it's not appropriate for you to play matchmaker. It's not polite, and you've embarrassed your guest."

Turning to Samantha, Caroline said, "Mother's right. I'm terribly sorry, Samantha. I just hate that Jonathan will be alone on my account."

"I have an idea," David Simpson interjected. "Is your friend Lou Berta going with anyone this evening?"

"I don't think so," Caroline cautiously answered. "Why?"

"Lou Berta's a sweet girl, and I'm sure she would love to be part of our group," David suggested. "Check with her, and we'll all go as one big happy crowd to your senior party."

"That's a great idea," Caroline smiled. "Lou Berta wouldn't mind being seen with Jonathan."

Jonathan squirmed at his end of the table, as Caroline looked to her mother for approval. Mrs. Kendall did not look pleased, but she refrained from saying anything.

"Check with her," David encouraged.

"You girls need to get ready," an impatient Mrs. Kendal instructed. "You need to be on your way."

"Yes, mother," Caroline replied as she and Samantha headed upstairs to finish preparing for graduation.

"That's great," Jonathan sighed after the girls left. "Going to party with Lou Berta will be like going with my sister."

"You *are* going with your sister," David replied with an impish grin. "Don't worry. We'll take the girls to their party. They'll get involved with their classmates, and we'll skip out to see our class."

"You got it all figured out," Jonathan said shaking his head skeptically. "Who's taking the Harvey girl anyway?"

"Woody Carlson," Augusta Kendall answered.

CHAPTER 14

John Kendall did not often take walks to clear his head, but the young woman his daughter invited to dinner caught him off guard. It was almost 6 o'clock, and the air was thick with humidity. A blue-steel bank of clouds billowed to the west, but bright sunshine cast a clear shadow in front of him as he walked aimlessly down the sidewalk.

The grass was damp from recent rains, and emerald-green patches of clover covered the lawns with little white flowers that looked like popcorn scattered upon the ground. John Kendall did not take time to appreciate the lush spring vegetation adorning the prosperous homes of Silk Stocking Row, however. With his eyes fixed two steps ahead, John Kendall walked slowly down the sidewalk while smoke from his pipe drifted lazily above his head in the calm, stale air.

The street was quiet, as families enjoyed their evening meal. Mr. Kendall knew the peaceful solitude would not last. It was graduation night. Some neighbors would go to the auditorium for the ceremony while others would attend a banquet for the past alumni of the community's high school. Stepping in front of the huge Conklin home, John Kendall watched Mrs. Conklin busily putting the final touches on her front porch decorations.

John Kendall knew his beloved daughter Caroline would be at the Conklin house later with David Simpson. He helped engineer this development, but now a queasy feeling rested in the pit of his stomach at the thought of that Harvey girl befriending Caroline. He breathed in the muggy air and slowly exhaled trying to purge the uneasy feeling from his soul.

"Looks like quite a shindig's planned for tonight," a deep, gravelly voice boomed from across the street.

Mr. Kendall looked over at Sam Bowles sitting on the porch of the Tilghman house holding a glass of iced tea.

"I think so, Sam," the almost squeaky voice of Mrs. Conklin replied. "I hope the children won't disturb you."

"I suppose they will," the former deputy chuckled. "I'd think they were up to something, if they didn't."

As Sam Bowles spoke to Mrs. Conklin, his inquisitive eyes shifted to John Kendall. The two men did not speak, but Mr. Kendall accepted the non-verbal invitation to join Sam.

"How's it going?" Mr. Kendall asked, as he stepped onto the porch.

"Good," Sam replied. "Looks like if might storm."

Mr. Kendall looked back to the west as clouds boiled in the distance before saying, "You might be right."

"Big night for you with the daughter graduating and all," Sam stated. "I noticed David Simpson's back in town."

"Yeah," Mr. Kendall admitted. "How'd you know?"

"It's my business to notice things," the former deputy said, as he turned his head to look at the Kendall house in the next block.

"David's back in town," Mr. Kendall said in a listless tone. "He's going to work at the gin."

"Have a seat, John," Sam offered. "Want some tea?"

"Not unless you got something extra in that tea," Mr. Kendall replied, as he took a seat next to Sam.

Sam Bowles smiled and replied, "You know me, John."

John Kendall smiled slightly and said, "I know you, deputy — a committed teetotaler."

"It's the law," Sam grinned.

John Kendall chuckled insincerely and looked again to the west toward his house, as towering thunderheads threatened to block the bright afternoon sun.

"Jonathan was by earlier," Sam observed.

"Headed to the rifle range, I suppose," Mr. Kendall surmised.

Sam nodded and said, "He was following a girl...a pretty girl at that."

"What?" Mr. Kendall asked.

Taking a sip of his tea, Sam said, "You had another guest for dinner tonight?"

Mr. Kendall stooped slightly and rubbed the palms of his hands together while looking at his feet.

"She looks a lot like her mother," Sam finally said.

Sitting up straight, John Kendall asked, "You know who the girl is?"

Sam nodded slightly while studying John Kendall's reaction.

"You know—" John Kendall began.

"I know a lot of things," Sam interrupted. "I rode with Sheriff Tilghman for a quarter of a century, and like I said, it's my business to notice things...and to know things."

"That was a long time ago," John Kendall said defiantly. "I didn't know they were still around."

"The girl and her father live east of town close to Indian Springs," Deputy Bowles shared.

"The mother?"

"Died a couple of years ago," Sam replied, as he watched John Kendall closely.

John Kendall took the pipe out of his mouth and held it in his hand has he bent down to look at his feet.

"The sins of some men are conspicuous while the sins of other appear later," Sam said thoughtfully.

"I'm no sinner," Mr. Kendall defended. "And you're no saint."

"We're all sinners," Sam corrected. "You're a respectable citizen, John, and seems like you've been good to your family, but that don't make what you done to those people right."

"I didn't break any laws," Mr. Kendall shot back.

Sam Bowles took another drink of tea before saying, "I've spent most my life trying to keep the peace and keep the law. The line between right and wrong's not always black and white...sometimes it's a little gray. You're a smart enough man to not break the law, but keeping the law don't make everything right. Doing business like you do's hard on people."

"Business is business," Mr. Kendall declared. "People know the rules. They come to me knowing the rent's got to be paid. I didn't do anything that wasn't my right, and you had a bigger hand in it than me."

"People are motivated by hope and fear," Sam explained, as his brow wrinkled in thought. "Most of these farmers live with fear most days wondering if the rains'll come, or if a flood'll wash it all away. They worry if prices'll hold or if the grasshoppers'll eat their crop clean. People are resilient, but when you squeeze all the hope out of 'em, they get desperate. Then I got to deal with them."

Mr. Kendall sternly replied, "I appreciate your keeping the peace, deputy, but you don't know what you're talking about."

"I know you turned white as a sheet when I said, Jonathan followed that girl earlier," Sam answered. "She seemed like a nice girl...at least to Jonathan."

"Jonathan doesn't know what he wants," Mr. Kendall sighed.

"Maybe you need to let him find out sometime," Sam suggested. "Jonathan's a good boy...he'll do the right thing."

"Maybe, but I won't have Jonathan associating with that Harvey girl," Mr. Kendall adamantly stated.

Sam Bowles looked at Mr. Kendall for a moment before saying with a raised eyebrow, "Sins of the father, tainting the son?"

"Something like that," Mr. Kendall sighed.

"The sins of some men are obvious, but the sins of other appear later," Sam quoted a second time. "Good deeds are also obvious, and even when they're not, they can't remain hidden."

"You make that up?" Mr. Kendall asked.

Shaking his head, Sam said, "Heard it in church last Sunday. It's from the preacher or the Bible. I'm not sure, but I've been thinking about it all week. Are you going to do the right thing, John?"

Standing up to leave, John Kendall sneered strangely and answered, "It's too late for the right thing."

Mr. Kendall nodded at Sam and walked toward the street.

When Mr. Kendall reached the gate at the front of the yard, Sam said, "It's never too late to do the right thing."

Mr. Kendall smiled sarcastically and walked away.

CHAPTER 15

SAMANTHA AND CAROLINE SCURRIED around the Kendall house getting ready, before making the short walk to the high school. Augusta Kendall aggravated her sister by giving unsolicited and blunt opinions about the color of her ribbon and the effects the evening's humidity was having on her sister's hair. When the girls finally left, it was as if peace had returned to the Kendall house.

"Let's take a quick look at the rifle range," David suggested to Jonathan, as Mrs. Kendall ordered her youngest daughter, Augusta, into the kitchen to finish cleaning as a reprimand for fussing with her older sister.

The National Guard rifle range was in a low area around Bell Cow Creek down the steep hill from the Kendall house. Recent rains left the area swampy, but the two friends stopped at the Statistical Building, which was located halfway down the hill. The building sat on a twenty-foot cliff of sandstone overlooking a cement wall 1,000 yards away where the targets were scored. As Jonathan walked with David, he glanced at his father sitting on the porch talking to Sam Bowles.

The two young men leaned against the rock wall of the vacant Statistical Building, as storm clouds boiled in the western sky. They talked about a variety of people and topics of local interest. The conversation was light-hearted and filled with recollections of their boyhood years.

The reminiscing stopped when David Simpson asked in a serious tone, "What was going on with you and that Harvey girl?"

Jonathan frowned, "She doesn't like me much."

"No joking," David agreed. "Did you insult her some way?"

"Not on purpose," Jonathan sighed.

David laughed and said, "Some things never change."

"What do you mean?" Jonathan asked defensively.

"Your way with ladies," David clarified. "There's never a girl that quite meets your standards, and when you do find someone you like, you fall all over yourself."

"Who says I like her?" Jonathan asked.

Smiling and shaking his head, David said, "I do. I've been around you enough to know when a girl's got your attention. What exactly did you do?"

"Nothing," Jonathan assured.

David looked stoically at his friend without replying.

After a brief silence Jonathan admitted, "At the train station when I was waiting for you—I was minding my own business when she walked by. I had seen her around town, but we'd never been introduced...I guess she's new to town—"

"What did you say?" David asked suspiciously.

Jonathan thought for a moment and said, "Good morning."

David looked suspiciously at his friend before saying, "And what else?"

"Nothing," Jonathan replied. "Honestly, I didn't say anything, but 'good morning,' but–"

Grinning broadly, David said, "Here it is...'but' what?"

"When I tipped my hat I looked down," Jonathan confessed. "I couldn't help but notice her shoes had a hole worn through the top. The shoes were crusted with red clay, so I figured she walked into town from the country. I didn't say anything."

David sighed deeply.

"What?" a frantic Jonathan asked.

Shaking his head, David said, "You really don't know anything about women, do you?"

Jonathan did not reply, knowing David was about to explain his shortcomings.

"To you and me, shoes are just shoes," David enlightened. "But to a woman...well to a woman her shoes are a statement of who she is. Just by looking at her shabby shoes, you insulted her."

"That doesn't make sense," Jonathan said dubiously.

"That's women," David smiled. "Nothing makes sense. You don't understand because you've always lived in that big house on Silk Stocking Row. You could walk around dressed in overalls and homemade moccasins and would still feel like you're...special."

"That's not true," Jonathan defended.

David shrugged and said, "We're not dealing with truth here...we're dealing with women."

Jonathan looked over the lush green field and did not reply, knowing anything he said would give David Simpson an excuse to tease him further.

"It does sound like the girl is a little irrational," David coaxed. "Are you sure that's all you said?"

Jonathan squirmed before admitting, "I ran into her this afternoon."

"What do you mean you ran into her?" David asked with a smirk.

"After you left the office, Dad and I had—a disagreement," Jonathan explained. "I was walking downtown and not paying attention. I knocked the poor girl to the ground. Before I had a chance to apologize, she took off and I tried to chase her down."

"You didn't," David said shaking his head.

Jonathan nodded sheepishly.

"You really need to learn about women," David sighed heavily. "Let me explain something. Girls don't want to be chased...the object is to get them to chase you."

"Like Caroline?" Jonathan interrupted.

"Leave Caroline out of this," David implored. "We're talking about you. You knocked the girl down, insulted her shabby shoes, and you're still wondering why she was horrified at Caroline suggesting you escort her?"

"I get it," Jonathan confessed. "I'm hopeless with women."

"Not hopeless," David smiled, "just not very hopeful."

Jonathan agreed with a sigh.

"She's a pretty girl," David finally admitted.

"I guess," Jonathan said indifferently.

"You guess?" David asked with a mischievous grin. "I can tell you, that girl's got something that'll turn any guy's head."

"She couldn't keep her eyes off of you," Jonathan sulked.

"So you did notice the girl's attractive?" David asked.

"I noticed," Jonathan admitted.

David Simpson looked at his old friend and was tempted to torment him more, but he decided instead to watch the clouds towering in the western sky.

After a time, Jonathan asked seriously, "What's going on?"

"Huh?" David responded.

Jonathan turned to face David and clarified, "What's going on with you and Caroline? I watched you at supper; you were flirting with that Harvey girl in front of her. You're moving back to town.

My dad's almost giddy with excitement. I'm confused. You don't seem that interested in Caroline."

David thought for a moment before saying, "Caroline's special. I went off to sow a little wild oats. I guess I didn't leave things with Caroline in a good way, but that's behind me now."

"Do you love her?" Jonathan asked.

"What a question," David sighed. "I don't even know what that means. Am I attracted to Caroline? Sure. Do I care for her? Of course. Caroline's always been able to make me feel...settled."

"That's not much of an answer," Jonathan replied.

"I do love her," David said more forcefully. "I'm planning to marry her."

David continued to look out across the empty field as if in deep thought while Jonathan studied his friend.

"Has my father helped orchestrate all this?" Jonathan finally felt compelled to ask.

David did not answer for a moment before saying, "What do you think? Your father came to see me every time he was in Oklahoma City and talked about all the opportunity I'd have in his land business. You know how he feels about me."

"It doesn't bother you that he's throwing Caroline at you?" Jonathan asked.

"He's not throwing her at me," David declared. "Caroline's a sweetheart, and I've known for a long time I'd ask her to marry me. If your dad thinks it's his idea, what difference does it make? I like your dad. I understand him a little bit."

"I'm glad someone understands him," Jonathan muttered. "I sure don't."

Throwing his arm on Jonathan's shoulder, David said, "You worry too much. I'm going to do right by your sister. I do love her, and we're going to be a great match...That'll make you and me brothers after all these years."

"I guess so," Jonathan said.

"Let's get to this graduation," David proclaimed. "We'll hit the senior party like we own the place and then cut out to see some of the old gang."

"I guess," Jonathan sighed.

"I know," David boasted. "That's the difference between you and me."

CHAPTER 16

NOTHING EXCEPTIONAL HAPPENED AT the dignified graduation, as Samantha watched her father sitting alone in the back of the auditorium. They had only recently moved to the area, and Samantha believed her father knew even fewer people than she did. Mr. Harvey looked lonely but content to see his daughter complete her high school education, and he was pleased to learn Samantha would attend the senior party.

The ceremony ended with the expected exclamation of joy and relief, as graduates hastened to meet family and well-wishers with big smiles. Samantha had only one person she wanted to hug, but as she searched the crowd, her father had vanished.

As she stretched to see where he might have gone, she heard the pleasant voice of David Simpson say, "You look lost."

"I'm fine," Samantha assured. "I'm looking for my father."

"Not sure I can help," David said, as he looked around the auditorium. "I don't know who your father is."

"He's not here," Samantha replied with a tone of concern.

"Maybe he went outside," David suggested. "Let's look."

Taking her gently by the arm, David guided her through the crowd and out the double doors of the auditorium. Samantha glanced at Caroline and her family on the way. Caroline was all smiles, as she talked energetically to the group. Samantha was relieved no one noticed David holding her by the arm.

As David and Samantha stepped outside, the noise and confusion subsided, as she looked through the evening dusk for her father. Clouds in the west now threatened and made the early evening seem much later than it actually was.

"There he is!" Samantha cried, as she pointed to the old man who was walking away nearly a half block down the street.

Samantha walked as quickly as her heeled shoes would allow, but it was nearly a block before she was close enough to call to her father.

"Papa!" Samantha shouted. "Papa!"

At first it appeared the old man did not hear his daughter, but as Samantha prepared to shout louder, he stopped to wait for her.

"Papa," Samantha greeted. "Where are you going?"

"Home," her father calmly explained.

"Why the rush?" Samantha asked. "I didn't even get a hug."

With a beaming smile, Mr. Harvey embraced his daughter while saying, "I wanted to get home before dark, and I knew you had plans."

As he continued to hug his daughter, Mr. Harvey asked, "Is this the young man escorting you to the party, Sammie?"

The question caught Samantha off guard, as she realized David Simpson had followed her.

Looking at the handsome David a few steps behind, she said, "No, this is David Simpson. He's a friend of Caroline."

"Good to meet you, David," the old man greeted warmly.

"I'm sorry," Samantha interrupted. "David, this is my father. Papa, this is David Simpson."

"Good to meet you, Mr. Harvey," David smiled.

"Aren't you glad you didn't miss your graduation?" Mr. Harvey asked his daughter.

"Yes," Samantha admitted.

Looking at David, Mr. Harvey said, "I bet you'll have a grand time at the party tonight."

Samantha blushed at her doting father's insinuation.

"Speaking of the party, we had better head to the Conklin house before this rain comes," David suggested.

"Yes," Mr. Harvey agreed. "You must get to your party, and I must get home before it storms. Young man, I trust you'll take good care of my daughter if the weather turns rough?"

"Absolutely," the confident David assured.

Mr. Harvey smiled at his daughter before stepping quickly down the street, while David and Samantha headed back to the auditorium.

After Mr. Harvey was out of earshot, David grinned, "Did he call you Sammie?"

"Yes," Samantha timidly admitted. "He's always called me Sammie since I was a little girl. I always thought that maybe he wanted a boy."

"Your dad is—" David began.

"Older," Samantha interrupted.

"I was going to say pleasant, but since you brought up the subject, he is...older," David said tactfully.

"Papa was married before he moved to Oklahoma," Samantha explained. "My mother was younger...Papa was fifty-eight when they were married and mother was twenty-five, so people have always thought Papa is my grandfather."

"I can see that," David said.

"Papa always worried about leaving mother and me alone, but she died about a year ago," Samantha continued. "I think it's a relief for him to see me through school."

"There you are!" Caroline yelled from the front steps of the auditorium.

The crowd had thinned out, and Caroline had gathered her group of Lou Berta, Woody, and Jonathan to go to the party.

"Where have you been?" Caroline asked.

"Samantha ran to see her father before he took off," David explained.

"Oh," Caroline replied, while Samantha stood conspicuously silent. "We better get to the house before it rains."

"Sure," David said as he moved smoothly to Caroline's side to hold her arm. "Let's go. I wouldn't want you to melt."

Caroline leaned into David's shoulder, as they headed up the hill. Woody looked awkwardly at Samantha, but she did not let him get as cozy as she followed David and Caroline up the hill while Woody tried to keep up. Jonathan politely offered his arm to Lou Berta, and all six began their walk to the Conklin house and the senior party.

CHAPTER 17

IRIDESCENT FLASHES OF LIGHTNING flickered on the western horizon, as the senior class hurried to the Conklin house on Silk Stocking Row. Mrs. Conklin had placed lights outside to outline the first and second floor porches. The house glowed in the dusk with the many lights.

Samantha felt out of place, but her uncertainties faded with the party's festive spirit. She had not been close to her classmates during the year, but her presence created some fascination especially with the young men, as several of them crowded around her.

"Haven't you boys bothered this girl enough?" David Simpson asked, as the boys tried to outdo each other with stories of their antics.

"We're just catching up with Samantha," one of them declared.

"Yeah," another added. "Why aren't you at your own party, anyway?"

David Simpson replied, "You boys better check that punch bowl—I saw Mr. Conklin sniffing around it earlier. I'd hate for him to walk over and get Deputy Bowles to investigate."

The concerned boys looked at each other before heeding David's advice to go make sure Mr. Conklin stayed away from the punch bowl, which had been supplemented with homebrew.

"That'll keep 'em busy for a while," David smiled. "Are you having a good time?"

"Surprisingly, I am," Samantha replied. "I was hesitant—"

"There you are," Caroline interrupted.

"Hey, Caroline," David greeted. "I just rescued Samantha from your knuckleheaded classmates."

"That's twice I've caught you with my guy," Caroline snickered while looking at Samantha.

"Oh no—I—I was just sitting here, and David was just being nice," Samantha awkwardly defended.

"I'm teasing," Caroline assured.

Turning to David, Caroline said, "Did you think maybe Samantha might like being bothered by the boys?"

"Knowing those guys, it never occurred to me," David joked.

"Come on," Caroline admonished. "They're about to start the dance."

"Yes ma'am," David replied, as he mockingly jumped to attention.

Samantha watched Caroline and David walk to the big center room, when Woody Carlson asked, "Would you like to dance?"

Samantha was speechless for a second before saying, "That's nice of you, Woody, but I don't dance."

"It'll be fun," Woody coaxed. "It's just a square dance."

As Samantha struggled to make an excuse, Lou Berta Cassidy exclaimed, "I'd like to dance!"

Seeing Lou Berta's escort was absent, Samantha said, "Why don't you two go ahead? I'm two left feet."

Woody looked at the eager Lou Berta and cheerfully asked, "How 'bout it?"

Lou Berta sweetly nodded her head, and they stepped quickly to the center room. Several other boys asked Samantha to dance, but she was content to watch the others.

"You're breaking a lot of hearts," Jonathan Kendall remarked, as Samantha stood alone.

"I doubt that," Samantha nervously replied.

"Trust me," Jonathan smiled. "I've been watching. The young bucks have been at your beck and call all evening."

Samantha blushed.

Realizing he had embarrassed the young woman, Jonathan said, "I'm sorry. I—I seem to have the ability to say or do the wrong thing every time I've seen you today. Could I possibly start over?"

A terse Samantha said, "I don't see how you could do any worse."

Jonathan swallowed hard and said with as much confidence as he could muster, "Hello, my name is Jonathan Kendall. I don't try to be the biggest oaf in town, but my friends...and family remind me often that I am. You seem to be a very nice girl, and I apologize for anything I've said...and probably for anything I might say."

Samantha tried to keep from grinning at Jonathan's honesty and self-conscious mannerisms.

"You smiled," Jonathan said. "I didn't think it possible, but you smiled."

"I smile quite a lot," Samantha said teasingly. "I've been told I have a lovely smile."

"I couldn't argue that," Jonathan said in a more comfortable tone.

"Why aren't you dancing, Mr. Kendall?" Samantha asked.

"Please don't call me, Mr. Kendall," Jonathan pleaded. "It makes me feel even older than I already feel at this party, and everyone calls my father Mr. Kendall."

"Okay," Samantha replied. "Why aren't you dancing – Jonathan?"

"It wouldn't be pretty," Jonathan admitted. "I would step on toes, turn the wrong way, and probably hurt someone. Do you see David out there?"

Samantha looked at the group of dancers and spotted David moving effortlessly through the caller's instructions.

"I see him," Samantha answered cautiously.

"Everything David's doing out there...I would do the opposite," Jonathan declared.

"He's magnificent," Samantha admired, as she continued looking at David Simpson.

"Everything's easy for David," Jonathan declared. "It always has been. We've been friends forever, and he's always been that way. We planned to be here a short time and then slip out to our own party, but David's always the center of attention, and I knew there would be no leaving once he got here."

"So," Samantha asked with a raised eyebrow. "I guess you're stuck talking with me?"

"Oh no – " Jonathan began to apologize.

"I was only teasing," Samantha said.

"See what I mean," Jonathan lamented. "Everything that's easy for David is hard for me."

"But you're still friends?" Samantha asked.

"The best," Jonathan assured. "There's nothing I wouldn't do for David."

"That's a good quality," Samantha said, as she watched David sashay through the dancers.

"What do you think of the Conklin's house?" Jonathan asked.

"It's wonderful," Samantha replied, "but I haven't seen much of it."

"You've got to look around," Jonathan encouraged. "It's one of the finest homes in town...I know Mrs. Conklin won't mind."

"That would be great," Samantha admitted.

"Come on," Jonathan encouraged, as he led her to the back of the house.

"Hello, Mrs. Conklin," Jonathan greeted the chaperon of the party.

"Hello, Jonathan," Mrs. Conklin replied cheerfully. "It's good to see you this evening."

"Good to be here," Jonathan said. "Have you met Samantha Harvey?"

"I've seen her at the party tonight, but I haven't really been introduced," Mrs. Conklin admitted.

After the introductions, Jonathan said, "Samantha's been admiring the house all night, and I was wondering if you would mind if I showed her the upstairs?"

"No, not at all," the pleasant Mrs. Conklin replied. "You know your way around, Jonathan. Make yourself at home."

CHAPTER 18

"How do you know your way around this house?" a curious Samantha asked as she and Jonathan Kendall headed upstairs.

"I used to see Mrs. Conklin's daughter—socially," Jonathan explained.

Samantha quizzed in a mocking tone, "Socially?"

An uneasy Jonathan nodded.

"What's her name?" Samantha asked.

"Elizabeth," Jonathan answered.

"Where is she now?"

Jonathan hesitated a moment, before saying, "Oklahoma City. Elizabeth went there to attend school, but I figured she followed David. Things didn't work out with him, but she's engaged to an attorney that works for Judge Robertson."

Feeling remorse for prying, Samantha said, "I'm sorry."

Surprised at her sudden empathy, Jonathan shrugged and said, "There's no reason...we were just friends and no more."

Samantha brushed the mahogany railing at the top of the stairway and admired the freshly painted walls.

Eager to change the subject, Jonathan said, "It's a statehood house."

"What?"

"The house was built the same year Oklahoma became a state," Jonathan explained.

"Everything looks so new," Samantha observed, as she peeked into the empty bedrooms.

At the end of the hall was a powder blue bedroom with stenciled roses on the wall. Samantha assumed the room had been Elizabeth's.

"Here's the door to the upstairs balcony," Jonathan said, as he opened the door for Samantha.

As Samantha stepped onto the balcony that covered two sides of the house, she noticed several couples had separated themselves from the square dance and Mrs. Conklin's watchful eye. The night was dark, warm, and humid. Samantha breathed in the moist air and looked east to see the outline of the courthouse a block away. Beyond the main street, Samantha could see fewer lights. The countryside surrounding her simple house was dark. Samantha thought of how far her home seemed from the fine homes on Silk Stocking Row. The view was peaceful, but made Samantha uneasy— reminding her she did not belong in this place.

After a few moments, Samantha noticed Jonathan had been silent since they stepped onto the porch.

"What are you thinking about?" Samantha asked.

Jonathan looked as if he was startled and replied, "I was just enjoying the view. I always liked it here."

"With Elizabeth?"

"Well, yes," Jonathan admitted, "but that's not what I was thinking about. I like being up high, away from the party and all the people."

Smiling unconsciously, Samantha said, "I know what you mean. I feel more comfortable by myself sometimes, too."

Samantha looked up and noticed a railing above them.

"What's that?" she asked pointing to the railing.

"I'll show you," Jonathan replied with a sly grin.

Leading her inside the house, Jonathan walked to the head of the staircase. A small door that looked like a closet opened up to a very narrow and steep stairway.

"I should've thought of bringing you here first," Jonathan said, as he headed up the stairway.

The stairs led to an attic area that was finished and looked as if it could have been used as a spare room. In the corner of the room was a ladder.

Looking at the ladder, Jonathan asked, "Do you think you can make it."

"Of course," Samantha confidently replied.

Jonathan climbed the ladder, as Samantha followed. When she reached the top, Jonathan extended his hand to assist her. Samantha was hesitant, but then took his hand. Jonathan's grip was firm but gentle as he lifted her to the deck. Samantha let go of his hand and found herself standing on a small deck on top of the house. It was about twelve feet square with a decorated spindle railing around it.

Samantha peered over the rail to the ground thirty feet below and immediately grabbed Jonathan's hand to settle herself, as she stepped back.

"It's high," she moaned.

"You okay?" Jonathan asked, as he held her hand securely.

"A little queasy," she explained. "I guess I'm not good with heights."

"I'm sorry," Jonathan apologized. "You want to head back down?"

"No," Samantha replied. "I'm fine standing away from the rail. Just give me a minute."

Samantha became uncomfortably aware that she still held Jonathan's hand. Although she would have liked to let go, it gave her a much-needed feeling of safety while standing on top of the tall deck.

"Maybe if you'd talk, it would take my mind off the height," Samantha rationalized.

"Oh—sure," Jonathan awkwardly stammered. "The house was built in 1907—Oh, I already said that."

"Did you come here often with Elizabeth?" Samantha asked.

"No," Jonathan replied. "I used to come here with her younger brother. Usually in the summertime, and we would watch the National Guard shoot on the rifle range. You can see the targets clearly in the daylight. Her brother was younger, but I loved to come up here. He said it was like being captain of a ship. In fact, in the light of day the hills to the west look like waves on the ocean."

"Thank you," Samantha interrupted. "You can let go of my hand now."

"Sure," Jonathan complied.

Laughing slightly, Jonathan added, "I guess it didn't take me long to bore you out of your vertigo."

"It's not that," Samantha tried to assure. "I'm just starting to get my sea legs."

Samantha stepped away from Jonathan and inched closer to the rail, looking west. Flickers of lightning flashed on the horizon, but the night was silent except for the faint sound of the fiddle from downstairs."

"It's like a fireworks show tonight, except there's no thunder," Samantha observed.

"The storm's too far away," Jonathan explained. "I'm afraid we'll see some rough weather, regardless of what David Simpson says."

Samantha perked up at the mention of Jonathan's handsome friend.

"What did David say?" Samantha coaxed.

"When I met him at the train this morning," Jonathan replied. "I told David it looked like it would storm today, but he said it wouldn't dare storm on his homecoming."

"What kind of homecoming?" Samantha asked.

Jonathan looked at the bright hazel eyes and attentive tilt of Samantha's head. Her interest in David Simpson caused him to smirk noticeably.

"Did I say something funny?" Samantha asked with a puzzled look.

"No," Jonathan assured. "It's just some things never change. Ever since I can remember, David Simpson has been a source of great curiosity to almost any female I've met."

"I'm not that interested in—" Samantha began to rebut.

"It's okay," Jonathan interrupted. "Girls can't help it."

Samantha's natural inclination was to take offense at Jonathan Kendall's accusation concerning her interest in David, but instead she flirtingly said, "Well then, tell me all about David Simpson."

Jonathan laughed insincerely, before saying, "Everyone wants to know about David."

"Are you jealous?" Samantha prodded.

Jonathan thought for a moment, before saying, "I am...and I guess I'm not. David's my best friend, and I love him like a brother. It's like we've been sewn at the hip since I can remember. David's the best friend you could want—funny, loyal. He makes you glad to be around him."

"So why are you jealous?" Samantha asked in a less insolent tone than before.

"Like I said," Jonathan explained. "David's my best friend. We've been through a whole lot of stuff together. I always see ourselves as equal partners in the friendship, and I think David does too, but to everyone else it's always David and his sidekick, Jonathan. Like our senior year of high school—our last day. David and I were always on the borderline of trouble with Mr. Fleming. We respected him, but were always pushing his limits. Mr. Fleming was giving his famous last day speech."

"He gave that lecture today," Samantha interrupted.

"He gives it every year," Jonathan said. "On the last day, he's giving his speech. Mr. Fleming keeps a coffee mug close to the radiator to keep it warm. I snuck out of class, because, of course, no one would miss me and I filled the cup with vinegar and a touch of iodine to give it some color."

"You didn't," Samantha gasped.

Jonathan nodded and said, "I did. You could hear him spewing it out from three doors down. Everyone immediately assumed David had pulled the prank. David wouldn't say anything to get me in trouble, so I went and confessed. The only punishment I received was a scolding from Mr. Fleming for trying to cover up for David Simpson. David did not get his diploma until a week after graduation."

"Sounds like David was being a good friend," Samantha said, as low-pitched, barely audible thunder rumbled in the distance.

"David's the best," Jonathan admitted, "but it was my prank. I should've been the one punished. The whole thing was typical. It doesn't matter what David and Jonathan do. David is always remembered, and I'm always forgotten. It didn't surprise me when you wanted to talk about David. I think almost every pretty girl I've ever met has been interested in only one area of my expertise—'What's David really like?'"

Samantha blushed slightly at the indirect complement from Jonathan about her attractiveness.

"So you want to know what David's like," Jonathan continued. "David's got personality and charisma to spare. He's smart, just not as smart as he thinks. He's athletic, just not as athletic as he thinks. He's much better at getting out of work than doing any. I'm as smart or smarter than David, can work circles around him, and even though David doesn't seem to notice, I'm considerably taller. But I'll tell you where David beats me and where he beats the world—it's that unmistakable confidence he has. David absolutely believes he can do anything, and he doesn't care a wit about what anyone else thinks. David's not afraid of anything."

"Sounds admirable to me," Samantha observed.

"I agree," Jonathan replied. "I just hope David's confidence and history of doing things easily doesn't catch up with him. Of course, there is that part of me that kind of wants to see David overcome some adversity."

"Your jealous part?" Samantha surmised.

Jonathan shrugged and said, "My feelings of jealousy come only from being under David's considerable shadow."

Jonathan hesitated a moment before saying, "Elizabeth Conklin—the girl I was telling you about. She had a crush on David and even followed him to school when she thought he was available. I guess it worked out for her. She's engaged to a young attorney now. It didn't take her long to forget me when she no longer needed information about David."

"What do you mean, 'he *was* available?'" a serious Samantha asked.

"David had a girl through high school," Jonathan explained. "David went away to school, and it appeared maybe he had left the girl behind."

"Who was it?"

"Caroline, of course," Jonathan stated factually. "David's older, but they've been an item since she was fourteen. It nearly broke Caroline's heart when he went away and didn't give her any assurances he would come back to Chandler."

"Until today?" Samantha asked.

"Yes," Jonathan answered. "David's taking a job in my father's business. David and I are going to be working together — back again, just like old times. I expect he and Caroline will be married soon and we'll be brothers-in-law."

"What kind of business are you in?" Samantha asked.

"We own the cotton gin on the south end of town," Jonathan boasted. "But there's a lot more to the business than that. Dad's acquired property all over the county and he rents it out. Dad says it's a constant battle to keep these farmers producing. He says most farmers can't manage the business end of a mule, so he has a man to keep tabs on them to make sure they're not wasting the seed or spending money they don't have."

Samantha became noticeably surly in her mannerisms and silent, as she bit her lower lip.

Trying to change the subject, Jonathan asked, "What does your father do?"

In a defeated voice, Samantha said, "He was a school principal, but he retired to do a little farming. Since we moved here, he's been a tenant farmer."

Jonathan Kendall stared blankly at her before saying, "I'm such a clod."

Samantha bluntly replied. "I'm sure you were only stating your true feelings."

Jonathan looked at Samantha and could see he had angered her.

"No," Jonathan tried to protest. "I *wasn't* stating my true feelings. I was repeating what I've heard my father say for years. I've tried hard not be like him, and now I find…I'm becoming more like him every day."

Samantha looked at Jonathan with a fury of resentment before replying in as civil a tone as she could muster, "Maybe you need to try harder."

A cool blast of air rushed over the top of the house and thunder rumbled ominously, as a contrite Jonathan suggested, "The storm's getting closer. We probably better get downstairs."

Samantha nodded before heading toward the small opening leading to the ladder. She felt embarrassed for scolding Jonathan and was annoyed at herself for venting her frustrations on him. He had tried to be kind to her, and she believed he had been sincere.

Before she reached the top of the ladder, Jonathan said, "You're right, you know. I do need to try harder. I've tried my whole life to please my father, and it never seems to be enough. He bullies and pushes everyone…and I let him do it to me as well."

The breeze whisked Samantha's sandy-brown hair across her freckled cheeks, as she stopped to say, "Courage is illusive. You read books and hear stories about being brave, but I think courage happens in those silent moments of solitude when no one is there to witness except our own souls. It's easy to act brave, to pretend to be bold, but the truth is…most of us live with our insecurities. I can't judge you…because I've not been courageous myself. I allowed myself to be intimidated without cause or reason. I haven't been able to believe in my own mind that I belong here, so I look for excuses — for people like your father to blame."

Samantha looked at the dark clouds starting to swirl above. Taking a moment to breathe deeply, she studied Jonathan and took satisfaction that he was listening.

"I don't really feel like I belong anywhere," Samantha sighed.

A sudden flash of lightning illuminated the entire house quickly followed by the ripping sound of thunder, as it tore through the sky before booming in a crescendo that shook the house.

"Where you belong now is inside!" Jonathan admonished.

Samantha did not need the encouragement as she scurried down the ladder to the safety of the second floor. Jonathan closed the opening leading to the roof and was quickly by her side. Another lightning strike shook the house again followed by the pattering of a few raindrops.

As Samantha hurried down the stairs to the first floor, the party was dispersing as many of the partygoers scurried out the door trying to beat the rain while a few others looked out the window at the impending storm.

"There you are!" David Simpson shouted. "We need to get home!"

Samantha and Jonathan did not argue, as they followed the decisive David and Caroline out the door, walking as fast as they could toward the Kendall home.

"Where's Lou Berta?" Jonathan yelled as Samantha grabbed hold of his arm to keep pace.

"She and Woody left a while ago," Caroline replied without looking back.

The wind intensified and lightning continued to flash above, although none of the crashes of thunder were as violent as before. A few large drops of rain fell, but the howling wind foreshadowed a deluge that was sure to come. Caroline and David moved quickly down the street, but Samantha struggled to keep up in the high-heeled shoes she had borrowed from Augusta.

As they hurried to the safety of the Kendall home, Sam Bowles watched the seniors scampering home. He knew the storm would mean less mischief than a typical graduation night. For a man who had lived most of his life hunting down dangerous men, he thought of how routine and safe his life had become in his old age. The deputy took a drink of his strong coffee as he watched Samantha Harvey hold tightly to Jonathan Kendall's arm. Sam Bowles did not know exactly what this meant, but he had his theories. Taking another gulp of coffee, he thought how interesting even routine interactions could be in a small town.

CHAPTER 19

Rain poured down in sheets, as David and Caroline stood safely on the Kendall porch watching Jonathan and Samantha trailing behind. Caroline had only a few damp spots on her shoulders, but Samantha was drenched even though she sprinted the last few yards while clinging to Jonathan's strong arm.

Caroline giggled while saying, "We barely made it."

"We didn't," Jonathan complained, as he used his fingers to comb wet hair away from his eyes.

"You're some escort," David teased. "You two are wet from head to toe."

"I'm so sorry," Samantha apologized to Caroline. "I hope I haven't ruined your sister's dress."

"It'll be fine," Caroline smiled, "but we need to get you inside and into some dry clothes."

"Oh my!" Mrs. Kendall screeched in her mousy voice when she saw Samantha standing in the doorway. "We need to get you out of those wet clothes right away."

"I'm sorry about the dress," Samantha apologized again.

"Don't worry about the dress," Mrs. Kendall replied, as she stepped quickly to the back of the house. "It'll dry."

In a moment, Mrs. Kendall returned with towels for Samantha and Jonathan.

"Caroline," Mrs. Kendall instructed. "Take Samantha upstairs and get her into some dry clothes before she catches her death."

The two girls hurried upstairs leaving Jonathan and David in the front parlor.

"No one seems worried that I might catch a cold," Jonathan complained, as he dried himself off.

"You weren't wearing Augusta's dress," David joked. "Besides, you look healthy enough."

"I guess," Jonathan smiled.

"That was a nice switch you pulled tonight," David said, "pawning Lou Berta off while making time with Samantha. Is there something going on I should know about?"

"Unfortunately not," Jonathan replied. "I think she just barely hates me."

Grinning mischievously, David said, "So there is some like on your part—stop the presses. And she barely hates you to boot."

"Stop it," Jonathan said in a whisper. "She'll hear you. I'll need to apologize to Lou Berta tomorrow."

Leaning in to speak in a low voice, David said, "Don't worry about that. Caroline told me Lou Berta has had her eye on Woody Carlson all year. She asked him to take her home as soon as there was the faintest hint of thunder, so you see, Lou Berta ditched you."

"That figures," Jonathan sighed, "at least Lou Berta had the good sense to know it was going to rain."

"It would have been a better plan, if they had walked toward Lou Berta's house, instead of down the hill," David smirked.

"What are you two whispering about?" Mr. Kendall asked, as he walked into the room.

"Nothing," Jonathan answered.

"What happened to you?" Mr. Kendall demanded. "It looks like you've been swimming."

"I got caught in the storm," Jonathan explained.

"I see David managed to stay dry," Mr. Kendall observed. "I trust you took good care of my Caroline?"

"She barely got a drop on her," David boasted.

Mr. Kendall laughed more heartily than was his custom at David's good humor. The rain seemed to intensify, as it beat down on the roof above.

"This rain's going to give my farmers along the Deep Fork an excuse to be late with the rent," Mr. Kendall fumed, as he looked out the window. "The whole country will be flooded if this keeps up."

"Don't you get paid on a percentage of the crop?" David asked.

"Sure," Mr. Kendall answered, "but the renters need tools, equipment, and supplies. We sell them on credit. It'll be okay — we may just have to wait longer to get our investment back."

"At a profit?" David added.

"Of course," Mr. Kendall smiled confidently. "The farmers work the land, and I take care of the business."

"Sounds like a win-win," David said.

"It doesn't matter to me," Mr. Kendall shrugged. "My loans are secured. Freddy Fletcher takes care of that."

Mr. Kendall was in a better mood than he had been earlier in the evening. Talking business with David Simpson acted like a tonic on his earlier surliness. Mr. Kendall's amiable rapport with David changed when he spotted Samantha Harvey coming down the stairs in her old dress and worn shoes.

Stepping quickly to his wife, Mr. Kendall whispered, "What's she doing here?"

"She got caught in the rain coming home from the party," Mrs. Kendall explained.

"Why isn't she with the Carlson boy?" Mr. Kendall asked urgently. "Why didn't he take her home?"

"Jonathan escorted her," Mrs. Kendall explained meekly. "It's a good thing we lived so close or the poor girl would've drowned."

"What?" Mr. Kendall responded.

"She would've drowned," Mrs. Kendall repeated.

"No," Mr. Kendall said impatiently. "You said Jonathan was with her?"

"Yes," Mrs. Kendall confirmed.

As Samantha approached, Mrs. Kendall asked, "How do you feel, dear?"

"Fine," Samantha smiled. "Again, I'm sorry for getting Augusta's dress wet."

"Don't think of it," Mrs. Kendall said pleasantly.

Leaning closer to Samantha, Mrs. Kendall said, "It frankly never looked as lovely on Augusta. It fit you perfectly."

"Thank you for being so kind," Samantha said.

Mr. Kendall stood noticeably silent as Mrs. Kendall was forced to take charge of the conversation.

"The rain doesn't look like its going to let up," Mrs. Kendall observed. "Maybe you should stay here tonight, Samantha?"

"No!" Mr. Kendall said abruptly.

Clearing his throat roughly, he added, "Her father will be worried. I think it's best for her to go home."

"She can't go home in this," Jonathan interjected. "It's pouring outside, and there's still lightning in the air."

Sensing the tension between them, Samantha said, "You're right, my father will be worried sick. I better go."

"You can't go out in this," Jonathan protested. "I'll drive you home."

"No!" Mr. Kendall exploded in a desperate tone bordering on a shout.

"Dad, you can't be serious?" Jonathan said in a more assertive tone than he usually used with his father.

"I need to talk business with you," Mr. Kendall lied.

"Tonight?" Jonathan protested.

"You were gone all afternoon," Mr. Kendall barked.

"Samantha doesn't want to leave her father alone, and I will not have her out in this weather," Jonathan assertively replied. "I'm driving her home."

"No," Mr. Kendall retracted desperately. "I wouldn't think of sending her out in this, either. David, would you mind driving Miss Harvey home?"

"Sure," a puzzled David replied.

"Take the car," Mr. Kendall ordered. "Jonathan and I can walk to the office tomorrow. If it's still raining in the morning, come pick us up. The keys are in the car."

"Dad," Jonathan interrupted. "I can drive her. It will only take a few minutes."

"No," Mr. Kendall insisted. "I need to talk to you."

Looking at Samantha, Mr. Kendall forced a smile and said, "You don't mind if David drives you, do you?"

A confused Samantha muttered, "Of course not."

"Good," Mr. Kendall sighed. "David, you better get going. The weather's not getting any better."

David agreed and opened the door for Samantha.

"I'll go with you," Caroline said, as she glared at her farther.

Mr. Kendall would have liked to have argued and sent Caroline to bed, but he was content to get Samantha out of his house for now and nodded his approval. He watched out the window as David drove into the stormy night.

"I'll be up in a moment," Mr. Kendall said kindly to his wife. "I need to talk to Jonathan for a few minutes."

Mrs. Kendall looked at her son and then followed the directive, sensing her husband wanted to talk to Jonathan alone.

"What was that about?" Jonathan asked after his mother left.

"Never mind that," Mr. Kendall directed. "I need to talk to you."

"What's going on?" Jonathan asked.

Mr. Kendall swallowed hard and said, "Jonathan, I know it seems that I'm hard on you. I've worked like a sharecropper to get this family to where we are, and I'll need you to carry on at some point. The things I do, you may not agree with, but you need to know I do them for your own good and for the welfare of your two sisters."

"I know that," Jonathan confessed.

"When your mother and I were married, I didn't have a barrel for seed corn," Mr. Kendall continued. "Her parents didn't think much of me, but I was determined to prove them wrong. With some money your mother had from her family, I started the business, and I've worked it like a field hand to get us where we are today. I've made plenty of tough decisions, and I know enough to realize the world won't work well for an idealist like you. That's why I'm always demanding more of you, to help you be the man you can be."

"You know I'll try, Dad," Jonathan replied.

"I know, son," Mr. Kendall said. "I'm proud of you, and I know I don't say that enough. I know you're a good boy...everyone reminds me of that, but I need you to do something for me and do something for you...no questions asked."

"Sure," Jonathan said, as he leaned slightly forward in anticipation.

"I need you to stay away from that Harvey girl," Mr. Kendall stated flatly.

A stunned Jonathan asked, "Because she's poor?"

"Don't be ridiculous," Mr. Kendall said bluntly. "She's no good for you, and I need you to stay away. I mean it!"

"I don't—" Jonathan began.

"You don't need to know why," Mr. Kendall interrupted. "Just stay away."

Staring sternly at Jonathan to emphasize his directive, Mr. Kendall left the bewildered Jonathan for the sanctuary of his upstairs bedroom. David Simpson dropped Caroline back home in half an hour after they drove Samantha Harvey home. Jonathan said goodnight to his sister and goodbye to his friend David without discussing his father's odd command. As Jonathan stepped to the front porch to watch the heavy rain continue, he knew he was going to do something he had never done before—defy his father's wishes.

PART 2

JONATHAN AND SAMANTHA

CHAPTER 20

SAMANTHA'S DOG GROWLED ANGRILY, waking her from a restless sleep. Beads of sweat glistened on her forehead from the muggy summer night, and the dog's husky barks had rescued her from an uneasy dream. It took a moment for her to remember the dog did not bark without reason, and she quickly jumped to her feet, searching for the shoes she had purchased the week before.

Samantha's father slept soundly so she did not wake him. Chasing the raccoons away had been Samantha's job since last summer. Samantha clutched her worn broom and crept outside trying to make as much noise as she could without disturbing her father.

"What do you see, Blue?" Samantha whispered as she stepped toward her barking dog.

The only light came from the myriad of twinkling stars in the moonless night. Samantha lit an oil lamp she kept on the porch and cautiously shined the light where the dog snarled. Samantha stepped toward the chicken coop and let out a muffled yelp, as a large raccoon stared at her from the shadowy light. The intruder was not intimidated as he stood his ground with remnants of egg around his whiskers.

"Git!" Samantha shouted angrily in a muffled tone, trying not to wake her father.

When the stubborn raccoon refused to move, Samantha slapped the broom on the ground eliciting a throaty growl from the animal, as it continued to stare at her. Placing the lantern gently on the ground, Samantha stepped back a few paces and found a rock that she threw at the animal. The raccoon finally waddled away defiantly into the dark night.

Samantha cautiously walked toward the chicken coop to inspect the damage. She was relieved to find her hens safe, but the incorrigible raccoon had eaten all the eggs. Samantha eased the light into the dark corner of the yard to make sure no other prowlers were raiding her chickens or fruit trees. Satisfied she had managed to drive the intruder away with her dog Blue's help, Samantha walked back to the small, wooden porch and extinguished the lantern.

The warm June breeze brushed Samantha's hair away from her face, as she sat on the porch staring into the darkness. She did not know the time but guessed it must be closer to dawn than midnight. The night was peaceful, but Samantha was not at peace. She looked at her new shoes in the moonlight. Samantha scrounged and saved for weeks for the simple purchase. The practical shoes now caused her to remember the pretty, white high-heels she had borrowed from Augusta Kendall several weeks earlier.

She felt loneliness bordering on despair. It was not her nature, but she was discouraged. Samantha felt like crying but did not see the point. As if sensing she needed him, her dog Blue nuzzled his nose against her arm inviting her to pet his coarse hair.

"Why didn't you chase that old coon away?" she playfully scolded.

The dog sat by her side, while she petted him gently.

"It's okay," Samantha sighed, as she continued to stroke the dog. "That coon was nearly as big as you, and I'm betting it was a lot younger."

Samantha looked into the dark, empty countryside. She had wanted to bake her father a cake for his birthday, but she needed eggs for that.

"Why don't those old coons steal food from the people rich enough to afford it," Samantha whispered to Blue, while the dog lazily sat by her side in the quiet darkness.

Samantha had never thought much about being poor, and her family's lack of money had not bothered her in the past. With an ailing father and pitiful little extra money to buy necessities, her poverty now seemed to dominate her thoughts in a disturbing way. She had wanted to go to college, but that would be impossible, even if she weren't a girl. The best she could hope for now was to teach at one of the small country schools next year. If her father did not get better, she did not know how she could even do that. She would have to find work doing something for them to survive. Her only relative was the brother of her late mother, but Uncle Huck seemed to be even more poverty stricken than her father.

Giving her dog Blue one last pat, Samantha said to the dog, "I got to get some sleep, old boy. Look's like I'll be making a trip to town to replace my eggs tomorrow."

The old dog looked faithfully at the young woman, as she returned to the stuffy house for a few hours rest, before facing another day of challenging chores.

CHAPTER 21

"You're goin' to join?" Jonathan Kendall excitedly asked David Simpson.

"I'll sign up in a week or two," David calmly assured, sitting at his desk at the Kendall Cotton Gin.

As an officer in the National Guard, Jonathan relished the idea of having rank over David Simpson, but he also knew having David in the unit would make the summer encampment more entertaining.

"I hope Bell Cow Creek dries up so we can pitch the tents," Jonathan said, as David looked over papers at his desk.

"It's not much of an encampment for you," David observed, as he continued to study the paperwork in front of him. "I could hit your house with a rock from the Statistical House."

The Statistical House, a rock structure overlooking the rifle range, was located halfway down the hill from the Kendall house. Officers kept all the records at the Statistical House for the many practice shots taken at the targets on the range. Further down the hill, a bathhouse in the same style had been built for the soldiers during their training in Chandler.

"When the fellas are all here, it's like you're a thousand miles away," Jonathan assured.

Mr. Kendall, who had been listening in the adjacent office roared, "If you'd spent as much time talking to David about this business as you do about that blasted guard, we wouldn't be so far behind."

"Behind on what?" Jonathan defended. "The cotton crop won't be in until the fall."

"There's plenty of work to do," Mr. Kendall fumed. "You're not thinking about getting involved with this soldiering are you, David?"

David Simpson squirmed in his chair and replied, "Jonathan says it's a good place to meet people, and I'm thinking about it."

Mr. Kendall sighed loudly while looking at a disappointed Jonathan, "I can teach you more in a single month than Jonathan's officers can teach you in a year."

"I was just thinking about it," David assured.

Mr. Kendall returned to his office with a discontented look as Jonathan stepped to David's desk and whispered, "You told me you would join."

David signaled Jonathan to discuss it later, when Mr. Kendall shouted, "Jonathan! Get in here."

Assuming his father planned to scold him for trying to coax David into participating in the summer drills, Jonathan reluctantly trudged to his father's office.

"I need you to run some errands this afternoon," Mr. Kendall stated. "It won't be too difficult, and I need to stay here to walk David through our ledgers."

"Sure," Jonathan replied, relieved his father did not overhear his whispers to David Simpson.

"Take this to the Union Bank," Mr. Kendall instructed as he handed Jonathan a small cash bag. "Don't dilly dally and take it straight to the bank."

"Yes, sir," Jonathan nodded.

Handing Jonathan a second parcel, Mr. Kendall said, "This envelope needs to go to the courthouse. Have the clerk file it; he'll know what to do. Take the bag to the bank first and then the courthouse. Can you handle that?"

"Go to the bank first, then the courthouse," Jonathan repeated. "Got it."

Mr. Kendall stepped back to his desk, and Jonathan hurriedly exited the office heading up the hill to downtown. Jonathan was glad to be out of the office. It was a warm, June day without a cloud in the sky. The walk up the hill from the cotton gin was steep, but Jonathan often hiked for miles in his military training.

The Union Bank was an impressive structure located a block south of the courthouse. The bank stood three stories tall with brick walls and an arched window in the front. The entrance situated at the corner of the building had a clock tower built over it that could be seen from one end of the business district to the other. Jonathan deposited the money from the bag and carefully placed the receipt from the deposit into the pocket of his jacket.

The courthouse was in the next block on the same side of the street. Jonathan did not delay in making his next stop. Being out of the office on such a fine day, put Jonathan in a particularly good mood. Glancing across the street, his attitude improved when he saw Samantha Harvey walking quickly in the same direction he was headed.

"Hey!" Jonathan shouted, as he waved.

Samantha Harvey wore the same plain dress she had worn the afternoon she first visited the Kendall home. She saw Jonathan and waved shyly before stepping into the grocery store across the street.

Jonathan stopped and looked at the entrance to the store. His first inclination was to cross the street and say hello. He stepped off the curb and onto the brick paved street when he stopped and looked at the small parcel he held in his hand. Stepping back onto the sidewalk, he hurried to the courthouse to make his delivery in hopes of catching Samantha before she finished shopping.

It took only minutes to make his delivery, and Jonathan hurried across the street to the grocery store. Jonathan stretched his neck to get a better vantage point, but he could not see Samantha among the shoppers. The ringing of the cash register indicated another customer would soon be leaving the store.

Jonathan asked the clerk, "Did you see a girl in here a moment ago—sandy-brown hair, wearing a brown dress?"

"Pretty girl?" the clerk asked.

"Yes," Jonathan replied. "That's her."

"She just left," the clerk informed. "Bought some eggs."

"Which way did she go?" a hurried Jonathan asked.

"Beats me," the clerk answered. "I just know she left."

"Thanks," Jonathan said as he walked quickly out the front door.

The street was not particularly crowded as Jonathan looked for Samantha. His business at the courthouse did not take long, and he believed she could not be far away. Jonathan thought she must have gone into another store but did not know which one. As he continued to use his height to look over the crowd, he spotted her one block down the street walking in front of Collar's Furniture Store.

Jonathan walked as quickly as he could without attracting undo attention and was closing the gap when he yelled, "Samantha!"

She did not hear him, but he was relieved to see her stop for a moment to look in a store window. Before he could get her attention, however, she stepped inside the store. Jonathan trotted to the front door and casually walked into the store to look for the girl he had not seen since the senior party several weeks earlier.

His view was blocked by a woman with a large, broad brimmed hat. As he moved to get a better look, another rather wide woman blocked his path.

About the time Jonathan realized he had walked into a women's dress shop, he heard the accusatory voice of Samantha Harvey say, "Are you following me?"

"No," Jonathan replied in a reflex lie.

Looking around the store, Jonathan noticed he was standing in front of a display of petticoats.

"No?" Samantha quizzed.

Jonathan was too flustered to answer as his cheeks glowed pink.

"It's okay if you are," Samantha finally said with a smile. "I saw you across the street earlier and thought you might come over."

"I—I," Jonathan stammered. "I did come to say hello, but I didn't pay attention to where I was going."

"You're not buying a petticoat for your mother?" Samantha teased. "Or do you have another girl I don't know about?"

"No," Jonathan said. "I—I better be going."

Angry with himself for being so clumsy with his words, Jonathan unceremoniously walked outside.

Standing in front of the store, he tried to muster the courage to attempt another conversation when from behind him Samantha said, "I need to go to City Drug to get some White Pine Cough Syrup for my father. Would you feel more comfortable there?"

Seeing Samantha was holding only her small sack of eggs, Jonathan asked, "You didn't buy anything? I didn't mean to interrupt your shopping."

Laughing pleasantly, Samantha replied, "I wasn't shopping, I was dreaming."

Taking hold of her old dress she added, "This dress seems to work fine, and I barely have enough to buy Papa's cough syrup, much less a dress."

Regaining his composure, Jonathan said, "I actually would feel more comfortable at the drugstore."

Samantha started walking a few doors down to the entrance of the City Drug Store when Jonathan asked, "Is your father okay?"

"Yes," Samantha replied. "He's just fighting a summer cold, and the cough syrup helps him sleep."

"I guess you didn't catch cold," Jonathan said, "from the night at the party."

Looking at him with a kind smirk, Samantha said, "I don't think getting wet is particularly dangerous. I've been known to bathe and even swim without 'catching my death.'"

"My mother's a little protective," Jonathan admitted.

"Your mother's very sweet," Samantha said. "It was kind of her to be so concerned about me."

"Mothers like to worry," Jonathan confessed. "Is your mother a worrier?"

Samantha was unfazed by the awkward question and as she entered the drugstore replied amiably, "My mother passed away last year."

Jonathan almost stopped breathing, as he was only able to mutter a pathetic, "Oh."

It was a lovely day, and Samantha had no desire to torment Jonathan like she had at their first meeting so she quickly said, "It's all right, you didn't know and yes — she was a worrier."

"I'm sorry," Jonathan apologized.

"That she was a worrier?" Samantha asked.

"No!" Jonathan stammered. "That she's — "

Before Jonathan could complete another awkward statement, Samantha asked, "Are you this smooth-talking with everyone, or do I bring out the best in you?"

"I'm not particularly good with anyone," Jonathan confessed, "but I seem to invent ways to offend you."

"I'm not that thin-skinned or offended," Samantha said as she picked up a bottle of the cough syrup while trying to calculate if she had the money to make the purchase.

Confident she had sufficient change in her purse, Samantha headed to the counter with Jonathan by her side.

"I'm glad you're not offended—at least not enough to hold it against me," Jonathan said trying to change the topic of the conversation. "My mother thought very highly of you."

"I don't think your father thinks much of me," Samantha said as she handed her coins to the druggist.

"Don't feel insulted," Jonathan tried to reassure. "There's a long list of people he doesn't approve of and an even longer list of people that don't get along with him."

"I guess that's where you get your charm," Samantha said with a good-natured smirk.

Jonathan looked at the floor in embarrassment at Samantha's assessment of him.

"That wasn't really fair," Samantha added, feeling guilty for reminding Jonathan of his earlier blunders.

In a sincere tone, she added, "I didn't really get a chance to tell you that I enjoyed our conversation on the roof. Things got—"

"Chaotic," Jonathan added.

Smiling, Samantha said, "Chaotic would be one word. My escort left with another girl, you got stuck having to entertain me, and David Simpson ended up driving me home—under Caroline's watchful eye. I think I know how the bread feels at the dinner table, I was passed around so much that evening."

"I'm really sorry," Jonathan apologized.

Stepping outside the drugstore, Samantha said, "I didn't mean to complain. I really did have a nice time talking with you on the roof."

Jonathan tried to restrain his enthusiasm at the comment as Samantha began walking down the street.

"Where are you going now?" Jonathan asked.

"Home," Samantha replied.

"Would you like to have an ice cream or a soda?" Jonathan asked, trying not to sound desperate.

Samantha thought seriously. Ice cream sounded perfect on such a warm day, and it had been months since she had splurged on anything so nonessential.

"My treat," Jonathan coaxed.

Samantha sighed heavily and replied, "I would love some ice cream, but I've got eggs, and I need to get home to finish some chores."

"Why does a country girl have to buy eggs?" Jonathan asked.

With a tone of disgust, Samantha answered, "Because the raccoons can't keep their paws out of my chicken coop, and my dog's too old to scare them away."

"You don't have a shotgun?"

"Papa's got a shotgun, but I'd just as likely shoot my dog as the coon."

"Sure you don't have time for ice cream?" Jonathan asked again.

Looking at her sack of eggs, she wistfully replied, "No, I really need to get home."

"Maybe some other time," Jonathan suggested.

"That would be nice," Samantha smiled. "I really need to get going, though."

Samantha took three steps before stopping abruptly. Jonathan had not moved and was looking at her as she stood silently thinking for a moment.

"I'm baking a cake for Papa tonight," Samantha finally said. "If you'd like to bring a pint of ice cream it would be perfect with the cake."

Straightening up, Jonathan said, "Ice cream is perfect with cake. Your father won't mind?"

Shaking her head, Samantha said, "He loves company."

"I'll be there," Jonathan said. "What time?"

"Come around six," Samantha smiled. "The cake should be baked by then."

"Great," Jonathan replied. "I'll see you at six."

Samantha turned the corner and headed down the hill to the trail leading across Indian Springs Creek to her home.

"Samantha!" Jonathan called as he ran up to her. "Don't let my father get to you. He takes some time to get to know. Believe me, I've tried a lifetime, and I'm not sure I'm used to him yet."

"Thanks," Samantha smiled.

"I'll see you at six," Jonathan reiterated.

"See you at six," Samantha replied as she turned to walk down the hill.

Jonathan watched Samantha until she was no longer in view before hurrying back to the office, hoping his father would not notice his delay.

CHAPTER 22

THE KENDALL COTTON GIN seemed like a more pleasant place to Jonathan when he returned from doing his father's errands. The landscape around town was lush and green with radiant sunshine and a blue sky above. Mr. Kendall was busy pointing out the details of the ledgers to David Simpson and barely noticed Jonathan's delayed return. The real charm of the afternoon for Jonathan, however, involved the invitation to visit Samantha Harvey that evening.

Samantha intrigued Jonathan in a way he did not understand. She spoke her mind more than any girl he had known. Her outspokenness, however, made her easier to talk to and more interesting than any girl he had ever met. Samantha possessed poise and confidence he admired. She was a pretty girl, but in a way that was hard to describe. All Jonathan knew was that he could not stop thinking about her throughout the afternoon. Even the admonishment of his father to not associate with the girl added to Jonathan's fascination about Samantha Harvey.

Jonathan spent the afternoon plotting his getaway from the office. He needed to get to the store before five to buy ice cream, meaning he needed to leave a few minutes early. Leaving work early was one of many pet peeves for Mr. Kendall, but Jonathan hoped David would distract his father. After getting the ice cream, he needed to go by his house to get a bucket of ice to keep the ice cream cold for the short trip and get directions from Caroline to Samantha's house. Then he needed to get across town to the country before his father came home.

Jonathan watched the clock nervously as it passed four o'clock, then four-fifteen, then four-thirty. At ten minutes to five, Jonathan breathed a sigh of relief as he slipped out the door and to the store. Caroline said Samantha lived just outside of town to the east beyond Indian Spring Creek. Jonathan recognized the directions as part of the old Brock place and headed out the door before his father arrived home. He made a detour two blocks north to lessen the chance that he might pass his father, before he headed east of town to the trail crossing Indian Spring Creek.

By five-thirty, the warm June afternoon had turned almost hot. Jonathan was a few minutes early, but he did not want to loiter with ice cream in the warm sun. The Harveys lived in a small cabin that had once been the caretaker's house at the Brock farm. When the Brock family moved to town and rented out parcels of their land, a number of sharecroppers had used the house, and it showed the wear and tear of having people living in the house with minimal means of maintaining the property.

A small shed outside the house stood next to a lean-to that looked like it might have been used as a chicken coop. The water well stood a few steps from the door. The sagging roof of the house had been patched in spots, but the place looked neat and clean.

An old dog lay lazily in the shade of the small shed and bellowed a throaty bark at Jonathan's arrival. The dog raised his head slightly and looked like he might stand, but he soon settled back to his previous position and gave a more apathetic bark. Jonathan nervously expected Samantha to greet him when the dog barked, but she was not in sight. As Jonathan realized the old dog was no threat, he walked slowly toward the open door to knock and announce his arrival. Before he made it to the porch, however, a frenzied and hurried Samantha walked quickly out the door.

"Oh!" she shrieked in surprise. "It's you."

Samantha's hair was matted and sweat glistened from her forehead, as she walked with a sense of urgency. Her overall appearance was strangely disheveled.

"I'm sorry, I'm early," Jonathan apologized as he had obviously caught her unprepared for a guest.

Samantha stopped for only a second to look at him before continuing to walk quickly to the well with a bucket in hand.

"I'm the one that should apologize," she explained. "I forgot about inviting you this evening."

As Samantha set the bucket down to pull water from a cylinder that went down into the well, Jonathan took control of the rope while offering, "Here, let me."

"Thank you," Samantha replied, as she quickly tried to wipe her face and straighten her mangled hair.

"What's wrong?" Jonathan asked, sensing her anxiety.

Biting her bottom lip and sighing heavily, Samantha answered, "Papa's much worse today and I've been trying to make him comfortable all afternoon. I'm sorry. I haven't baked a cake and I've wasted your trip out here."

"There's no such thing as wasted ice cream," Jonathan pleasantly replied, trying to make her feel better.

As Samantha began to pick up the bucket filled with water, Jonathan reached down and took it from her. Samantha hesitated at first as if to resist his offer of assistance, but she had wrestled the heavy bucket all afternoon. Samantha paused again at the door before letting Jonathan come into her small home. The house had four rooms that were neatly swept: a front room with two chairs and a small table, a utilitarian kitchen with a wood-burning stove, a bedroom to the back, and a larger bedroom to the front.

Samantha walked to the back bedroom as she took the bucket from Jonathan's hand. She intended for him to stay in the front room, but Jonathan followed her to a bedroom where her father lay. A shocked Jonathan stared in amazement at the advanced years of the man. Caroline had mentioned the age of Samantha's father, but Jonathan was surprised at how old and feeble the man looked.

"He's really sick," Samantha said worriedly. "He was like this when I got home."

Jonathan moved by her and touched the forehead of the man lying in the bed.

"He's burning up," Jonathan said, as the man lay unaware of the young man's presence.

"He's been like this all afternoon," Samantha fretted.

"He needs a doctor," Jonathan stated. "I'll get Doc Richardson for you."

Jonathan moved quickly to get the doctor and was already off the porch when Samantha said, "I think he'll be okay, the fever will break."

"Maybe, but I'll feel better if a doctor has a look," Jonathan replied.

Jonathan began to leave again when Samantha shrieked in a strange, pathetic voice, "Wait!"

Stepping to Jonathan, Samantha said with tears in her eyes, "I don't have the money for a doctor."

Jonathan had not thought about the cost of a doctor. Samantha tried valiantly to avoid crying in front of him, but she was tired and out of answers. The girl had always seemed so in control to Jonathan, but now she seemed vulnerable, helpless, and alone.

"Don't worry," Jonathan said in a calm, reassuring voice. "Doc Richardson's a friend of mine, and he owes me a favor."

Before Samantha could protest, Jonathan bolted up the hill toward town. An embarrassed Samantha hated taking charity, but when she thought of her poor father suffering through the night, she did not protest. Stepping back into the house, she put a rag into the cool bucket of water and tried to comfort her father.

CHAPTER 23

JONATHAN DESCRIBED MR. HARVEY'S appearance to Dr. Richardson and asked the doctor to come to Samantha's house. Dr. Richardson knew Jonathan well enough to know he was not prone to exaggeration. In less than an hour, Jonathan arrived with the doctor at the Harvey home.

"Samantha!" Jonathan called from the yard.

A frantic but relieved Samantha immediately came to the door.

"He's in the back bedroom," Jonathan explained to the doctor.

Dr. Richardson headed to the door when Samantha timidly said, "I don't know when I'll be able to pay—"

"Let's not worry about that now," the doctor smiled kindly. "Let's check on your father."

After looking into the bedroom, he turned and said in a calm tone, "Jonathan, why don't you take the young lady outside for some air so I can properly examine her father?"

Jonathan nodded and escorted an exhausted Samantha outside.

"He'll be fine," Jonathan tried to assure.

Samantha did not reply, but followed Jonathan out of the house.

Taking a deep, cleansing breath, she said, "Thank you—thank you for getting a doctor."

"He's the best in Chandler," Jonathan boasted.

"How many doctors are there?" a serious Samantha asked.

"One," Jonathan deadpanned.

Samantha had a faint hint of a smile before saying, "I guess he is the best."

"How about you?" Jonathan asked. "How are you holding up?"

Reaching up to touch her hair, Samantha said, "I must look a mess."

"But how are you doing?" Jonathan asked again.

"Better," she smiled. "Thanks to you."

"I didn't have anything better to do this evening," Jonathan replied.

Samantha suddenly remembered the purpose of Jonathan's trip and said, "Your ice cream."

Jonathan looked at the small bucket he had used to carry the ice cream.

He stepped over to inspect it and said, "It's more cream than ice now."

"It would have been so good on the cake I was going to bake," Samantha lamented.

Jonathan looked at her a second before impishly sticking his finger in the gooey container.

"Quick," he instructed. "Get a spoon. It's still cool."

Samantha resisted at first. Enjoying ice cream, even melted ice cream, did not seem appropriate when the doctor was looking after her sick father. Something about Jonathan's silly antic, however, caused her to race into the house. In a moment, she returned with two spoons.

"Ladies first," Jonathan smiled.

Samantha put her spoon into the soft mush and shoveled the melted cream into her mouth.

"Umm," she moaned with delight. "It's still delicious. Try some."

Jonathan complied, and soon the two were alternating turns dipping their spoons into the soupy remains of the ice cream.

When Samantha had her fill she said, "That's the most fun I've had since—well since you took me on top of the Conklin house and we got drenched in the rain."

"You need to get out more," Jonathan teased. "When did you have fun before that?"

Samantha became strangely silent as she dipped her spoon into the remains of the cream for one last taste.

"Before my mother died," she finally said as she looked worriedly at the house where her sick father lay.

Before she could go and check on her father, Dr. Richardson came out of the house wiping his forehead.

"How is he?" an anxious Samantha asked.

"He's fine for tonight," the doctor explained. "I gave him aspirin for the fever and codeine to help him sleep. How old is your father?"

Embarrassed by the question, Samantha timidly said, "Seventy-six, I think."

The doctor nodded and said, "The medicine will make him feel better, but try to get as much water in him as possible."

Samantha nodded, but felt the doctor was not telling her everything.

"Is he going to be okay?" she asked.

"He'll be fine," the doctor tried to convince, "but he's an old man. A sickness like this can take a lot out of him. Try to keep him comfortable, and we'll see how he does. I don't think he's in any immediate danger, but if that high fever returns, come get me.

Otherwise, I'll try to check back in a week or two. He should sleep through the night now."

"Thank you," Samantha said.

"I'll write a prescription that will help with the pain," the doctor said.

Looking over the plain surroundings, the doctor dug around in his bag and said, "There's no need for a prescription, I've got some of it here."

Handing a bottle to Samantha, Dr. Richardson said, "Give him one of these before bed, and it'll help him sleep."

"Okay," Samantha nodded.

"Are you riding back with me?" Dr. Richardson asked Jonathan.

Looking around at the empty house, Jonathan said, "I think I'll help out here for a while. It's not far, I can walk."

Dr. Richardson looked at Samantha and then at Jonathan before saying with a smile, "Suit yourself."

The doctor did not tarry and walked back toward his automobile.

Samantha went inside the house to check on her father, so Jonathan moved to the doctor's car before he drove off.

"Thanks for coming," Jonathan said. "I'll come by in a day or two to take care of the bill."

"They can pay when Mr. Harvey's back on his feet," the doctor offered.

"I'll take care of things," Jonathan replied.

Samantha stepped back onto the porch, but was out of earshot.

As the doctor looked at the girl, he said, "I'll be seeing you, Jonathan."

"One more thing," Jonathan said. "Could you not tell my father you were out here?"

"That might be a good idea," the doctor smiled.

Jonathan watched the doctor drive off as Samantha walked toward him.

"You don't have to stay," Samantha said. "I'll be fine."

"It's not dark yet," Jonathan observed. "Do you mind if I stay?"

"Not at all," Samantha smiled.

Jonathan spent the next hour on the porch learning about Samantha Harvey. He would have liked to have stayed longer, but he had to make his way back to town before the night was too dark to navigate the trail. The walk up the hill was long and tiring, but Jonathan had an energy to his step that defied the late hour. The worry he felt about the questions his father might ask about his whereabouts were overwhelmed by his growing infatuation for the girl that lived across Indian Spring Creek. Jonathan's mind devised schemes and excuses to return to the Harvey home as soon as possible.

CHAPTER 24

JONATHAN LEFT FOR WORK early, enjoying the fresh summer air. He watched carefully for Samantha as he walked the streets, although he knew she would not likely be in town at such an early hour. Thoughts of Samantha made him grin unconsciously as he thought of the time they spent together the previous evening. He considered taking a detour to check on her father, but knew he could not get there and back before the start of work. Jonathan opened the door of the cotton gin and settled into his desk. The office was peaceful, but Jonathan doubted that would last once his father arrived.

"This is a surprise," Mr. Kendall stated with a raised eyebrow. "You're on time for once? Could it be you're starting to take this business seriously?"

"Just getting ready for the day," Jonathan replied, as he organized papers on his desk.

"What time did you get in last night?" his father asked.

"A little after dark," Jonathan answered, as an uneasy feeling churned in his stomach.

"You and that guard business," his father frowned, assuming Jonathan had gone down to check on the condition of the wet grounds for the upcoming encampment.

"We've got to be ready," Jonathan smiled, as he avoided lying to his father without being completely truthful.

"I'm glad you're ready to work this morning," Mr. Kendall said. "I've got a special job for you and David today. Come to my office when he gets here."

Mr. Kendall took his suit coat off and began working through the assorted papers on his desk. Freddy Fletcher came in a few minutes later, waddling across the room on his short, thick legs, before flopping in the chair behind his desk.

"Good morning," Freddy greeted curtly in his heavy German accent. "See you're on time for a change."

"Good to see you too, Mr. Fletcher," Jonathan replied, as the older man buried his head in the morning paper.

Almost a half hour later, David Simpson wandered in as if he did not have a care in the world.

"Where've you been?" Jonathan asked urgently, knowing his father was waiting.

"Stopped for some coffee at the diner," David replied.

Freddy Fletcher growled under his breath and exhaled a strange laugh.

David in an overly polite voice asked, "How are things, Fletch?"

The older man grunted, "You're 'bout to find out, for sure you are."

David did not pay any mind to the round-faced German, but Jonathan knew exactly what Freddy Fletcher meant.

"We're supposed to meet with Dad," Jonathan explained. "He wanted to see us as soon as you got in."

Freddy Fletcher did not look up from his morning paper but laughed again to himself. David did not seem concerned and straightened his tie before following Jonathan into Mr. Kendall's office.

"There you are!" Mr. Kendall roared. "I told you to bring David as soon as he got in, Jonathan."

"It was my fault," David interjected. "We were catching up on the local news with Mr. Fletcher."

Jonathan braced for the speech about responsibility he had heard from his father many times.

"Good," Mr. Kendall said to Jonathan's surprise. "You got to keep up with local happenings, and you can learn a lot from Freddy. That's one of the things I want to talk to you boys about."

David and Jonathan sat in chairs facing Mr. Kendall's desk.

"Running this cotton gin is a pretty straightforward proposition," Mr. Kendall explained. "The farmers bring in their crop and gin it for a percentage. It the farmer does good, we do good. The problem is the farmers don't do so well every year, so as businessmen we've got to protect ourselves, the cash flow, and our investments. That's why we sell seed, help finance equipment, and manage the land. The secret is to sell as high as possible, but the real money is made when you buy low. Watching the business cycles and having your funds available to take advantage of opportunities is how to make money."

David sat on the edge of his seat, while Jonathan said, "Buy low, sell high — sounds simple."

Heaving a sigh, Mr. Kendall continued, "It's not simple. It takes timing, know-how, and smarts. That's why I'm sending you with Freddy this morning to look at a piece of property going up for auction in a couple of days. Look it over and take notes. Don't say anything to anyone and don't look too eager. Watch Freddy and learn."

Tearing off a piece of paper from a notepad on his desk, Mr. Kendall said, "Give this to Freddy. Go about mid-morning. There's sure to be other buyers, but I want that piece of land."

David took the piece of paper from Mr. Kendall and said, "We'll see you get it."

Mr. Kendall smiled awkwardly at David's enthusiasm and then continued working. David and Jonathan went back to their desks, excited that they would get to spend part of this beautiful day outdoors, even if it was going to be with Freddy Fletcher.

CHAPTER 25

FREDDY FLETCHER DROVE ACROSS a viaduct that connected the east side of Chandler with the west side. The railroad connecting Oklahoma City with Tulsa went through a low area running north and south through town. The hill to the west contained the business district and the homes on Silk Stocking Row; the east side featured more modest residential areas. A bridge over the railroad connected the two hills and was known as the viaduct.

The conversation on the short trip was limited as David and Jonathan smiled at each other while Freddy Fletcher grumbled in an almost unintelligible accent about having to bring them. After crossing the viaduct, Jonathan looked down the narrow trail leading to the east to Indian Springs where the Harveys lived. Freddy Fletcher turned north and stopped at a small house on the edge of town.

Jonathan had been distracted by the trail leading to Samantha Harvey's home and had not noticed the neighborhood to which Mr. Fletcher had driven them.

"This is the Cassidy house," Jonathan observed.

"Yep," Freddy Fletcher grunted as he stepped out of the car.

"What are we doing here?" Jonathan asked.

"This is the house we's looking over," Mr. Fletcher replied factually.

Jonathan looked at David and said, "Did you know this was the place being auctioned?"

"No," David replied, while Mr. Fletcher stopped at the front yard gate.

"This must be a mistake," Jonathan said as he walked beside Mr. Fletcher.

"No mistake," Freddy replied. "This is the address and look…there's the posting on the door. Bein' sold for taxes."

"This is Lou Berta Cassidy's house," Jonathan argued.

"I don't know about that," Mr. Fletcher shrugged. "Property's property to me and this is the place your father wants to buy."

Before Jonathan could inquire more, he was interrupted by the squeak of the front door as Lou Berta Cassidy stood looking at them. The small girl appeared terrified with embarrassment and looked as if she wished she had stayed inside.

Before she could retreat, David said, "Hello, Lou Berta."

"Hello, David," she greeted in a guarded tone. "Hello, Jonathan."

Jonathan and David left Freddy Fletcher, who was making notes on his pad as they walked to the front porch.

"What's going on, Lou Berta?" a concerned Jonathan asked.

Lou Berta's eyes shifted from Jonathan to David before answering, "I don't know. The sheriff came by a few days ago and talked to Daddy, but I don't know about what. They talked for a long time, and then the sheriff said, 'I'm sorry,' and posted the public notice on the door. It has something to do with taxes."

"That's terrible," Jonathan consoled.

"I guess we'll be moving," Lou Berta lamented. "What are you doing here?"

Jonathan was speechless, but David Simpson responded, "We heard they were going to auction a piece of property, but we didn't know it was your place. Is there anything we can do?"

Lou Berta shook her head and said, "I don't know. I—I don't know what we will do."

"Git over here!" Freddy Fletcher shouted from the front yard.

Jonathan and David looked at the short, gruff man, but before they could reply, Lou Berta said, "I better get inside and help mother."

Lou Berta disappeared into the house leaving David and Jonathan facing Freddy Fletcher.

"Take a look at the items in the back and mark their condition," Freddy Fletcher ordered, as he handed them a piece of paper with a list of property scheduled for auction. "Mark it good, fair, or poor."

Mr. Fletcher left them to walk brazenly around the property occasionally uttering phrases in his thick accent like "good" or "not too good."

Jonathan timidly went with David to inspect a small building in the back and some household items stacked for the auction. They did not see Lou Berta or her family again, but Jonathan felt as if poor Lou Berta watched his every move from inside the house. Jonathan and David did not say much and were glad when Freddy Fletcher pulled away from the Cassidy house.

"This isn't right," Jonathan sighed. "Lou Berta is Caroline's friend, and we're picking at their property like vultures."

"Their loss is our gain," Freddy groused as he drove back to the office. "That's the way da' world works. When someone loses, somebody else wins."

"That's not right," Jonathan replied.

"That's business," Freddy Fletcher bellowed back. "It don't have nothing to do with people. It's just an opportunity."

"I don't like it," Jonathan said. "I don't like it one bit."

Freddy Fletcher muttered something under his breath, but Jonathan was in no mood to argue business ethics with the older man. The ride to the office was silent except for the hum of the tires on the brick road. Jonathan looked at David Simpson and was agitated at his friend's calm demeanor. Even though David was his friend, Jonathan had long felt David's cavalier attitude bordered on self-serving. Jonathan was particularly disheartened at David's apparent indifference. He felt compelled to do something, but did not know what that might be.

CHAPTER 26

BY THE TIME FREDDY Fletcher parked in front of the office at the cotton gin, Jonathan was determined to do one thing—talk to this father. Mr. Kendall was outside his office when they arrived. Freddy Fletcher immediately went to his desk to sit down as Mr. Kendall followed him, anxious for a complete update.

"Well," Mr. Kendall asked. "What did it look like?"

"Looks good," Freddy replied with his uncomfortable grin. "I didn't see other buyers, and the property's in tip-top shape."

"Good," Mr. Kendall smiled.

"Dad," Jonathan interrupted. "I've got a problem with this."

"A problem with what?" Mr. Kendall asked.

"A problem taking advantage of the Cassidys' bad luck," Jonathan explained.

"Nonsense," Mr. Kendall replied bluntly. "There's no such thing as luck. I'm taking advantage of nothing but an opportunity, and I've done nothing to hurt these people. They're the ones that are behind on their taxes."

"I still don't feel good about it," Jonathan said. "Mr. Cassidy was sick last year. Shouldn't we try to help them?"

"We are," Mr. Kendall defended. "We're buying the property so Mr. Cassidy can pay the back taxes and stay out of jail. They'll get whatever's left to start over."

"Why don't you just buy the property directly from Mr. Cassidy and save them the humiliation of the auction?" Jonathan asked.

"That'd be stupid," Freddy Fletcher interrupted. "We'll buy it at auction for a good price."

"Good for us!" Jonathan interjected hotly.

"Yes!" Freddy replied in a condescending tone. "That's good business!"

"Dad," Jonathan said, looking at his father. "You can't feel good about this. Lou Berta Cassidy is one of Caroline's best friends. She's at our house all the time."

"It's not about feeling good," Mr. Kendall defended. "Opportunity's an opportunity…you can't do business on what you think feels good."

"Mr. Kendall," David interrupted. "Could I say something?"

"Sure," Mr. Kendall said. "What is it David?"

"I looked at the property, and I'd agree with Mr. Fletcher that it's in good condition," David began. "But Jonathan has a point. I don't think this is the right property for this business."

"You don't know what you're talking about," Freddy Fletcher said bluntly. "I saw the property, and we can make a bunch of money reselling it."

"Maybe," David replied, unfazed by Freddy Fletcher's bullying tone. "But it doesn't fit what we do. I've looked at our inventory of property and our customer list. We deal with farmers — people that need seed, equipment, and credit. You've said it yourself, the cotton gin's just a part of the business, but our business deals with developing and using those relationships as a basis for everything."

"You're right, David," Mr. Kendall confessed, "but diversification's important. If we can get this property at a good price, we can resell it quick and make a profit. I don't see that that's anything but good business."

"Of course we could make a profit," David replied, "but it would tie up some of your cash while we wait for a buyer. I've been studying the land records and there's several properties likely to be auctioned this fall…especially if things don't dry up soon. These places have some agricultural usage. If we acquire them, we can rent them out and not only generate cash, but build seed and equipment customers."

"I see your point," Mr. Kendall replied, "but if we can get the Cassidy place at a good price and sell it quick, I don't see how it would keep us from buying up more farms in the fall."

"You bet'cha," Mr. Fletcher added. "Don't let good money go by."

Stepping closer to Mr. Kendall, David said, "Business is business, but I'm thinking of Caroline, too."

Mr. Kendall elevated his head and listened more intently to his new employee.

"She's friends with Lou Berta," David continued. "I'm betting they'll be involved with a lot of activities this summer. They'll be on the party planning committee for the upcoming encampment, they'll be doing all those girl club things they like to do, and…they're at the age when they'll be married soon and…do you really want to be involved in the foreclosure of one of your daughter's bridesmaids?"

Mr. Kendall had a hard time containing his smile at the insinuations of a possible marriage between David and Caroline.

"I see your point," Mr. Kendall smiled.

"What point?" Freddy Fletcher exploded.

Before Freddy could say more, Mr. Kendall said, "David's right. We need to stay focused on farms and leave this business with the Cassidys alone."

"That's the stupidest thing I've heard this upstart say yet!" Freddy Fletcher sneered.

"I've spoken, Freddy," Mr. Kendall said sternly. "David has a point. We can pass on this deal."

Freddy Fletcher looked like he might say more but instead turned to his desk shaking his head and grumbling under his breath. Mr. Kendall did not give him further opportunity to argue the point and returned to his office.

In a few minutes, Jonathan walked to David's desk and said, "That was smooth."

"What?" David coyly asked.

"The way you got Dad to back out of that Cassidy deal," Jonathan answered. "I didn't think Dad could ever change his mind."

"It was nothing," David claimed.

"Nothing," Jonathan replied. "You don't know my father very well. He's not one to change his mind, especially when an easy profit's to be made."

Looking at Jonathan, David said, "I know your father well. That's how I kept him from creating an awkward situation for Caroline. You tried to reason with your father based on the idea of fairness. That would never work on your dad."

"Because he's unreasonable?" Jonathan asked.

"No," David explained. "It's not that your dad's a bad person. He's just wired to ignore fairness when it comes to a business deal. In his mind, he didn't cause the situation, so he was entitled to profit without feeling guilty. It's simple psychology. You tried to appeal to his sense of fairness while I tried to appeal to something he cares about...this business. People don't argue with their own ideas, so I simply used some of the things he's been telling me the past weeks to convince him to at least think of the alternatives. I gave him an option. Once he was thinking, I threw in the part about it being awkward for Caroline. I wanted the same thing you did — I just went about it differently."

"Pretty manipulative," Jonathan said.

"It's such a fine line between manipulation and influence," David smiled. "I wasn't just blowing smoke though. I've been looking over these papers, and there's a real chance that there'll be a flood of good land available soon. A surplus of land on the market will drive prices down and provide an opportunity for those with the resources to buy."

Jonathan did not reply, but his body language conveyed he was impressed by his friend's logic.

"I'm a little more diligent than you give me credit for," David said. "We just do things differently."

"I'm glad you got us out of that Cassidy deal," Jonathan confessed.

"Me too," David replied with a sigh, "but it won't matter much."

"What do you mean?" Jonathan asked.

"Your dad's right," David explained. "The property's going to be auctioned and someone will buy it at a good price…it just won't be us. The fact we're not buying the land won't help the Cassidys at all."

"Why did you do it then?" Jonathan asked.

"Caroline's going to get married soon," David factually stated. "She'll want to ask Lou Berta to be a bridesmaid. I wanted to avoid an awkward situation."

"You've asked Caroline to marry you?" Jonathan gasped.

"Not yet," David said in a lower tone of voice, "but soon."

"How do you know she'll accept?" Jonathan quizzed. "You've been gone a year and back a few weeks…how do you know she'll want to marry you?"

"I know people," David replied. "It's the one thing I'm good at. Caroline will want to marry, your father will be thrilled, we'll all live happily ever after."

"I don't believe in 'happily ever after,'" Jonathan smirked. "When are you going to ask?"

Mr. Kendall interrupted the conversation when he came out of his office to say, "I've got a lunch meeting with a commissioner today. David, why don't you join me?"

Standing up from his desk, David replied, "Sure."

As David followed Mr. Kendall out the front door, he turned to wink at Jonathan and said, "Soon."

CHAPTER 27

JONATHAN LOOKED ACROSS THE office at Freddy Fletcher, who was in an even grumpier demeanor than normal. Since the two men were alone in the office, the afternoon proved tense. Thankfully for Jonathan, Freddy was content to rummage through his desk without talking or complaining about the Cassidy deal.

The door opening did not attract Jonathan's attention at first, but in a few seconds, he realized Freddy was not greeting the visitor. Timid steps patted across the wood floor interrupting the otherwise silent office. Looking up, Jonathan saw Samantha Harvey standing in front of him.

Blood rushed to his face, as his initial surprise quickly turned to exhilaration at seeing the young woman, who had filled his thoughts all day, standing in the office. Jonathan breathed a sigh of relief as his brutish colleague hid behind the paper, seeming to have no interest in the girl's visit.

"Samantha?" Jonathan greeted. "I didn't expect to see you here."

Samantha looked around nervously before saying, "I hope I'm not interrupting."

"No," Jonathan assured, relieved his father had taken a long lunch. "Not at all. How's your father?"

"He's doing much better, thanks to you," she replied.

"I didn't do anything but fetch the doctor," Jonathan said.

"It meant more than anything to me," she said sincerely. "I wanted to thank you."

Jonathan blushed and said, "You're welcome, but it was really nothing."

"I brought you something," Samantha beamed with a tinge of excitement as she handed Jonathan a pan. "It's the chocolate cake I promised."

Jonathan took the small cake from her and said, "It looks delicious."

"I'm sorry I didn't bring ice cream," Samantha said, "but I hope you enjoy it."

"I will," Jonathan assured. "But ice cream would be good — we're having a little trouble coordinating our timing."

"I guess," Samantha laughed politely.

"Would you like a piece now?" Jonathan asked.

"No," Samantha answered. "I need to get back to Papa."

"You're sure?" Jonathan asked.

"Maybe some other time, but I really need to be running right now," she said sweetly.

"Okay," Jonathan replied, trying to hide his disappointment.

"I better go," Samantha said awkwardly as she headed outside.

Samantha was out the door before Jonathan worked up the courage to follow her.

"Samantha!" he yelled as she walked toward downtown.

Samantha turned around to see Jonathan approach her.

Taking a deep breath, Jonathan asked, "Maybe I can come visit sometime…to see how your father's doing."

"That would be fine," Samantha replied abruptly.

She glanced away for a moment and appeared uncharacteristically unsure of herself before looking at him with a slightly tilted head to say in a reserved voice, "What I mean to say is that I would like that—very much."

A relieved Jonathan said, "Good. I'll come by sometime...very soon...maybe this afternoon."

Samantha smiled and hurried up the hill toward downtown while Jonathan walked back to his office. Stepping inside, Jonathan noticed Freddy Fletcher looking at him.

The older man had ignored Jonathan since they had returned from the Cassidy place, so he was surprised when Freddy Fletcher asked, "Was that the Harvey girl?"

"Yes," a confused Jonathan replied.

"The Harveys from around Warwick and Wellston?" he probed again.

"I believe so," Jonathan answered.

Freddy Fletcher leaned back in his chair and smiled oddly at Jonathan. The sometimes-gruff man laughed softly to himself as if sharing a secret joke only he could hear.

"What's wrong?" Jonathan asked.

"Nothing," Freddy Fletcher said as he continued to chuckle. "Life's just funny somehow—that Harvey girl bringing you a cake and all."

"What do you mean?" a confused Jonathan asked.

Laughing a little louder, Freddy Fletcher said, "I guess you can have your cake and eat it too."

"Do you know that girl?" Jonathan asked.

Freddy Fletcher stopped laughing suddenly and said, "No! I don't know that girl but—"

Mr. Kendall and David Simpson returned from lunch, interrupting Jonathan's interrogation. Freddy Fletcher said no more, and Jonathan's visitor remained a secret. Jonathan was edgy about

Freddy Fletcher talking to his father about Samantha's visit, but the brooding employee did not speak to Jonathan's father the rest of the afternoon.

CHAPTER 28

SAMANTHA HARVEY WALKED AWAY from the Kendall Cotton Gin relieved, yet anxious. She convinced herself the cake she baked for Jonathan Kendall was a gesture of appreciation, but knew it was more. Samantha had enjoyed talking to the young man the night of her senior party, but their conversation on her porch the preceding evening had been more than entertainment. A more relaxed and comfortable Jonathan made her realize he was not the person she had first thought, and that he was different from his overbearing father.

Knowing Jonathan wanted to see her again caused Samantha to smile, but she was apprehensive about their different backgrounds. Jonathan's family owned property, had the trappings of prosperity, and held prestige in the community, while Samantha's background included poverty and a past of which she knew little. Samantha had only known Jonathan a few weeks, but her practical nature thought about the advantages a marriage with someone of Jonathan's status would mean. She always believed there would be more romance in regard to the man she might marry, but with an ailing father, pitiful little money, and a family she barely knew, Samantha could not help considering the possibility that Jonathan might be attracted to her.

None of the complexities of her life bothered her this afternoon, however. The day was sunny and warm, but the heat of summer had not fully taken hold. She had delivered her cake to Jonathan Kendall, and he promised to come see her again. Not even the pesky raccoons that continued to steal her eggs could get her down this afternoon.

"Samantha?" a strange voice greeted from the alley behind Collar's Furniture Store.

A startled Samantha watched a man step awkwardly toward her, wearing well-worn overalls that looked like they belonged to someone thirty pounds heavier. The lean man looked nervous, and his eyes shifted erratically as if expecting some calamity.

"Yes," Samantha replied cautiously.

"I'll be," the man smiled, showing several missing teeth. "You don't recognize me, do you?"

Looking at the shabby, strange-acting man, Samantha confessed, "No. Should I?"

The man looked around nervously and said in a dejected tone, "No, I guess not. I—knew your ma. You sure look like her—pretty as a peach."

"You knew my mother?" Samantha timidly asked.

"Yeah," the man replied with a slight sparkle in his sad, tired eyes.

Samantha smiled politely and asked, "How'd you know my mother?"

The question seemed to confuse the man, and he finally said, "I knew her a long time ago—I—I just knew her."

The man looked as if he might say more, but instead he looked around the corner anxiously as if he were trying to stay out of sight. Samantha, on the other hand, was determined not to be lured into the alley with the strange man. Samantha wanted to leave the man, but did not want to turn her back.

Samantha stepped back slightly before saying, "Who are you?"

"Marcus Lutz," the man replied. "Come on over here...I won't hurt you."

"Stay away from me," Samantha warned as she stepped back. "If you know my mother, why didn't you know she passed away?"

The question again seemed to puzzle the man as he stared at her silently.

"She passed away last year...before we moved to Chandler," Samantha said in an accusatory tone.

The man finally responded and said, "I'm sorry to hear that. I've been away for a while. I hadn't heard."

The man's mannerisms made her uneasy. He seemed overly friendly, yet withdrawn. She wanted to find out what the stranger knew about her mother, but she also wanted to get away from him. As she stepped backward, the man started to follow her before suddenly stopping. Samantha looked to see who had caught his attention, and when she turned back around, the man had vanished. Although he had left, it felt as if Marcus Lutz was still watching her.

Samantha decided to make a detour home and turned away from her usual path to walk down Silk Stocking Row to ensure the man did not follow her. Samantha stopped several times to make sure she was walking alone, when she nearly walked into Sam Bowles.

"Oh!" Samantha exclaimed, as she quickly stepped to miss the deputy.

"Excuse me," Sam Bowles politely offered.

"No, excuse me," Samantha said as she looked quickly behind her.

"Don't tell me Jonathan Kendall's chasing you again?" Sam asked.

"Huh?" Samantha stammered before remembering her previous meeting with the deputy. "Oh no, I was just walking home."

Sam Bowles did not say anything about Samantha walking the wrong direction when she said, "I'm sorry, I'm Samantha Harvey...I'm afraid I didn't introduce myself last time we met."

"Sam Bowles," the deputy introduced.

"You must have thought me silly, running away from Jonathan and into his house?" Samantha blushed, remembering her last encounter with Sam.

He chuckled and said, "I didn't think you were silly, but I did get a good laugh."

Samantha looked back toward downtown again as Sam asked, "Are you okay, Miss Harvey?"

Turning back around, Samantha asked, "Do you know a Marcus Lutz?"

The question was answered by the reaction of Sam Bowles, as he wrinkled his forehead and said, "Yes. Why do you ask?"

"I met him a few minutes ago," Samantha revealed. "He's a very strange man."

In a serious tone, Sam Bowles asked, "You saw Marcus Lutz here...in Chandler?"

"Over by the furniture store on my way here," Samantha replied.

"Excuse me," Sam Bowles, said urgently as he began to walk away. "I'd like to see him, if he's in town."

Samantha watched in bewilderment, as the old deputy walked as fast as his short legs would move in the direction of where she said Marcus Lutz had been a few minutes earlier.

Samantha wanted to ask more questions, but Sam Bowles shouted as he walked away, "You'll want to tell your pa you seen Marcus."

Samantha, left alone on the street, walked in front of Jonathan Kendall's house to stand for a few seconds before circling back to her world on the edge of town across Indian Spring Creek. Samantha walked quickly and cautiously. It was a peaceful, summer day, but she had the uneasy feeling she was being watched, and every sound in the woods caused her heart to jump. Samantha felt a surge of relief as she stepped onto the safety of her porch. She did not know what Marcus Lutz was doing in town, but Samantha wished she had never met the peculiar-acting man.

CHAPTER 29

"You came!" a cheerful Samantha Harvey greeted as Jonathan walked up to the Harvey house.

Samantha had been on edge since meeting the stranger named Marcus Lutz. She had not bothered to tell her father and did not want to do anything that might upset him. Samantha had kept a watchful eye on the trail leading to town and was relieved to see Jonathan coming to visit.

"Hope I'm not intruding?" Jonathan replied.

"Not at all," Samantha assured. "It's good to have company."

"How's your father?" Jonathan asked.

"He's doing better," Samantha replied. "Would you like to see him?"

"In a little bit," Jonathan said. "I'd like to know about your day first."

"Not much to my day," Samantha lamented. "The coons stole all my eggs again and killed one of my hens. If old Blue here doesn't do a better job of scaring them away, I'm going to have to sleep in the chicken coop. I tried putting a string of cans around to frighten them, but so far the raccoons have been smarter than me."

"Sammie!" Mr. Harvey yelled from inside the house. "Who's out there?"

"It's Jonathan," Samantha replied.

"The boy you were telling me about?" Mr. Harvey asked.

"Yes!" Samantha shouted back in embarrassment.

Turning to Jonathan, Samantha said, "I'll be right back." She disappeared for a moment before returning.

"Sammie?" Jonathan whispered with a sly smile.

"Yeah," Samantha affirmed. "It's what Papa calls me."

"I like it," Jonathan said. "Sounds like a ballplayer."

"Thanks a lot," Samantha said while rolling her eyes. "How was your day?"

"Pretty good, I guess," Jonathan replied.

"You don't seem too excited," Samantha observed.

"There's really not that much to get excited about," Jonathan shrugged. "It's kind of slow until harvest."

"Would you like to come in and meet my father?" Samantha asked.

"Sure," Jonathan replied.

Samantha led him into the small house. Jonathan had observed how neat it was kept on his first visit, but this time there were wildflowers in a vase decorating the front window. Jonathan also noticed a photograph hanging on the wall of a woman who looked somewhat like Samantha, which Jonathan assumed to be her deceased mother.

"Papa," Samantha said to the old man sitting in a chair in the front room. "This is Jonathan. He's the boy that got the doctor."

"This isn't the boy I met a couple of weeks ago," Mr. Harvey said while looking at Samantha.

A frustrated Samantha said, "I told you this is a different boy. He's the one that came to see me."

Mr. Harvey looked confused and said, "The boy I was thinking about was shorter—"

"I think you're talking about David Simpson," Jonathan interrupted. "He's a friend of mine."

"David was his name," Mr. Harvey declared, "but you're not him."

"No," Jonathan patiently replied. "My name is Jonathan."

"Jonathan?" the old man said in a confused tone. "Have I met you?"

"Papa," Samantha scolded mildly. "I told you Jonathan's the boy that came to the house. You haven't met him yet."

Mr. Harvey still seemed slightly confused so Jonathan held out his hand and said, "Hello, Mr. Harvey, I'm Jonathan Kendall."

The old man gripped Jonathan's hand firmly while looking at the young man's face and said, "Kendall?"

"Yes, sir," Jonathan confirmed.

"You're a friend of Sammie's?" Mr. Harvey asked.

"Yes," Jonathan said while stealing a look at Samantha, who was becoming impatient at her father's confusion.

"Have a seat," the old man offered in a lower tone of voice.

Jonathan sat in the chair across from Mr. Harvey, while Samantha pulled up a chair from the table.

"Any relation to the Kendall that has the cotton gin?" Mr. Harvey asked.

"Yes," Jonathan affirmed. "My father owns it."

"John Kendall?" Mr. Harvey asked.

Jonathan had rarely heard anyone, call his father anything, but Mr. Kendall.

"That's right," Jonathan answered. "Do you know him?"

"Not well," Mr. Harvey said.

"How are you feeling, sir?" Jonathan asked.

Mr. Harvey seemed to be lost in thought for a moment before saying, "Better. I'm still a little weak, but the fever's been gone today, and I'm feeling better."

"I'm glad to hear it," Jonathan said.

Seeming to be more clearheaded than before, Mr. Harvey asked, "Sammie tells me you're the one that found the doctor?"

"Yes, sir," Jonathan acknowledged. "He's a neighbor of mine and was glad to help."

"Thank you," the old man said politely.

"You're welcome," Jonathan replied.

"You work with your father, or do you attend school?" Mr. Harvey asked.

"I'm through with school and have been working with my father the past year," Jonathan explained.

"How's that been?" Mr. Harvey asked.

"Okay," Jonathan said.

"You don't sound too convinced," Mr. Harvey observed.

Smiling, Jonathan said, "I guess I'm sure most days."

"Your father's a hard man," Mr. Harvey said.

"He is on me," Jonathan confessed. "How do you know my father?"

Mr. Harvey looked at the young man for a moment before saying, "It's not important. I would much rather learn more about you. Sammie and I don't receive many visitors, and I don't get to town much."

"There's not much to learn about me," Jonathan said, "at least not much that's interesting."

"I doubt that," Mr. Harvey said with a smile. "What do I always tell you, Sammie?"

Samantha was listening nervously to her father's inquisition of her new friend when she said, "Everyone's interesting, if you take the time to get to know them."

Mr. Harvey was noticeably pleased with his daughter's answer as he said, "What do you like to do besides gin cotton?"

"Almost anything," Jonathan replied. "The cotton gin's just where I work. I wouldn't say I like it."

Mr. Harvey had a concerned contortion to his face, as he said, "A man should like what he does. You're likely to spend much of your life doing it."

"Not according to my father," Jonathan revealed. "According to him, business is business…and everything else is foolishness."

"What do you like to do, then?" Mr. Harvey pressed.

"I like serving with the guard," Jonathan revealed.

"I forgot to tell you Jonathan was a soldier," Samantha said.

"I'm just a part-time officer," Jonathan blushed.

"An officer?" Mr. Harvey said.

"Yes, sir."

"You're rank?" Mr. Harvey asked.

"Lieutenant," Jonathan replied.

"Sammie," Mr. Harvey called to his daughter. "Bring me the small box that's in the chest by my bed."

In a moment, Samantha handed the small cedar box to her father. He gently looked through the contents before picking out a picture.

"Take a look at that," Mr. Harvey said as he handed the picture to Jonathan.

Samantha moved behind Jonathan to get a look at the picture.

"Is that you, Papa?" Samantha asked.

Mr. Harvey nodded.

"You were a captain?" Jonathan asked as he looked at the insignia.

Mr. Harvey nodded again.

"The Union army?" Jonathan asked rhetorically.

"The Army of the Potomac," Mr. Harvey clarified. "The 145th Regiment of the Pennsylvania Volunteers from Mercer County."

"Wow!" Jonathan exclaimed. "Did you see action?"

"Too much," Mr. Harvey frowned, as Jonathan handed him back the picture.

"I didn't know you were in the army," Samantha said.

"It was a long time ago," Mr. Harvey explained. "I never saw the need to bore you."

"What was it like?" Jonathan asked.

"Boring most of the time, accented by moments of sheer terror," Mr. Harvey shared.

"What battles were you in?" Jonathan asked.

Mr. Harvey had a twinkle in his eye as he barked out, "Fredericksburg, Chancellorsville, Gettysburg…Antietam."

"It must have been something," Jonathan said.

"Like hell on earth," Mr. Harvey said nervously. "Horrible things…things you don't like to talk about or remember."

"I'm sorry," Jonathan apologized.

"Not your fault," Mr. Harvey said pleasantly. "I'm the one that brought it up. I saw a lot of good men die…I suppose on both sides if I'd had the opportunity to know the men across the fields from me. Our first day on duty we were placed outside of Sharpsburg face to face with Stonewall Jackson's men. We were in reserve and didn't see much real action until they sent us to tend to the wounded and bury the dead…I'll never forget the stench. Half my men were sick afterwards at the sight. By the time we were pinned at Marye's Heights near Fredericksburg in the winter, we were so used to death that using the bodies of our dead to shield us through the night seemed normal. Death in war's not like death ought to be…it's different…it changes a man."

"I've read about that battle," Jonathan said with genuine interest. "You were at Marye's Heights?"

Mr. Harvey nodded. Jonathan would have liked to have asked more questions but had the feeling Mr. Harvey did not want to remember the past—at least not in front of his daughter."

"Let's talk about something more pleasant," Mr. Harvey suggested. "How do you know my daughter?"

"She's a friend of my sister," Jonathan explained.

"And you think my daughter is pretty?" Mr. Harvey asked with a mischievous grin.

"Papa!" a horrified Samantha scolded.

"Yes," Jonathan said without hesitation.

Mr. Harvey winked at his glaring daughter and said, "I think I better rest before supper. Would you like to stay for supper, Jonathan?"

Jonathan looked at Samantha for approval and said, "If it's no trouble."

Mr. Harvey laughed and said, "I don't know much about young people anymore, but I'm sure my daughter won't mind setting another plate."

Jonathan stayed for supper that evening and became a regular visitor to the Harvey house for the next couple of weeks. Mr. Harvey was always pleasant to Jonathan but never again talked so plainly about his war experiences—nor did he ask questions about Jonathan's father. Jonathan did not understand at the time, but Mr. Harvey knew more about his father than Jonathan's father knew about himself.

CHAPTER 30

"I CAN'T BELIEVE THE audacity of that man!" Mr. Kendall roared at the dinner table as Mrs. Kendall, Caroline, Augusta, Jonathan, and David Simpson listened meekly. "Freddy Fletcher's worked for me ten years and to do this."

"Let's not talk business at the dinner table," Mrs. Kendall suggested.

"This isn't business," Mr. Kendall fumed. "It's betrayal. It was one thing for him to go behind my back and buy that Cassidy place after I decided not to bid, but bidding against me for that Johnson place! He's worked for me ten years and used that against me!"

"We still got the Johnson place," David Simpson tried to console.

"It cost me twenty percent more!" Mr. Kendall seethed. "And after all I've done for that man."

Freddy Fletcher had been Mr. Kendall's right hand man for many years, collecting rents and doing the legwork on land acquisitions. He was hardworking, aggressive, and efficient — others would add ruthless to the description. Freddy felt Mr. Kendall made a mistake listening to David Simpson concerning the Cassidy property. When the place was auctioned, Freddy bought it himself.

Since most in town believed Mr. Kendall would be bidding, there were few other bidders.

Mr. Kendall had harsh words with his employee, but before he could fire him, Freddy Fletcher quit. The former employee quickly sold his new acquisition and was now bidding against his former boss, loaded with inside information he had obtained through the years.

Jonathan knew his father would not be appeased about the matter, so he sat quietly through dinner listening to Mr. Kendall's rants, and his contrived logic. Jonathan had worked with his father long enough to know his attitude toward the former employee was more than anger—Mr. Kendall was afraid. He had depended on Freddy Fletcher for many years, and now he would have to rely on David and Jonathan to produce results. Jonathan was relieved when his father disappeared for an evening walk. With David courting Caroline in the front room and Augusta helping Mrs. Kendall in the kitchen, Jonathan retrieved a sleeping roll he had prepared earlier. He had a special job this evening and was glad to disappear without questions.

Mr. Kendall walked toward the courthouse with his pipe in hand. The evening air was warm and moist as he took a puff and blew the smoke skyward. Sam Bowles sat on the Tilghman's porch as he did most evenings.

"What's bothering you, John?" Sam Bowles greeted, as Mr. Kendall walked past.

"What makes you think I'm bothered?" Mr. Kendall asked.

Sam laughed good-naturedly and said, "You only seem to go for walks when something's on your mind, and you look serious tonight."

Mr. Kendall stepped toward the porch and said, "I guess you've heard about Freddy Fletcher?"

"Of course," Sam replied. "This is a small town. News travels fast."

"After ten years, to have that German brute be my competitor," Mr. Kendall sighed.

"Are you afraid you've trained him too well?" Sam asked.

"Actually, yes," Mr. Kendall confessed. "I've got David Simpson working with me now who's smart as a tack and Jonathan's...well Jonathan's reliable, but Freddy had that killer instinct."

"Like you used to have?"

Frowning, Mr. Kendall said, "Yes."

"Listen, John," Sam said in a conciliatory tone, "I didn't get a chance to tell you that I respected what you did about that Cassidy deal."

"It didn't help the Cassidys much," Mr. Kendall reasoned. "I just let Freddy Fletcher steal that place. It'd been better for them if I would've bid on it. I'd at least made Fletcher pay a decent price."

"The Cassidys are good people," Sam replied. "They got caught in a bad situation. You wouldn't have wanted to meet them in town knowing you'd been the one who'd taken advantage of them."

"I guess," Mr. Kendall sighed, knowing he had taken advantage of his share of people down on their luck.

"The Cassidys'll be all right," Sam informed. "They've rented a nice little place in town, and Mrs. Cassidy's going to teach school next year."

"That's good to know," Mr. Kendall fumed in an apathetic tone.

"I notice David Simpson's at your house again," Sam observed.

"Yes," Mr. Kendall replied with a tinge of excitement in his voice. "I think things are going very well between those two."

"You approve, I assume?" Sam smiled crookedly.

Mr. Kendall nodded and said, "David's smart, and he would be a good match for Caroline."

"How about Jonathan?" Sam asked. "I notice he's out most nights. Is he seeing someone special?"

"Jonathan?" Mr. Kendall smirked. "I wish he'd find a good girl and settle down. He's too involved in pretending to be a soldier."

"He may not be pretending much longer," Sam suggested. "If this thing in Europe keeps going on, I'm afraid we're headed for a fight."

"I don't see what things in Europe have to do with us," Mr. Kendall said.

"Maybe not," Sam replied, "but it probably doesn't hurt Jonathan much to practice his soldiering."

Sam Bowles did not say anything for a moment before observing, "I saw Jonathan with that Harvey girl a few weeks ago after the senior party."

The hairs on the back of John Kendall's neck bristled at the deputy's observation.

"I talked to Jonathan about that," Mr. Kendall said. "He won't be seeing her again."

"She's a pretty girl," Sam said. "I've heard people say she's a good girl."

"That's good to know," Mr. Kendall nervously responded, "but she's not good enough for Jonathan."

"Is there something I don't know?" Sam asked with a raised eyebrow.

"What do you know?" Mr. Kendall timidly replied.

Sam Bowles studied John Kendall for a moment before saying, "Not much more than most people. Her mother was one of the Hellwigs down south of Warwick—German immigrants that lined up like a lot of us to stake their claim during the run. Found a nice piece of river bottomland and plenty of water...right next to the place you staked. Being immigrants, they didn't have much money and not speaking the language so well, they didn't have much chance of getting any.

"You helped with seed money and took a percentage of their crop as payment. They had two boys and two girls. Looked like they might make it farming, but their neighbor didn't exactly explain how to pay the taxes on the land. They'd made enough of the place to get a bank loan to pay the taxes, but two bad years of crops and the bank foreclosed. You managed to buy the place at a bargain and made enough off the deal to move to Chandler. A couple of boys tried stealing. One got sent to prison, and one got shot dead. The girl married the old school teacher, Mr. Harvey, and had the daughter soon after. A family ruined and you pick up the pieces at a profit. Is there anything else I need to know?"

Mr. Kendall swallowed hard and said meekly, "You know enough. It wasn't my fault. The river flooded one year, and the drought hit hard the next. It was bad luck for them."

"You came out okay," Sam noted.

"It was just business," Mr. Kendall replied in a slightly more defiant tone.

"Your business ruined a lot of people," Sam sharply replied.

"That was a long time ago," Mr. Kendall said, as he took another puff on his pipe. "It was a bad business, I'll agree, but it's something I can't take back. I don't see any good coming from Jonathan getting involved with them now."

"It wouldn't have anything to do with the brother that's left out there?" Sam probed. "You worried he still might hold a grudge?"

"Maybe," Mr. Kendall sighed. "I've got to be going, deputy."

Mr. Kendall walked to the front yard before stopping to say, "There's more to the story."

Sam leaned forward in his chair to listen.

"I tried to do right," Mr. Kendall said. "I know it don't look like it from your point of view, but I tried to do right. Sometimes things get to a point they can't be fixed except to walk away. That's what brought me to Chandler, and it's been good for my family."

"That don't change that boy going into the bank and getting shot," Sam said.

Mr. Kendall looked at him and said, "I didn't shoot the boy, deputy. You did."

Sam Bowles leaned back in his chair and watched Mr. Kendall walk peacefully back to his home.

CHAPTER 31

"WHERE ARE YOU GOING with a bedroll?" Mr. Kendall asked, as Jonathan headed out the door.

Stammering for a second, Jonathan lied, "I'm helping Captain Gilstrap set up for the encampment."

"I didn't think they were going to have an encampment this year," Mr. Kendall asked with a raised eyebrow. "Isn't it too wet?"

"It's wet," Jonathan admitted, "but there'll still be some units coming to use the range."

Mr. Kendall studied the nervous Jonathan for a moment before saying, "Don't be late for work tomorrow."

"Tomorrow's Saturday," Jonathan protested.

"I know the day!" Mr. Kendall retorted. "We've got to figure out this Freddy Fletcher mess."

Looking at his son, Mr. Kendall sighed heavily and said, "Be in by nine."

"I'll see you in the morning," Jonathan replied as he headed down the hill to the Statistical Building while his father watched.

A long, outdoor stairway led from the top of the hill to the rifle range located below. Jonathan stopped at the Statistical House to look up the steep slope, making sure his father had not followed. Jonathan walked past the vacant Statistical House and headed south to walk around the hill where the houses of Silk Stocking Row were located. By the time he reached the path leading toward the Harvey home, long shadows of the late afternoon stretched before him along the wooded path. As Jonathan approached the Harvey house, Samantha was bent over pulling weeds from her vegetable garden.

A startled Samantha rose quickly to straighten her apron before saying, "I didn't think you were coming this afternoon. It'll be dark soon."

"I got delayed," Jonathan replied. "What are you doing?"

"Trying to keep the weeds out of my tomatoes," Samantha explained. "I try to do a little each day so it's not a big job. I don't know why I bother. The pesky raccoons will eat more of the tomatoes than I will."

Jonathan smiled broadly and said, "I might be able to help with that."

Samantha lifted her head to listen as Jonathan explained, "I thought I might sleep out here tonight and shoot a coon or two, if you and your father don't mind a little noise."

"They wake me up most nights," Samantha shrugged. "Come in and I'll ask Papa."

"Hello, Mr. Harvey," Jonathan greeted as he followed Samantha into the small house.

"Looky here!" Mr. Harvey replied from his rocking chair. "We've got a visitor!"

"Keep your seat, Mr. Harvey," Jonathan encouraged as the older man attempted to stand.

Falling back into his chair, Mr. Harvey asked, "What brings you this way — again?"

"I thought I might help Samantha with her raccoon problem this evening," Jonathan sheepishly answered.

Rocking back in his chair, Mr. Harvey teased, "So, Sammie's soldier friend is declaring war on the raccoons. Did you recruit him for this mission, Sammie?"

"No, Papa," Samantha blushed. "Jonathan's just heard me complaining about them stealing our eggs."

Leaning forward in his chair, Mr. Harvey asked in a whisper, "What's your plan?"

"I don't really have a plan besides sleeping outside and taking a shot at one of them with my pistol," Jonathan explained.

Mr. Harvey studied Jonathan slyly, knowing his real strategy was to impress Samantha.

"Let me see your weapon," Mr. Harvey said.

Jonathan opened his bedroll to reveal a Colt pistol and holster.

"I was going to offer you my shotgun," Mr. Harvey continued, "but it looks like you're set."

"I was afraid a shotgun might kill as many chickens as raccoons," Jonathan said.

"Would you like to have some cake?" Mr. Harvey invited while winking at his daughter. "I don't know why, but Sammie made another one today."

Jonathan accepted the invitation and visited further with Mr. Harvey as Samantha prepared their dessert. It was dark by the time Mr. Harvey announced it was past his bedtime. Jonathan and Samantha took the opportunity to sit on the small porch and enjoy an evening breeze.

"Your father's an interesting man," Jonathan announced.

"I think so," Samantha acknowledged. "He likes you...I can tell."

"Your father strikes me as a man who likes most people," Jonathan observed.

"I guess you're right," Samantha admitted, "but you two always find the most interesting things to talk about."

"Like firearms and battles?" Jonathan asked suspiciously.

"Not exactly that," Samantha admitted. "I just enjoy listening to you talk to him."

"He's easier to talk to than my father," Jonathan said. "I think everyone is."

"Why is that?" Samantha asked. "I've not been around your father much, but I can sense the tension."

"I don't know," Jonathan admitted. "He's a hard man."

"There's more to it than that," Samantha bluntly stated, "I've seen him with David Simpson and Caroline. He's not a hard man with them."

"That's different," Jonathan sarcastically laughed. "He likes David."

"I think he expects more from you," Samantha noted.

"What?" Jonathan questioned.

"You're his oldest son," Samantha explained. "You're smart, reliable…he has high expectations for you."

"I'm not so sure," Jonathan replied.

"Papa's the same way with me sometimes," Samantha continued.

"Your father's nothing like mine," Jonathan protested.

"They have different personalities," Samantha admitted, "but Papa worries about me, like your father worries about you."

"You think so?" Jonathan quizzed, as he thought about Samantha's theory.

"Papa changed after mother passed away," Samantha said softly. "He worries about me."

"You seem to do all right," Jonathan observed.

Samantha smiled at Jonathan and said, "You're a man. You wouldn't understand."

"Understand what?" a puzzled Jonathan asked.

"It's different for a girl," Samantha explained. "What becomes of a girl like me? No money, no property...my father's old, and those things worry him. It's not like I can get any job I want. I can't even vote. I had the best grades in high school, and I can't even think about college. I'd wanted to be a nurse or a pharmacist, but that's just a dream. My father worries about what will become of me, and I think your father worries about you."

"You may be right," Jonathan sighed, as he looked at the stars above.

"What are you going to do with your life, Jonathan?" Samantha asked seriously.

"What do you mean?" Jonathan replied with a raised eyebrow.

Before Samantha could answer a rustling noise from the darkness interrupted her. Jonathan instinctively reached for his pistol.

"Is it the coons?" Samantha whispered.

"I don't think so," Jonathan replied, as he pointed his pistol into the darkness.

CHAPTER 32

"**Whoa!**" **a voice with** a heavy drawl shouted from the darkness. "Don't shoot."

"Who goes there?" Jonathan demanded.

Marcus Lutz lumbered slowly into the light, fixing his eyes on Jonathan like a wild animal on the prowl.

"It's me, Samantha," Marcus Lutz greeted with his hands held passively at his side.

"Do you know him?" Jonathan whispered to Samantha as the dangerous looking man approached.

"Yes," Samantha replied tensely. "He met me in town the other day and says he knew my mother."

"What are you doing out here this time of night?" Jonathan demanded.

"Take it easy," the man replied. "I was just looking for a place to camp for the evening. Someone in town told me the Harveys lived out here."

"What business do you have with the Harveys?" Jonathan questioned.

The scruffy man with a lean glint in his eyes came uncomfortably close. His overly familiar smile made Jonathan uneasy. The man looked to be nearly forty years old, with patched overalls and a worn straw hat. He looked like he might be a farmer, but his skin was less tanned than any farmer Jonathan had ever seen.

"Maybe I should be asking what you're doin' here at this hour?" the man asked

Jonathan kept his pistol near and said, "I'm out here to take care of some raccoons been bothering the chickens."

"Coons, huh?" the man shrugged.

"Your dad around, Samantha?" Marcus Lutz asked.

"He's asleep," Samantha explained. "Unless this commotion woke him."

The man looked at the house and took a few steps back to peer around the side to see there were no lights visible from inside.

"I don't want to bother him, I reckon," Marcus said. "You sure this boy ain't bothering you?"

"He's helpin' me chase the coons away," Samantha answered firmly.

The man looked Jonathan over and said, "I guess I'll go find a place to stay far enough away that I don't get mistaken for a critter."

"I'll tell Papa you came by," Samantha nervously said.

The man stared at Jonathan a moment and then slipped back into the dark night without another word. Samantha had moved close to Jonathan and held tightly to his arm. Both looked into the darkness unable to see which way the man traveled.

"Did you know him?" Jonathan whispered after the man had left.

"Not really," Samantha replied. "He—He knows me somehow, but he makes me uneasy. He takes for granted that we're familiar. Maybe he knows Papa."

"He was bold to come to a strange place in the dark," Jonathan observed.

Still holding his arm, Samantha said, "I was glad you were here."

Jonathan looked at Samantha and did something he did not plan. Without thinking, he leaned toward her and kissed her cheek. A startled Samantha did not move for a second, then put her arm around Jonathan's neck and held him before the awkward Jonathan had a chance to apologize for the kiss.

Still holding him, Samantha said, "Thank you for being here tonight. I feel safe for the first time in a very long time."

Jonathan held Samantha gently. He did not know what to say, but felt tranquil knowing Samantha wanted him there.

CHAPTER 33

AFTER MARCUS LUTZ DISAPPEARED into the night, Jonathan spent the rest of the night talking with Samantha. Midnight passed before she went to bed, leaving Jonathan to sleep on the porch. Thoughts of Samantha holding his arm tightly, the kiss he had placed on her cheek, and their long conversation afterwards kept Jonathan awake in his bedroll, as he waited for the raccoons with Samantha's dog beside him and his pistol within reach.

The peaceful night would have been perfect, if Marcus Lutz had not interrupted the evening. Jonathan realized the man frightened Samantha, and her misgivings about him were enough to concern Jonathan.

As Jonathan lay in his bedroll watching for signs of the raccoons, he noticed the stillness and quiet of the night. The silence put his nerves on edge. Jonathan hunted and knew the sounds of the night. Tonight there were no tree frogs, katydids, or owls hooting in the darkness, just unsettling silence. Jonathan kept his gun close listening for an intruder, but he heard none. He did not think he had slept, but the creak of the front door woke him as Samantha peeked outside as sunrise threatened to overtake the dawn light.

"Good morning," she whispered. "I didn't hear any shots."

"I think the raccoons stayed away," Jonathan groggily replied.

Samantha was already dressed and stepped around Jonathan to inspect her hens. In a few minutes, she returned with an apron full of fresh eggs and a cheerful disposition.

"You must have scared the coons away," Samantha smiled.

"Yeah," Jonathan said as he packed his bedroll.

Jonathan wondered if Marcus Lutz camping nearby might have been the real reason the raccoons stayed away, but he decided not to worry Samantha this morning. It was still a few minutes before sunrise. Samantha looked fresh with her tanned cheeks glowing and her sandy brown hair looking as if it had already been brushed.

"How'd you sleep?" Samantha asked.

"Fine," Jonathan lied, having stayed up most of the night wondering if a raccoon or Marcus Lutz might come prowling.

"I think that's the first time I've slept through the night in weeks," Samantha gleamed.

Jonathan smiled at Samantha's enthusiasm for a good night's sleep.

"Will you stay for eggs?" Samantha asked.

"I need to get back to town, but I have time for breakfast," Jonathan replied.

"Good," Samantha chirped, as she headed inside to stoke the morning fire.

Jonathan finished packing his bedroll when Mr. Harvey said, "Good morning. I didn't hear any shooting, so I'm guessing the raccoons didn't attack last night."

"No," Jonathan said, as Mr. Harvey stood on the porch with him looking at the morning haze.

"You're probably disappointed," Mr. Harvey kindly observed. "At least we'll enjoy fresh eggs this morning."

"Yes, sir," Jonathan replied.

Mr. Harvey leaned against the rail of the porch and said, "I think my Sammie has taken a liking to you."

Jonathan blushed and said, "She's a little more friendly than the first time we met."

Mr. Harvey chuckled to himself before saying, "Sammie can be frank...It's her way of keeping people at arms length until she decides if she'll let them get close. I can tell by the way she whistles when she's making a chocolate cake for you or how she straightens her hair when you showed up that she's decided to trust you. That's not an easy thing for Sammie. I'm pretty much all she's got."

"Why do you call her Sammie?" Jonathan asked.

Mr. Harvey looked inside the house to make sure Samantha was not within listening range when he whispered, "Sammie thinks it's because I wanted a boy, but that's not it. She's always been a little bit of a tomboy. She used to drive her mother crazy by insisting on wearing overalls most days but Sunday. I got in the habit of calling her Sammie to tease her mother, and the name stuck."

Taking a more careful look inside the house, Mr. Harvey leaned in to say, "Until two years ago, she was built like a boy, but she's filled out since then. When her mother died, she had to take on the responsibilities of being the woman of the house. I haven't seen her wear overalls since we moved to Chandler."

"What brought you to Chandler?" Jonathan asked.

"The old farm was too much for me to keep even with Sammie's help," Mr. Harvey explained. "The bank owned nearly as much of it as I did, so I decided to sell while I could get a little out of it. We found this place to rent, to keep a few chickens and a cow. It was close to a high school, and I wanted Sammie to have an education. I'd planned to send her to college but then got sick, and we've spent most of the money on doctors and medicine."

Jonathan could tell by Mr. Harvey's tone that his daughter's future concerned him.

In a more upbeat voice, Mr. Harvey said, "Things have worked out okay. Sammie finished school and she's making some friends. She's got a boy coming to see her now."

"Who?" Jonathan asked with a raised eyebrow.

"You," Mr. Harvey said, with a sly grin.

"Oh," Jonathan replied, while Mr. Harvey looked at him.

"You like my daughter?" Mr. Harvey bluntly asked.

"Yes," Jonathan replied seriously. "I like her very much, as a matter of fact."

Mr. Harvey did not reply, but he studied Jonathan as he encouraged the young man to say more.

"She's different than most of the girls around here," Jonathan tried to explain.

"How so?" Mr. Harvey asked.

Jonathan thought hard for a moment and then said, "She's — she's not as silly as most girls I've known. There's something about her that — 'practical' is probably not the right word, but she's smart, easy to talk to. I — It's difficult to say exactly."

Mr. Harvey chuckled aloud at Jonathan's clumsy attempt to express his feelings about Samantha.

"What's so funny?" Samantha asked as she stepped outside.

Jonathan stared in horror, as Mr. Harvey calmly said, "Nothing that would interest you. Jonathan's just telling me about how practical he finds things in Chandler."

"Oh," Samantha shrugged. "I'll start the eggs in a little bit once the fire's hot."

Samantha disappeared into the house as Mr. Harvey smiled mischievously at Jonathan.

"It's kind of hard to explain," Jonathan said, trying to finish his thoughts about Samantha.

Mr. Harvey did not laugh but smiled at Jonathan's honesty.

Stepping closer to Jonathan, Mr. Harvey said in a more solemn voice, "I know what you mean. I wasn't always old. I can vaguely remember what it was like to be a young man."

Looking at Jonathan, Mr. Harvey added, "I know you have feelings for my daughter."

"I want to assure you my intensions are honorable," Jonathan interrupted.

"I know they are," Mr. Harvey said. "If I'd thought different, I'd have run you off with my shotgun the first night. There are some things you need to know, though."

Jonathan listened intently before Mr. Harvey said, "Things won't be easy, if you continue seeing Sammie."

"What do you mean?" Jonathan asked.

"You two are from different worlds," Mr. Harvey tried to explain.

"We both live in Chandler right now," a confused Jonathan observed.

"I'm not talking about geography," Mr. Harvey stated. "Your family has property, a business—I'm suspecting your father has plans for you."

"Yes," Jonathan admitted.

"Me and Sammie," Mr. Harvey continued. "We're simple folk—poor folk to a man like your father. People like him own things and get the most out of their investments, while people like us—"

"This is the twentieth century," Jonathan boldly protested. "I can assure you Samantha's economic condition has nothing to do with my feelings for her."

"I don't doubt you," Mr. Harvey said, as he rubbed his forehead. "It's not you, it's—Let me ask you a question."

"Okay."

"Have you told your father about Sammie?" Mr. Harvey asked.

"No," Jonathan admitted.

"And why not?"

Jonathan squirmed for a second before saying, "Dealing with my father is complicated."

"You're afraid," Mr. Harvey stated. "Don't feel badly. You've made my point. You haven't talked to your father about this girl that you're finding excuses to see every night, because you know deep down he will not approve."

"Are you saying I shouldn't see Samantha any more?" Jonathan asked.

Mr. Harvey shook his head and said, "I'm not saying that at all. You make my daughter happy and that makes me happy. I'm trying to tell you that you'll be forced to make some hard choices — courageous choices, and I don't want my daughter hurt."

"I wouldn't hurt Samantha," Jonathan defended.

"Not on purpose," Mr. Harvey agreed. "That doesn't mean she wouldn't be hurt in a conflict between yourself and Mr. Kendall."

"Do you know my father?" Jonathan asked.

Mr. Harvey nodded his head.

"There's some history between the Harveys and the Kendalls," Mr. Harvey admitted. "Samantha's mother was a Hellwig. They lived around Warwick in west Lincoln County. The Hellwigs were farmers, until they lost their land to the bank. Your father bought their place and made them sharecroppers. Things worked well for a time, but eventually bad weather and bad luck caught up with them. The Hellwigs blamed your father — I was a teacher at the school and I probably blamed him too. One of the boys and a friend went looking for your father. They had been drinking, and when they couldn't find John Kendall, they decided to rob the bank. Lawrence Hellwig was shot dead in the mess and the other boy was sent to prison. It ruined the Hellwigs. Mr. Hellwig died the next spring. The rest of the family moved south. I married Samantha's mother, and she was all that was left of the Hellwigs in Lincoln County."

"I'm sorry," Jonathan apologized.

"Wasn't your fault," Mr. Harvey said. "You can't be responsible for your father's doings. You probably weren't more than two or three years old at the time. It was a long time ago."

"I'm still sorry," Jonathan sighed. "No wonder my father was so adamant about me not seeing Samantha."

"So you have talked to your father?" Mr. Harvey asked with a raised eyebrow.

"Not exactly," Jonathan answered. "He met Samantha the night of her graduation. She was at the house. She borrowed my sister's dress that evening."

"I remember the dress," Mr. Harvey said.

"Dad told me that night he didn't want me seeing 'that Harvey girl,'" Jonathan explained. "I guess I know now."

"I don't know if we really know all the reasons behind a man's life," Mr. Harvey admonished. "You've got to be your own man."

"That's what I've been told," Jonathan sighed.

Mr. Harvey smiled kindly and said, "I see why my Sammie likes you. I think maybe you do have courage that's not apparent on first appearance."

"Do you know a Marcus Lutz?" Jonathan asked.

Mr. Harvey's body language communicated he recognized the man before he said, "I haven't heard that name in years. How did you know?"

"Know what?" Jonathan asked.

Mr. Harvey looked confused and said, "How did you know Marcus Lutz was the man who robbed the bank with Lawrence Hellwig?"

"I didn't," Jonathan replied.

"Marcus Lutz married my wife's sister," Mr. Harvey explained. "He went to town with Lawrence when they robbed the bank.

Lawrence got shot, and Marcus Lutz was sent to prison. His wife died a few months later. I haven't heard from him since."

Jonathan looked at Mr. Harvey and said, "He was here last night. He talked to Samantha and wanted to see you. You were asleep, and Samantha didn't want to wake you."

"Marcus Lutz was here?" Mr. Harvey asked.

Jonathan looked at Mr. Harvey to see that he was surprised by the news, but the older man did not seem alarmed.

"Yes," Jonathan said, "last night."

Mr. Harvey rubbed his chin and said, "That's interesting. I didn't know where he was at. You said he spoke to Sammie?"

"Yes."

"Did he say if he would be back?" Mr. Harvey asked.

"I didn't hear him say," Jonathan replied, somewhat surprised at Mr. Harvey's calm demeanor at having a convicted felon roaming around his place.

Mr. Harvey thought for a moment before he said, "Did he know you were John Kendall's son?"

"I don't think so," Jonathan answered. "The subject didn't come up."

Mr. Harvey was silent for a few seconds before he said, "You better stay away from Marcus until I have a chance to talk with him. I wouldn't think he'd be here to cause trouble, but I'd like to find out why he's here.

"Breakfast is ready," a cheerful Samantha called from inside the house.

As Jonathan headed inside, Mr. Harvey grabbed him by the sleeve to delay the young man and said, "I didn't tell you those things about the Hellwigs to make it difficult between you and your father. What's done is done in my book, but if you keep seeing Sammie you can't keep it from him in a town this size. Sammie will put you between a rock and a hard place with your father — and I don't want her being hurt again by that man."

"I understand," Jonathan said, as Mr. Harvey released his hold on his arm.

"I don't think you do," Mr. Harvey replied seriously. "But I do believe you'll do the right thing."

Jonathan enjoyed his eggs with Samantha and Mr. Harvey. Samantha apologized several times for not having any bacon, but her biscuits were flaky, and the butter she had churned was sweet. Jonathan headed across Indian Springs and toward town well before eight o'clock. He did not want to be late for work and have to answer prying questions from his father. What he wanted from his father was answers, but as he walked to town on the peaceful morning, Jonathan was at a loss on how to get them.

CHAPTER 34

BY LATE JUNE, JONATHAN Kendall became a nightly visitor at the Harvey home. He liked visiting with Mr. Harvey and hearing stories about the great Civil War, but he especially enjoyed evenings on the porch with Samantha after the old gentleman retired for the evening. The rifle range for the National Guard had been underwater most of the spring. In previous years, this would have been a concern to Jonathan, but he had not been to the Statistical House where they kept records for the rifle range in many days. There had been rumors of the war in Europe for months, but Jonathan's interests were all on Samantha Harvey during the summer of 1916.

Jonathan kissed Samantha good night and promised to see her the next evening as he started his long walk back to town. The clock on the courthouse showed a little after ten o'clock as he strolled lazily onto Silk Stocking Row and toward his house. The memory of the pleasant conversation with Samantha was replaced only by his plans to see her the next evening.

As Jonathan walked the street, a stern voice from the Tilghman's front porch startled him by saying, "Jonathan?"

The voice was not from Deputy Bowles who watched the place, but was the familiar bark of his father.

"Is that you?" Mr. Kendall asked in a more urgent tone.

"It's me," Jonathan replied.

Looking past the iron fence, Jonathan saw his father and Sam Bowles sitting on the porch.

"Where have you been?" Mr. Kendall asked.

"I've been walking," Jonathan vaguely replied.

"Where?" Mr. Kendall asked. "And don't tell me you've been around the rifle range, because Captain Gilstrap tells me he hasn't seen you in weeks."

"I've been busy," Jonathan answered.

"I'm going to turn in," Sam Bowles interrupted.

"I'll see you, Sam," Mr. Kendall replied as he stepped toward Jonathan.

Jonathan started walking, hoping the inquisition was over when Mr. Kendall stepped to his son's side as the two headed toward the Kendall home.

"Where have you been?" Mr. Kendall asked again.

"I've been busy," Jonathan replied.

"Don't give me that!" Mr. Kendall roared in a voice loud enough that Jonathan feared he might wake some neighbors. "You can't do anything, especially work, without talking or wasting your time with that blasted guard, and now you're too busy?"

Jonathan's heart raced as he realized his father was not going to let the subject drop.

"I've been to see Samantha Harvey," Jonathan explained.

"What?" Mr. Kendall replied in a strange, timid voice. "You can't—I won't allow it."

"What does it matter to you?' Jonathan asked.

Regaining his bravado, Mr. Kendall replied, "It matters plenty! I won't have a son of mine throwing his life away on a girl like that."

"You know nothing about her," Jonathan challenged in an uncharacteristic tone of defiance.

"I know enough!" Mr. Kendall shouted in a voice that caused several neighborhood dogs to bark.

In a more controlled tone of voice Mr. Kendall added, "I know that you can't be with that girl. I know I'll never permit it."

Jonathan looked at his father and realized for the first time that John Kendall was afraid of his son's independence.

This knowledge bolstered Jonathan's boldness as he said, "It's not really your choice, Father — It's mine."

As Mr. Kendall stood speechless, Jonathan said, "Good night, Father."

Jonathan left his father standing on their front porch as he disappeared to the sanctuary of his room. Jonathan's heart was pumping as he closed the door to his upstairs bedroom. He expected his father to knock on the door to confront him for the defiance. A smile eased on Jonathan's face as each minute passed without an interruption from his father. He had stood up to his father and had taken a stand for Samantha's sake. The sense of triumph felt good, but Jonathan believed the issue would not be forgotten.

CHAPTER 35

JONATHAN WOKE BEFORE SUNRISE with a terrible sense of dread. He had confronted his father the night before and understood there would be consequences this morning. He walked slowly down the stairs and almost stopped when he saw his father reading the morning paper at the dining table. Fortunately, Caroline was there serving pancakes, and Jonathan believed his sister might insulate him from some of his father's fury.

"Good morning," Caroline greeted, as Jonathan walked to the table.

"Good morning," Jonathan replied, as he kept a wary eye on his father.

"Would you like some pancakes?" Caroline asked cheerfully.

"Sure," Jonathan replied. "Why are you in such a good mood this morning?"

A beaming Caroline said, "David's taking me on a picnic this afternoon. I think he may have something he wants to talk about."

"Really?" Jonathan smiled, knowing his friend David Simpson had been threatening to ask his sister to marry him for weeks.

"David won't be able to make it this afternoon," Mr. Kendall coldly informed.

"What?" Caroline asked.

"I need David at work today," Mr. Kendall replied.

"You promised him the afternoon off," Caroline protested. "He's been working so hard."

"I'm sorry," Mr. Kendall stated. "Business is business. David can take you another time."

"Anything I should know about?" Jonathan timidly asked.

Mr. Kendall looked over his paper and said, "No. I need David this afternoon, and of course I'll need you to be on time this morning."

Jonathan was relieved his father was so cordial, because he was not sure he still had a job after his confrontation the night before.

"I'll be on time," Jonathan said, as he sat at the opposite end of the table.

A deflated Caroline did not protest and brought Jonathan a plate of pancakes. Mr. Kendall did not say more and soon left for the office, much to Jonathan's relief. Jonathan felt sorry for Caroline, who had been looking forward to her time with David for several days, but he was thankful his father had business, which might distract him from his prejudice against Samantha Harvey.

Jonathan walked quickly through town and down the hill to the Kendall Cotton Gin. The June morning was already warm, but the air smelled fresh. He looked to the edge of town to the trail leading to Indian Springs and to the Harvey place. Jonathan thought about Samantha cooking breakfast and would have loved to have seen her that morning. He did not dare be late, however, and he continued to walk.

Mr. Kendall was in his office with the door closed. A grateful Jonathan slid quietly behind his small desk and began sorting files.

David Simpson arrived a half hour later and asked Jonathan, "What's going on?"

"I have no idea," Jonathan shrugged, although he felt his relationship with Samantha Harvey had something to do with his father's strange behavior.

"I was planning to take Caroline on a picnic," David explained. "Your dad seemed like that was the best idea since iced tea and then sent me this note to come in today."

"Something's come up," Jonathan replied.

"Guess I better see what it is," David said in a carefree way as he knocked on Mr. Kendall's door.

David Simpson disappeared into Mr. Kendall's office for most of the morning, while Jonathan was left in the outer office wandering what was so urgent. A little before lunch, David exited the office with a look Jonathan was not used to seeing from his friend — confusion and uncertainty.

"What's going on?" Jonathan whispered, trying to not draw the attention of his father.

David studied Jonathan for a second before saying, "There's a land deal that has to be done today."

"Where?" Jonathan asked.

David hesitated to reveal the details of his conversation, and before he could answer, Mr. Kendall called, "Jonathan! Get in here."

Jonathan looked at his friend to see if he would give him a clue about the conversation to come, but by then David had decided to let Jonathan find out the details from Mr. Kendall.

"Hurry up!" the impatient Mr. Kendall insisted.

When Jonathan entered the office, Mr. Kendall shouted, "You can go to lunch, David. I'll see you in the morning."

Jonathan looked back and watched David calmly put on his hat and walk into the bright sunshine toward town.

"What going on?" Jonathan asked.

"I'm sending David to inspect some land this afternoon," Mr. Kendall explained.

"You want me to go with him?" Jonathan asked.

"I would," Mr. Kendall said with a forced smile. "But David can handle things. Besides I have a more important job for you."

Jonathan looked at his father suspiciously, as Mr. Kendall said, "It's time you take a little more responsibility around here. I've got a special job for you."

"What?" Jonathan asked.

"I'm sending you to Oklahoma City," Mr. Kendall answered. "I have some important papers I want you to deliver to Judge Robertson's office."

"Since when do you have anything to do with Judge Robertson?" Jonathan pointedly asked.

"This is business, not politics," Mr. Kendall scolded. "These papers are important, and I don't want to send them by mail. I'm sending Caroline with you, as well."

"What for?" Jonathan responded, confused as to why Caroline would need to go with him.

"I want you to take Caroline to Edmond while you're there," Mr. Kendall said. "She's going to the Normal School next year, and I need you to escort her and find a nice place to board. I'm sending two hundred dollars with you. That should be sufficient."

Jonathan was caught by surprise at this revelation. He believed Caroline expected to be engaged and she did not seem to have an interest in continuing her education.

"What's going on?" Jonathan asked. "I thought David —"

"You thought wrong," Mr. Kendall pointedly replied. "David's too busy to think about Caroline, and it will be good for her to be away for a while."

"Does David know you're planning to send Caroline to school?" Jonathan inquired.

"You have enough questions this morning," Mr. Kendall huffed. "I had a conversation this morning with David, and he understands everything. Now if you have no further questions, there are two train tickets for you and Caroline. The train leaves in an hour, so you better get packed. I left instructions for Caroline to be ready, and I'll have a man in Oklahoma City get you a hotel room. I think you should be able to get everything done in three days."

Jonathan had more questions, but Mr. Kendall stared at him and said, "I've got work to do. Have a good trip, and I'll see you Friday."

Mr. Kendall's tone of voice indicated he would be taking no more questions, and he immediately busied himself with the work on his desk. Jonathan left the office with the train tickets in hand. He had as confused a look as David Simpson had earlier.

Jonathan hurried up the hill to his house to pack and bring Caroline to the train depot. As he passed the viaduct that led to the other side of town, he looked toward the Harvey home. He wanted to say good-bye to Samantha, but with only an hour before the train pulled out of town, he had no time. Instead, Jonathan made a quick stop at the Western Union office to send a message to Samantha saying he would return in three days.

CHAPTER 36

CAROLINE KENDALL'S PUFFY EYES showed her disappointment about making the trip to Oklahoma City, although she put on a brave face pretending to be excited. Traveling to the city with spending money and no parental supervision would normally have been a thrill, but the brokenhearted Caroline did not want to be away from David.

Jonathan loved his younger sister. He remembered how Caroline's birth had brought the family together. Jonathan was only four years old at the time, but his father was rarely around before her birth. Jonathan and his mother had been living in Michigan with family, but they moved to Oklahoma to the big house on Silk Stocking Row soon after Caroline was added to the family.

Caroline tactfully talked about David Simpson on the train ride inventing a variety of excuses for his sudden interest in business over spending an afternoon with her. She managed to bring up David's many good qualities in the conversation, but Jonathan could tell his good-natured sister was concerned about being away from him for even a few days. Jonathan did not talk about his budding romance with Samantha Harvey, fearing Caroline would tease him or tell Mr. Kendall. Jonathan worried his infatuation was only in his mind, and he doubted Samantha Harvey thought of him as more than a friend.

Jonathan and Caroline observed impressive homes and businesses under construction as they arrived in Oklahoma City. Caroline pointed at the new state capital building on the north side of town. The impressive structure looked like a Greek temple rising from the prairie, as scaffolding adorned the half-finished building. Cows grazed lazily nearby as workers feverishly manned hand cranes to move the large stones. The Santa Fe line ran downtown on raised tracks, and the Colcord Hotel where Jonathan and Caroline would stay stood twelve stories into the blue sky.

Oklahoma City was a whirl of activity as automobiles competed with horse-drawn carriages for the right of way. Compared to the serene town of Chandler, the city was chaotic and exciting. Jonathan and Caroline found Oklahoma City to be an enticing place especially at night with electric lights illuminating the streets. Jonathan soon forgot the hurried events sending him to the city, and he believed even Caroline was glad she had made the trip.

The next day Jonathan delivered the papers for his father, before he and Caroline spent the day sightseeing and shopping. He took Caroline to Edmond, a few miles north of Oklahoma City by train, the next day to look at the Normal School located in a stately rock building with a clock tower looming over the small campus. There was not much activity, but Jonathan saw several pretty girls enrolling for fall classes. Caroline had wanted to go to school before David Simpson moved back to Chandler, but now she looked over the campus apathetically. Jonathan located a nice place where he rented a room for his sister in the fall. After visiting the Normal School, Jonathan was ready to return home and eager to see Samantha.

Friday's train arrived in Chandler a little after lunch under a hot June sun. Jonathan sent his bag with Caroline and headed to see Samantha. He picked wildflowers growing along the trail and walked with a spirited stride to see the girl he had missed during his trip. As the Harvey house came into his view, his high spirits sunk as he saw Samantha sitting on the porch entertaining a visitor.

CHAPTER 37

THE WIND GENTLY BLEW Samantha Harvey's long, sandy-brown hair across her face, while the sun made her cheeks glow. She gracefully removed the strands of hair from her radiant face while leaning against the porch rail. What bothered Jonathan was the way she giggled with delight at David Simpson's conversation.

"David?" Jonathan said in a bewildered voice as he approached.

David turned around and replied calmly, "You're back."

"Yeah," Jonathan confirmed as he moved closer.

"Hi, Samantha," Jonathan greeted.

"Hello," she coolly replied.

Jonathan lowered his head slightly while looking at Samantha and asked, "Is everything all right?"

"Fine," she snapped. "What are you doing here?"

"I came to see you," Jonathan explained wearily.

"Hum," Samantha replied in a dismissive tone.

"What's wrong?" Jonathan asked.

David Simpson interrupted the question and said, "I better get going. I'll see you tonight, Sammie?"

"Sure," Samantha replied cordially. "I'll see you tonight."

"See you at the office," David said to Jonathan, as he tilted his hat and headed back to town.

As Jonathan stood speechless, David walked away, while Samantha turned without a word and headed into the small house.

"Wait!" Jonathan implored. "What's wrong?"

Samantha stopped and said, "Nothing."

"Something's wrong," Jonathan observed.

Samantha sighed heavily and said, "Where have you been?"

"Oklahoma City," Jonathan explained. "I sent you a note."

Looking unconvinced, Samantha said, "What note?"

"I sent you a note from the Western Union office saying I was out of town," Jonathan replied.

"I didn't get a message," Samantha said in a slightly more civil tone.

"I'm sorry," Jonathan said. "My father sent me to Oklahoma City on business on short notice. I didn't have time to come by."

"You spent three days in the city?" Samantha said.

"David didn't tell you?" Jonathan asked.

Samantha did not respond.

"What was David doing here?" Jonathan asked.

"He just came by," Samantha said.

Jonathan did not reply, which forced Samantha to say, "He came by Wednesday. He said he was just passing by the house. He asked me to go to the magician show at the St. Cloud Hotel. I told him I didn't want to because I thought you'd be coming to see me. He came by yesterday afternoon and again today. I didn't know where you were…I figured you got tired of my company…so I told David I'd go to the show tonight."

"I see," a disheartened Jonathan said.

"I thought maybe you'd lost interest…in me," Samantha said. "David said it had happened before with other girls."

"What other girls?" Jonathan snapped back trying to keep his composure.

"Elizabeth Conklin, for one," Samantha fumed.

"What did David say exactly?" Jonathan asked.

"Not anything really," Samantha admitted. "He said you were in love with Elizabeth Conklin and that she wasn't engaged any longer."

"David said I went to see Elizabeth?"

"Not exactly," Samantha replied with pursed lips. "He said your old girl was unattached and you hadn't been around. I just put two and two together."

"I told you about Elizabeth the first night we met," Jonathan observed pointedly. "She doesn't have any feelings for me, and I can't believe you'd think I'd have any feelings for her...or any girl but you after the past weeks."

Samantha did not respond for a moment and then said with a sigh, "I thought—I thought maybe your father had reasoned with you. I thought maybe you'd come to realize I don't have many prospects like Elizabeth Conklin with her good family and coming from a fine house—I assumed you might prefer a girl like that."

"And David just happened to be here," Jonathan muttered to himself.

"What?" Samantha asked.

"Nothing," Jonathan said. "I was just talking to myself."

"I heard you say David's name," Samantha said.

"Yeah," Jonathan groaned. "It didn't take David long to come in and—well, to come in and impress you."

Samantha looked at Jonathan for a moment and said, "He didn't impress me much. He's just been persistent. I'd never have agreed to go with him to town, if I thought—"

"Thought what?" Jonathan interrupted.

"If I thought you cared," Samantha answered frankly.

Jonathan stepped to Samantha and took her by the shoulders to make her face him and said sincerely, "I do care—I care very much."

Samantha's cheeks flushed as she quickly wiped a tear from her eye and cried, "I'm so confused."

Jonathan put his arms around her and said, "Something's going on and I'm going to get to the bottom of it. Will you see me tomorrow?"

Samantha nodded as she said, "Of course."

"I've got to go," Jonathan explained. "I will see you tomorrow—No, I'll see you tonight."

"But David," Samantha sniffled. "I promised him—"

"I don't expect you to break your promise," Jonathan said. "But will you see me tonight after the show?"

"Yes."

"Good," Jonathan smiled. "I'll be back, but I've got business in town this afternoon."

Without further explanation, Jonathan left Samantha and sprinted up the hill toward town.

CHAPTER 38

JONATHAN HOPED TO CATCH David Simpson before he got to town. By the time Jonathan reached downtown, sweat glistened from his forehead, but he did not see David anywhere. A frustrated Jonathan looked at the Western Union office where he had left a message a few days before when he boarded the train to Oklahoma City.

"Hello Jonathan," Mr. Wellington greeted as the young man entered the office.

"I sent a message on Tuesday," Jonathan abruptly stated. "I was wondering why it wasn't delivered?"

Mr. Willington looked worriedly at Jonathan and said, "I—I don't know, but I'll find out."

"Samuel!" he shouted. "Get out here!"

"Yes, sir," a young boy of about fourteen answered from the back.

"Didn't I ask you to deliver, Mr. Kendall's message the other day?" Mr. Wellington sternly asked.

"Yes, sir," the boy answered.

"Why didn't you deliver the message?" Mr. Wellington quizzed.

"I did," the boy replied.

"The message didn't get there," Jonathan charged.

"Your pa took it," the boy explained.

Mr. Wellington looked at the stunned Jonathan and said to the boy, "Get back to work and I'll deal with you later."

The boy left, and Mr. Wellington said to Jonathan, "I'm sorry, Jonathan. Our policy is to deliver only to the addressee, but the boy—"

"Don't blame the boy," Jonathan interrupted. "Good day, Mr. Wellington."

Before Mr. Wellington could respond, Jonathan was out the door. Taking one more look down the street on the chances of seeing David Simpson, he walked down the hill toward the Kendall Cotton Gin. He did not know if he would find David Simpson there, but he knew he would find his father.

Jonathan entered the cotton gin and slammed the door as hard as he dared without breaking the glass. David was nowhere to be seen, and it appeared the office was empty. Still sweating and breathing heavily, he walked directly to his father's door and opened it without an invitation.

"You're back," Mr. Kendall calmly stated as he barely looked up from his desk.

"How could you?" Jonathan charged.

Mr. Kendall stopped what he was doing and examined his son who stood before him with flaring nostrils and angry eyes.

"I don't know, son," Mr. Kendall said. "I've done so much for this family; I don't know exactly what you're talking about."

Jonathan's anger boiled as he tried to calm his shaking voice before saying with a sneer, "How could you do that to Caroline?"

"Caroline?" Mr. Kendall asked in surprise. "I've done nothing to Caroline, but see to it that she gets a good education."

"You've broken her heart!" Jonathan shouted angrily. "You know how she feels about David, and still you threw him at

Samantha like he was a bull in the herd. Is it really that important to you to keep me away from Samantha Harvey?"

"Yes," Mr. Kendall blatantly replied. "To me it was worth it, even if it did break Caroline's heart, and even if it broke yours."

"Why?" Jonathan asked.

Mr. Kendall did not answer immediately, but he rose from his desk to look Jonathan square in the eye.

"She's no good for you," Mr. Kendall finally stated plainly.

Jonathan did not blink and responded quickly by saying, "That's not good enough."

"Fine!" Mr. Kendall shouted back angrily. "Sit down, and I'll tell you the whole story."

Jonathan took a seat and waited for an explanation.

Mr. Kendall paced a few steps before saying, "I'll admit sending David Simpson to the Harvey house was a bad idea. I found out you'd been sniffing around out there, and I panicked. I can't have you associating with those kind of people."

"Mr. Harvey and Samantha are very pleasant and decent people," Jonathan defiantly stated.

Mr. Kendall fought back his temper to keep control of the conversation and said flatly, "It's got nothing to do with being 'pleasant.' I'll admit I sent David out there because I know he's easy with the ladies, and I thought once you saw how the girl went after a young man of equal means that you'd wake up to how foolish a relationship is with this girl. David's sensible enough not to get entangled with a girl like that. He knows how to have his fun and run. I know you'd get involve emotionally, and…trust me…it would cost everyone."

"Samantha's not like that," Jonathan defended.

Mr. Kendall sighed heavily and said, "There's more. That girl's a Hellwig. The poorest excuse for pig farmers you've ever seen."

"I know about the Hellwigs," Jonathan interrupted.

"You know nothing!" Mr. Kendall scolded. "Are you going to shut up so I can tell you what you nearly got tangled up with?"

Jonathan could barely control his urge to strike his father, but his curiosity about Mr. Kendall's resentment toward this family caused him to nod his head to his bullying father.

"Let me ask you a question," Mr. Kendall said in a calmer tone. "Do you like your life?"

"What do you mean?"

"Do you like the home you live in?"

"Yes," Jonathan timidly admitted.

"Like going to Oklahoma City a couple of times a year to shop for clothes?"

"Sure."

"Like having people do you favors and treat you like you're something special just because you're a Kendall?"

"What's your point?" Jonathan asked, uncomfortable at the questioning.

"Those things didn't happen by accident," Mr. Kendall explained. "They happened because I worked like a field hand in this business. Because I've taken advantage of opportunity, been smarter, and more willing to take risk than any man in this county! I didn't inherit money or advantage. I've worked for everything I've got, and I've worked mainly to give you and Caroline and Augusta a better life. I've done it by cunning, and quick wits, and calculations, and I'm not ashamed, because you don't get ahead in this world without making a few enemies, and you can't worry about being friends with everyone when it comes to business. You got to realize that some people can handle business and some can't. For some, prosperity would be a burden because their own stupidity and laziness would cause them to lose it all. It would be worse for them to get a taste of success before their inevitable failure dragged them into pitiful ruin."

"People like the Hellwigs?" Jonathan snidely asked.

Mr. Kendall turned red, as if he might lose his temper, before saying, "Let me tell you about the Hellwigs. They staked a claim without enough to buy beans much less seed and tools and equipment. They'd have starved, the whole lot of 'em, without help. The mom and dad could barely speak English and signed some papers that would have left them out in the cold of winter because they didn't make the required improvements to keep the land by the rules of the run. When the bank threatened to take their land, I came to help. Bought 'em the seed they needed and rented the tools. All I asked was payment, and since they had no money I took a part of the crop.

"They made the crop the first year, and you'd thought I was a relative from the old country. They fed me that sausage they made and told me how they'd never have made it without my help. Then the weather turned bad a couple of years, and they had a couple of years planting at the wrong time. The oldest boy drank more than he plowed. I had no choice but to foreclose to protect my investment. I was no friend then."

"Is that when Lawrence Hellwig and Marcus Lutz came after you?" Jonathan interrupted.

Mr. Kendall's face turned ashen as he said, "How did you know that?"

"Mr. Harvey told me," Jonathan replied.

"That old fool doesn't know anything!" Mr. Kendall replied nervously.

"He knows lots of things," Jonathan slyly stated. "He told me those boys came looking for you. When they didn't find you, they decided to rob a bank. One died and the other went to prison."

"Like I said," Mr. Kendall lectured. "Some people are bred for stupidity."

Jonathan shook his head and said, "All for some land that's probably flooded most years. Marcus Lutz came by to see Mr. Harvey, and he told me the whole story."

"Marcus Lutz told you that story!" Mr. Kendall exclaimed.

"No," Jonathan said. "Mr. Harvey told me the story after Marcus came by his house."

"Marcus Lutz is out of prison?" Mr. Kendall said almost to himself.

"Are you afraid he's still looking for you?" Jonathan asked.

Mr. Kendall looked oddly relieved at the question and answered, "I guess I wouldn't blame him, but I'll put the sheriff on notice just the same. Marcus Lutz doesn't have any business in Lincoln County, and the sheriff won't have much patience for a vagrant felon prowling around town."

"You're not worried?" Jonathan asked.

"For you, yes," Mr. Kendall replied as he pulled back his coat pocket to reveal a handgun in a shoulder holster. "For me, I always keep a little extra protection."

Mr. Kendall put his jacket back in place to cover up the pistol and said, "Now you know why I've tried to protect you from that girl. That family's bad news, and although she puts on a veneer of civility, she's bad news too. Marcus Lutz is a brother-in-law or something, and she's got another Uncle down south that's meaner than him. You mess around with that girl and they find out you're a Kendall, they're going to mess around with you."

Jonathan stood up from his chair and straightened his hair before saying, "I guess I'll have to take my chances."

"Where are you going?" Mr. Kendall demanded.

"I've got business with David Simpson before evening comes," Jonathan explained as he stopped by the door.

"David was just doing what I told him to do," Mr. Kendall said. "He was checking on some land for me and just happened to be by the Harvey place."

"Don't worry," Jonathan fumed. "I'll straighten everything out."

"You've got work to do," Mr. Kendall stated in a commanding voice.

"Not any more," Jonathan said with a strange smile. "I quit."

"What!" Mr. Kendall roared.

"I'm not like you," Jonathan said. "If this is what it takes to make it in the land business, I'm doing something else."

"What are you going to do?" Mr. Kendall sneered.

"Frankly, I don't know," Jonathan said in a more confident voice than he thought he could muster. "But I plan to do it with Samantha Harvey."

Mr. Kendall exploded with a string of threats and insults, but Jonathan walked away without listening. Jonathan did not know what life offered outside of the protection his father, but he felt a freedom and relief he had never experienced. As he walked away from the Kendall Cotton Gin, he was not intimidated by his father's anger. His thoughts focused on Samantha Harvey, but first he had to find David Simpson.

CHAPTER 39

"I'M GOING TO TOWN, Papa!" Samantha shouted as she headed out of the house with her basket. "The raccoons got my eggs again."

"Okay," Mr. Harvey replied from inside the house. "Did I hear Jonathan earlier?"

Samantha stepped back into the house to say, "Yes."

"Did he say where he'd been keeping himself?" Mr. Harvey asked.

"Said he'd been to Oklahoma City," Samantha answered.

After a slight hesitation she added, "He said he sent a message, but I didn't get it."

Mr. Harvey smiled and said, "A lot of things get lost on the way out here."

Samantha blushed and said, "He's supposed to come by tonight."

"I thought you were going to a show," Mr. Harvey said with a raised eyebrow.

Frowning, Samantha said, "I am, but Jonathan said he would come by later."

"You're a busy girl all of the sudden," Mr. Harvey smiled.

"Not that busy," Samantha assured, "but I do need to go to town for a few things."

Samantha stepped off the front porch and walked quickly toward town with high spirits while Mr. Harvey sat in his chair listening to the silence of the countryside. Mr. Harvey knew his daughter had been anxious about Jonathan Kendall's three-day absence, and he sensed her relief at the young man's return. Mr. Harvey knew about worry. He had been concerned about Samantha's future since the death of her mother.

The loneliness of a summer afternoon was quickly interrupted by slow, deliberate steps Mr. Harvey heard from outside. He knew Samantha could not be back from town, and the footsteps sounded heavy, like a man wearing boots.

Mr. Harvey struggled to rise from his chair to meet the intruder, but before he could stand, he heard a voice call, "Anyone home?"

"I'm in here," Mr. Harvey shouted back. "Come in."

Mr. Harvey had not heard the man's voice in nearly twenty years, but he knew it immediately. He had mixed feelings about hearing Marcus Lutz calling from outside. For most of his married life, he had lived in fear of Marcus Lutz. With his wife now dead, he listened to the man approach with more curiosity than fear.

Marcus Lutz stepped into the doorway to look at the old man sitting inside. The last time Mr. Harvey had seen his visitor, Marcus was a brash young man with ambition and too much temper. Marcus looked similar to the man Mr. Harvey had known, but twenty years of prison had taken its toll. Marcus's face looked hard and his skin pale.

Mr. Harvey did not know what to expect from the man, but said, "Come in, Marcus. I've been expecting you."

Marcus Lutz stepped through the door and tipped his dirty hat.

"Have a seat," Mr. Harvey offered while pointing to an empty chair.

The man agreed and took a seat without speaking as his eyes shifted around the room nervously.

"What brings you to Chandler?" Mr. Harvey asked.

"I could ask you the same," Marcus replied.

Mr. Harvey cleared his throat and said, "I couldn't keep the old place any more. Samantha wanted to go to high school, so this seemed a good place."

"I seen the girl, the other night," Marcus grimly observed. "Looks like her mother."

"I suppose so," Mr. Harvey replied. "You see a person every day, and you don't notice so much. I think Samantha will always be a little girl to me."

"I ain't seen much of anyone in nearly twenty years," Marcus stated bluntly.

"I know," Mr. Harvey apologized. "It must have been hard."

"Some days," Marcus shrugged. "After a while, it seemed all days blend into one."

"How are you doing now?" Mr. Harvey hesitantly asked.

Marcus Lutz had a strange twisted expression on his face as he inclined his head and said, "Adjustin' I guess. A fella gets used to being told everything to do and watching over his shoulder all the time…I guess I thought it'd be different."

Marcus squinted his eyes as if in deep thought before continuing, "I thought about getting out every day, thinking the whole time it weren't going to happen…but then they let me out…Mr. Harvey, I've got to tell you, I didn't think I'd be so afraid being out."

"You didn't say why you came to Chandler," Mr. Harvey said kindly.

"To see you," Marcus said flatly, "and to see…the girl."

"She's gone to town," Mr. Harvey said.

"I know," Marcus said. "I saw her walk up the hill before I came out of the woods."

"Have you been watching us?" Mr. Harvey asked.

Marcus nodded and said, "Sometimes. I saw the girl…Samantha a few weeks ago, and I think I scared her some. She's with some fella that looked like he knew I didn't belong here. That's why I waited 'till she went before I came to see you. I've been needin' to talk to you."

Mr. Harvey leaned forward slightly as if to give the shy man permission to speak.

Marcus looked at his worn shoes for a moment before saying, "I went to prison with a lot of hate in my soul. I's mad at pretty much everyone…even you. You'd tried to tell me to settle down, and if I'd listened, I'd had a different life—wonderin' what could've been instead of what was. I just wanted to tell ya' that I'm out now and don't have no grudges 'gainst anyone."

"Even John Kendall?" Mr. Harvey asked.

Marcus straightened in his seat and said, "Probably ought to have some hate left for him, but…I'd probably be back in prison if'n I ran into him. It'd be better for both of us if I stay clear."

Mr. Harvey had a puzzled look on his face and said, "You didn't come to Chandler looking for John Kendall?"

"No," Marcus said with a look of bewilderment that showed he did not know John Kendall lived in the town.

"That's good," Mr. Harvey said. "I've been worried since Samantha told me you were in town."

"John Kendall lives in Chandler now?" Marcus asked slowly.

Mr. Harvey nodded as Marcus Lutz's neck turned a crimson tone.

"Are you okay, Marcus?" Mr. Harvey asked, concerned at the man's agitated body language.

Marcus did not answer for a second before saying, "I didn't know he was here."

Marcus got up and looked as if he might march into town before Mr. Harvey said, "Stay a little longer, Marcus. I would like to talk to you about Sammie."

Marcus obeyed the elderly man and returned to his chair.

Marcus finally said. "Look's like you did a right fine job raising her."

"I had help," Mr. Harvey said. "Mrs. Harvey was a wonderful mother...and wife."

"Sarah always would do anything for family," Marcus said while fighting back a tone of sarcasm.

"Yes she would," Mr. Harvey said sternly. "Sarah was a wonderful woman. You of all people should know that!"

Marcus looked at the picture of Sarah Harvey hanging on the wall and said, "You're right, I'm stuck in the past."

"What are you going to do now?" a concerned Mr. Harvey asked.

"I'm going to a place close to Huck," Marcus said. "He's got some good land down south of Keokuk Falls in Seminole County."

"In the Econtuska bottom?" Mr. Harvey asked.

"No," Marcus sighed. "The Hellwigs'll never have a piece of property that rich, but he's still got a spread south of there. Huck's got an old cabin...ain't much more than a shed, but I'm fixin' it up and doing odd jobs. I've got to get back tomorrow to help pick the squash...that's why I finally worked up the courage to come see you."

"Huck's got him a farm," Mr. Harvey said.

"It's his, too," Marcus bragged. "Huck's no sharecropper."

"Sounds like he's doing okay," Mr. Harvey said.

"He's treated me decent," Marcus said.

"Huck's a decent man," Mr. Harvey replied. "At least he always has been."

"Yes, sir," Marcus agreed, "and so have you."

Mr. Harvey smiled at the complement and was also relieved at the tone of the conversation. He reached next to his chair and retrieved some stationary and his old pen.

"Would you mind taking Huck a note for me?" Mr. Harvey asked.

"Of course not," Marcus replied.

Mr. Harvey quickly wrote while explaining to Marcus Lutz, "Samantha's got no family left up here and I'd like for Huck to consider sending me the directions to his place. Just in case something happens to me."

"I've got the directions with me," Marcus interrupted. "At least I got the directions to my cabin, and I'm right next door."

"Good," Mr. Harvey said, as he took down the directions and continued writing his note.

"Like I said, I got to be getting back," Marcus nervously stated. "I've got to catch the train shortly, and I thought...well...I don't know that many people from back at the old place...at least not people that might like to visit. I was thinkin' you and the girl'd like to come down sometime to see me or Huck."

"That would be a wonderful trip," Mr. Harvey encouraged.

Marcus smiled for the first time since he had entered the room. His teeth were yellowed with several missing from a smile that had been nearly perfect when he was a younger man. A sense of sadness came over Mr. Harvey, as he looked at the man who had so much promise, but who had traded it all away in one rash act.

"I've got a train to catch," Marcus said.

"Can't you change the ticket?" Mr. Harvey asked.

"Ain't got no ticket," Marcus smiled sheepishly. "There's a freight train runnin' that I can catch goin' toward Shawnee then to

Seminole. I can't miss that train. If I spend one more night in these woods I think the chiggers'll eat me alive."

Mr. Harvey strained to get up and walk his guest to the door.

"It was good to see you, Marcus," Mr. Harvey said.

Looking at the floor, Marcus Lutz replied, "It was good to see you, too."

"I wished you'd got a chance to meet Sammie," Mr. Harvey said.

With his sad smile, Marcus said, "I did. In fact, I seen her twice. Once in town and once here on the porch with that fella."

"Did you know who that young man was?" Mr. Harvey hesitantly asked.

"No," Marcus said. "But he's an arrogant—"

Before Marcus could say more, Mr. Harvey interrupted and said, "That was John Kendall's son."

Marcus Lutz's face turned pale.

"He and Sammie have become...friends," Mr. Harvey explained.

"And you permit that!" Marcus replied with a flash of anger.

"Not at first," Mr. Harvey said. "But I've spent time with him, and he seems to be an upstanding young man."

"His father seemed upstanding, too," Marcus hissed.

"I'm a pretty good judge of character," Mr. Harvey defended. "Maybe it's because I'm old, but I think you'll agree that I'm not easily taken in by people. I tried to warn the Hellwigs about John Kendall back in Warwick. I will tell you, the boy's not like his father, and I believe he has honorable intensions toward Sammie."

Marcus shook his head violently and said, "I can't agree to that. John Kendall's caused that family and that girl more grief than she'll ever know. There ain't no good can come from a son of John Kendall around a Hellwig woman."

"The sins of the father can't be held against the son," Mr. Harvey reasoned. "You of all people should understand that."

"Maybe so," Marcus said, "but—"

Marcus stopped talking as if searching for the right thing to say before finally sighing heavily and continuing, "But, I guess it's not my say. It was good to see you Mr. Harvey. I'd like it if you and Samantha could come for a visit sometime."

"We will," Mr. Harvey assured.

"I got to go," Marcus said, as he turned to walk back toward town.

Mr. Harvey leaned against the post to the porch and watched Marcus Lutz step quickly down the trail. He was a sad figure in so many ways. His time in prison gave him an unusual gait that made him appear unsure of himself. Mr. Harvey was confident Marcus would try to salvage something of his life, but the older man lamented the future that could have been for the man. As Mr. Harvey watched Marcus Lutz disappear, he wondered if he had made a mistake telling him about Jonathan Kendall. It would have been easier to have avoided the subject, but Mr. Harvey knew better than anyone that people had refused to deal with the truth for too many years and that procrastination had harmed Samantha he was sure. He determined it was time to reveal some truth, at least to his daughter. When he felt better, he would take Samantha south of Keokuk Falls to see a family she had never really known.

CHAPTER 40

JONATHAN FRANTICALLY SEARCHED THE town for David Simpson after the confrontation with his father. He felt a strange mixture of liberation and anxiety at the same time. Failing to find David, Jonathan leaned against the railing of the viaduct, staring down the train tracks, contemplating the hectic day.

"You're not jumping are you?" David Simpson asked, interrupting Jonathan's solitude.

Jonathan immediately straightened to confront David, who walked toward him with a carefree gait that contrasted with his own troubled demeanor.

Walking to within striking distance, David said, "Bet you've been looking for me?"

Jonathan did not know how to respond. His first instinct was to punch David, but his friend's calm persona disarmed him. Jonathan did not say anything but turned to lean against the railing of the viaduct and look down the train tracks leading out of town.

David said, "Train tracks are exciting and lonely at the same time."

"How could you do it?" Jonathan finally asked.

"Do what?" David innocently replied.

"Break Caroline's heart like that," Jonathan clarified.

"Whoa, a second," David responded. "I've not done anything to your sister."

Shaking his head, Jonathan said bitterly, "It didn't take you long to find your way to Samantha's house when my sister left town!"

"Hang on," David replied sternly. "I went out to the Harvey's on business—for your father. He's buying the old Brock place, and the Harvey house is on part of it."

"It didn't look like business to me," Jonathan said pointedly.

David studied Jonathan for a moment and said, "You're serious about this girl?"

"What did you think?"

"I thought you'd have a good time and maybe have a few laughs."

"I'm not like you, David," Jonathan explained. "I do have a good time with her—but—there's more. I—I think Samantha's special."

David whistled and said, "I had no idea. Your dad sent me there to visit the place. Said it'd be good to know about it in case we had to evict."

"What?" Jonathan asked.

"Your dad owns the Harvey place as of Thursday," David explained. "I thought you would have known."

"Didn't you know what he was up to?" Jonathan asked hotly.

David did not answer but looked away from Jonathan and back down the tracks.

"I can't believe my father would sink that low," Jonathan fumed.

"Jonathan," David said. "You can't be serious about this girl."

"Why not?"

"First, your dad will never approve," David factually explained. "Secondly, she's the tenant, and you're the landlord. How do you think that's going to work out? Haven't you ever suspected that she sees your family's big house and the successful business and sees you as a way out?"

"Samantha's not like that," Jonathan replied hotly. "She's independent, intelligent—"

"She's a woman," David interrupted. "What better way to put her intelligence to work than marrying the son of one of the most successful land men in the county, and don't think she hasn't thought about it."

"You don't know what you're talking about," Jonathan said as he and David continued looking down the tracks side by side.

"I know women," David boasted. "I've spent enough time with Samantha to know she's set her sights on you."

"That's why you asked her out tonight?" Jonathan sarcastically asked. "To show me you can have any girl—even mine?"

"I didn't know you were serious about her," David smiled uneasily. "It took some doing and a little charm, but I convinced her to broaden her social horizons. Besides, I'm just a puppet on a string."

"What do you mean by that," a terse Jonathan replied.

"Not all of us are born with a father that can make things happen like your dad can," David explained. "I need this job, and I need to keep your father happy. I am sorry, but I was just doing my job."

Jonathan did not reply, but studied David for a moment. David always seemed confident and in control, but Jonathan could see in David an uncertainty in his friend he had rarely seen.

David shrugged, as if trying to convince himself, and said, "I was just trying to do you a favor. Your dad'd have a cow if you got messed up with a girl like that."

"Dad'll have to have a cow then," Jonathan replied. "I quit the cotton gin this afternoon and I suspect I'll be moving out tonight."

"What!" David exclaimed. "You quit the business?"

Jonathan nodded.

"That's the stupidest plan I've ever heard of," David said shaking his head. "What are you going to do?"

Jonathan struggled with this question the entire afternoon. He had always lived with his family and worked in the family business. Jonathan had felt a rush of satisfaction when he told his father he was quitting, but he had not thought much about what he might do.

"I'll find something," Jonathan muttered.

David Simpson laughed sympathetically and said, "Three days."

"What?" a puzzled Jonathan replied.

"Three days until you come to your dad with your tail between your legs," David explained.

Jonathan did not respond.

Leaning closer to his friend, David said, "You can stay at my house in the meantime."

"Thanks," Jonathan replied.

David handed Jonathan a small envelope and said, "Take these tickets for the show tonight. I've spent enough time with Samantha to know she'd rather go with you."

"Really?" Jonathan said as he took the envelope. "But they're your tickets."

David laughed good-naturedly and said, "You're plenty of entertainment for me."

"Thanks," Jonathan said as he took the tickets for the magic show.

"She's a clever girl," David noted. "Every time I tried to talk about my favorite subject—me—she twisted it around to talk about you. I really didn't know you were serious about her and sure didn't know Caroline would be back in town this evening. Good luck—because I think you're going to need it."

David tipped his cap slightly to Jonathan and headed back across the viaduct to his home on the more modest side of town.

"I may be taking you up on that offer for a place to sleep!" Jonathan shouted as David walked away.

Turning to look at his friend, David said, "If you use those tickets, I'm sure of it."

CHAPTER 41

JONATHAN ARRIVED AT THE Harvey home unsure if Samantha would be pleased to see him as a substitute for David. Samantha greeted him with a pleasant smile before throwing her arms around his neck to hold him tight. On the walk to town, Jonathan explained the strange day he had while a cheerful Samantha seemed content to listen.

The magician teased the crowd at the St. Cloud Hotel with tricks and illusions. Jonathan was fascinated at the magician's ability to suspend reality and create deceptions so effortlessly. Samantha held his hand when the lights went low, and Jonathan felt all was right with the world.

Exiting the small theater in the back of the hotel and stepping into the warm summer air, Jonathan looked forward to a long walk to Samantha's home. The sun was setting in the west. He had so much he wanted to say and was beginning to believe Samantha cared for him as much as he cared for her.

"Jonathan!" a voice shouted from the street interrupting his stroll down the town's main street.

Running across the street, Woody Carlson waved to ensure he had Jonathan's attention.

Jonathan, still holding Samantha's arm, stopped as Woody said excitedly, "Have you heard?"

"Heard what?" Jonathan replied.

"They're mobilizing the National Guard!" Woody explained. "Captain Gilstrap's been looking for you all afternoon."

"We're mobilizing?" Jonathan clarified.

"In a couple of days," Woody panted, out of breath from his quick walk to catch up to Jonathan. "Captain Gilstrap wants to see you as soon as possible."

"I'll take Samantha home and be right there," Jonathan said.

"I don't think that'll be a good idea," Woody replied. "The captain's been expecting you for a while. It's crazy down there."

Jonathan looked at Samantha and then back at Woody's urgent body language before saying to the young man, "Could you see that Samantha gets home?"

"Yes, sir," Woody said in an almost military tone.

"I' m sorry—" Jonathan began to apologize.

"Don't be," Samantha assured. "I can see myself home."

Stepping close to her, Jonathan said, "I'd feel better if Private Carlson escorted you."

Samantha blushed slightly at the attention and said, "If it will make you feel better."

"I'll come see you once I know what all this is about," Jonathan said. "This wouldn't be the first time we've had a drill. I can't think what it could be about."

"I'll see you tomorrow," Samantha said before giving Jonathan a peck on the cheek.

As Samantha walked away with Woody Carlson close behind, she looked over her shoulder and smiled. Jonathan watched Samantha disappear into the night, before he quickly walked to the National Guard's Statistical House to find Captain Gilstrap.

CHAPTER 42

JONATHAN ARRIVED AT CAPTAIN Gilstrap's office with the sun sinking below the horizon in the west. Opening the door, Jonathan interrupted his father who was having an animated conversation with the captain.

"I'll be going," Mr. Kendall said nervously as he stood. "I just wanted you to know my thoughts."

Mr. Kendall barely looked at his son as he quickly exited the room leaving Jonathan alone with Captain Gilstrap.

"Where've you been?" Captain Gilstrap asked as he looked through papers stacked on his desk.

"The magic show at the St. Cloud," Jonathan explained. "What was my father doing here?"

"Making sure you'd be going to Mexico," Captain Gilstrap stated.

"What?" Jonathan gasped.

"Your father thinks you won't want to go with the company," Captain Gilstrap informed with a raised eyebrow.

Jonathan did not respond immediately, but then stated factually, "He wants me out of town."

Captain Gilstrap said authoritatively, "I don't know what's happening between you and your father, but it doesn't matter. You're an officer in the Oklahoma National Guard, and I expect you to do your duty."

"Yes, sir," Jonathan affirmed.

"Good," Captain Gilstrap replied. "We've got orders to ship out by train to Fort Sill Monday morning. I've sent couriers, but I'll need you to make sure your men are ready."

"Yes, sir," Jonathan nodded.

"We'll organize at Fort Sill," Captain Gilstrap continued. "There's no question we'll be headed to the border to hunt Pancho Villa and his bandits. I don't know much more than that at this point, but we'll be ready."

"Yes, sir," Jonathan stoically replied.

"That'll be all," Captain Gilstrap said dismissing Jonathan for the evening.

As Jonathan stepped to the door, Captain Gilstrap said in a more casual tone, "Lieutenant Kendall, you better say good-bye to that girl of yours for a while. It doesn't matter what your father said, you're likely to be gone several months."

"What did my father say?" Jonathan asked.

"Not much," Captain Gilstrap shrugged. "I just know he was anxious for you to get out of town and to Mexico. I've known your father for a few years, and I've never got the sense before that he cared much for your service in the militia."

"No, sir," Jonathan replied. "His interest in my guard duty is a new development."

"I want you to know, it didn't matter," Captain Gilstrap explained. "We're getting shipped out whether your father came here tonight or not. I thought you should know."

"Thank you, sir," Jonathan said.

Smiling, Captain Gilstrap said, "If she's as pretty as everyone says, she'll be worth the wait."

"I know," Jonathan said, before nodding at the captain and stepping into the warm June night.

Jonathan wanted to see Samantha, but darkness shrouded the countryside, and he decided to wait until morning. Jonathan started the short walk up the long stairway leading from the Statistical House where Captain Gilstrap's office was located to his family's home on top of the hill. His mind busily thought of the many men he needed to contact over the weekend. The news of the deployment would travel fast, but he still wanted to make sure all of the men were ready.

Jonathan stood outside his house for a few moments listening to the tree frogs and other sounds of the summer night. He swallowed hard before opening the door to confront his father.

"Jonathan?" the voice of his father greeted even before the door fully opened.

Jonathan's instincts were to retreat to the safety of the night. Instead, he pushed the door open to see his father sitting in the front room with a cheerier demeanor than was his norm. Jonathan would normally have been relieved to see his father in a rare good mood, but this evening, Mr. Kendall's jovial attitude irritated him.

"When does the company ship out?" Mr. Kendall asked in an overly interested tone.

Jonathan stared coldly at his father. Mr. Kendall must have known Company B would leave Monday morning. Jonathan believed the whole town knew by now, and his father had met with the captain not an hour earlier. Mr. Kendall had always been critical of his son's service in the National Guard, and his father's false tone of concern angered Jonathan.

"Monday," Jonathan answered curtly.

"You'll have a thousand things to do," Mr. Kendall replied, ignoring his son's obvious annoyance.

"We'll be ready," Jonathan said pointedly.

"Good, good," Mr. Kendall smiled. "It will be quite an adventure in Mexico. Thank God you're not being dragged into the mess in Europe. If I was a few years younger, I'd be tempted to enlist myself for the kind of stories you boys will have to tell."

Jonathan looked at his jubilant father and said, "It won't matter."

"What?" Mr. Kendall asked, still smiling.

"Being away from Samantha," Jonathan answered. "It won't change the way I feel about her."

Mr. Kendall's countenance transformed from carefree interest in Jonathan's upcoming trip to Mexico to one of strained apprehension. Mr. Kendall studied his son carefully, trying to make sure he said the right thing.

"Jonathan," Mr. Kendall finally said. "I know what it's like to be a young man, but you've got to believe I'm trying to look out for your long-term interest. I know you're infatuated with this young woman, but you hardly know her, and I'm afraid your main attraction is the fact that I don't approve."

"I love her," Jonathan said without thinking.

Mr. Kendall fought back his instinct to respond authoritatively and instead said, "I believe you think you do…and maybe you do, but you owe it to yourself to think this through…to at least take some time to make sure this is right for you."

Jonathan was caught off guard by his father's rational reply and did not know how to respond.

Mr. Kendall took the opportunity to say, "I know things about this girl's past and her family, but it won't make any difference to you now…not as long as you're driven by your feelings. Trust me, I know the passions of a young man, and you're seeing this beautiful young woman without any flaws, but I'm afraid...I'm afraid for you."

"What are you afraid of, Father?" Jonathan asked calmly.

"I'm afraid the main attraction of this girl is the fact that I've been so adamant about my disapproval," Mr. Kendall explained sincerely. "I fear you're not seeing things clearly because you're rebelling against me. You've certainly heard the whispers of the people around town about her family and her mother?"

"No," Jonathan defended. "I haven't."

"It doesn't matter," Mr. Kendall replied shaking his head. "You're going away, and it will give you time to think. I won't stand in your way any longer. If you come back and still think this girl is worth your attention, I'll discuss it with you."

"Thank you," Jonathan said confused at his father's uncharacteristic sensibility.

"Only one thing," Mr. Kendall added.

"Yes."

"Promise me you won't do anything stupid until you get back from Mexico and we can talk," Mr. Kendall pleaded.

"I won't do anything stupid," Jonathan agreed.

"I mean it," Mr. Kendall warned. "Don't get married —"

"Married!" Jonathan exclaimed. "We're not even engaged."

"I know how young men are when they're heading off to war," Mr. Kendall said seriously. "I know how persuasive young women can be to get what they want."

"What are you saying?" Jonathan said bluntly.

"I'm saying a girl like her might do anything to get you to commit to marriage," Mr. Kendall said plainly. "It wouldn't be the first time, and I don't want you forced into a marriage with a girl that would trap you like that. I certainly don't want you going off to play soldier leaving a bastard child behind."

The calmness Jonathan had felt at the tone of his father's conversation evaporated as his face flushed with anger.

Struggling to say the right thing, Jonathan finally said is a quivering voice, "You don't know anything about Samantha Harvey! I won't be doing anything 'stupid,' but my time in Mexico won't change how I feel about her, and that—you can count on."

Before his father had a chance to respond, Jonathan walked defiantly to his room and firmly shut the door in case his father had intentions of continuing the conversation. Mr. Kendall took a deep breath and sighed heavily. His attempt to reason with his son had not gone well, but he was comfortable knowing his son would soon be far away from Samantha Harvey. Mr. Kendall was confident the girl would not be an issue for his son when Jonathan returned to Chandler.

As Mr. Kendall turned off the light in the front room to head to bed, Mrs. Kendall watched from the shadows at the top of the stairs now knowing why her son could never be with Samantha Harvey. She was as determined as her husband to keep the two apart, but was convinced Jonathan could never know why.

CHAPTER 43

JONATHAN PACKED HIS BAGS and left the Kendall house before dawn the next morning. He headed across the viaduct to the trail leading toward Indian Springs and the Harvey place.

Samantha leaned against the fence by the chicken house as Jonathan approached. She did not see him at first and looked into the countryside as if lost in thought.

"What are you looking at?" Jonathan asked as he walked up to her.

Slightly startled, Samantha smiled sweetly saying, "I'm looking at the mimosa tree. The blooms are out. I like looking at them in the morning breeze."

Jonathan looked at a large mimosa tree in full bloom and said, "It's peaceful here, isn't it?"

Samantha shrugged and turned to Jonathan, "Sometimes. It's quiet, that's for sure. When do you leave?"

"Monday," Jonathan replied.

"Where are you going?" Samantha asked. "I heard the company's headed to Mexico."

"We'll go to Fort Sill first," Jonathan answered.

A melancholy Samantha turned to look at the mimosa tree and asked, "How long will you be gone?"

"I don't know," Jonathan said as he looked at the despondent girl. "Are you okay?"

Forcing a smile, Samantha answered, "I'm fine. I'm just tired. Father's not feeling well, and I didn't sleep much last night."

"Is there anything I can do?" Jonathan offered.

"No," Samantha replied.

Sensing there was something Samantha was not saying, Jonathan asked, "Are you going to tell me?"

"Tell you what?"

"Are you going to tell me what's really bothering you?"

Samantha breathed deeply and said, "Don't you know?"

Jonathan shook his head in puzzlement as he continued to watch her carefully.

"You," Samantha finally answered. "You're going away...that kept me up last night. I've gotten used to you taking care of me and seeing you every day and now...now you'll be gone for who knows how long."

"It's not like I won't come back," Jonathan smiled.

"I know," Samantha said. "I'm being silly."

Samantha knew Jonathan could not understand her feelings. He was not a woman, and he had not experienced the despair of poverty. She had become fond of Jonathan the past weeks but felt embarrassed that she had considered a marriage to him would make her life easier. Samantha wished her mother were alive to help her know how to feel or how to act. Thinking of Jonathan going away made her feel desperate, and she did not like the sensation of not being in control.

"I'll write," Jonathan tried to assure.

Samantha looked compassionately at Jonathan, thinking of their differences. He could not understand buying postage would be anything but an incidental expense. Samantha would have to become even more frugal to keep in touch with Jonathan. His trip to Mexico would be an adventure for him, but to Samantha his departure threatened her security.

Samantha smiled at Jonathan's naivety and said, "It won't be the same."

"I know," Jonathan confessed. "But it'll make coming home that much sweeter."

Samantha smiled and threw her arms around Jonathan and hugged him tightly.

"Maybe I need to leave more often," Jonathan joked, as he enjoyed the embrace.

"Don't tease me now," Samantha sobbed as she buried her face in Jonathan's shoulder.

Jonathan stroked the back of her head and said, "It's going to be all right. Don't worry."

Worry was all Samantha had done since learning Jonathan was leaving, but she said, "I won't."

After a few moments, Samantha asked, "Will you come see me tonight?"

"Of course," Jonathan replied.

"Will you bring your bedroll and sleep on the porch?" Samantha asked. "To chase the raccoons away?"

Samantha's request startled Jonathan. He was eager for any excuse to come to the Harvey place, but the words of his father from the previous night haunted him. He had been offended and upset at his father's slur on Samantha's virtue. The idea she would even think of trapping him polluted his opinion of her innocent request and made him angry with his father for thinking so crassly.

"Are the raccoons stealing your eggs?" he finally asked.

Samantha said, "Not so much, but it will be nice having you right outside."

Jonathan smiled awkwardly at the invitation and said, "I should be able to guard your henhouse for a night or two."

Samantha straighten Jonathan's collar and said, "Can you stay for breakfast?"

"I'd like to, but I've got a lot of things to do today," Jonathan replied. "I'll see you this evening."

Samantha kissed Jonathan before he began the long walk back to town, and held him tightly, not wanting him to go. Jonathan had many things to do before leaving on Monday, but he spent his last two nights on the Harvey's front porch talking to Samantha late into the night.

The soldiers of Company B were eager for service, yet most found the unexpected call to duty an inconvenience. Jonathan Kendall was no different. The prospect of seeing new places was tempered by leaving Samantha. She walked Jonathan to the train depot Monday morning amongst a whirl of activity. The soldiers marched down Manvel Street with crowds cheering on both sides of the street. The station was filled with excitement and anxiety as family, friends, and neighbors came to see their soldiers leave. Mr. Kendall stared coldly at Samantha as she held tightly to Jonathan's arm. Jonathan noticed his father's intent look, but he chose to ignore it and savor his last few moments with Samantha.

"I want you to have this," Samantha said, as she handed Jonathan a photograph. "It's not much, but it's the only picture I have of myself."

"I'll look at it every day," Jonathan promised.

Jonathan gazed into Samantha's eyes one last time before embracing her tightly. He was the last to board, and the train was rolling by the time he reached his seat. Samantha Harvey watched the train chug around the bend toward Oklahoma City, not knowing when Jonathan might return.

Samantha turned to walk home when she saw Mr. Kendall watching her. Caroline stood by her father's side and looked like she wanted to speak to Samantha, but Mr. Kendall restrained her. Mr. Kendall led Caroline away, leaving Samantha alone. The empty train station almost made Samantha cry, but life had been too difficult the past year to let loneliness cause her to weep. She walked home to look after her ailing father, wondering when she would see Jonathan again.

PART 3

GONE AWAY

CHAPTER 44

SOLDIERS IN THE CROWDED train buzzed with excitement as Company B rumbled toward Oklahoma City. The exhilarated young men told stories, made jokes, and teased each other during the short trip. Jonathan Kendall, however, had no time for their crude amusements. Captain Gilstrap used the travel time to organize his officers, and Jonathan listened carefully as his commander explained their itinerary. After a brief stop in Oklahoma City, they would travel to Fort Sill near Lawton. Captain Gilstrap explained Company B would deploy in San Benito, a small Texas town close to the border of Mexico and 20 miles from the Gulf of Mexico.

By the time the train stopped in Oklahoma City, the troops were still in high spirits. Jonathan had made many trips to the city, but for some of the farm boys, it was their first look at the tall buildings and busy streets of an urban area. Company B exited the train and boarded the Interurban for a short trip to the fairgrounds northeast of the downtown area. In the distance, the soldiers saw the new state capital building being constructed and surrounded by scaffolding.

Units from across the state caused a near riot as men scrabbled for any information about their immediate destination. A large tent served as a processing office for the nearly three thousand soldiers gathered there. Captain Gilstrap looked like he might explode at the confusion before Company B returned to the trains for the two-hour trip to Lawton and Fort Sill.

Jonathan had never been west of Oklahoma City and was captivated by the vast expanse of empty plains stretching to the horizon. In the distance, he saw granite hills rising from the prairie and an outcropping of the Wichita Mountains in the distance. This was the Oklahoma depicted in popular literature, and the landscape contrasted greatly with the hilly countryside surrounding Chandler. The train rumbled to a stop at the Fort Sill depot. Captain Gilstrap gave his lieutenants instructions, and Jonathan barked orders like the other officers.

Fort Sill had a neatly groomed square of antique-looking rock buildings that baked in the western afternoon sun. The fort originally served as a cavalry outpost during the Indian Wars, but had been the School of Fire for Field Artillery since 1911. Geronimo, the famous Apache warrior, had been a prisoner at the fort until his death seven years earlier, and his body was buried in the Apache Indian Prisoner of War cemetery at the fort.

Company B trained for three weeks at Fort Sill as part of the 1st Infantry of the Oklahoma National Guard. Colonel Roy Hoffman, the senior officer, arrived in camp to review the troops. Colonel Hoffman took special interest in Company B from his hometown of Chandler causing Captain Gilstrap to be even more diligent in training.

Jonathan took an excursion to the tourist village of Medicine Park one weekend, which was located a few miles north of the base. Cobblestone buildings situated around a cool lake and stream, provided a refreshing retreat from the summer heat. There were plenty of young women to entertain the officers, but Jonathan could only think of his Samantha and was very poor company for anyone. There was a dance in the evening, but Jonathan passed on the social and spent his evening looking at the reflection of granite mountains off the glimmering water.

In late July, the Oklahoma National Guard traveled to San Benito in the far southern part of Texas. The train left at six o'clock in the morning and did not reach its destination until nearly eight o'clock that night. The dusty, brown landscape looked stark and rugged with mesquite and scrub brush dotting the otherwise bare scenery. The drab surroundings were different than the exotic adventure the men had imagined.

A small wood building for the mess represented the only useable structure. The tired soldiers worked late into the dark night to raise their tents and stow their gear. It was nearly midnight before Jonathan rested in his canvas cot, exhausted from the day's trip. The sparse surroundings made his home in Chandler seem far away. Looking out the door of his stuffy tent, Jonathan gazed at a brilliant star-filled sky and wondered if Samantha might be looking at the same stars. Jonathan took out her photo and looked at it by candlelight. He smiled—his first of the day, thinking of Samantha and her raccoons. The smile faded as he thought how much he would like to be on her front porch that evening.

CHAPTER 45

"You're up early," Samantha greeted as her father looked out the window.

"Thought I would enjoy the cool of the morning," Mr. Harvey smiled.

The early September afternoons were still hot, but the morning provided relief from the oppressive heat they endured in July and August.

"Are you feeling better today?" Samantha asked, as she prepared to go outside for her morning chores.

"Some," Mr. Harvey replied.

"Good."

"Will you be going to town this morning?" Mr. Harvey asked.

Samantha blushed slightly and said, "Yes."

"To the post office?" Mr. Harvey added.

"Yes."

"Is there a day you don't receive a letter?"

"Not many."

"How's Jonathan?" Mr. Harvey pried.

"Good," Samantha smiled. "I think he's disappointed he didn't get to march into Mexico and hunt down Pancho Villa. He says San Benito is a little short on entertainment. I think he spends most of his time doing drills."

"So you two are still…communicating?" Mr. Harvey asked.

"I write about half the letters that Jonathan sends," Samantha pined, "but my letters are longer."

"When I met your mother, we corresponded by mail for many months," Mr. Harvey revealed. "She saved most of them, and they're sappy, incoherent dribble. I remember she got testy when I went back to Pennsylvania for a time. I intended to be gone a few weeks but ended up gone several months. I think she almost lost patience with me."

"I miss Jonathan," Samantha admitted. "I read every letter several times looking for some hint of what he might be thinking or feeling."

Mr. Harvey put his arm around his daughter and said, "I found writing letters a good way to get to know Sarah…your mother. Writing made me think. It was a good way to get to know her. Maybe this is a good way for you to get to know Jonathan."

"What was mother like?" Samantha asked. "I mean, what was she like when you first met?"

"Like a spring day," Mr. Harvey answered. "I left Pennsylvania after my first wife passed away. Our son died of the pox the year before, and it was too much for her. I came to Oklahoma because…well, I thought it was a brand new country and I could start over. I never thought I'd marry again. Your mother was much younger than me, but she had a mature soul. She was smart and very frank when I first met her. She was a Hellwig, and they were dirt-poor farmers. Sarah was embarrassed about her lack of refinement, but I never met a finer woman than your mother. She was loyal, kind, trustworthy, and pretty as a peach…just like you."

"When did you know you loved her?" Samantha asked.

Mr. Harvey looked affectionately at his daughter and said, "It depends on what you call 'love.'"

"What do you mean?"

Mr. Harvey took a deep breath before saying, "There's that thing we call love that's a big knot in your stomach...a feeling you have about a person. I felt that for Sarah almost the first time I saw her. I was too old for her, but we had a connection. I can't answer or guess what she saw in me. After a few months of knowing her and the family, I became more comfortable in my natural affections for her, and she seemed to find me at least tolerable."

"So you knew right away?" Samantha clarified.

"I didn't say that," Mr. Harvey smiled. "I knew right away I was attracted to Sarah, but like any relationship, I *learned* to love her, and I think she learned to love me. Love's not an emotion as much as an attitude we have toward others. It's the way you treat another person. Your mother was easy to love. She always looked for the best in others. She sacrificed everything for you, and that was her best quality."

"I miss her," Samantha sighed.

"I know you do," Mr. Harvey consoled. "I miss her, too."

"I better get the chores done," Samantha said, as she stepped to the door.

"So," Mr. Harvey interrupted. "I take it you have a knot in your stomach for Jonathan Kendall?"

Samantha's cheeks flushed as she nodded and said, "I do. I...I think he feels the same way about me."

"He'd be a fool not to," Mr. Harvey assured.

Samantha beamed while her father studied her carefully.

Mr. Harvey finally added, "You're a special girl, Sammie. I hope you know that. I've tried to do the best I could for you, but I've always felt you were going to do fine with or without me. I think Jonathan's a fine young man, but don't get too wrapped up in depending on another person to make you happy. You've got to be happy with yourself. I don't want to see you hurt."

"Jonathan's—" Samantha began.

"I know," Mr. Harvey interrupted. "Jonathan's different, but sometimes things happen that can't be helped. I've seen people put all their hope in someone else, and then life happens. I just want you to be happy."

"I am happy," Samantha assured.

"I'm glad," her father replied. "When you go to town today, see if you can find someone to watch the place for a day or two...you know, milk the cow, feed the chickens."

"Why?" Samantha asked.

"I want to take you somewhere for a few days," Mr. Harvey answered.

"Where?"

"Your Uncle Huck has a place close to Keokuk Falls about twenty miles south and east of here," Mr. Harvey explained. "He's your mother's brother, and I think you need to get to know some of her family. They're about all the kin you have left besides me."

"I've heard you and mother talk about Uncle Huck, but I'm not sure I've ever met him," Samantha said.

"You saw him when you were very little, but you wouldn't remember," Mr. Harvey said.

"When will we go?" Samantha asked.

"I'd like to go this weekend," Mr. Harvey said.

"So soon," Samantha replied. "Do you feel up to a trip like that?"

"It's not that far, and I'll be fine," Mr. Harvey assured.

"I'll try to find someone," Samantha said.

Samantha stepped into the cool morning to begin her day. Her father watched her with a sense of satisfaction, but also a feeling of regret. He hoped Jonathan Kendall could make his daughter happy, but he learned long ago to not depend on the Kendalls. Samantha had grown into a poised, smart, and beautiful young woman, but Mr. Harvey worried about his failing health knowing a young woman like Samantha should not be on her own. Introducing her to a family she barely knew seemed the only remedy to his concern. He telegraphed Huck Hellwig a few weeks earlier, but had not heard back from his wife's brother. Mr. Harvey would take a chance on dropping by to try to give Samantha a safety net he was not sure he would be able to provide much longer.

CHAPTER 46

SAMANTHA WALKED TO THE post office a little before ten o'clock where a letter from Jonathan greeted her. She sat on the bench in front of the courthouse to read the letter before placing it in her lap and relaxing in the bright sunshine. She sensed Jonathan's disappointment at having routine assignments, but she was relieved to hear he was safe.

Samantha's father asked her to find someone to look after their place, but this assignment reminded her of how few people she really knew in Chandler. Looking at Jonathan's letter one more time, she decided to take a walk.

Chandler was peaceful this mid-morning, as townspeople went about their daily routine. Samantha walked west of the courthouse and headed down Eighth Street past the impressive houses on Silk Stocking Row. Samantha enjoyed walking by Jonathan's home imagining how he must have been as a small child, but she was always careful to avoid Mr. Kendall.

She wanted to stop at the Kendall house, but Caroline had moved to Edmond to attend school the week earlier. Samantha looked at the house as she continued to walk, unsure she would be warmly received even by Mrs. Kendall. Samantha did not understand why but sensed both Mr. and Mrs. Kendall had misgivings about their son's attachment to her.

Walking past the Kendall house, Samantha strolled down the steps to the Statistical House where the campgrounds for the National Guard stood eerily empty. Samantha wondered why she made the walk down the hill. The vacant parade grounds and silent rifle range reminded her that Jonathan was far away. Heading back to town, Samantha walked past the Kendall house again on her way home.

"Kind of empty down there ain't it?" the strong voice of Sam Bowles greeted from the front porch of the Tilghman house.

"Yes," Samantha answered as she used her hand to block the sun to see Sam sitting in a rocking chair. "It's sad to me."

"Have you heard from him?" Sam asked.

"Jonathan?" Samantha asked.

"Of course, Jonathan," Sam impatiently replied.

"I got a letter today," Samantha admitted. "I think he's bored."

"Not quite the adventure he thought?" Mr. Bowles suggested. "How's your pa doing?"

"Better," Samantha said. "We're taking a trip south in a few days."

"Where to?" the former deputy asked.

"Some place called Keokuk Falls," Samantha answered.

Sam Bowles let out a long whistle and said, "Keokuk Falls! I could tell you some stories."

"I've got a minute," Samantha smiled as she stepped close to the porch.

Sam Bowles sat up in his rocking chair and said, "Keokuk Falls was the rowdiest place in all of Oklahoma Territory, and that's sayin' something. The town, if that's what you want to call it, sat in the panhandle of Pott County right on the North Canadian River next to the falls and half a mile from the county line to the east. The place was half a mile from the Creek Nation, and the Seminole Nation was right across the river. You couldn't sell liquor in the old Indian Territories, but you could make all you wanted on the Oklahoma side. Operators set up shop close to the borders so they could make quick retreats from the law. All those border towns were rough, but Keokuk was the worst.

"Prague, the town just north of there, was filled with those Bohemians. They loved to brew beer, but the city folks decided to clean up the town. They ran the riff-raff out, but no one could clean up Keokuk. The town had some of the roughest saloons in the whole territory. One old stagecoach driver used to say, 'Welcome to Keokuk Falls. Stay around twenty minutes and see a man get shot!' I'm sure the place has changed since the old days. What are you doin' goin' down there?"

"Papa says we have family there," Samantha answered as she listened intently to the old deputy's tales.

Sam scratched the back of his head and thought for a moment before saying, "Who is it? Huck?"

"That's what Papa said," Samantha replied. "Do you know him?"

"Used to," Sam Bowles admitted in a more timid voice than was his nature. "Didn't know he was back in these parts."

"You knew my family?" Samantha asked.

Sam nodded his head and said, "A long time ago."

"What were they like?" Samantha asked.

"Hard luck people," Sam replied. "Huck moved away after the family lost the farm at Warwick. He had a brother that got shot dead trying to rob a bank with another fellow named Marcus Lutz, but that was just bad luck."

"Marcus Lutz?" Samantha asked.

"Yeah," the deputy confirmed. "I think he was engaged to Huck's sister or something."

"My mother?" Samantha questioned.

"No," Deputy Bowles said. "The other sister...your mom's younger sister."

"I've never met her," Samantha said.

"She died along time ago," the deputy said. "It was a bad business."

"What happened?" Samantha asked.

Sam looked at her, but was uncharacteristically quiet.

"Tell me what you know," Samantha pleaded. "I know something happened. I can't walk down the streets of this town without hearing people whisper about my family and 'that Harvey girl.' Please."

Sam sighed heavily as he looked around to confirm they were alone and said, "What do you know?"

"Nothing really," Samantha mused. "I know my mother's family lost a farm around Warwick. Beyond that, I've never met any of the Hellwigs."

Sam looked at the girl as if debating whether to speak before saying, "The Hellwigs staked a claim to a decent piece of land south of Warwick during the run, your grandpa and grandma and four kids. Huck was the oldest. Sarah, your ma, was only a year younger. The youngest girl was a cute thing—I think her name was Suzanne. The youngest boy was named Lawrence."

Deputy Bowles thought for a moment before wrinkling his forehead and saying, "They got their land but didn't have nothing else, so they mortgaged the place to buy tools and seed. They made a crop for a few years but never made much more than the cost of the seed and couldn't pay back the bank. Your mother taught school in Warwick. That's where she met Mr. Harvey, I believe. A drought hit one year and a flood the next. Crop prices failed, and it seemed one disaster happened on top another until the bank foreclosed. A businessman bought the property, and then something happened."

"What happened?" an eager, but apprehensive Samantha asked.

Sam Bowles sighed heavily again and said, "I don't know all the details, but the sheriff had to move the Hellwigs off their farm. Your grandpa and grandma left with the oldest boy Huck to live south of here."

After a hesitation, Sam continued, "The youngest boy, Lawrence, was rambunctious. He and Marcus Lutz decided to take things in their own hands. They'd been drinkin' and went to find the businessman they blamed. When they couldn't find him, they decided to hold up the bank. Lawrence was shot dead, and Marcus Lutz went to prison for it. Marcus was engaged to your aunt, but she went away. The next thing I heard, the poor girl was buried…died of a broken heart some said. Your mother married Mr. Harvey—a few months later, had you."

Samantha looked at the deputy with her forehead wrinkled in concern, "How many months later."

"I don't recall," Sam replied nervously while looking away.

"Who bought the place?" Samantha demanded.

A puzzled Sam looked at the girl before saying, "You don't know?"

"No," Samantha replied tersely.

Looking down the street at the Kendall house, Sam said, "It was John Kendall. I thought you knew."

Blood flowed out of Samantha's cheeks and she felt dizzy, as she muttered, "No. I didn't know Mr. Kendall knew my family."

Sam looked at the sad girl and regretted telling her the story. Although he believed he had been truthful, he knew he had not told her everything.

After a moment of silence, Sam said in a tone of voice that was less boisterous than his norm, "John Kendall knew your family well. He spent a lot of time there. I guess that's why they felt so betrayed.

The Hellwigs never forgave John Kendall. There's something else you should know."

Not really listening any more, Samantha mumbled, "What?"

Hesitating a second to make sure the young girl was paying attention, Sam waited until Samantha's hazel blue eyes met his.

Taking a deep breath, he said, "I'm the one that shot Lawrence — your uncle. I saw the commotion in the bank and heard someone yell there was a robbery. Lawrence was the first out of the bank holding a pouch of cash and what I thought was a pistol. It turned out to be a bottle of whiskey. I shot him through the chest before I knew what happened. Marcus Lutz surrendered without a fight."

Looking at the former deputy, Samantha said, "That must have been terrible."

"There's hardly a day goes by that I don't see that boy's face," Sam said softly. "It was a bad day, but it was worse for the Hellwigs...for that, I'm sorry."

Samantha did not know what to think, but she knew she did not want to know more about her family's tragedy as she said, "Thank you for telling me the truth. I need to go."

The old deputy did not reply as Samantha walked away in a daze. The sun still shined brightly, and birds continued to chirp in the autumn air, but darkness seemed to descend on her spirit. She felt as if she were walking in thick molasses. Samantha always believed her family had dreadful secrets, but now she wished they had stayed a mystery. Her mind was cluttered by Sam's revelations, and she wondered what other dark secrets might haunt her.

"Samantha!" a voice from across the street shouted, causing her to snap back to reality.

Samantha turned to see Augusta Kendall running toward her. Augusta was Jonathan's tall and somewhat gawky youngest sister, who had a bubbly personality and a frankness Samantha had always liked.

"Hello, Augusta," Samantha cordially greeted.

"I saw you walking down the street and was afraid I'd miss you," Augusta said.

"I'm heading home," Samantha replied.

"You never come by the house," Augusta pouted. "I was wondering if you had heard from my brother."

Samantha had always been intimidated by the Kendall house and especially Mr. Kendall. She now wondered if she would ever feel comfortable there.

"I got a letter today," Samantha revealed to Augusta.

Augusta smiled and said, "I knew he would write you more than me. What did he say?"

Samantha fumbled for the letter for a moment and then said pleasantly, "Why don't you read for yourself?"

The eager Augusta grabbed the letter and quickly began reading its contents, while Samantha carefully watched the twelve-year-old girl.

"He really likes you," Augusta noted with a mischievous grin.

Samantha had not remembered some of Jonathan's attempts to impress her before she handed the letter to Augusta and sheepishly said, "I think maybe so."

"I think maybe a lot," Augusta bubbled. "I definitely won't be telling Father about this letter."

An embarrassed Samantha said, "That would be best. I don't think your father thinks much of me."

Continuing to read the letter, Augusta shrugged and casually said, "That's okay. Father doesn't like anyone much."

Normally a glib statement from the candid Augusta would have caused Samantha to laugh, but today it did not bring her any pleasure. When Augusta finished reading the letter, she handed it back to the distracted Samantha.

"Is everything all right?" Augusta asked.

Surprised at the question and unaware of her preoccupied appearance, Samantha forced herself to smile and said, "Everything's fine."

"You look like something's bothering you," the outspoken Augusta noted.

"I'm just thinking about a trip Papa and I are about to take," Samantha said. "In fact, could I get you to do me a favor?"

"Sure," Augusta replied. "What is it?"

"We'll be gone for a couple of days, and I need someone to feed the chickens and collect the eggs," Samantha said before adding, "and to milk the cow."

"I can do that," Augusta smiled. "When?"

"If you could check on it the day after tomorrow, that's when we'll be gone," Samantha explained.

"Sure," Augusta affirmed. "Where are you going?"

"We're headed south to a place called Keokuk Falls to see some family," Samantha said.

After confirming the details with Augusta, Samantha walked home, wondering if her trip to Keokuk Falls would shed any more light on the mysteries of her family's past.

CHAPTER 47

THE TRIP TO KEOKUK Falls was less than thirty miles, but no direct roads connected it with Chandler. Mr. Harvey and Samantha boarded a morning train on the St. Louis and San Francisco line running between Oklahoma City and Tulsa to Daggett seven miles away just outside of Davenport. The train barely came to a stop in Daggett, to let passengers off before they caught the Atchison, Topeka, and Santa Fe line running south. Mr. Harvey and Samantha stayed on the train only as far as the tiny stop at Sparks seven miles away. After waiting nearly an hour, they boarded a much older train on the Fort Smith and Western line to Prague. The train trip took the better part of three hours and involved changing trains three times.

Prague, located in the far southeast corner of Lincoln County, was about the same size as Chandler, but it had a more casual atmosphere. The buildings were simple and practical. Samantha thought the people friendly, but tight knit. Named after the ancient European city, most of the early settlers were Bohemian, Czech, and German. The people were frugal and hardworking.

"We need to find a livery stable," Mr. Harvey said as he looked around the area surrounding the train station.

"Why don't you let me?" Samantha offered. "Have a seat and rest."

Mr. Harvey agreed and Samantha searched the small town looking for a place to rent a horse and carriage. Main Street was anchored by the First National Bank and the Prague National Bank. The nearby Busy Bee Café prepared for lunch customers. Samantha looked down the street to see Whitmore's Gin and the Union Cotton Oil Company, which caused her to think of Jonathan. On the far end of town, a modest sign for the Prague Livery and Blacksmithing offered mules for rent. Samantha secured a sturdy carriage and mule at a reasonable price. The large man renting her the rig gave her directions to Keokuk Falls. In less than thirty minutes, she managed to drive the mule back to the station to meet her father.

"That was quick," Mr. Harvey smiled as he climbed aboard.

"Prague's an efficient town," Samantha smiled. "The man rented this mule for a dollar once he found out I wasn't going to plow with her."

"It must've been a special price for pretty girls," Mr. Harvey teased.

Samantha blushed and gently tapped the mule to nudge the carriage south of town. It was a pleasant day, and the two travelers enjoyed a lunch Samantha had prepared.

The rolling hills turned to open fields as they approached the North Canadian River five miles south of Prague in the panhandle of Pottawatomie County. The Pottawatomie County panhandle was a small stretch of land about seven miles east to west and about five miles north to south. The panhandle had been located in the old Oklahoma Territory close to the borders of the Creek and Seminole lands, which made it the perfect base to export illegal liquor into the Indian Territory.

Before coming to the river, Samantha turned the mule east on a road that was not more than a trail for another three miles before turning south to the little town of Keokuk Falls located on the river.

Keokuk Falls was a notorious border town, but as Samantha looked over the place, it was a ghost of its former self. Unpainted buildings lined a wide street, but most were vacant. A general store still operated in one of the old saloons, but it looked like it had seen few customers this day.

Samantha nudged the mule through the remnants of the town toward the end of the street, where rushing water gently roared from the falls on the North Canadian River. The falls were only two to three feet tall with an abandoned gristmill on the far side of the falls. Logs and other debris littered the top of the rapids, while a dog enjoyed swimming in the tranquil water under the falls. The scene was peaceful compared to the rowdy past of the once notorious town. An old man, who looked old enough to tell stories that would have been hard to believe, charged a dime to take Samantha and Mr. Harvey across the river on a flat-bottomed ferry into Seminole County.

The topography of the land south of the river was hillier than the flat bottomland north of the river. Small open fields were surrounded by intimidating pockets of forest that looked like patches of jungle. A few miles south of Keokuk Falls, Mr. Harvey directed Samantha to drive the wagon between a thick stand of trees to a small field with a run-down shack situated in the corner by the trees.

"Hello!" Mr. Harvey shouted, as they approached the house.

The small house appeared to be vacant, and the derelict barn showed no activity.

"Are you sure this is the place?" a concerned Samantha asked.

"This is where I was told to come," Mr. Harvey said, as he got down from the wagon to walk around.

"You's shouldn't be here!" a boy of about 12 years old shouted, as he came out of the house.

"Dad'd not like it!" the boy continued with a gibbering manner of speech that made it hard to understand.

"Hello," Mr. Harvey said in a calm voice.

"You's shouldn't be botherin' us," the agitated boy repeated.

Mr. Harvey kept his distance and said, "I didn't mean to disturb you, but I'm Mr. Harvey. Is this the Hellwig place?"

The boy's eyes darted back and forth as if he was unsure of what to do and he repeated, "Dad said you's shouldn't be botherin' us."

The young boy continued to act erratically and stammered in his speech. Samantha stepped down from the wagon and walked cautiously toward the boy.

"Hello," she said kindly. "I'm Samantha. What's your name?"

The boy looked at her as if mesmerized and said, "Harold."

Samantha looked at her father and then back at Harold and said, "Hello, Harold. I'm Samantha Harvey."

"Hello," Harold replied shyly.

"We're looking for the Hellwig place," she explained.

Harold's forehead wrinkled and he repeated, "You's shouldn't be botherin' us."

"I don't want to bother anyone," Samantha assured as she stepped closer to the strange boy. "Do you live here?"

"Yeah," Harold replied.

"Is your last name Hellwig?" she asked.

The boy thought for a second as if debating whether to answer before saying, "Yeah."

Samantha smiled pleasantly and said, "It's good to meet you, Harold Hellwig. What's your father's name?"

The boy looked puzzled and said, "Dad."

Samantha smiled as Mr. Harvey said, "Someone's coming."

At the end of the field about one hundred yards away, four men noticed the wagon in the front of the house and began walking quickly toward them. One large man seemed to lead the others. Halfway to the house, one of the men stopped and turned around while the other three continued toward the visitors. When the men were closer, Samantha could tell one of them looked to be in his early twenties while the other was perhaps her age or a year younger.

As the three men approached, Mr. Harvey shouted, "Huck?"

The large man walked closer, squinting into the sun and answered, "Mr. Harvey?"

"Yes," Mr. Harvey answered. "Good to see you, Huck."

The large man Mr. Harvey called Huck continued to walk forcefully toward the house giving no indication if he was annoyed or pleased at the intrusion.

"What'r you doin' out here?" Huck finally asked, as he stepped toward Mr. Harvey to shake hands.

"I brought Sammie to meet some of her kin," Mr. Harvey explained.

Looking at Samantha, Huck said, "She looks like her mother."

Smiling at his daughter, Mr. Harvey said, "Yes, she does. Are these your boys?"

"Yeah," Huck admitted. "Haskell's the oldest, and the other boy's Howard. You've met Harold I see."

"Who was the other man in the field?" Samantha asked.

The men looked at her for a moment as if they were surprised at her outspokenness before Huck said, "That's Marcus. He lives on the other side of them woods, but he likes to keep to himself, particularly around strangers. He didn't know it was you two up here, so he skedaddled back into the woods."

Samantha looked across the empty field and said, "That's odd."

"Marcus likes keeping to himself," Huck defended.

"He came to visit me a few months back," Mr. Harvey said.

"Marcus?" Huck asked.

Mr. Harvey nodded.

"He always thought a lot of you," Huck shrugged.

Huck looked at his middle son Howard and said, "Go fetch Marcus, if he'll come. Tell him Mr. Harvey's here."

The boy nodded obediently and headed across the field toward the woods.

"Could I speak with you, Huck?" Mr. Harvey asked. "In private."

Huck looked around at the few people around and said, "Sure. Haskell show Samantha around the place. Me and Mr. Harvey are goin' around by the barn to talk a little."

Haskell nodded and walked toward the house with Harold and Samantha trailing behind.

Huck started walking to a secluded spot behind the barn and said, "I guess you want to talk about the girl?"

CHAPTER 48

Samantha thought Haskell Hellwig a handsome young man with a pleasant personality, but their conversation was awkward. Haskell was Samantha's cousin, but she knew nothing about him. If they had met in other circumstances, they might have been friends, but now they were forced together with nothing to talk about.

Harold Hellwig was a different matter. The young boy talked in short bursts of excited speech that Samantha had difficulty understanding. Haskell patiently interpreted and answered the boy's many questions, but the older brother seemed nervous that Harold would say something inappropriate.

"Nice place you got here," Samantha said politely as she walked around the outside of the small house.

Calling the Hellwig place "nice" was a stretch. The small cabin needed paint and appeared to have only four rooms. Almost an inch of dirt decorated the front porch and the inside looked more like a barn than a house. The fields looked neat and orderly, but the old barn where her father talked with Huck Hellwig looked as if it might fall down.

"It ain't much," Haskell shrugged, "but it's home and it's ours...or at least ours and the bank's."

Samantha stepped inside the small house and was greeted by a stiff stench of body odor. It was obvious the Hellwig boys did not waste time on household chores.

"Where's your mother?" Samantha asked.

The question caused a reaction from Harold, who became agitated. Haskell calmed him down and gave Harold the job of picking up the cluttered house.

"Let's sit outside," an embarrassed Haskell said, realizing the cluttered house was not the best place to entertain a visitor.

"Ma died when Harold was born," Haskell explained. "I don't think Harold understands much about what a mom is...he's a little light in the head if you hadn't figured."

"I'm sorry I asked," Samantha said.

"You couldn't have known," Haskell smiled. "I guess the place shows that we don't have much of a woman's touch around here."

"A little," Samantha replied.

"We work in the fields all day and don't pay much attention to the housekeeping," Haskell apologized. "Dad's real proud of ownin' this land, but it takes about all the hours in the day to pay the mortgage."

"The fields look good," Samantha noted.

"Cotton's goin' to be good, I think," Haskell replied. "We'll know for sure in a month, I expect."

The clumsy conversation was interrupted when Harold came outside the house to ask Haskell a question. Haskell excused himself to check on his brother. Samantha could see her father and Huck engaged in their private conversation by the barn so she walked the other direction to inspect the cotton fields. The autumn day was warm, and the trees still had most of their browning leaves, while the short sumac trees had transformed to a brilliant red. The cotton was waist high, and Samantha could have easily disappeared in the field. She fondly remembered when her father and mother grew corn, and she would often play hide and go seek with her mother on autumn days before the harvest.

Samantha's pleasant memory was disturbed by the sound of crunching leaves in the dense woods. A startled Samantha bent down to hide herself in the cotton field peering between the plants to see who might be coming. Feeling foolish, she was about to stand up when she spotted a man standing twenty steps into the trees. He had a rough desperate look and wore old, ragged overalls. Samantha felt sure he must have spotted her, but the man did not seem to be aware of her presence. He moved slowly watching the house.

As the man edged closer, Samantha's heart raced as she recognized Marcus Lutz. The sinister man moved to the edge of the tree line, and Samantha watched him scanning the fields for signs of danger. Feeling trapped, Samantha crouched in the field hoping the man would go away.

Marcus Lutz looked like he had not shaved in several days while his neck and arms were sunburned. He had a menacing scar over his left cheek and dark, suspicious eyes, which continuously shifted as if searching for unseen threats. An overall appearance of hardness to the medium-size man caused Samantha to easily believe him to be a convict.

"Marcus!" the shrill shout from Herbert Hellwig called from behind him.

Marcus Lutz looked into the woods and walked toward the hidden voice. Samantha watched until he disappeared and then walked quickly back to the house and to safety.

"There you are," Haskell greeted as he walked around the house. "Where'd you get off to?"

A sheepish Samantha answered, "I was looking at the fields."

"Did you see Marcus out there?" Haskell asked.

"No," Samantha quickly replied, "just cotton."

"Funny," Haskell said, while scratching behind his ear, "because Marcus and Herbert are coming up behind you."

Samantha looked over her shoulder to see Marcus Lutz and Herbert walking toward her. She swallowed nervously knowing Marcus must know she had been hiding in the fields. As the two men walked toward her, she felt trapped.

"Hey, Marcus!" Haskell shouted, as he waved. "We got company...kin folk from up around Chandler."

Marcus continued walking silently toward them, and Samantha saw his eyes fixed on her. He did not speak, but his solemn countenance conveyed his displeasure about her spying.

"This is Samantha, Marcus," Haskell introduced as the man stopped not more than five steps away.

Samantha wiggled nervously as the man continued to stare at her and timidly said, "Hello."

Marcus smiled, revealing several missing teeth, and he said, "Hello, I—"

Marcus stopped as if he would say more but hesitated before saying, "You look just like your mother."

Samantha blushed as Marcus, Haskell, Harold, and Herbert all looked at her as she said, "People say that, but I don't think so much."

Marcus watched her as if studying every detail before saying, "I saw you in Chandler a while back. Hope I didn't scare you too much."

Regaining her composure, Samantha said confidently, "I don't scare that easy."

Trying to keep from smiling and showing his missing teeth Marcus said, "That's good...that's good that you're a strong girl."

"Uncle Marcus told us about seeing you in Chandler," Herbert confessed.

Marcus quit looking at Samantha for a moment to stare at Herbert and say bluntly, "You don't have to say everything you think."

Herbert did not seem intimidated by the warning and said to Samantha, "Don't let Uncle Marcus bother you none. He's mean lookin' but easy going."

"You're an uncle?" Samantha asked.

Marcus looked back at the young girl and said, "Sort of. I was married to Huck's sister, Suzanne, and Huck still claims me. These knuckleheaded nephews of mine are about all the family I've got left."

"Me too, I guess," Samantha admitted to the stranger.

"There he is," the strong voice of Huck Hellwig rang from behind Samantha as he approached from the barn with Mr. Harvey. "You didn't know you had company when you disappeared."

"Never know who's a coming," Marcus greeted. "How are you, Mr. Harvey?"

The nervous-acting Marcus reached out to shake the old man's hand.

"I'm doing better now," Mr. Harvey said as he shook the man's hand.

Looking at his boys, Huck said, "We're getting a new neighbor next spring. Mr. Harvey and Samantha are moving from Chandler."

Chandler had only been Samantha's home for a short time, but she was shocked to hear her father reveal they were moving. Her newfound relatives seemed to be nice people, but she could not see them as neighbors. When she looked at her father for confirmation that this was a mistake, he winked casually at her.

"You're moving here?" Marcus asked.

"Yes," Mr. Harvey stated. "I've got to sell off a few things, but we've got to vacate our place by the spring, and Huck said I could build a house on the edge of his farm."

"Why?" Samantha blurted out, trying not to show her horror at the prospect of being the only woman in the colony of unhygienic men.

Mr. Harvey smiled pleasantly and answered, "I can't take care of the place anymore and you're through with school. These boys could use a woman around the house to clean and cook. We'll be with family."

Samantha did not argue with her father, but she was frustrated he had not consulted her before deciding to move. Huck invited the Harveys to stay the night, but Mr. Harvey claimed they needed to get back to town. Samantha was relieved she did not have to share the house with the men. It was late afternoon by the time Samantha and her father crossed the North Canadian River at Keokuk Falls and headed back to Prague.

"You're quiet," Mr. Harvey commented, as they drove past the decaying town of Keokuk Falls and headed across the open fields leading back to Lincoln County.

Samantha gently patted the back of the old mule with her reins and said, "I'm studying the landscape...since this will be home."

"I'm sorry the news came as a surprise to you," Mr. Harvey sighed.

"Why?" Samantha asked as she continued to look down the narrow road. "Why didn't you discuss this with me?"

"I wanted to talk to Huck to see what my options were," Mr. Harvey explained.

"What about my options?" Samantha replied sharply.

"That's what I was discussing with Huck," Mr. Harvey replied. "I can't keep the place up at Chandler, and the rent's using up what money we have left. You're through with school and it'll be good to be near family."

"Family?" Samantha snorted. "I barely know those people, and they didn't seem much like family to me."

"Nevertheless," Mr. Harvey continued. "They are your family. Huck's a good man, and he seems to have three hardworking, responsible sons."

"He's got a convict living next door," Samantha noted. "That doesn't make me feel any safer."

"Marcus would never hurt anyone," Mr. Harvey claimed.

"According to Sam Bowles, he already has," Samantha said.

"That was a sad circumstance," Mr. Harvey defended. "Huck will take care of Marcus, like I know he'll take care of you."

"I don't need to be taken care of," Samantha stated defiantly.

Mr. Harvey did not reply as the wagon continued north. About two hours of daylight remained, and what had been a warm afternoon showed signs of turning to a chilly evening.

After a moment, Mr. Harvey said stoically, "I'm not well, Sammie."

Samantha listened as her father continued, "I'm old, and I'm sick. You know it, and...well the doctor knows it too. He's told me I don't have much time to enjoy God's green earth before he takes me away."

Turning to her father, Samantha asked in a worried tone, "What has the doctor said?"

Mr. Harvey sighed heavily again and said, "He doesn't exactly know. Says my heart beats irregular, and the congestion in my chest seems to be getting worse."

"What can we do?" Samantha frantically asked.

In a calm tone, her father said, "Make plans to take care of you."

Sensing his daughter's worry, Mr. Harvey added, "I'm an old man, Sammie. I've lived a good life, and now I have you. You're a fine young woman and I wish I could see all that your life will be, but I fear the doctor's right in saying my time is short. I'm not leaving you much, but I want to do what I can to provide for you."

"Does Uncle Huck know?" Samantha asked in a defeated tone.

"He does now," Mr. Harvey smiled. "That's why I needed to talk to him. He's agreed to let me build a small cabin on his place, and he's assured me you'll be taken care of if anything happens to me. I have no insurance and very little of—anything. He's got those boys, and looks like the place could use a little womanly attention."

"That place needs an army of womanly attention," Samantha moaned.

Samantha stared straight ahead as if she were driving in a dream. The prospect of losing her father and the thought of having to live with the Hellwigs caused her forehead to furrow in anxiety.

Mr. Harvey laughed to himself and said, "Don't worry, dear. It'll cause your face to wrinkle when you're old. See my wrinkles? They're all pointing to a smile."

"Don't tease me," Samantha pleaded.

In a serious tone, Mr. Harvey said, "I didn't mean to tease you. I'm just trying to be practical. I couldn't go on thinking of leaving you in debt, trying to make it in the place we're at."

"You mean to make it alone," Samantha sneered.

Taken back by his daughter's typical frankness, Mr. Harvey said, "Yes. This is a hard country for anyone, but for a single woman...it does worry me."

"I'll be fine," Samantha retorted.

Mr. Harvey smiled at his daughter's self-assurance and said, "I guess I know that, but I'll still feel better knowing you've got some family...Can you pacify an old man?"

In a serious tone, Samantha said, "I'll be fine, but I don't believe you're as bad as the doctor says. I'll do whatever makes you happy...even if it means living next to the Hellwigs."

Mr. Harvey seemed satisfied as he slapped his knee and said, "It'll be too late to catch the train tonight. I didn't think you wanted to share a room with your cousins, so I thought we'd splurge some and get a hotel in Prague with a good dinner tonight. How does that sound?"

With a sly grin, Samantha said, "I think the livery stable would be an improvement over staying with Uncle Huck, but dinner with my father and a night at the hotel sounds like a fine idea."

The Harveys returned the rented mule and secured a room at the Barta Hotel. The hotel was modest but clean, and Samantha looked forward to sleeping without the disruption of raccoons raiding her henhouse. Mr. Harvey took Samantha to the Busy Bee Café for a simple meal of roast beef and mashed potatoes. The next morning the two caught the first train back to Chandler and discussed many things they would need to do to prepare for their move. Samantha did not tell her father, but she secretly hoped Jonathan Kendall would return from Texas in time to make her move to Keokuk Falls unnecessary.

CHAPTER 49

THE SOUTH TEXAS LANDSCAPE looked stark and empty on a cool February morning. The solitude of the sunrise penetrated Jonathan Kendall's soul, as the loneliness of the camp reminded him of Samantha. The people of San Benito had been excited to see the soldiers come to town, but the mass influx of men overwhelmed the citizens, and they were now anxious for the visitors to leave. Jonathan clutched his latest letter from Samantha and felt isolated although surrounded by thousands of men.

Eight months had passed since Jonathan left Samantha, but it seemed longer to him. Samantha's letters and her picture had been his best companion during his stay in San Benito. The letters elevated his opinion of the insightful girl, and he savored each correspondence. Her latest letter, however, pained Jonathan, as he looked over the rows of tents and the empty countryside grieving for his beloved Samantha.

"You're up early," Captain Gilstrap said, as he sipped his morning coffee.

"Yes, sir," Jonathan replied.

The captain grunted and said, "It's too early in the morning for 'sirs.'"

Jonathan nodded apathetically as his commander took another drink of hot coffee.

"Bad news?" Captain Gilstrap asked, as he nodded his head toward the letter Jonathan held in his hand.

"Why do you ask?" Jonathan replied.

The captain laughed insincerely and said, "You're a good soldier, Jonathan. In time you'll be a fine officer, and then you'll need to pay attention to details concerning the morale of your men. This hasn't been an easy deployment, but we're a better outfit for it. You've got more letters than any young man I've ever known, and they've put you in a good mood most days, but today you seem distant. I can only guess that letter you're holding is bad news. I'm betting it involves the girl."

"Her father passed away," Jonathan admitted. "He'd been sick, but I didn't know how serious it was."

"I'm sorry," Captain Gilstrap replied. "Is there anything I can do?"

"The funeral's today, so I won't be there," Jonathan lamented. "I was wondering, though, if I could get a pass to see Samantha."

Jonathan hated to ask for the leave. He had denied many requests from his men who had become homesick or imagined some calamity back home. Captain Gilstrap talked often to his officers about the need to maintain morale and keep the men in camp, but Jonathan felt Samantha needed him.

Captain Gilstrap took a drink of coffee and said, "I would Jonathan, but that'll be pointless. I got word last night we're being deactivated. We'll be back in Oklahoma in a week or two—all the troops will."

"Thank God," Jonathan sighed. "I don't think we could keep a lid on these guys much longer."

"I agree," the captain replied. "I won't miss San Benito. The men are starved for entertainment when they show up to watch the Indian boys do their war dance."

The Oklahoma Guard had swelled in numbers in a burst of patriotic excitement at the mobilization. The adventure the men envisioned, however, turned into a numbing routine of drills, training exercises, and marches. Serving in a support role for the regular army meant they were immune from even minor clashes with the bandits across the border. The Oklahoma Guard had many Indian soldiers who put on a traditional war dance to entertain their comrades.

"The men will be glad to head home," Jonathan said.

"And you?" Captain Gilstrap asked with a raised eyebrow.

"I won't miss San Benito," Jonathan replied.

"And getting back to Chandler?" Captain Gilstrap coaxed.

"I'm ready to see home," Jonathan admitted.

"Your girl?" Captain Gilstrap asked.

"I'm especially ready to get back to her," Jonathan nodded. "Letters are fine, but I'm looking forward to being with her again."

Captain Gilstrap laughed causing Jonathan to ask, "What's so funny?"

"Nothing's funny," Captain Gilstrap smiled. "I was just thinking how serious you've been these past months whenever you read your letters. It reminds me of how I courted my wife when I was in Cuba. I think you'll marry this girl—regardless of your father."

"You're right," Jonathan replied seriously. "I plan to marry her as soon as possible. I had hoped to ask her father, but I waited too late for that."

"Do you have any doubts?" Captain Gilstrap asked.

"About Samantha...no," Jonathan smiled. "My father'll have to adjust his attitude."

Captain Gilstrap laughed loudly as he poured out the rest of his coffee on the dusty ground and said, "The 1st Oklahoma Infantry may not have seen much combat in Texas, but knowing your father's aptitude for changing his attitude and your stubbornness, I think we may witness a real brouhaha when we make it back home."

CHAPTER 50

CHANDLER'S TRAIN STATION WAS alive with excitement, although a sharp, late February wind blew through the crowd gathered to welcome home the soldiers from Company B. Even though the exuberant crowd pushed against her, Samantha felt completely alone. Her father had died two weeks earlier, and she had thought of little else than his death until she received the letter from Jonathan saying he would be home today.

Samantha's father had planned to move, but he became too sick over the winter to think of relocating. Uncle Huck came to the funeral and invited Samantha to stay with the Hellwigs. She had been able to pay rent on the place until the end of March and delayed becoming part of the Hellwig household, but was unsure of her future after that. The prospect of being the woman of the house at Uncle Huck's seemed a real possibility. Jonathan was coming back today, however, and Samantha hoped that would change her prospects. Jonathan had all but proposed in the letters, and Samantha believed they would be happy together.

John Kendall and his family stood on the other side of the platform waiting for their son to arrive. Caroline was still at school, but Augusta waved enthusiastically at Samantha. Mr. Kendall stared coldly at Samantha, as if willing her to leave the station before Jonathan's train arrived. Mrs. Kendall was always more tactful and diplomatic, but her angst about Samantha's presence could not be masqueraded.

The crowd hushed momentarily as the first sound of the train's whistle echoed in the distance before they exploded in shouts of excitement anxiously waiting for the train to come into view. The buzz built to a deafening level as the train screeched to a stop with one last gasp of steam blanketing the platform before the conductor jumped out to open the exits. A steady stream of soldiers stepped into the clear, cold February air to be greeted with hugs and handshakes from friends and family. The many soldiers coming off the train added to the chaos and confusion as Samantha strained for a glimpse of Jonathan.

Samantha looked quickly at Mr. Kendall to make sure she had not missed seeing Jonathan when he emerged at the door of the rear passenger car looking over the mass of people.

Mr. Kendall yelled and waved at his son, while Jonathan continued to search the crowd. After a few seconds, his eyes found Samantha as he bolted to hold the young woman.

Jonathan's eyes did not look away from Samantha as he pushed and maneuvered through the crowd. Several soldiers under his care stopped to say farewell. Jonathan shook hands and smiled at the soldiers, but never took his eyes off Samantha. Without a word, Jonathan threw his arms around Samantha and held her tightly.

Before Jonathan could speak, the voice of his father roared, "Jonathan!"

Continuing to hold Samantha, Jonathan turned his head to see his father standing twenty feet away.

Without acknowledging his father, Jonathan looked into Samantha's eyes and said, "I missed you so much."

"I missed you, too," Samantha smiled.

"I've had in my head how beautiful you are, and now I see you...my imagination was not even close to how wonderful you look," Jonathan said without taking his eyes off her.

Samantha blushed and said, "Don't you think you need to talk to your family?"

Jonathan dispassionately replied, "No."

"Jonathan," Samantha coaxed. "See to your family."

Jonathan grudgingly looked at his father and ended his embrace but continued holding onto Samantha's hand.

"Hello, father," Jonathan finally sighed. "Mother, Augusta, you look well."

Mr. Kendall stared spitefully at Samantha as Jonathan held her hand. Mrs. Kendall stepped past her husband and threw her arms around Jonathan.

Crying, Mrs. Kendall said, "It's so good to see you."

"It's good to be home," Jonathan said as he patted his mother's back with his free hand.

Seeing Augusta, Jonathan said pleasantly, "Look at this girl. She's practically grown."

Augusta smiled enthusiastically and said, "You wouldn't know it by how Mom and Dad talk to me. I'm glad to have you home. With Caroline and you both gone, I've gotten way too much attention."

"How's Caroline?" Jonathan asked, while looking at his mother.

"She's fine," Mr. Kendall interjected. "She had a good first semester and seems to be making many friends."

"She wanted to come, but she had something she had to go to," Mrs. Kendall added.

Clearing his voice, Mr. Kendall said, "Would you mind letting go of that girl's hand. You're making a spectacle out here."

Jonathan pulled Samantha closer to him, causing Mr. Kendall's brow to wrinkle as he fidgeted in disapproval.

Samantha gently pushed Jonathan's arm away and said meekly, "Your father's right, Jonathan. You need to be with your family...I've got things to do anyway."

"Samantha—" Jonathan began to protest.

Samantha interrupted his objection and said kindly, "I'll see you later."

Trying to hide her disappointment at the cool reception she received from Jonathan's parents, Samantha politely said, "Mr. Kendall, Mrs. Kendall, it was good to see you."

Neither parent replied, but Augusta unpretentiously said, "It was good to see you Samantha. Maybe you'll come by sometime."

Samantha smiled at Augusta's genuine friendliness and said, "I'll try, Augusta."

"Samantha," Jonathan said as she stepped away. "Are you heading home?"

Samantha nodded.

"I'll come by to see you as soon as I can," Jonathan assured in a tone of voice his father could not miss.

Samantha nodded uncomfortably and walked away from the train depot, ignoring an audible gasp from Mrs. Kendall.

When Samantha was a distance away, Jonathan said, "I hope you're happy."

"I'm not happy at all," Mr. Kendall forcefully replied. "I thought you would have gotten this nonsense out of your system."

"Jonathan!" Mrs. Kendall interrupted. "You can't go to that girl's house without a chaperon. It wouldn't be proper."

"You, too?" Jonathan asked, looking at his mother.

"Jonathan, your father and I just want what's best for you," Mrs. Kendall pleaded.

"I don't know why you can't see what I see in Samantha?" Jonathan pleaded. "Can't you see that she's extraordinary?"

Mr. and Mrs. Kendall looked at each other as the easygoing voice of David Simpson interrupted the conversation by shouting, "There's the old bandit chaser, himself."

Grateful for the break in conversation with his parents, Jonathan replied, "Hey, David."

David Simpson walked confidently up to his friend and shook Jonathan's hand while saying, "It's great to see you back."

"You should have been with us," Jonathan said.

"Maybe next time," David chirped.

Looking at the Kendalls, David Simpson said, "Good to see you, this morning. Have you heard from that daughter of yours?"

Mr. and Mrs. Kendall looked at each other before Mrs. Kendall said, "Caroline's doing well. School seems to agree with her."

"I hadn't seen her in a while," David said. "Make sure you say hello."

"We will," Mrs. Kendall said.

"We've got to be going!" Mr. Kendall barked. "I'll see you at the office, David."

"Yes, sir," David said as the Kendall family headed up the hill toward town.

"What was that about?" Jonathan asked after his father had left.

"It's a mystery to me," David shrugged.

Mr. Kendall had always been overly friendly with David Simpson and treated him more like a long-time chum than a friend of one of his children. Jonathan had been away for eight months, but he could tell something had changed in the relationship.

"Don't give me that," Jonathan said. "I know you well enough to know you always have a pretty good idea of what's going on."

David began to walk away from the train platform to the more secluded street when he said, "I think it has something to do with your girl, Samantha."

"What does Samantha have to do with you?" Jonathan asked in a concerned tone.

"You know your father tried to throw me at her," David factually stated.

"Yeah?" Jonathan answered suspiciously.

"He sent Caroline away, and I think he figured something might happen between me and Samantha," David said.

"Did it?" Jonathan anxiously quizzed.

David looked at Jonathan with a sly grin and said, "Not a chance. I have got to know her since you went to the border. But —"

"But what?" an eager Jonathan asked.

David carefully watched his friend as he continued, "Your dad sent Caroline to school, and he kept finding projects for me to do around the Harvey place. I've checked every land record for any piece of property those people ever set foot on, I think. I guess I figured if my best friend's crazy about this girl, I might as well get to know why."

"You've been spending time with Samantha?" Jonathan redirected.

"Relax," David replied. "Like I said, I got to know her pretty good, and the one thing I learned while you were gone is that she's crazy about you. You must be some letter writer."

"Are you serious?" Jonathan asked.

David laughed and said, "If I know anything, it's women. Any conversation with her evolved into only one subject, 'What's Jonathan really like?'"

Jonathan smiled broadly at David's information, but he noticed something different in his old friend's swagger.

"There's more?" Jonathan asked.

David took a few steps and said, "I was just spending time with Samantha. I had planned to ask Caroline to marry me, but kept putting it off. I think your dad sent Caroline to school trying to push me closer to Samantha. Funny thing is, I'm not sure Caroline's that interested in me any more."

"You're thick in the head," Jonathan replied. "Caroline's been crazy for you forever."

David shrugged and said, "Maybe, but like I said, I do know women, and Caroline's not the same. She doesn't come home much, and she seldom writes. I've watched Samantha Harvey closely the past months, and I know what a girl's like when her guy's away. Caroline's not like that with me…at least not now."

"I don't believe it," Jonathan said. "Caroline's probably just trying to keep up with school."

"Maybe," David said. "But there's more. You had to notice your dad. He's always treated me like the son he never had…no offense."

"Trust me, I know what you're talking about," Jonathan smiled.

"Things are different somehow," David continued. "I'm just an employee now. If Freddie Fletcher hadn't quit, and if you'd been in town, I'm not sure I'd still have a job. I figure I probably don't have a job now you're back."

"I'm not going back to work for my father," Jonathan stated flatly.

David smiled, "Does he know?"

"I don't care," Jonathan replied. "He's trying to ruin my life, and it sounds like he may have already done that for you and Caroline."

"I can't blame Caroline or your father," David stoically said. "She's a great girl and I took her for granted. She went away and discovered she didn't need me to make her happy. Your dad sending me to sweet talk Samantha Harvey didn't help, but it was all my fault. What about you?"

"What do you mean?" Jonathan asked in confusion.

"You won't take Samantha for granted, will you?" David asked.

"Not a chance," Jonathan affirmed.

"Well," David said, while gently nudging Jonathan. "Go to her."

Jonathan looked around the quickly emptying train station and smiled at his friend. Jonathan always believed David Simpson would be his biggest rival for Samantha Harvey's affections, but his friend's affirmation of Samantha's feelings bolstered his resolve. Without saying another word, Jonathan nodded and headed across the tracks and toward the trail leading to Samantha Harvey's house.

David watched Jonathan disappear over the hill leading to her house and sighed heavily knowing Jonathan would find a warm reception from the young woman at the end of the trail. David looked back toward town and the cotton gin. Working for Mr. Kendall had quit being enjoyable several weeks earlier when it became apparent Caroline Kendall's attentions no longer belonged to him. David had not told his friend that Caroline had found someone in Oklahoma City that had caught her eye. David straightened his hat and walked slowly to the office, knowing his boss would not be in a good mood this day.

CHAPTER 51

THE FEBRUARY LANDSCAPE WAS stark and cold as Jonathan walked toward the Harvey home. The trees stood leafless with only a few cedars breaking the monotony of the brown scenery. The winter silence was somehow different from the summer trips he had made to the place the previous year. As Jonathan approached, he saw a section of fence leaning against the tall grass, and the door of the chicken coop hanging crookedly. The Harvey place had never looked prosperous but now needed repairs. Bluish-gray smoke drifted from the chimney, but otherwise the property looked vacant. Jonathan walked toward the porch when he noticed Samantha leaning against the side of the small barn looking into the lifeless woods. Jonathan's boot crunching against dead leaves caused a crying Samantha to turn toward him.

After a brief hesitation, she ran into Jonathan's arms and buried her face into the wool shoulder of his jacket and whimpered, "You came."

"Of course, I came," Jonathan assured. "Why are you standing in the cold?"

"I needed the air," Samantha sniveled.

"Your face is cold," Jonathan said, as he rubbed his cheek against Samantha's.

Samantha did not reply but seemed content to cradle her head on Jonathan's neck.

"I'm sorry about my parents," Jonathan apologized.

"It's not that," Samantha said.

"I was sorry to hear about your father," Jonathan sighed.

Samantha burst into the tears she had been trying to suppress, as Jonathan said, "What can I do?"

"Just hold me," Samantha asked. "It feels so good to be held…I've felt so alone these past weeks."

"I wanted to come to the funeral," Jonathan said, "but we were being mustered out."

"I'm glad you're here now," Samantha smiled through the tears. "Would you go with me to the cemetery?"

"Sure," Jonathan smiled. "Is he buried at Oak Park?"

Samantha nodded. After Samantha retrieved a heavier coat, Jonathan walked hand in hand with her to the Oak Park Cemetery to see her father's grave. Oak Park Cemetery was located on the other side of Chandler. It was about a twenty-minute walk from the Harvey place to the center of town and another thirty minutes to walk to the hill on the west of town to the cemetery's location. The route took the two past the courthouse, down Silk Stocking Row, and past the Kendall home. The streets were quiet as the winter wind made the walk less than comfortable. Jonathan had worried that after months of letter writing, the couple might quickly exhaust topics for conversation, but his anxiety was unmerited. The couple's walk was filled with conversation, and the long trip to the cemetery seemed to take a short time.

Walking close to the fresh grave with a simple marker, Jonathan pulled Samantha close to him and said, "I wish I'd have known him better."

"He liked you," Samantha assured. "I would've liked to have purchased a bigger stone, but this one seems to fit him. Papa was a simple man but strong in his own way."

Samantha looked toward the town where the fine houses on Silk Stocking Row could be seen clearly across the bare winter landscape.

"It's peaceful here, isn't it?" Jonathan noted.

Leaning deeper into his arm, Samantha said, "Yes, it is. I can see your house from here."

"It's not my house any more," Jonathan stated coldly.

Stepping away from Jonathan to look into his eyes, Samantha said, "You shouldn't say that, Jonathan. That is your home…it's your family."

"Not after the way they treated you," Jonathan fumed.

"You can't blame them," Samantha said.

"Of course I can," Jonathan replied. "My father's behavior is inexcusable."

Samantha laughed insincerely and said, "You're not seeing things clearly."

"What do you mean?"

"Your father's an important man in town," Samantha explained. "How could he be excited about his only son involved with a poor girl with no prospects and little family? I'll have to move in with the Hellwigs down at Keokuk Falls, and I'm not sure they're not part outlaw."

"You're moving from your place?" Jonathan asked.

"It's not mine," Samantha smiled. "Papa had it rented until the end of March, but then I'm homeless. Papa made arrangements for me to live with relatives down south. Maybe that will make your father happy."

"I'm not worried about my father's happiness," Jonathan rebelled.

"I suspect he'll be happier once I've moved," Samantha mused. "He didn't take any chances, you know? He bought the property where our farm is. He's the one that wouldn't renew Papa's lease."

"What!" Jonathan roared.

"It doesn't matter," Samantha assured. "I couldn't afford to pay the rent anyway. It took about all I had left to bury Papa."

Looking down at her father's modest grave, Samantha said, "Papa wouldn't have approved of me spending this much, but I felt he deserved it...and I needed to."

Jonathan walked around the site looking in the distance at his family's home on Silk Stocking Row before saying, "Your father's ten times the man mine is!"

In a low, peaceful tone Samantha admonished, "You shouldn't say that Jonathan. Trust me, I have no family left, and you need to value the family you're blessed with."

"You're wrong," Jonathan smiled.

"About what?" a confused Samantha asked.

"You have family," Jonathan replied.

"I have the Hellwigs down at Keokuk," Samantha said.

Shaking his head, Jonathan took her hand and said, "You don't understand...you have me. Samantha, I'm asking...Will you marry me?"

Samantha's head ticked involuntarily in shock. She had written Jonathan hundreds of letters and had hoped for a proposal in time, but his asking on the first day they were together was a surprise. Samantha was sure she loved Jonathan but felt guilty at the timing. She hated the thought of living with the Hellwigs, and marriage to Jonathan would solve her immediate problem. Her excitement was tempered with the knowledge Jonathan's family would not approve and feelings that she had somehow pressured him into asking.

"Your silence can't be good?" Jonathan timidly said.

"Of course, I'll marry you," Samantha finally replied as she embraced Jonathan. "Are you sure...Are you sure you want to marry me?"

Gazing into her teary eyes, Jonathan said, "I've never been more sure of anything in my life."

CHAPTER 52

A COLD WIND BLEW as Jonathan and Samantha walked from the cemetery toward town. Jonathan's heart, however, glowed warmly at the thought of Samantha as his wife. The couple walked up the steps toward Silk Stocking Row and past the Kendall house without stopping. They ate a sandwich at the café across from the courthouse before Jonathan walked hand-in-hand with Samantha across the railroad tracks to her home on the east side of Chandler. The couple decided to keep the engagement a secret, although Samantha wanted Jonathan to tell his parents.

Jonathan promised to marry Samantha at the courthouse as soon as he could secure a job and rent a small place in town. Samantha had to leave her house across from Indian Springs by the end of March, and Jonathan was confident he could have things in order by then. Jonathan stayed with Samantha until sunset on the winter day. By six o'clock, he said good-bye and made the walk back to town. Although he would have liked to have avoided his father altogether by staying with David Simpson, he trudged through town to the Kendall house. Timidly opening the front door, he was temporarily relieved to see the front room empty.

Two steps inside the house, however, Jonathan's mother looked out from the kitchen and screeched, "There you are!"

Jonathan heard the rumble of footsteps from upstairs, as his sister Augusta flew down the stairs in excitement to hug her brother's neck. Mrs. Kendall was close behind to squeeze her son tight.

"Where have you been?" Mrs. Kendall asked as she hugged her son.

"I walked around town," Jonathan replied. "Is Father here?"

"No," Mrs. Kendall said. "He had a meeting at church this evening. We already ate, but I can fix you something."

"No," Jonathan said, "I've eaten."

"Where?" Mrs. Kendall asked.

"I ate with Samantha in town," Jonathan replied.

Mrs. Kendall's relaxed manner changed as she said stiffly, "Oh."

Jonathan looked at his smiling sister and said, "What grade are you in this year?"

"Eighth," Augusta proclaimed.

"I bet you're driving the eighth-grade boys crazy," Jonathan teased.

"And some of the freshmen," Augusta boasted.

Jonathan laughed at the always opinionated and self-confident Augusta and said, "I'll bet you are."

"Augusta," Mrs. Kendall interrupted in a serious tone, "Go upstairs and finish your homework."

"I'm finished," Augusta protested.

"I need to talk to Jonathan alone," Mrs. Kendall demanded.

When her daughter refused to react, Mrs. Kendall ordered sternly, "Now!"

Augusta frowned and said, "You know I can hear everything from my room."

"If you eavesdrop, I'll tan your hide," Mrs. Kendall threatened.

Augusta did not protest further but stomped upstairs demonstrating her displeasure at being dismissed.

"She's growing up," Jonathan commented pleasantly.

Ignoring her son's conversation, Mrs. Kendall said, "Jonathan we need to talk, before your father comes home."

"About what?" Jonathan asked.

"That Harvey girl," Mrs. Kendall replied with a slight tone of disdain in her voice.

Jonathan sighed heavily and said, "Not you, too."

"I don't dislike the young lady," Mrs. Kendall defended. "I just don't think it's a good idea for you to be out alone."

"Why?"

"She's living by herself in that place," Mrs. Kendall explained. "It was bad enough when her father was there to chaperone, but it's not proper, and it's not right for you to be alone with a girl—especially that girl."

"What do you mean by that?" Jonathan asked in a tone of anger he had never used with his mother.

Mrs. Kendall paced across the room before saying in a low voice, "The girl's mother was of questionable morals. It was well known in Warwick and some people in this town know it's quite possible Mr. Harvey was not the girl's real father."

"That's slanderous!" Jonathan roared.

Mrs. Kendall signaled with her petite hands for Jonathan to speak softer and said, "I don't want you to get trapped by a girl like that...I don't see any good coming from your association."

"Trapped?" Jonathan responded in a quieter voice. "I've spent eight months writing this girl trying to entice her!"

"Jonathan, you haven't!" Mrs. Kendall gasped.

Trying to comfort his mother, Jonathan said, "Don't you trust me...haven't you always?"

"Of course," Mrs. Kendall replied.

"Then trust me now," Jonathan pleaded.

Mrs. Kendall looked at her son with a twisted expression and said, "I do trust you, but you don't know…you have so little experience with a girl like that."

Facing his mother, Jonathan grabbed her gently by the shoulders and said, "It's you that doesn't understand a girl like Samantha. She's smart. She's sweet…and her virtue is beyond reproach."

Mrs. Kendall began to cry and said, "Your father will never approve, and she's already put a wedge between you two…what kind of girl would do that?"

"You can't blame Samantha for father being unreasonable," Jonathan countered.

Mrs. Kendall regained her composure and said, "Your father is just looking out for your best interest…your future. There will be no peace as long as you continue seeing that girl."

"Then there will be no peace," Jonathan promised. "I plan to marry Samantha as soon as I find a job."

Mrs. Kendall looked pale as she whispered, "Jonathan, please think of what you're doing."

"I have," Jonathan replied. "I've thought of little else for eight months."

Jonathan stepped to the front door as his mother tearfully said, "Where are you going?"

Jonathan stopped and said, "I'm going to David's house…he's not nearly as judgmental."

Without saying more, Jonathan stepped into the cold, February night and walked past the fine homes on Silk Stocking Row toward the more modest neighborhood where David Simpson lived with his mother. Mrs. Kendall went to the window and watched her son walk away from the house of his youth and from his family. The distraught Mrs. Kendall thought of the irony of her son going to

David Simpson. She had believed the two friends would have been brothers-in-law by now, but Mrs. Kendall knew that was not likely and believed Samantha Harvey was the reason.

The empathy she once felt for the girl was now replaced by anger at Samantha Harvey's disruption to her family's happiness. Mrs. Kendall hated to share news of Jonathan's engagement with Mr. Kendall. She knew it would cause days if not weeks of anguish in the Kendall household.

Mr. Kendall will know what to do, however, she thought to herself. If she had learned anything about her husband in their years together, it was that John Kendall always knew how to take care of things.

CHAPTER 53

EARLY MARCH REMAINED CHILLY in Chandler, but the days grew longer as spring approached. Jonathan Kendall's optimism for his future with Samantha Harvey grew each day he spent with the enchanting young woman. Jonathan's parents showed no sign of accepting Samantha as his fiancé, but that did not matter to him. Jonathan had learned independence in his eight months in Texas and felt confident he could provide for his soon-to-be-bride without his family's blessing.

Jonathan had been apprehensive about finding a job, since his father was active and respected in town. Mr. Hellman, however, had a general store and was pleased to find someone with Jonathan's personality and bookkeeping experience. Jonathan worked six days a week. Every night, he walked to Samantha's to spend his evenings. Although Jonathan was sleeping on David Simpson's floor, he was practically living at the Harvey house and helping Samantha sell off the few possessions she owned to prepare for their move to town.

Jonathan expected his father to confront him about his time with Samantha Harvey, but was surprised when his father appeared to be letting him make his own decisions for once.

March 31st was a sunny, Saturday with warmer than normal temperatures. Jonathan took his lunch hour to make a deposit on a room he had found to rent off Allison Street close to the viaduct. Jonathan arranged to move Samantha into the room and marry her the following Monday at the courthouse.

Jonathan looked down Eighth Street at the stately homes on Silk Stocking Row and stopped for a moment. His head dropped as he looked at the brick pavement before grudgingly walking down the street to his parent's house. He had wanted to marry Samantha without informing his family of the date, but she had demanded he talk to them. Jonathan did not look forward to the inevitable conflict with his father. He looked at the Maxwell automobile Mr. Kendall now owned and knew his father was home for lunch. Swallowing hard, he tapped timidly on the front door.

Jonathan heard footsteps inside the house and then the voice of his father shouting, "Is someone going to get the door?"

The door opened and Augusta squealed, "Jonathan!"

A variety of sounds were heard from inside, but the most ominous was the noise from his father's chair scooting on the wood floor.

Somehow his father did not look as intimidating as Jonathan remembered, but Jonathan feared his news would result in an eruption of anger.

"Jonathan," his father said politely. "Come in."

"I don't have time," Jonathan explained. "I'm on my lunch hour and just have a minute."

"You're working at Hellmen's, I hear," Mr. Kendall said.

"Yes," Jonathan acknowledged. "I came to tell you I'm getting married…Monday afternoon."

Mr. Kendall looked shaken as he stared at his son before finally saying, "I guess you're not getting married at a church."

"No," Jonathan replied. "We'll be married at the courthouse by the judge."

Mrs. Kendall was standing behind her husband and began to cry, but Mr. Kendall just looked at his son without saying a word.

After the awkward silence, Jonathan said, "I thought you should know."

Jonathan left his father in the doorway and headed back toward downtown. Before he reached the street, Jonathan heard his father's footsteps behind him.

"Jonathan," Mr. Kendall said in a more conciliatory tone than Jonathan expected. "Wait."

Jonathan turned to watch his father walk close to him.

In a low whisper, Mr. Kendall asked urgently, "You're not having to get married...are you?"

Blood rushed into Jonathan's face at the insinuations and he said, "No, and I don't appreciate the insult! You really know nothing about Samantha."

"You know my feelings about the girl," Mr. Kendall forcefully replied.

"Oh yes," Jonathan smugly answered. "I know how you tried to throw David Simpson at Samantha and ruined your daughter's happiness. I know how you bought the property and planned to evict Samantha out of town. I'm quite familiar with your opinions about my fiancé."

Mr. Kendall did not respond, and Jonathan walked quickly away from his father. Jonathan's heart pounded, and he tried to compose himself when he saw Lee Gilstrap running toward him. Jonathan assumed the young man, who was a relative of Captain Gilstrap and the bugler for Company B, was headed down the hill to the Statistical House. As the boy approached, however, it became obvious he was looking for Jonathan.

"Lieutenant Kendall!" Lee Gilstrap shouted as he approached.

"What's the hurry?" Jonathan asked, as the boy rushed to him.

"Captain's lookin' for you," Lee said, as he panted for breath. "I've been looking all over town for you."

"What's he want?" Jonathan asked.

"I can't say," the excited boy explained. "But the Guard's being mobilized."

"Mobilized!" Jonathan repeated. "That's not possible. The government just deactivated us a month ago. There's nothing new happening on the border."

"All I know is the captain wants to see you right now," Lee Gilstrap said.

Jonathan looked at his watch. He intended to use his lunchtime to finalize the rental of his room, but the Statistical House was only a few hundred yards away.

"Let's go," Jonathan said as he stepped quickly back toward the Kendall house and down the hill to the National Guard office in the Statistical House.

Lee Gilstrap talked excitedly about a telegram Captain Gilstrap had received. Although the boy kept claiming he could not talk about the contents of the telegram, he incessantly chattered about his speculation about the war. Jonathan was relieved when he was able to leave the babbling Lee outside the door and get the news from Captain Gilstrap.

"You wanted to see me?" Jonathan asked, as his commander looked over papers on his desk.

Captain Gilstrap's serious demeanor told Jonathan something unusual was happening.

"We're being mobilized...again," Captain Gilstrap informed.

Jonathan tried not to act surprised and asked, "When?"

"For the officers, right now," Captain Gilstrap explained.

"I've taken a job, sir," Jonathan replied. "I had no idea."

"Neither did I," Captain Gilstrap stated flatly. "I've talked to Mr. Hellman, and he understands you're back on active duty."

"What's going on?" Jonathan asked. "Why are they mobilizing us?"

"It has to do with that Zimmerman telegram, I imagine," Captain Gilstrap replied. "I think we're going to war...in Europe. The American army's a myth right now. We have about 130,000 regular army troops and another 180,000 National Guard troops. None of us with much more experience than chasing bandits in Mexico. The Germans have millions, and they've been slugging it out in the trenches for years now. We're going to need every man that can shoulder a rifle."

"I'm getting married, Monday!" Jonathan frantically replied.

"I need you this afternoon to go over the rosters," Captain Gilstrap said in a less commanding tone. "You can talk to your girl tonight. We should be here in Chandler a week or two. Then we'll ship out to Oklahoma City, and from there...only God knows."

"Yes, sir," Jonathan replied.

"Are you really getting married Monday?" Captain Gilstrap asked.

"Yes, sir," Jonathan answered.

"It'll all work out," Captain Gilstrap assured. "You can ask Mrs. Gilstrap...a soldier's wife always finds a way to make things work. You'll have a couple of weeks to honeymoon."

With a sly grin, Captain Gilstrap said, "Who knows...after two weeks, she may be glad to see you gone."

Jonathan spent the rest of the day sorting through the personnel records of Company B of the 1st Oklahoma Infantry. He was anxious to see Samantha. He dreaded telling her the bad news but was sure in a small town like Chandler, she would know before he arrived. Captain Gilstrap was willing to give Lee any job that would take him out of the office, so Jonathan sent the deposit for the room with him and sent a message to Samantha saying he would see her that evening to help her get settled into the new room. Jonathan's afternoon was a blur of reports and rosters until Lee Gilstrap returned.

"Did you get the deposit made?" Jonathan asked without taking time to look up.

"Yes, sir," Lee Gilstrap replied. "I got the room and the keys."

"And you sent the message to Samantha with the keys?" Jonathan continued.

"Didn't have to, Lieutenant Kendall," Lee Gilstrap informed.

"What?" Jonathan said as he looked up from his work. "I had other errands to run for Captain Gilstrap so your father took the keys and the message for me…seemed happy to do it."

Jonathan looked strangely at the boy and asked, "How long ago?"

Lee Gilstrap could tell Jonathan was not pleased and he said timidly, "Two or three hours…It was right after I left here. I saw your father on top of the hill and told him the news."

"And he said he would take the message to Samantha?" Jonathan anxiously clarified.

"Yes, sir," Lee Gilstrap replied. "Hope that was okay?"

Jonathan looked at the clock and it was nearly five o'clock. He excused himself and headed out the door hoping his father had not further insulted his bride-to-be. It usually took a half hour to walk to Samantha's house. Jonathan was sure he could make it in half that time this day.

CHAPTER 54

IT HAD BEEN COINCIDENCE that John Kendall ran into the young Lee Gilstrap. Mr. Kendall, with his hat on his head and briefcase in hand, was already on his way to see Samantha Harvey. He had been working on a plan for a couple of weeks to deal with the situation, but Jonathan's announcement about a marriage scheduled for Monday forced him to act sooner rather than later.

Mr. Kendall took the note from Lee Gilstrap and asked him to keep busy with his other errands for a couple of hours. The young bugler seemed to have plenty to do and left the message with the older man. After the boy left, Mr. Kendall opened the message and read his son's note. The message seemed sincere, if not sappy, to Mr. Kendall. He hated the way circumstances had unfolded but was prepared to end the mess this day. After a quick stop at the train depot, He drove his automobile to the Harvey home.

As Mr. Kendall stepped out of the car, he noticed how bleak and vacant the place appeared. The chickens and cow had been sold, the place looked clean, but he could see little use for it, although the property now belonged to him. The porch leading to the small house was void of any decoration, and it was obvious the girl planned to leave the place today. Mr. Kendall felt guilty that the poor girl did not know how far she would be going.

Ten steps from the front door, Samantha happened to come out of the house.

"Mr. Kendall!" she gasped. "I...I didn't expect to see you today."

Mr. Kendall looked at the beautiful young woman. He could see the attraction his son had for the girl, and it sickened him to think he would have to destroy that infatuation for his son.

"No," he said politely. "I don't expect you did."

Samantha stood awkwardly on the porch before Mr. Kendall asked, "Can I come in?"

Samantha looked around anxiously before saying, "I suppose so, but there's not much left."

Mr. Kendall followed the girl into the near vacant house that had little more than two wood chairs that looked as if they were ready to be packed.

"Can I sit down?" Mr. Kendall invited himself.

As he sat in one of the chairs, Samantha said, "Of course."

"Have a seat," Mr. Kendall coaxed. "We need to have a talk."

Samantha nervously obeyed and carefully watched Mr. Kendall.

Looking around the sparse house, Mr. Kendall said, "It looks like you're moving."

Straightening in her chair and regaining some composure, Samantha replied. "I suspect you knew that before you drove here."

"Yes," Mr. Kendall replied in a matter-of-fact tone so casual it made Samantha uneasy. "I know a great many things."

"You know Jonathan and I plan to marry?" Samantha asked, although she was sure she knew the answer.

"Yes," Mr. Kendall said trying to remain calm.

"You approve?" Samantha asked hopefully.

Shaking his head methodically, Mr. Kendall said, "I think I've made it plain that I very much disapprove."

Trying to take charge of the conversation, Samantha said, "I love him...and Jonathan loves me."

With a labored sigh, Mr. Kendall admitted, "I know that. I've tried to deny it, but that's out of my control now."

"So you'll give Jonathan your blessing?"

"No," Mr. Kendall said calmly. "I don't expect that you'll be here to marry Jonathan."

"What?" a confused Samantha replied.

Slowly opening his briefcase, Mr. Kendall said, "I understand you wanted to go to school."

"I did," Samantha said warily.

"My daughter Caroline's at school," Mr. Kendall stated. "She seems to like it."

"That's what David Simpson told me," Samantha replied.

This response seemed to agitate Mr. Kendall who appeared intent on being businesslike in his discussion.

"Yes, I suppose David would know," Mr. Kendall responded while looking at Samantha. "You know things would have been much better if you'd taken a liking to David."

"David's not Jonathan," Samantha said defiantly. "Besides, David already has Caroline."

"*Had* Caroline," Mr. Kendall interjected.

Samantha raised her eyebrow and Mr. Kendall added, "Like I say, college opens up a world of opportunity and new experiences."

"What's your point?" Samantha bluntly asked.

Mr. Kendall tried to contain a sly smile and said, "I have an envelope with a thousand dollars and a receipt for paid tuition at Hope College in Holland, Michigan. My brother has agreed to let you live with him and his wife for a time until you can get settled."

A puzzled Samantha looked at the papers when Mr. Kendall tossed a train ticket on top of the pile and said, "All you have to do is get on the train this afternoon."

Shaking her head, Samantha said in an annoyed voice, "What kind of girl do you think I am?"

"I'm hoping the kind that can see an opportunity," Mr. Kendall said coldly.

Handing Samantha another file full of papers, Mr. Kendall continued, "Do you see this?"

"What is it?" Samantha asked.

"It's the mortgage to the Hellwig place south of Keokuk Falls...your family's place," Mr. Kendall explained.

"What's that got to do with me?" Samantha inquired sheepishly.

Mr. Kendall said, "This is the last place you have left to go to when Jonathan leaves town to go to the war."

"Jonathan's been released from the army," Samantha replied.

"Until today," Mr. Kendall gleamed. "He's been called back to service...I have the note he sent you right here."

Mr. Kendall handed Samantha the message from Jonathan to read.

"How did you get this?" Samantha asked.

"Don't you mind that," Mr. Kendall instructed. "Just read it."

"Jonathan says he'll marry me Monday anyway," Samantha said.

"Yes," Mr. Kendall smiled. "But can he keep you in a place on a soldier's pay...without any family to help? If you look at the mortgage on the Hellwig place, you'll see I now own it. I know you don't know those people well, but they are your family, and you're all that's keeping them from foreclosure right now."

"You wouldn't," Samantha answered in disbelief.

"I've done worse," Mr. Kendall said. "But I don't want to. All you have to do is get on the train and tell my son you never want to see him again. Go to college, live a happy life far from here. I can't imagine you're too interested in living with all those Hellwig men and Marcus Lutz?"

"I can't do it," Samantha replied hotly. "I love Jonathan. What kind of woman would I be to break his heart for a train ticket and your money?"

A despondent Mr. Kendall replied, "If you were that kind of woman, I wouldn't have a problem."

"You should leave!" Samantha demanded as she stood up to encourage her unwanted guest to go.

"Sit down," Mr. Kendall forcefully requested.

When Samantha hesitated at following his directive, Mr. Kendall said in a kinder voice, "Please sit down, Samantha...I think you'll need to for what I have to say."

Samantha reluctantly followed his directive and seated herself in the chair.

Mr. Kendall sighed heavily and said, "It's easy to see why Jonathan's so fond of you. I'd hoped to have handled this differently, but I know you love Jonathan. I didn't want to believe it at first, but I'm sure you do now."

"Why don't you want us together?" Samantha pleaded. "I know you think I'm just a poor girl looking to snag a man to take care of me. I'll have to admit, a girl in my circumstance can't help but think those things, but I do love him, and I'll make him happy."

Mr. Kendall looked at the girl as if looking through her and said, "You remind me of your mother. She had a kind heart and virtue you could admire, too. She was a lovely woman."

"What do you know of my mother?" Samantha asked.

Ignoring the question, Mr. Kendall continued, "She wasn't nearly as outspoken or as headstrong as you...I guess you get that from me."

Samantha listened to the man sitting across from her, but it was as if his words were not real. Hot flashes followed by cool beads of sweat made her forehead feel unearthly, as the room appeared to spin. Mr. Kendall looked at the girl patiently as his words overwhelmed her denial.

Mr. Kendall thought she might slump into the floor, but when it became clear she would not, he continued, "The reason I must keep you and Jonathan apart is that I fear you are my daughter."

"What?" Samantha said in a voice so low it was barely audible.

Mr. Kendall leaned forward slightly and said kindly, "You can't tell me there haven't been times…since you became a woman that you've doubted Mr. Harvey was your real father."

"He'll always be my Papa," Samantha whimpered helplessly.

"Of course he will," Mr. Kendall tried to assure. "He was a fine man…he took care of your mother and you…when I couldn't."

"I don't understand," Samantha protested. "This can't be."

"I'm afraid it can," Mr. Kendall said with regret. "When I moved to Oklahoma, Mrs. Kendall stayed behind with Jonathan…he was only a baby. We had our troubles as a couple…married much too young. I believed we would divorce, and she would stay in Michigan. I got to know the Hellwigs and tried to help them. Your mother was like a beautiful flower on the prairie. She thought a marriage to me would be advantageous to her family. I know that sounds old-fashioned now, but those were different times."

Mr. Kendall looked at Samantha's unbelieving eyes and continued, "I loved your mother very much, but when Mrs. Kendall's family convinced her to follow me back to Oklahoma, she became pregnant with Caroline, and I had to break it off with Sarah. The Hellwigs didn't take it well, and your mother refused to talk to me again. She went away and married Mr. Harvey. Less than nine months later, she showed back up in Warwick with you. I offered to help, but your mother would not discuss it. I moved to Chandler and got on with life…until you showed up in town."

"You're saying I'm a mistake!" Samantha finally replied angrily. "You're saying my mother was—"

"I'm saying it was my mistake," Mr. Kendall interrupted. "A mistake I thought I could run away from, but one that I'm now prepared to make right."

"How?" Samantha shouted back. "By sending me away and covering up your indiscretion so the family you took care of won't know? You're not trying to do right by me...you just don't want Mrs. Kendall and—"

"That's right," Mr. Kendall interjected. "I don't want Jonathan to find out...and I believe you do not want Jonathan to find out either."

Samantha's face turned pale, and her anger transformed into confused anguish. As much as she hated John Kendall now, she knew he was right. This situation could do nothing but destroy Jonathan. Mr. Kendall might have deserved to have his family know the truth, but Samantha knew it would be an awful thing for Augusta, Caroline, and Jonathan to discover.

Samantha buried her head in her lap and cried uncontrollably in the chaos of her emotions. Deep down she knew the man she had always called Papa was not her real father and the man that made her life so hard, was now taking her hopes for happiness away in a cruel irony she could never explain to Jonathan.

When Mr. Kendall's hand gently rubbed her back, Samantha bristled and said, "Don't you touch me! Don't you ever touch me!"

"Samantha—" Mr. Kendall tried to comfort.

Samantha glared angrily at the man and shouted, "Don't pretend you care about me now! I'm nothing but a bastard to you...an inconvenience you haven't been able to sweep away!"

Mr. Kendall took his scolding in silence while Samantha continued to cry.

After a minute, a teary Samantha sat up to straighten her clothes and said, "You had...arrangements for me?"

"Yes," Mr. Kendall sheepishly replied. "I have a thousand dollars cash. That's a lot of money, and I've made arrangements for you to stay with my brother in Michigan. You'll have tuition at a fine school and there will be more if you need it or ask for it."

"When does the train leave?" a dazed Samantha asked.

"Three o'clock," Mr. Kendall informed. "How long will you need to pack?"

Samantha laughed pathetically and said, "You see all I have. My whole life is in that trunk."

"Life will get better now," Mr. Kendall tried to assure.

"My life was fine before today," Samantha tersely replied.

"Do you want to leave Jonathan a note, or do you want me to tell him?" Mr. Kendall said.

"What will you tell him?" Samantha asked warily.

A calculating Mr. Kendall said, "I'll tell him I offered you money to go away and you took it."

"He won't believe it," Samantha replied.

"Not at first," Mr. Kendall agreed, "but when you're gone...and stay away. Jonathan will believe."

Laughing insincerely, Samantha said, "I'll be the little tramp you always claimed I would be?"

"To protect Jonathan," Mr. Kendall tried to reason.

Placing the money and train ticket in her worn coat, Samantha picked up the trunk with all her belongings and headed to Mr. Kendall's car.

Mr. Kendall picked up the other end of the small trunk and said, "Who knows, maybe someday when Jonathan settles down and marries, we can tell him he has a third sister."

Samantha dropped her end of the trunk and vehemently said, "Jonathan must never know. Promise me...Jonathan can never know where I've gone or what you've done."

Mr. Kendall nodded and drove Samantha to the lonely train depot to put her on the train out of town. Mr. Kendall looked around nervously, hoping Jonathan would be pre-occupied at the Statistical House long enough for Samantha to leave town. After tipping the porter to handle her bags, he looked at the girl he was sending away and wondered what might have been.

"Samantha?" the voice of David Simpson called from inside the train.

In a moment, David Simpson stepped out of the train to speak with Samantha. David had not seen Mr. Kendall at first. Before Mr. Kendall could retreat, David Simpson spotted him.

Samantha noticed the awkward silence between the two men and said to David in a tone of disappointment, "Are you in on this, too?"

Innocently, David said, "In on what?"

Looking at Mr. Kendall, Samantha could tell David did not know of Mr. Kendall's clandestine family secrets.

In a friendlier tone of voice, Samantha said to David, "Nothing."

"What are you doing here?" a confused David asked.

"I'm leaving town," Samantha said.

"I thought you were getting married," David replied.

Samantha glanced at Mr. Kendall and said, "Things didn't work out. Jonathan's going back into the army."

"I hadn't heard," David said suspiciously, sensing the topic did not need to be probed further. "I'm leaving Chandler, too."

Samantha tilted her head in surprise as David added, "Things didn't work out so well for me, either. I'm going to Tulsa to find work in one of the oil refineries."

In a flirting tone, Samantha glared at Mr. Kendall and said to David, "I guess we'll be sharing a ride to Tulsa."

Samantha moved toward the train to follow David into the passenger car when Mr. Kendall frantically bellowed, "Samantha!"

"Find us a seat, David," Samantha smiled. "I'll be there in a second."

After David stepped inside, Samantha walked to Mr. Kendall and said, "Don't worry, your secret's safe. I wouldn't do anything to help you, but I'd do anything to keep from hurting Jonathan."

With a facetious and artificial smile Samantha added, "Dad."

Mr. Kendall breathed a sigh of relief seeing Samantha go. He felt it unfortunate David Simpson took the same train, but Mr. Kendall was confident Samantha would keep his secret — for Jonathan's sake. Mr. Kendall was relieved to have Samantha gone, but feelings of regret overwhelmed any pleasure he had for his hollow victory. Jonathan would hate him for a long time, he knew, but Mr. Kendall believed he had saved his only son from a scandal that would have ruined the both of them. Mr. Kendall looked down the now-empty train tracks leading north knowing he may have saved a son, but he had lost a daughter forever to cover up an indiscretion from long ago.

CHAPTER 55

Mr. Kendall drove to the Harvey home to await the firestorm sure to erupt when Jonathan came for Samantha. As he sat quietly in the small house, he wondered what Samantha must have been like in it. The house looked stark and depressing now. Any joy from the place vanished with Samantha's departure. Mr. Kendall lost track of time as his thoughts filled with remorse, guilt, and shame at what could have been for everyone. His mournful meditations were interrupted by the sound of Jonathan gently opening the door.

"What are you doing here?" Jonathan asked bluntly.

Mr. Kendall did not answer immediately, which prompted Jonathan to ask, "Where's Samantha?"

When Mr. Kendall still did not reply, a more agitated Jonathan demanded, "Where is she?"

"She's gone," Mr. Kendall said in almost a whisper.

Jonathan looked quickly through the small house to see it was empty before taking a frantic look outside.

"What have you done?" Jonathan shouted as he stormed back into the vacant house. "Where is Samantha?"

"She went away, son," Mr. Kendall explained quietly.

In a tone of disbelief, Jonathan said, "She didn't just go. Where is she?"

"Samantha left on a train about an hour ago," Mr. Kendall assured. "You can ask the ticket man at the station. He'll tell you."

"What have you done?" Jonathan charged angrily.

In a calm, sad tone, Mr. Kendall said, "I sent her away."

"What do you mean?" Jonathan snapped back.

"I gave her one thousand dollars to leave," Mr. Kendall explained. "She took the next train out of town,"

"Liar!" Jonathan shouted as he once again looked outside as if Samantha might be hiding as part of a sick practical joke.

"I don't lie about money," Mr. Kendall stoically explained.

"Samantha would never take your money…I don't care if it was ten thousand dollars," Jonathan sneered.

Looking coldly at his son, Mr. Kendall said, "I would have gone as high as five thousand, but she settled for a thousand — at least she was a cheap flirt. That's the problem with the poor…they don't understand the value of the important things."

Jonathan punched his father in the face and screamed, "Liar!"

Mr. Kendall did not retaliate, but straightened himself and wiped his face before saying, "You can think what you like, but the girl's not here and won't be coming back. You can check my bankbook to verify the amount."

Jonathan wanted to beat his father senseless, but Mr. Kendall's calm demeanor served to unnerve the younger man.

"Are you coming to the house or spending the night here?" Mr. Kendall asked. "It makes no difference to me — we own them both now."

Jonathan could not muster a response and could only stare blankly at the empty house. Mr. Kendall put on his hat and walked slowly to the door while Jonathan stood still, seemingly suspended in time.

Stopping at the doorway, Mr. Kendall said, "You're upset. In time you'll see this is for the best."

Without saying more, Mr. Kendall left his distraught son in the empty house and walked slowly to his car. A few hours of daylight remained, but Mr. Kendall knew Jonathan would not leave the Harvey house. Mr. Kendall believed Jonathan would wait through the night hoping his Samantha would come back to him — a hope Mr. Kendall knew was ruined.

PART 4

HOLLAND, MICHIGAN

CHAPTER 56

THE TRAIN LUNGED FORWARD violently, before gaining momentum as it chugged away from Chandler. Samantha wanted to be alone but could not avoid David Simpson. The two sat silently on the wood bench of the passenger car until the train began clicking along regularly through the countryside.

"You're the last person I expected to see on this train," David said, as Samantha looked blankly out the window at the late afternoon landscape that showed only a hint of springtime.

Turning her attention to her travel companion, Samantha smiled politely, but apathetically and replied, "I'm the last person I expected to see here, too."

"Do you want to talk about it?" David asked.

"About what?" Samantha replied cautiously and suspiciously.

"About why you're headed out of town...without Jonathan," David innocently explained.

"Not really...no," Samantha said.

David did not say anything for a few moments before stating, "I was surprised to see Mr. Kendall at the train depot."

"He wanted to make sure I left town," Samantha admitted. "He finally got what he wanted."

"I'm sorry," David replied, feeling guilty for his role in being a roadblock to her relationship with Jonathan.

"There's nothing to be sorry about," Samantha replied, trying to guard her emotions. "Things will be better for Jonathan, and...well, I'm going to school. I've always wanted to go to college. Things will be better for me."

Desperate to change the subject, Samantha asked, "What are you doing on this train?"

David smiled before saying, "Mr. Kendall was running out of uses for me."

"What do you mean?"

"Caroline's engaged," David explained. "She met a man in Oklahoma City from a well-to-do family. That pleased Mr. Kendall. I was becoming a distraction."

"I'm sorry," Samantha said.

"No reason to be," David replied blithely. "It probably worked out for the best...for the both of us."

"You're moving to Tulsa?"

"Yes, if I can find a job," David answered. "I hear the place is booming. I lived in Oklahoma City for a year and like living in the city."

"I think I'll always be a country girl," Samantha said.

"Where are you heading, then?" David asked.

Samantha hesitated in answering but finally said, "Somewhere in western Michigan."

"Somewhere?"

"A college called Hope in a town called Holland," Samantha elaborated.

"The name at least sounds cheerful," David smiled.

Samantha reciprocated the smile and said in an optimistic tone, "It does...doesn't it?"

David watched her carefully before asking, "What did Jonathan think about you going away?"

Samantha's false exuberance vanished as she said, "Jonathan doesn't know yet."

David contained his surprise and sighed, "Oh."

Being close to Mr. Kendall the past year, David knew enough about the man's tactics to understand the gist of the circumstance, if not the details.

Sensing David's discomfort Samantha added, "Things will work for the best...it will be best for Jonathan."

"Don't you think Jonathan should have a say?"

Samantha fought back tears of regret and bravely said, "He should, but I couldn't let him."

David tactically summarized, "Jonathan thinks you took the money and left him, but that's not the reason, is it?"

"You know Mr. Kendall well," Samantha grimaced.

"Too well," David admitted. "Do you need anything...money?"

Samantha shook her head and said, "Mr. Kendall made my exodus profitable."

"Do you need me to say anything to Jonathan?" David offered. "I've known him a long time, and I think he'll understand."

"Understand?" a puzzled Samantha asked. "You know?"

David hung his head and said, "I figured it out today...before I quit. I think Jonathan—"

"No!" Samantha frantically declined. "Jonathan can't know where I am, what I've done—or who I am. It would be better if he never knew you and I talked."

David looked at Samantha without responding.

"You have to promise me," Samantha demanded. "I don't care what you think about me, but you have to promise, you'll never tell Jonathan we talked."

A bewildered David replied, "I promise."

Samantha studied David intently to insure he took the pledge seriously. Samantha looked out the window to forget the pain this pitiful day had brought. David respected her need for privacy and was content to let the train click along the rhythmic tracks on the two-hour trip to Tulsa.

A few miles outside of Tulsa, David asked, "Would you like to get a bite to eat?"

"I don't have time," Samantha replied.

"Come on," David cheerfully chided with his amiable smile. "Everyone's got to eat. I always thought we got along well enough?"

David's invitation unsettled Samantha. She had liked David from their first meeting, but his hospitality now reminded her how much she had grown to rely on Jonathan. Samantha often questioned whether her infatuation with Jonathan had been about the security he could offer or her feelings for him. Her financial future was now secure, but David's kind manners made her realize the safety Jonathan offered was inconsequential to the connection she shared with him—the deep feeling she held that they belonged together.

"I can't," Samantha sighed.

David looked at her, wishing he had not been so insistent.

"I wished I'd fallen for you, David," Samantha explained. "I bet I'm one of the few girls that hasn't. I know you're trying to help, but every time I look at you, I think of Jonathan and thinking of Jonathan makes me feel like a mess inside—I think it always will."

"I understand," David replied meekly. "Are you sure you're going to be okay?"

"I'll be fine," Samantha smiled. "I'm ready for a new start."

"Sure you won't get something to eat at the station," David invited one more time, as he stepped off the train. "No ulterior motives, I promise."

"I really don't have time," Samantha explained. "I'm changing trains in Tulsa and traveling on a Pullman to Chicago...I've never been in a sleeping car."

"You're moving up in the world," David smiled.

"I suppose," Samantha replied.

David stayed with Samantha until her train pulled out of the station toward Chicago. David glanced at the busy train station and the bustling streets of Tulsa that looked like opportunity to him. Gazing down the tracks at the train, which quickly disappeared into the night, he felt sorry for the lonely girl heading north. David wondered when or if he would see Samantha again.

CHAPTER 57

MR. KENDALL LEFT JONATHAN at the abandoned Harvey home and drove to the Western Union office to pick up a telegram. The simple message caused him to take a deep breath as it confirmed Samantha Harvey's train left Tulsa for Chicago and she was aboard. Mr. Kendall arrived home with electric lights creating a glow inside his house, but he felt little satisfaction in his day's work.

The door made a slight creak as Mr. Kendall gently opened it. Augusta was upstairs listening to her phonograph, but Mrs. Kendall peeked around the corner of the kitchen to see her husband had returned.

Mrs. Kendall walked up to her husband and asked lifelessly, "Well?"

"The girl's gone," Mr. Kendall factually stated. "She knows and Jonathan doesn't...that's all that matters."

Mrs. Kendall stared coldly at her husband and said, "I hope you're happy."

"No, Mrs. Kendall," he replied. "I'm far from happy. My son hates me...you're upset, David Simpson's gone...I'm not happy at all, but the thing's done, and at least Jonathan's saved from humiliation, and he can get back to the family business."

Mrs. Kendall brusquely replied, "Don't try to make yourself feel better. You didn't do this for Jonathan...you did this to save your reputation. I should have known what you did back then and stayed with Jonathan in Michigan. A divorce would have been preferable to this."

"You're leaving me?" Mr. Kendall asked.

Mrs. Kendall shook her head and said sternly, "No, dear. I won't have my children's reputation ruined by their father's indiscretions."

"It was a mistake," Mr. Kendall tried to defend. "It happened so long ago."

"Some mistakes your family never stops paying for!" Mrs. Kendall answered in as loud a voice as she dared without being heard by Augusta. "I've lived with this one for twenty years! I'm afraid Jonathan will pay for your little fling for a long time, so don't pretend you're some kind of hero for keeping your son away from that girl. Save your theatrics for the people in town. I know you too well to be entertained by the show."

Mrs. Kendall left her husband standing in the front room as she returned to prepare dinner. Mr. Kendall could hear his wife weeping softly in the next room, but he knew he had no capacity to comfort her. He had used up her trust long ago and knew it would take more than empty words to heal his family. He sat in his chair and waited for supper, preparing once again to put on the act of being the caring father for Augusta. Mr. Kendall knew his wife would also display a veneer of happiness for the sake of her children. Alone in his chair, Mr. Kendall could not stop thinking about Jonathan sitting alone in the empty cabin, knowing his son was still paying the price for his forbidden infatuation with a woman he could barely remember.

CHAPTER 58

JONATHAN SAT SILENTLY IN the dark cabin. An oil lamp cast an amber glow, which created gloomy shadows in the bare room. He confidently waited for Samantha. He knew she would be home soon, and he would take her in his arms, laughing at his father's delusions of manipulating her out of his life. With each passing hour, however, that confidence turned to worry and then desperation. Jonathan did not think he slept during the long night, but the cold chill of the room woke him from a restless slumber.

The chilly morning sobered Jonathan, and for a brief moment he felt peaceful, believing the night had been a bad dream. Jonathan looked at the empty room where he had waited for Samantha, however, and realized the nightmare had been too real. Samantha had not returned to the house for him. For Jonathan, the thought of his father being right about Samantha was almost worse than being jilted.

Rubbing his hands together and briskly patting his face, Jonathan started thinking. He hurriedly checked Samantha's bedroom to make sure she had not come during the night. With the room empty, he frantically searched outside and confirmed he was alone. There was no use waiting for Samantha, he thought to himself. He needed to find her and convinced himself a simple explanation was eluding him.

Jonathan was at wits end as to where Samantha might have stayed the night. He did not know of any friends or family in the area, but he walked swiftly through town searching for any clues or ideas about her whereabouts. In desperation, Jonathan finally decided to wake David Simpson. David was always clearheaded, and Jonathan believed he might have some insight.

The sun was up, but few people were stirring when Jonathan stepped on the porch of the Simpson's modest home and knocked frantically on the door. It only took a moment for Jonathan to hear movement inside the house and in a few seconds, Mrs. Simpson opened the door.

"Jonathan?" Mrs. Simpson greeted. "What are you doing out so early?"

"Sorry to disturb you, Mrs. Simpson—"

"It's fine," Mrs. Simpson interrupted. "I was up."

"I'm looking for David," Jonathan explained.

Mrs. Simpson looked perplexed and said, "David's not here."

"What?"

"I thought he would've talked to you," Mrs. Simpson said in a distant voice. "David's moved."

"Moved!" Jonathan exclaimed.

"Yes."

"From Chandler?"

"Yes."

"For good?"

Mrs. Simpson smiled and said, "You know David. It's hard to say anything's forever with him. I thought he would have talked to you."

"He didn't," Jonathan sharply replied. "Where did he go?"

"Tulsa," Mrs. Simpson answered. "He went to work in the oil fields."

"When did he leave?" Jonathan asked.

"Yesterday evening," Mrs. Simpson replied. "He took the last train to Tulsa, yesterday."

"Thank you," Jonathan said hurriedly as he excused himself and trotted to the train depot.

The train depot was deserted when Jonathan arrived. He looked at his watch, and it was not quite seven o'clock. Jonathan knew the ticket office would not open until eight. A knotting uneasy feeling grew in his stomach. Jonathan could not get his mind around the disequilibrium of the past hours, but he was beginning to feel an overwhelming sense of dread. Instead of wasting an hour fuming at the train station, Jonathan decided to walk to the Statistical House and try to clear his mind until eight o'clock.

Jonathan would have preferred not walking past his father's house, but that was the shortest distance to the Statistical House, and he was in no mood for a detour this morning. As Jonathan passed the courthouse and started down Eighth Street, he spotted the Presbyterian Church waiting for its members on a quiet Sunday morning.

The train station won't be open for hours, Jonathan thought to himself.

Walking slower now, Jonathan walked past the Conklin house where he had his first conversation with Samantha Harvey. Looking at the small deck on top of the third floor, he remembered how the moonlight made her eyes sparkle and hair shine. He remembered the lightning storm and how electric he had felt that evening. Jonathan continued anxiously past his parent's home and shuffled quickly down the steps leading to the Statistical House. Jonathan chuckled to himself and shook his head as Lee Gilstrap frantically swept the front steps.

"Don't you ever sleep?" Jonathan asked the boy.

"Not much, sir," Lee Gilstrap replied with inflated bravado. "Not when there's a war to fight."

Looking around the lonely encampment, Jonathan said, "I don't think the Germans are attacking this morning. Why don't you go home and go to church with your mother?"

"Yes, sir," Lee replied with less bluster in his tone of voice.

As Lee put his broom down and headed for the stairs leading up the hill, he stopped suddenly and said, "Lieutenant Kendall, I'm sorry about not deliverin' your message like you ordered yesterday. I should've given it to the girl myself."

"It's okay," Jonathan assured.

"I was so busy," Lee Gilstrap continued. "The captain had me running all over town. If I'd hung on to it, I'd seen Miss Harvey at the train station later anyway."

The sounds of the morning seemed to mute for Jonathan as he turned his full attention to the young man.

"You saw Samantha yesterday?" Jonathan asked excitedly.

"Yes, sir," Lee Gilstrap confirmed. "She got on the last train yesterday afternoon."

"You saw her get on the train?"

"Yes, sir," Lee repeated. "Your father was there with her. She left on the train with your friend David."

"David Simpson?"

"Yes, sir," Lee continued. "Your father watched them both get on the train."

Jonathan felt dizzy as the blood rushed from his face. The cool breeze felt strange and unreal to him as he thought about Lee's encounter.

"Are you okay, Lieutenant Kendall?" Lee asked.

"Huh?" Jonathan muttered.

"You don't look so well," Lee observed.

Making himself focus attention on the young man, Jonathan forced a smile and said, "I'm fine."

"I'm awful sorry about the message," Lee apologized, feeling his failure to follow directives caused Jonathan's strange reaction.

"It's fine," Jonathan assured. "Get up the hill and see your mother. If Captain Gilstrap lets you muster out with us, she'll want to be with you."

"Yes, sir," Lee said as he started up the hill.

Jonathan took a seat on the steps of the Statistical House and buried his head in his hands for a moment before roughly rubbing his eyes and forehead. He looked around at what was turning out to be a beautiful, sunny morning. For Jonathan, however, everything looked dull and gray. He could not believe Samantha had left him. After the many letters and the time they had spent the last month, he believed he knew the girl he had so loved. Jonathan prided himself on being rational, and he could not deny the facts. His father had been right. Samantha had only been interested in advancing her social standing. With his father's cash in hand, Samantha had been free to leave with David.

Taking a deep breath, Jonathan resolved to commit himself to the one thing that still made sense to him: Company B would head to war in a matter of weeks, and his job was to prepare. With Samantha gone, Jonathan was ready to leave the memories of this place — even if that meant Europe.

CHAPTER 59

A POLITE PORTER SHOWED Samantha to her private berth in the Pullman car as it rolled out of Tulsa toward St. Louis and then Chicago. Samantha had never been this far on a train and certainly had never been in a Pullman sleeping car. David Simpson had been pleasant to her on the trip from Chandler to Tulsa, but as the train gained its full speed through the rolling hills of eastern Oklahoma, she was content to be alone.

Samantha felt the soft velvet seats and admired the lush compartment. Such luxury made her strangely uneasy, however. The rich surroundings reminded her of the unsavory circumstances of her exile. The rhythm of the train would have normally relaxed her, but her mind drifted to the painful memory of Jonathan. Sitting alone in the compartment, she tried to block out thoughts about him, but a tap on the door interrupted her tragic daydreaming.

Samantha was not aware that her forehead was wrinkled until the porter said, "You okay, miss?"

"Yes," Samantha replied.

"The way your forehead was wrinkled up, I thought maybe you's doin' mathematics or something," the porter said with a broad smile.

"No," Samantha said while returning the smile. "It's just been a long day."

"Are you taking supper tonight?" the porter asked.

Samantha had not thought about food, although it had been hours since she had eaten anything.

"I guess, I could eat," Samantha replied.

The porter looked over the young girl and said, "Is this your first time on a Pullman?"

"Yes," Samantha admitted.

The porter smiled and said, "Don't you worry none because I'm here to take care of everything...you don't have to think about anything as long as you're on this train."

Samantha giggled slightly at the man's enthusiasm and said, "Your name is George, right?"

The porter looked around and said, in a low voice, "Ma'am all the passengers calls us Pullman porters George, but you can call me Irving...Irving Prevost from Port Arthur, Texas at your service."

"You're a long way from home?" Samantha noted.

"This train's my second home ma'am," Irving stated. "I travel all over the country, and I know every turn on this trip...and I know the roast beef will be gone in an hour, and I recommend you try some."

The conversation with Irving was one of the few times Samantha had not felt hopeless all day. His suggestion about the roast beef reminded her how hungry she had become.

"I won't want to miss it," Samantha said. "Where do I go?"

"The dining room's one car back," Irving replied. "Follow me, and I'll show you the way."

"Thank you," Samantha said as she followed the tall, black man to the dining car.

"If you don't mind me asking," Irving said as he walked down the narrow, shifting isle of the train. "What's a pretty girl like you doin' travelin' alone?"

The helpful porter had only been trying to make polite conversation, but the question put Samantha back into the melancholy mood she had endured since being sent away from Chandler.

The smiling Irving stopped to open the door and noticed Samantha's change in demeanor.

"I'm sorry ma'am," he apologized. "I wasn't trying to pry."

"It's okay," Samantha assured. "It's just been a long day. Thank you for your kindness and showing me where to get supper. I'm sure I'll feel better after a good meal."

"Don't thank me," Irving instructed. "It's my job to take care of folks. Being it's your first time on one of my Pullman cars, I'm going to take special care of you. You enjoy your dinner. I'm going to talk to the cook to make sure he makes yours special good. I'll come by later to fold out your bed. You've never slept until you've slept on a Pullman bed as we click off the miles."

Samantha thanked the man again and took her seat in the dining car. She was joined by an old preacher and his wife who were traveling to St. Louis to see a son. Samantha had never met the couple and did not have much in common with them, but the idle conversation took her mind off the events of the day, and the preacher reminded her somewhat of her father. Irving came by later and folded out her bed, and she slept soundly until the train made its stop in St. Louis. Samantha found it easy to sleep with the calming sounds of the train tracks drowning out her thoughts, but she was glad to be awake to see the train cross the Mississippi River, although it was so dark she could see little of it.

By the time Samantha awoke, the sun was up, and the train chugged through the empty farmland of Illinois as it approached the mighty city of Chicago. She had slept much later than she anticipated and dressed hurriedly. Irving helped fold up the bed so she could watch Chicago approach in the distance. Tall buildings contrasted with the vast expanse of Lake Michigan. Samantha marveled at the emerald waters and how the flat surface of the lake made the jagged skyline look ominous. The train coasted to a stop under a two-hundred-yard-long canopy. The train shed stretched across ten rows of tracks. As she looked at the nine-story building housing the station with a thirteen-story clock tower, Samantha thought the station might have more people in it than the entire town of Chandler.

Samantha said good-bye to Irving and prepared for a three-hour wait to catch a train that would run into Michigan and the town of Holland on the eastern shore of Lake Michigan. Central Station was one of six train depots in Chicago and was located at the southern end of Grant Park. Samantha was cautious at first but soon worked up the courage to take a quick walk through the expansive park. She had never seen a farm as big as the landscaped park. Samantha marveled at the size of the city and the tall buildings lining the street across from the park.

As fascinated as Samantha was with the city, she was relieved to board the train for Holland. The car was simpler and less opulent than the sleeping car she had taken to Chicago, but she had a good view of the tall trees of southern Michigan as the train rolled into some of the most beautiful forests Samantha had ever seen.

The weather in Chicago had been cold and breezy. Samantha looked at the massive trees still bare from the winter and decided spring must still be a few weeks away. She was anxious to see Lake Michigan but discovered the train did not offer a good view of the lake. Samantha settled into her seat as the new landscape soon became monotonous.

She would be in a new place in less than two hours and did not know what to expect. The excitement of Chicago and the trip had temporarily taken her mind off her troubles, but as she approached her final destination, Samantha began to doubt her decision to come north. She thought of the Hellwigs scratching out a living close to the raw town of Keokuk Falls and wondered if she would have been happier living in that rustic setting having never known the Kendalls. Samantha had no time to think about being happy, as she focused on surviving her new life. In two hours, she would know more about her future. Samantha was sure of one thing: it would be a long time before she could get the hopes she shared with Jonathan Kendall out of her head.

CHAPTER 60

ANTICIPATION AND ANXIETY OVERWHELMED Samantha as the train stopped with a final shriek of steam at the Holland, Michigan, train station. She looked at the brown brick station cloaked in the lengthening shadows of the approaching evening. It was April 1, 1917, and it seemed a lifetime since she hurriedly left Chandler, although her journey started only the day before. Her legs wobbled slightly as she stepped off the train, and a cold chill of a westerly breeze raked across her face. It felt more like February to her than early spring as she pulled her thin wrap tight to block out the cold. The baggage handler tossed her large trunk to the platform as she stood alone in the strange town.

Samantha pulled the heavy trunk to the canopy running next to the tracks when a young porter at the station asked politely, "Can I get that for you, miss?"

Before the boy could move the trunk an ominous voice said, "Put it in that car."

The man's voice caused Samantha to wince. Samantha turned to face a man that must have been Mr. Kendall's brother. The man was shorter with a balding head and looked at least ten years older, but his commanding tone of voice and stern face, which appeared as if he did not smile often, was unmistakably like John Kendall's voice.

"Mr. Kendall?" Samantha timidly asked.

The man looked at her for what seemed to Samantha to be minutes before saying, "Yes...you must be...Samantha."

Samantha nodded fearfully.

"Where's the rest of your luggage?" he asked.

"The trunk's all I have," Samantha answered, as she struggled to look the unsmiling man in the eye.

The man heaved an audible sigh before saying, "I was told you would be staying for a time...I would have thought you would have packed more."

"No, sir," Samantha apologized.

"We'd best be going," Mr. Kendall stoically pronounced as he walked to a large black car parked close to the station.

Samantha watched the austere man and was almost too terrified to follow. Mr. Kendall drove away from the station without saying more. Samantha scanned the scenery to see that Holland was a neat and picturesque town, although the trees were still weeks away from showing any leaves, giving the place a stark, wintery appearance. Mr. Kendall drove a few blocks past a downtown area that was larger and with taller buildings than what she was accustomed to, but nothing as intimidating as Chicago.

"You know about me?" Samantha finally asked.

Keeping his eyes fixed on the road, Mr. Kendall nodded.

"I'm guessing you're not too excited to have me sent to you?" Samantha observed.

Mr. Kendall did not answer for a second before saying, "I haven't seen my brother in nearly twenty years and have heard little from him, and then he sends me a message saying he has a daughter in trouble. Well...he's my brother still. Are you with child?"

"No!" Samantha quickly replied. "It's nothing like that."

"What other kind of trouble is there for a young girl that would send her away," Mr. Kendall asked.

Samantha answered, "Your brother didn't tell you?"

"He didn't say anything," Mr. Kendall replied. "He asked if his—"

Mr. Kendall hesitated until Samantha added, "Illegitimate daughter."

"Yes," Mr. Kendall affirmed. "I just assumed—"

"You assumed I must be with child?" Samantha said.

Mr. Kendall shrugged, "What other kind of trouble can a young girl get into?"

"There was a man," Samantha said, sensing Mr. Kendall was not aware of her circumstance. "Your brother did not approve of him."

"My brother would know the kind of men to stay away from," Mr. Kendall said. "He has been that man enough times. Won't the man come find you?"

"No," Samantha answered. "He doesn't know where I am."

"Was he cruel to you?" Mr. Kendall asked.

Thinking of Jonathan and having to answer questions about a mistake that was not her own, caused Samantha to become teary eyed as she said, "No...He was kind and sweet to me always. It was just complicated, and...well his parents would never approve. It was better for me to leave."

Mr. Kendall did not ask further questions and pushed the accelerator as the car sped through town. Samantha was strangely relieved that the people in Holland did not know about Jonathan. Samantha shook her head silently thinking how ironic is was for her to be glad that the people she would be living with thought she was only the illegitimate child of their black sheep brother.

A park was situated in the center of town with a large, white church building to the west close to a couple of stately buildings that looked like they might be part of the college. Samantha wanted to ask if the buildings were Hope College but decided to let Mr. Kendall drive uninterrupted. Mr. Kendall turned the automobile to the east, as Samantha looked at well-kept yards and homes down a wide street. Less than a half mile from the park, Mr. Kendall made a sudden turn into the gravel drive of a large, white two-story house.

Mr. Kendall did not speak, as he exited the car and proceeded to remove Samantha's trunk from the back of the car. Samantha hesitantly opened the car door and looked at the stately home lit by the amber glow of electric lights inside. Samantha turned to see if she could help Mr. Kendall when she heard the door of the house open behind her.

Before Samantha could turn around, a high-pitched and overly excited voice squealed, "This must be the girl!"

Samantha turned around to see a woman who she supposed was Mrs. Kendall. The woman was short, and everything about her seemed round including her pudgy face capped with a white bonnet. The woman did not wait for Samantha to walk to the door as she waddled out and threw her hefty arms around Samantha and squeezed her tight.

"It's so good to see you," the woman exclaimed. "I'm Margaret, and it's good to have company."

"Thank you," Samantha stammered, not knowing how to respond to the hospitable welcome that contrasted with Mr. Kendall's cool reception.

"George," the woman barked to her husband. "Put her bags in the upstairs bedroom on the right. I've got everything ready."

"Yes, dear," George Kendall humbly replied.

Samantha smiled at Margaret Kendall's energy and said, "This is a beautiful house."

"Thank you," Margaret replied. "It'll be so nice to have such a lovely young woman back in the house. George and I have been in this big house all alone since my youngest daughter married three years ago."

Leaning into Samantha to whisper, Margaret added, "Mr. Kendall is a fine man, but he's not much for conversation. I've been excited all day to have you stay with us."

George Kendall dragged the large trunk through the front door when Margaret shouted to him, "How come you didn't tell me how pretty she was?"

The stoic Mr. Kendall answered back, "I've never seen the girl. I didn't know she even existed until a week ago."

Samantha's smile evaporated at Mr. Kendall's realistic assessment of her situation.

Margaret Kendall turned back to Samantha and said, "Don't pay that old grouch any mind. He's as glad as me to have the company. How many more bags do you have?"

"None," Samantha replied.

Margaret Kendall smiled broadly and said, "Then we'll go shopping tomorrow. Mr. Kendall's as tight with a dollar as my corset, and I've needed a good excuse to go shopping."

"I'll be fine," Samantha assured.

"Fine is fine, but we'll go shopping anyway," Margaret smiled. "You must be starving."

"I could eat," Samantha admitted.

"What kind of host am I, sitting out here talking to you when you're starving?" Margaret scolded herself. "Come inside, I'll have dinner ready for you in a minute."

Samantha finished a filling dinner and listened to Margaret Kendall talk continually as Mr. Kendall listened patiently. Margaret prepared a nicely furnished bedroom for Samantha and told her to make herself at home. As Samantha settled into the soft bed, her mind went over the chaotic events of the past days. Samantha somehow felt at home in this strange house in this new town thanks to the hospitality of Margaret Kendall. Samantha did not know what the future held, but she now hoped her stay with Margaret Kendall might give her time to sort out the confusion. Samantha was tired, but she found sleep did not come easily. She tried to block out memories of Jonathan Kendall, but thoughts of their plans haunted her and would haunt for years to come.

CHAPTER 61

APRIL 2, 1917, WAS a bright, sunshiny day in Chandler, but for Jonathan Kendall it seemed hopeless and gloomy. The weekend had been agonizingly tedious. His fiancé left town two days before their marriage, coerced by bribery and intimidation from his father. Worse, Jonathan learned Samantha had left town with his best friend, David Simpson. Jonathan's initial anger at his meddling father transformed to growing resentment toward Samantha Harvey. His father had seduced the young woman out of town, Jonathan reasoned, but he began to question what kind of girl would abandon her fiancé without a word. Jonathan wondered if the girl possessed the bad character of which his father warned.

Jonathan still harbored faint hope, however, as he sat in front of the courthouse on the chance Samantha had fooled his father and would show up to be his wife. As noon approached, Jonathan held equal resentment for his father, David Simpson, and Samantha as it became clear everything he had learned the past day was true.

Dejected, Jonathan returned to the one thing in his world that made sense — his military duty. He walked away from the courthouse and did not care if he ever saw the stately building again. Trees were leafed out and spring was in the air as he walked down

Silk Stocking Row on his way to the Statistical House to prepare for the departure of Company B in a matter of weeks.

Jonathan was lost in thought, trying to admire a beautiful spring day, when he heard a woman's voice call timidly, "Jonathan!"

Jonathan did not immediately recognize the voice but turned in the direction of the Conklin house to see a young woman sitting on the porch.

"Elizabeth?" Jonathan answered, as he stopped to look at her.

Jonathan hesitated to walk across the street for a moment. He had convinced himself that he did not want to talk to anyone this day, but Elizabeth was a friend he had not seen in over a year, so he finally sauntered toward the Conklin house. Elizabeth Conklin had been his girlfriend before she moved to Oklahoma City. The last he heard, she was engaged to a young attorney working in Judge Robertson's office after she too had chased after David Simpson. Elizabeth was an attractive girl with brown hair and a fair complexion. Seeing her only reminded him of Samantha's leaving.

"What are you doing in town?" Jonathan asked as he stepped to the porch.

Elizabeth looked around the empty street and said, "I decided to come home for a while."

"It's a pretty day," Jonathan noted in a tone emphasizing he had little to say.

"Yes," Elizabeth smiled.

"I was headed to the guard office," Jonathan explained. "We're shipping out in a couple of weeks."

"I heard," Elizabeth said. "You're a lieutenant now?"

"Yes," Jonathan blushed. "I guess a lot has changed since you left town."

"Some things have," Elizabeth replied. "But the thing I like best about coming back to Chandler is that somehow most things stay the same. It makes me feel good to know I can count on some things being dependable."

"I guess," Jonathan shrugged.

"You've changed, though," Elizabeth noted.

"How?" Jonathan asked.

"It's hard to tell, but something's different," Elizabeth said as she looked closely at him. "You were always so serious, but now...well, now it's like you're sad too."

"I don't have time for such silly emotions," Jonathan bristled. "I'm serious because Company B is being activated and we're likely headed to Europe."

"You're right," Elizabeth retracted. "I'm sorry."

"I've got to go," Jonathan said as he turned to leave.

Before Jonathan had taken a step, he heard Elizabeth faintly sobbing behind him. His first instinct was to walk away, but after a step, he turned to look at the teary eyed and weeping girl.

"I'm sorry," Jonathan apologized. "I shouldn't have been so blunt."

"It's not you," Elizabeth sniveled. "It's me...I...I came home because my fiancé broke our engagement. I was through with school, but didn't know where to come but home. I'm the one that should be sorry."

"No," Jonathan assured as he stepped closer. "You're going through a tough time, and I should have been more sensitive. I know how much it hurts to lose someone."

Elizabeth broke down into an almost uncontrollable cry as Jonathan stepped to her with a handkerchief.

"It's going to be okay," Jonathan tried to assure as he gently patted the girl on the back.

"I'm so sorry," Elizabeth said again.

"There's no reason," Jonathan replied.

"Yes, there is," Elizabeth stated. "I went away to Oklahoma City and broke up with you. Of all the people I know, you should be happy to see me this way."

"I'm not happy," Jonathan replied. "I know you Elizabeth, and this guy is...well...he isn't worth crying about. If he's not smart enough to see what he's missing in you...forget about him!"

Jonathan was talking to himself as much as he was encouraging Elizabeth. His brash statement caused her to giggle slightly through her tears.

After a few moments of letting Elizabeth cry into his shoulder, Jonathan said, "I really do have to go. It was nice seeing you, Elizabeth."

Elizabeth nodded and released her grip on Jonathan.

As Jonathan walked away, Elizabeth said, "Thanks, Jonathan. I've been dreading seeing you, but you made everything okay...just like the old days."

Jonathan smiled and started to walk away when Elizabeth said, "I'll be home for good now. Do you think you might want to come...and just talk some time?"

Jonathan was surprised by the question, but after thinking a second, he nodded his head in acknowledgement before walking away.

The next several weeks kept Jonathan busy, and he liked the hectic job of organizing the company for action. The demanding hours and work helped keep his mind off Samantha Harvey. Jonathan spent so many hours at the Statistical House that Captain Gilstrap sent Jonathan home a couple of nights to force him to sleep. Captain Gilstrap did not know the details about Samantha Harvey's exodus from Chandler, but he knew it had made Jonathan Kendall a more serious and determined soldier.

Jonathan managed to spend a couple of evenings at the Conklin house. Mrs. Conklin had been almost overjoyed at Jonathan's visit the first night. Elizabeth Conklin seemed to enjoy Jonathan's company, but she was somewhat distant and distracted. Jonathan could tell the girl's behavior frustrated Mrs. Conklin, but Jonathan understood completely. Although seeing Elizabeth was pleasant, his thoughts always drifted back to Samantha. Elizabeth was a sweet girl, but Jonathan could tell she was not over her broken engagement. As much as Jonathan tried, he was still not over Samantha Harvey.

CHAPTER 62

THE UNITED STATES OFFICIALLY declared war on Germany on April 6, 1917. Jonathan Kendall had been feverishly preparing Company B of the 1st Oklahoma Infantry for mobilization. After their monotonous duty in Texas on the Mexican border, the troops were eager to see some real action. Jonathan's tireless work under the direction of Captain Gilstrap had occupied his time and distracted him from thinking constantly about Samantha Harvey.

Jonathan believed Company B would be deployed to Europe by the end of April, although Captain Gilstrap reminded his young officer that the wheels of the military often turned slowly. As May turned into June, Jonathan wondered if Company B would ever get out of Chandler. Jonathan lived in the small room he had rented for Samantha and himself. Although his days were filled with activity, the nights were lonely, and his rented room served as a reminder to his happiness lost.

Elizabeth Conklin provided some relief for Jonathan's feelings of abandonment. Elizabeth had also recently been victim of a broken engagement, and Jonathan ended up spending hours talking to her about their shared loss. Mr. Kendall would have been pleased at Jonathan's attention to Elizabeth Conklin, but Jonathan refused to speak to his father, going as far as to cross the street to avoid an encounter. Jonathan was estranged from his family and waited anxiously for his orders to Europe.

On July 4, 1917, the first contingent of the American Expeditionary Force arrived in Paris, but its appearance was symbolic. For all the enthusiasm of men like Jonathan Kendall, the United States was unprepared for war. The troops that served on the Mexican border represented the only scant combat experience in the American army. The American commanders were learning their army was short of men, supplies, experience, and training. Jonathan Kendall found out the next day that the Oklahoma troops would move to Fort Sill for training.

Most of the town showed up at the train station to say good-bye to their troops. Jonathan Kendall saw his father at the station but refused to acknowledge his presence. Augusta Kendall gave her brother a hug, almost causing Jonathan to become emotional. He did not have time for emotions, however, as he carefully watched the men load into the crowded train that would take them to camp.

Just before Jonathan stepped onto the train, Elizabeth Conklin called, "Jonathan!"

Stopping to say good-bye, Jonathan said, "You came."

"Of course I came," Elizabeth replied. "Jonathan I'll miss you...please be careful."

"I will," Jonathan assured.

"I'll write!" Elizabeth raised her voice as the train's whistle sounded the signal for all aboard.

As the train began to move, Jonathan nodded and said, "That'll be nice."

Jonathan hurried to his seat but looked out the window to wave at Elizabeth. Settling into the wooden seat, Jonathan's smile turned to a frown as he thought of the many letters he had shared with Samantha Harvey. He closed his eyes and tried to sleep on the three-hour trip to Lawton and to forget about the past.

Fort Sill was familiar to the 1st Oklahoma Infantry, and they believed they would be sent to fight the Germans from there. A collective groan could be heard from the troops when they learned a few days later they would be sent to Camp Bowie near Fort Worth, Texas. The Oklahoma Guard had spent eight long months in Texas guarding the border, and they were not anxious to return. The scorching heat of Lawton would be replaced by the scorching heat of Fort Worth, as the 1st Oklahoma Infantry boarded trains to its new camp.

Morale for the Oklahoma soldiers did not improve at Camp Bowie. Most men believed they would be fighting Germans in the trenches by this time. Instead, the officers of the Texas and Oklahoma guard units fought with the army. Both states wanted separate divisions, but the Oklahoma contingent was too small, so the Texas and Oklahoma units were soon reorganized into the 36th Division of the United States Army. To make matters worse, officers from the regular army replaced many of the senior National Guard officers. Brigadier General Hoffman from Chandler was one of the few exceptions as he took command of the third brigade of the new 36th Division.

Jonathan, who believed he had proved himself as an able officer on the Mexican border, found his experience mattered little in the new division. Animosity brewed in the camp as soldiers waited for supplies and training. Captain Gilstrap was reassigned during the organization of the division as the Company B of the 1st Oklahoma Infantry was merged to the 142nd Infantry of the 36th Division of the United States Army.

Jonathan's straightforward personality soon earned him respect with his new commanders, however. Petty squabbles between the Texas and Oklahoma troops evaporated as the new division took shape and the men endured harsher than expected conditions at Camp Bowie. September presented an unusually cold autumn that left the men cold and eventually sick. Jonathan described the conditions as chaotic in a letter to Elizabeth Conklin as the army seemed to be out of everything including adequate clothing.

With over 25,000 men in camp, the place was like a city with large canvas tents laid out in a pyramid pattern and street signs with the names of the regiments between the tents. Each tent housed seven privates and a corporal but as the men continued to arrive, ten or more men were often crowded together. Things seemed under control until flooding and cold weather caused many men to become sick with measles, pneumonia, meningitis, and other respiratory ailments. Jonathan described to Elizabeth the "36th division cough" which erupted into a loud chorus of hacking fits when the men woke each morning.

The epidemic spread during October, causing the camp to be quarantined. By early November over 1,800 men crowded into the hospital and morale reached an all time low before Christmas. There were no signs the 36th Division was ready for war or would be anytime soon. With over 5,000 men sick during the fall and over 60 deaths due to disease, Jonathan wondered if the army would ever make it out of camp.

Jonathan spent the lonely, cold nights in Camp Bowie reading letters from Elizabeth. She carefully documented the happenings in Chandler in much more detail than Samantha Harvey had. Elizabeth's letters were an oasis of comfort from the dire conditions of the camp, but Jonathan felt despondent reading the thoughtful letters, because they reminded him of Samantha.

Elizabeth was an accomplished young woman, but her writing did not affect him as Samantha Harvey's had the year before. As much as he tried, Jonathan could not block Samantha Harvey from his thoughts. Although he had received no word from her, he still reclined in his cot each night looking at Samantha's picture and wondering where she had gone.

CHAPTER 63

"Cow needs milking," Samantha Harvey heard her father say from the dim reality of her dream.

Startled, Samantha sat up in her soft bed in a room illuminated by morning sunshine. The mid-May morning promised a delightful day. She had lived with the Kendalls in Holland for nearly six weeks and quickly became accustomed to Margaret Kendall's pampering. Samantha's meager wardrobe grew substantially as Margaret relished shopping for her young guest.

Samantha often dreamt about her papa. She loved waking up in the mornings with pleasant memories of him. Those memories, however, were often tainted with nightmares about Jonathan's father revealing she was the child he did not want. Samantha wanted to forget Jonathan Kendall, but being surrounded by the Kendall family in Holland made that difficult.

Margaret Kendall raised six children, all of whom were married and living in the area. George Kendall had been a furniture maker before retiring, and several of his sons now worked for furniture factories in nearby Grand Rapids. Margaret's two daughters, Elsie and Greta, were raising families of their own, and Samantha spent most of her time with the round and jovial Margaret.

"Good morning, sleepyhead," Margaret greeted cheerfully as Samantha came down the stairs for breakfast.

"Good morning," Samantha replied.

"This Michigan weather seems to agree with you," Margaret smiled.

Samantha looked out the window to see the towering trees casting long shadows over the green lawn and brightly colored tulips. Samantha had not been accustomed to the cold weather of April in Michigan and had always asked for a heavier coat. The warmer days of May, however, were to her liking, and Samantha enjoyed the older woman's kind teasing. Samantha sat at the table and drank the hot coffee Margaret placed before her.

"Has Mr. Kendall gone?" Samantha asked.

"Yes," Margaret affirmed. "One of the boys was having trouble with a lathe at the shop, and George still thinks he can tinker with anything and make it work."

"Mr. Kendall's different than I thought," Samantha said as she sipped her coffee.

"He takes some getting used to," Margaret grinned, "but he's a good man."

"He's a lot different than his brother," Samantha blurted out without thinking.

Margaret Kendall stopped what she was doing and took a seat next to Samantha.

"That's the first time you've said anything about John," Margaret observed. "Would you like to talk about it?"

"About what?" a red-faced Samantha asked.

Margaret sighed and said pleasantly, "You've been here six weeks, and you don't talk about why you came or about the man who sent you. We hadn't heard from John in twenty years, and he sends a telegram asking us to keep his daughter, and you don't act like he's your father."

"He's not!" Samantha replied sharply.

Taking a second to calm down, Samantha said, "I didn't mean to snap—It's complicated."

Leaning close to the Samantha, Margaret squeezed the girl's cheeks gently in her hands and said, "I've grown fond of you these past weeks...Mr. Kendall has too, but I can tell you're not happy. Such a lovely girl should be happy. Won't you talk to me? Maybe I can help."

Samantha looked blankly at the kind woman and said, "I don't know if I deserve to be happy."

"Everyone deserves to be happy," Margaret preached. "When my parents came from the Netherlands they said America is the place for 'life, liberty, and the pursuit of happiness.' Of course, you deserve to be happy. Talking about whatever is bothering will help."

Samantha hesitated a moment before confiding, "I didn't know John Kendall was my father until the day he sent me to you."

Samantha looked carefully to measure Margaret Kendall's reaction. She had grown to love the older woman and did not wish to upset her.

After determining Margaret was not passing judgment, Samantha continued, "My Papa was a dear sweet man. He was older. I guess Mr. Kendall...John Kendall had known my mother. He said he had loved her, but he had his own family."

"Why did he wait so long to tell you?" Margaret asked.

Samantha looked down at the floor and said, "I was engaged to marry Jonathan...Mr. Kendall's son—"

Samantha could not continue as she began to cry.

"It's okay," Margaret said as she hugged the younger woman.

"It's been so confusing," Samantha wept.

"Of course it has," Margaret said as she continued to console Samantha. "Tell me what Jonathan's like...I haven't seen him since he was a baby."

Samantha was still crying as she said, "Jonathan was sweet and kind. He was awkward and sometimes stubborn too. He reminds me of your husband a little."

"There, there," Margaret coaxed as she continued to console Samantha. "No wonder you've been so quiet. It's not your fault."

"I know," Samantha sobbed, "but I feel so guilty."

Margaret let Samantha cry into her shoulder for a while then said, "A man reaps what he sows."

"What do you mean?" Samantha asked, looking at Margaret.

Margaret said, "John Kendall was always a rambunctious young man. A more boisterous and ambitious person I never knew. John was nearly eight years younger than George. Maybe that's why they have such different temperaments. The Kendalls were a hardworking family that prospered even if they weren't considered rich. The Kendalls were not Dutch, and in these parts that was unusual. My family name was Westerveldt. My father was a farmer and a good one. They weren't too happy to see me marry a Kendall, but George was a good man, and they soon approved.

"John set his sights on Gertrude Van Antwerp. Her family owned timberland in western Michigan and had a shipping business as well. The big white house overlooking the lake was theirs. The Van Antwerps were not excited to see John Kendall courting their youngest daughter, but John could be charming when it was in his best interest. I don't know if John loved Gertrude as much as he loved the ambiance of the Van Antwerp's wealth. The family did not approve of John but suddenly arranged a hasty wedding. Needless to say, Jonathan was born six months later. It was a scandal that irritated the Van Antwerps and humiliated the Kendalls.

"John soon found out Mr. Van Antwerp had no intention of funding any of his schemes or business ventures, and after a few years, he left and went to Oklahoma. Divorce was unheard of in the Reformed Church, and after John went away, Mr. Van Antwerp threatened to cut off the money. John came home for a time, and soon after, Gertrude was expecting their second child. John moved the family south. I never knew the details, but always suspected the Van Antwerp family paid John to move to avoid further embarrassment."

"That must have been when he was seeing my mother," Samantha surmised. "Maybe he did love her."

"Love for John Kendall was always more of a convenience than a commitment," Margaret harshly observed.

"He seemed committed to his family in Chandler," Samantha defended.

"I guess a man can change," Margaret said, "but it still doesn't excuse his treatment of you."

Samantha smiled at the supportive Margaret and said sweetly, "Maybe not, but I had nowhere to go except to some relatives I don't even know. At least he sent me to you...I hope I haven't been too much of a bother."

"No bother at all," Margaret assured. "You've been a joy to this house."

Samantha smiled and somehow did feel better having talked to Margaret about her circumstance. Samantha thought of all the confusion of her life the past weeks, and her brief smile vanished into an unconscious frown.

"There's something else, isn't there?" Margaret asked. "There's something else bothering you, dear."

Samantha bit her lower lip and did not know how to respond. There were so many things still troubling her, but she felt the need to be guarded. She still thought of Jonathan Kendall as a man she loved instead of a brother, but there was something else that had been gnawing at her.

"My family back in Oklahoma," Samantha finally said. "I left without telling anyone. I know they won't be worried...they barely know me."

"What's the matter dear?" Margaret asked.

Samantha thought of ways to express herself without incriminating John Kendall any further when she said, "The family I left in Oklahoma are in a bad way. They work hard, but I'm afraid they don't do much better than survive. They have a mortgage."

Samantha hesitated again before saying, "Mr. Kendall gave me money to help with school. I have plenty, and I can find a job. I felt guilty taking the money, but I've felt even more guilty knowin' they're back home struggling. I was wondering if you could help me wire some money…to help out."

Samantha did not reveal that John Kendall was the man who held the mortgage and had used his financial leverage over the Hellwigs to coerce Samantha away from Jonathan.

"Of course, I can," Margaret replied, impressed by Samantha's kind heart. "You're a good girl. We'll go to town this morning and take care of it."

"Thank you," Samantha smiled.

"Do you feel better now?" Margaret asked.

"Some," Samantha replied.

CHAPTER 64

SAMANTHA WIRED MONEY TO the Hellwigs in Keokuk Falls for their mortgage. Helping her family seemed the right thing to do, and she had never felt comfortable accepting John Kendall's money. Margaret invited Samantha to her quilting club, but the young girl politely declined and decided to take a walk in the afternoon sunshine. Samantha strolled casually through town looking at window displays and enjoying the day.

In a window, Samantha saw a "help wanted" sign and stopped to inquire about the position. The pharmacy was a cluttered assortment of apothecary items on one side and a soda fountain on the other with cosmetics and home remedies in between. The store seemed vacant, and Samantha thought the store might be closed for lunch before hearing rustling sounds from the back.

"Can I help you?" a man who looked to be in his early thirties asked.

Samantha cleared her throat and said, "I noticed the sign on the door said, 'Help Wanted.'"

"Yes," the man said as he straightened his apron. "You have a brother or perhaps your husband's looking for work?"

"No," Samantha explained. "I was thinking of work for myself."

"Oh," the man replied. "I've always hired young men in the past. The job requires making deliveries, and I need someone who can ride a bicycle."

"I can ride," Samantha claimed, although she had never ridden a bicycle.

"I'm sorry," the man said with a sympathetic tilt to his head. "I've always hired men, and I'm looking for someone who might be interested in learning pharmacy."

"I would be interested," Samantha boldly proclaimed.

The man looked around the empty store and said politely, "But you're a woman. Perhaps you could try the dress store across the street or maybe the telephone company?"

Samantha did not want to argue, but remembered a brochure she had seen and said, "Women go to school to become pharmacists. I received a pamphlet from the University of Oklahoma saying it was a wonderful profession for women."

The man looked at her carefully and then asked, "Are you from Oklahoma?"

"Yes, sir."

"That explains the accent," the man said with a smirk. "What brings you here looking for work?"

Samantha was always guarded about questions related to her trip to Michigan, but she replied, "I'm staying with relatives and plan to attend college at Hope in the fall."

"It's a good school," the man said. "Again, I'm sorry, but you're just not what I had in mind."

"Any chance of you changing your mind?" Samantha smiled.

"You're an outspoken young lady," the man grinned.

"Yes, sir."

The man looked around the empty store again before saying, "Most of the young men in town have either signed up for the navy or been drafted into the army. I guess maybe I can't be too picky. I'm Isaac Vandaveer, this is my store."

Isaac Vandaveer walked up to Samantha with a noticeable limp favoring his right leg. He was of medium build, with brown hair, and would have been the most average-looking man if not for the limp. Not knowing exactly how to greet the young woman, Isaac awkwardly stuck out his hand.

"The job pays seventy-five cents a day, and the winters can be brutal," Isaac Vandaveer explained. "Why don't you try it for a week or two, and we'll see how things work out?"

"Really?" Samantha squealed while grabbing his hand to shake it.

Isaac nodded his head and said, "Can you start tomorrow?"

"I can start today," Samantha excitedly affirmed.

"I got things under control today," he smiled. "Tomorrow will be fine."

"Thank you, Mr. Vandaveer," Samantha smiled.

"Please, just call me Isaac," he admonished. "I'm too young to feel like an old man."

Samantha nodded before heading out the door when, Isaac asked, "Can you really ride a bicycle?"

With a confident grin, Samantha said, "I'm going to learn right now."

Samantha left the pharmacy feeling as if she were walking on air as she practically ran to the Kendall house several blocks away. After changing clothes, she rummaged through the storage building and found an old bicycle. After several tries in the grass, Samantha was able to control the wobbly bicycle enough to head down the road. She steered west down a gravel street running parallel to Lake Macatawa, a large inland body of water connected to Lake Michigan by a canal.

After twenty minutes, the road ended and Samantha came to a clumsy halt at the foot of a sand dune. The brisk breeze blew fine sand into her face, causing her to turn her head for protection. The chirp of gulls in the wind was accented by the crash of waves on the other side of the dune. Samantha could not believe how quickly she had been able to ride to the beach. Leaning her bicycle against a tree, she athletically climbed the shifting sand until she reached the pinnacle and could see Lake Michigan stretching out into the western horizon.

Samantha breathed deeply admiring the view for a moment before skipping down the steep sandy slope to the water's edge. Samantha was in such a good mood she did not care if she tumbled down the dune, she was happy just to be in this moment — temporarily away from the painful memories of the past weeks. Removing her shoes, Samantha danced with the waves as she stepped into the wet sand and tried to beat the large waves cresting on the sandy beach. After she tired of wading in the waves, Samantha dried her feet and decided to walk out on the pier to the lighthouse at the opening to the canal.

The canal connecting the port in Lake Macatawa to Lake Michigan was dug by the Dutch immigrants when they first established the town of Holland in 1847. The first years of settlement had been hard, but the hardy people dug the canal as a testament to their persistence. At the end of a pier, a lighthouse guided ships through to the safety of the harbor. The lighthouse looked like a small house at the base with a tower for the light rising above. Painted pale yellow with a dark maroon base, the lighthouse had a steam whistle that could be heard in town on foggy nights. Samantha always felt the lighthouse looked lonely and strong at the same time. She liked to think of herself as being like the lighthouse and did not miss an opportunity to see it.

Samantha walked by the picturesque lighthouse and traversed the rocky barrier protecting the canal from the persistent waves. The breakwater stretched into Lake Michigan another two hundred yards. When Samantha reached the end of the pier, she faced the sun. With her eyes closed, she listened to restless waves crashing against the rocks. The churning water seemed to overwhelm her feelings of turmoil, and for the moment, her problems vanished, while she reveled in the nirvana of the moment.

"Don't fall in," a man's voice interrupted her peaceful meditations.

Turning around, Samantha faced a man who looked to be in his early twenties with dark, wavy hair and a fine, pencil mustache over an infectious smile. The man sported a white wool sweater and pleated khaki pants. A cap tilted confidently on his head and a colorful apricot scarf blew in the breeze. His eyes were hidden by dark sunglasses. Samantha could not speak as she stared at the attractive man.

"There's a strong riptide," the handsome man explained over the sound of the surf. "I wouldn't want you to fall in."

Samantha timidly took the man's hand and stepped back from the edge of the raging water.

"I'm Simon Dupree," the man smiled from behind his dark sunglasses.

Samantha was speechless for a moment before finally saying, "I'm Samantha Harvey."

"Nice to meet you Samantha," Simon casually replied as he looked over the crashing surf of Lake Michigan. "It's quite a sight, isn't it?"

"Yes," Samantha replied. "I never get tired of it."

"You're not from around here," the man suggested.

"Is it that obvious?" Samantha asked.

"It's the accent," Simon explained. "Texas?"

"No!" Samantha exclaimed. "Oklahoma."

"Oklahoma," the man said mockingly. "Are you Indian?"

"Nooo..." Samantha confusingly stammered.

Simon Dupree flashed a broad grin and said, "The light hair and blue eyes should've tipped me off."

"You were kidding," Samantha dejectedly replied.

"I was," he laughed. "What brings you to the shores of Lake Michigan?"

"I'm going to school in the fall...at Hope College," Samantha answered. "I'm staying with...some relatives this summer."

"My family owns the house on the hill," Simon said pointing at a large white house on the hill.

"It's lovely," Samantha said, as she shielded her eyes from the sun and looked up the hill.

"The view's spectacular," Simon said.

"I bet," Samantha replied. "How long have you lived in Holland?"

"I don't live here," Simon informed. "My family's from Chicago. This is a vacation home."

Samantha looked at the palatial home and could not imagine anyone needing more than one home so fine.

"We come here for a week in the spring to see the flowers bloom and for a month during July," Simon explained. "It's a great place to get away...when it's not winter."

"I'd love to see it," Samantha said before thinking the request was too presumptive.

"Do you have a minute?" Simon asked.

Samantha hesitated before saying, "Sure."

Simon confidently led Samantha by the hand, off the pier, and helped her up the steep dune to a set of stairs leading to the house. A large deck adorned the back of the house, and Samantha took a deep breath before looking out over the lake and miles of tan beaches.

"It's breathtaking!" Samantha exclaimed.

"It's a wonderful place to watch a sunset," Simon smiled.

"I would never want to leave," Samantha noted.

"It makes for a nice vacation from the city," Simon replied.

Samantha could not see anyone around until Simon invited her into the stately home. Inside the house, a butler and maid busily dusted and moved furniture.

"Are you having a party?" Samantha asked, as she watched the two workers busily attending to their tasks.

Simon laughed, "We will in about a month. They're getting the house ready to shut down. The family has already headed back to Chicago. I'm leaving tomorrow."

"Oh," Samantha sighed.

"Do you have plans tonight?" Simon asked.

"No," Samantha answered.

"How about I take you out this evening?" Simon suggested. "It's my last night in town."

"I don't know," Samantha hesitated. "I'd have to ask...the woman I'm staying with, but I don't see that she would mind."

"Where are you staying?" Simon asked. "I'll come by about seven...just in case she says yes."

Samantha laughed at Simon's easy charm and jotted down the address. After saying good-bye, Samantha took her shoes off to walk down the steep sand dune to her bicycle parked below. As she mounted her bicycle to peddle home, she glanced up at the large house on the hill to see Simon Dupree waving from his deck.

CHAPTER 65

"SIMON DUPREE!" MARGARET KENDALL shrieked. "You're telling me Simon Dupree is coming here?"

"Yes," Samantha replied. "I hope that's all right?"

"All right?" Margaret repeated. "Here I've been wondering how to find you a man with this war going on, and you went and found the biggest fish in the sea on your own!"

Samantha looked puzzled, as Margaret explained, "The Duprees own ships, oil, and…well, about anything else you could own in the Midwest. They bought that old Van Antwerp place like I'd go to town and buy a shawl. Simon Dupree is the most eligible bachelor in Chicago if not the whole country! And he's coming to see you?"

"If that's okay?" Samantha said.

Fanning herself, Margaret said, "Of course its okay…only I've got to straighten this place up."

For the next hour, Margaret Kendall inspected and cleaned every inch of her always spotless house. Samantha tried to help, until Margaret demanded she go upstairs to get ready. Mr. Kendall sat patiently in the living room without saying a word. His calm demeanor contrasted to Margaret's frantic antics amused Samantha, as she walked up the stairs. He looked like an old sailor weathering a squall, as Margaret worked around him. Samantha could barely get ready because Margaret kept coming in to give her suggestions on dresses, hair, and even make-up, which Samantha did not usually wear.

Margaret also gave Samantha some conversational advice by saying, "You know I love you dear, but promise me one thing—please, please try not to be so outspoken tonight."

"You've always told me to be myself," Samantha coyly replied.

"I know, I know," Margaret frantically instructed. "Only...Only don't feel obligated to say everything you think...Try to develop *his* interest."

Samantha replied with a fake salute and said, "Don't worry...I'll shut up and listen just for this one night."

Before Margaret could give more advice, a knock on the door caused her to whisper, "He's here!"

The rotund Margaret pulled up the hem of her skirt and hustled down the stairs with more agility than Samantha would have thought possible. When the more leisurely Samantha arrived down the stairs, Margaret anxiously waited to answer the door. After Margaret's overly polite welcome and George Kendall's equally apathetic greeting, the dapper Simon Dupree offered Samantha his arm and walked her to a large car. Margaret Kendall discreetly watched out the window until the automobile vanished around the corner.

"They didn't ask you to go along?" George Kendall asked with a mocking deadpan tone, as he read his evening paper.

"What?" Margaret asked somewhat frustrated at her husband.

"I thought maybe you'd go with them," Mr. Kendall said. "It looked to me like you were more excited than Samantha."

"Of course I'm excited," Margaret Kendall stated bluntly. "Who wouldn't be excited about a handsome, rich suitor like Simon Dupree calling?"

"He's not a suitor," George observed. "He's a man on vacation that's having supper with a pretty girl."

"How can you be so indifferent?" Margaret asked.

Mr. Kendall put down the paper and said seriously, "I'm not indifferent about the girl. She seems sensible and...a very good girl. I've grown fond of her. Have you forgotten what happened to my brother in that very same house?"

"Samantha's different," Margaret defended. "She's not like your brother."

"I'll grant that," George replied. "But people with money don't change. The boy's family won't be excited about a girl like Samantha no matter how much we dress her up in respectability. I just don't want to see her get hurt."

Margaret rarely lost her temper, but answered hotly, "You're old fashioned and stuck in the past. Families don't marry their children off like royalty in the dark ages. I've seen Simon's eyes—he fancies her."

"Fancying a girl and marrying her are two different things," George noted.

"You're wrong," Margaret blurted out in frustration.

George Kendall took a moment before saying softly, "I hope I am...for Samantha's sake, I hope I'm as wrong as can be."

Margaret did not have the energy to argue with her husband, so she let him return to his paper while she continued to fiddle with the details of her front room. After an hour, Margaret made a point to look out the window every fifteen minutes to check for traffic. After two hours, Margaret heard a car door shut. Before she could peek out the window, the door opened and Samantha entered. Margaret's presence startled Samantha.

"Well?" Margaret asked anxiously. "Is he coming in?"

"No," Samantha said. "He's leaving for Chicago on the early train so he's headed back."

Margaret could not hide her disappointment as she asked, "Where did you go?"

"He took me to the little restaurant by the lake," Samantha replied. "He had the chef make me a special dish…and had a violinist at the table."

Looking at her husband who was still looking over the paper, Margaret said, "It sounds like this boy might like you a little."

"Oh…I don't know," Samantha smiled shyly. "He drove me out by the lake to see the moonlight on the water."

"And then?" Margaret prodded.

"And then he drove me home," Samantha explained curtly.

"Will he see you again?" Margaret asked.

"I don't know," Samantha replied. "I suppose we might run into each other when he comes back in July. It's a small town, and he said he would be back then."

"Did you hear that?" Margaret said to her husband who did not respond.

Samantha watched Margaret's enthusiasm and said, "I'm tired…I'm going to turn in."

"Okay," an almost giddy Margaret replied although she was eager for more details.

As Samantha walked upstairs, George Kendall watched his young guest acting more indifferent to her social encounter than he would have thought. Samantha reached the top of the stairs and closed her door before crying quietly into her trembling hands. Simon Dupree was polite and considerate despite his tendency to talk about himself. It had been Samantha's idea to drive to the beach to see the moonlight flicker off the waves. She had not been prepared for him to kiss her so aggressively. Simon was a very self-assured man, and Samantha tried to convince herself that he had not been out of line.

Samantha continued to cry quietly as she buried her head into her pillow. The kiss bothered her because it reminded her of the feelings she shared with Jonathan and the guilt she now felt for so many things. As much as she tried to put Jonathan out of her mind, it seemed everything, including a kiss, reminded her of him. She had liked Simon Dupree and believed he had liked her too, but she was less than confident her reaction would entice him to call again. Her emotions were like one of the crashing waves of Lake Michigan, and Samantha wondered if she would ever feel calm again. As she lay in her dark room holding her pillow to muffle her sobbing, all she could think to do was cry.

CHAPTER 66

SAMANTHA SOON FORGOT HER inexperienced response to Simon Dupree's kiss as she began her new job at the pharmacy. Margaret Kendall had not been excited about her working, but George thought it was a sensible thing for a girl to learn a skill. The first few days had been rough, as she struggled to find addresses in the strange town and learn a new job. She expected Isaac Vandaveer would let her go after the first week, but he was a patient and kind man who Samantha found easy to like.

Isaac Vandaveer was in his early thirties, with strong arms and a compassionate face. Although he was not a handsome man, he was very pleasant and well groomed. Samantha could tell immediately that he related well to his customers.

After a few weeks, Isaac began explaining some of the rudimentary principles of pharmacy. Samantha had never worked anywhere but the farm, but with Isaac's help she adjusted well and soon picked up his knack of building a positive rapport with people who came into the store.

In late June of 1917, Mr. Vandaveer spent many hours reading journals to come up with substitutes for chemicals and drugs that were not available because of the war. He was on a stepstool stocking the shelves when Samantha heard a loud crash, as he fell and sprawled awkwardly on the floor.

"I'm all right!" Isaac frantically informed as he struggled to regain his feet.

Samantha gasped as she rounded the counter and saw him on the floor with his pant leg ripped from the fall.

Isaac tried hurriedly to pick himself up from the floor when Samantha said, "Let me help."

"No!" Isaac replied in a stern and panicked voice, "I can do it."

Samantha watched as Isaac righted himself using his thick arms before reaching down and straightening his artificial right leg that had been knocked askew during the fall. Samantha did not know what to do as she looked helplessly at him. She could not ignore the man's unique feature but felt she could not ask about the missing leg. Samantha had noticed Isaac's noticeable limp from her first meeting with him, but he had managed so well that in a short time Samantha viewed the limp as normal.

"I'm sorry you had to see that," Isaac finally sighed. "It must be a shock."

"No," Samantha stammered. "Are you okay?"

Isaac checked the wooden leg to make sure he was balanced and said, "Yeah...I'm fine."

"What happened?" Samantha asked.

"I reached a little too high and tripped," Isaac explained.

"No," Samantha flatly asked. "What happened to your leg?"

Isaac had become accustomed to his young employee's tendency to speak her mind, when he answered lightheartedly, "You mean my friend 'Woody?'"

Samantha nodded and watched carefully as Isaac knocked on the wooden leg.

Seeing the store was empty for a few minutes, Isaac said, "You didn't think I was always a pharmacist did you? I used to cut wood when I was younger. Hard work, but the money was good. I was trying to figure out what to do with my life, and cuttin' timber gave me plenty of time to think. Thing was, I thought too much and didn't pay attention enough. A tree got uphill from me and rolled over my leg and crushed it flat. The doc couldn't do anything but cut it off and fit me with this when I was seventeen. Me and Woody have been a pair since then."

"I'm so sorry," Samantha groaned thinking of the painful accident.

"I don't think much about it anymore," Isaac shrugged. "It helped me figure out what I wanted to do. I spent months in the hospital and asked questions about the medicine. I was squeamish about blood, but mixing the medicines seemed useful and something I could do. That was eleven years ago, and I own my store now, so things could be worse."

"That's a good attitude," Samantha noted.

"Attitude's about how you deal with things not about the things that happen to you," Isaac smiled. "Now, since you know my secret, I won't mind asking you to put these canisters on the top shelf for me."

Samantha smiled at Isaac's good nature and climbed on a chair to complete the task. Samantha learned over the next several weeks that Isaac had borrowed the money from his father to buy the store and was going to have him paid back in two years. Isaac had grown up in Holland and still liked to go to the pier to fish, saying it was the only sport he could really excel at with one leg. Spring turned to summer, and Samantha began thinking she might want to study pharmacy. Isaac gave her tips on courses to take and even went with her to Hope College to enroll. The day Samantha enrolled in Hope College should have been one of the happiest of her stay in Holland, but even Isaac Vandaveer could tell something was bothering his young helper.

"What's wrong?" Isaac asked as they walked slowly across the park and toward the store.

"Nothing," Samantha replied as she stared at the gravel walkway in front of her.

After a few more steps, Isaac said, "I've always thought you had trouble keeping your thoughts to yourself, but I'm learning you're even worse at keeping your feelings hidden."

Samantha smiled at her boss's good-natured coaxing and finally said, "Enrolling today caused me to think of home for some reason."

Samantha had been reminded during the enrollment process that John Kendall had paid for her tuition. It had been weeks since she had thought about the tragic events that sent her to Michigan. Samantha could not think of the cold-hearted John Kendall without remembering her beloved Jonathan. For the first time in days, Samantha thought about Jonathan, wondering where he was and if he was safe. So many of the young men had been sent to fight in the war, and she was sure Isaac Vandaveer would have been there as well if not for his accident.

"Homesick?" Isaac asked.

"Not really," Samantha smiled, trying to be pleasant. "I appreciate your help today."

"It was no trouble," Isaac replied. "I think you'll do very well at Hope."

Samantha appreciated the encouragement but was not in the mood to talk. She enjoyed the summer day, and Isaac was content to escort her silently back to the store.

CHAPTER 67

ISAAC VANDAVEER DROVE SAMANTHA to the lake to watch fireworks on the Fourth of July. It was a warm summer day, and people cooled themselves by wading or swimming in the lake. To Samantha, it was nothing like the hot summers she was used to in Oklahoma, and she could not imagine getting more than her ankles wet in Lake Michigan's surf. Isaac had many friends, and Samantha enjoyed exploring the dunes and beaches on the holiday.

The Fourth of July was particularly patriotic this year. The Americans had sent their first symbolic troops to Europe, but the vast majority of the American army was located in camps across the country training and trying to acquire adequate equipment for the battles to come. The breeze was light this evening as Samantha watched the sun set across the small waves tickling the sandy beaches.

"Do you want to watch the fireworks from the hill?" Simon Dupree asked as he walked up behind Samantha.

"You're back," Samantha commented, as she turned to see Simon.

"Every July," he smiled pleasantly. "How about it? The view's wonderful up there."

"I don't know," Samantha replied. "I rode here with a friend."

"Not a boyfriend, I hope," Simon teased.

No," Samantha clarified. "Actually my boss drove me."

Seeing no one around, Simon said, "Then I'd be doing him a favor by taking you home later."

"I suppose," Samantha reasoned. "Give me a minute to find him, and I'll be back."

"I'll wait," Simon pleasantly answered.

In a few moments, Samantha located Isaac and informed him she had a ride back to town. Isaac questioned her since the beach was nearly five miles from town, but Samantha assured him she had a ride and headed back to find Simon. He stood in ankle deep water with his pant legs rolled up, looking like a picture in a magazine.

"Are you ready?" Simon eagerly asked. "It'll be dark soon."

"Let's go," Samantha smiled.

Simon took Samantha by the hand and led her up the sand dune toward the Dupree house on top of the hill. Once they arrived, about two dozen fashionably dressed people, with servants taking care of their every whim, stood casually on the deck. A band played, and all the partygoers looked over the crowd of people below like Greek gods watching from Olympus.

"Here," Simon said, as he grabbed a glass from a man wearing a white jacket.

Taking a sip, Samantha asked, "What is it?"

"Champagne, silly," Simon laughed.

"I don't drink," Samantha said nervously.

"It's not liquor," Simon assured. "It's like grape juice with bubbles."

Samantha took another sip of the pleasant, yet slightly bitter drink that tickled her nose.

"It's good," she smiled.

Someone called Simon's name from inside the house, and he left Samantha standing alone on the edge of the large deck overlooking Lake Michigan and the beach. Samantha normally exuded an assured demeanor, but looking around at the other guests, she felt terribly out of place in her simple cotton dress. She was thankful the others seemed to ignore her presence and Samantha was content to remain invisible standing with her arms folded looking over the lake. As twilight seduced the first rocket to paint the darkening sky, Samantha looked at the house to see Simon talking to an older woman who she assumed was his mother. The woman had a stern glare and did not look happy. Before Samantha could look away, she made eye contact with the woman and felt she might be the reason for the woman's grumpy appearance.

Samantha sighed heavily and turned back to the peaceful scenery of the lake. She was frustrated at herself for letting little things like an unkind look cause her to remember the way John Kendall had made her feel when he tried to separate her from Jonathan. Samantha was thankful she was not left alone to her thoughts for too long, as Simon returned to her side.

"Is everything okay?" Samantha asked.

"Peachy," the cocky Simon said. "I just had to take care of a small matter inside."

Looking back at the house, Samantha noticed the stern-looking woman watching her, but the woman turned away upon seeing Samantha.

"Is that your mother?" Samantha asked.

A surprised Simon turned to see the woman standing in the window and said, "Yes."

"She's not coming out?" Samantha inquired.

Simon smiled and said, "My mother endures the beach house more than enjoys it. She much prefers being inside."

A loud bang indicated the show was about to begin as Simon said, "I'm glad you decided to come. I hope you enjoy the view."

Samantha smiled pleasantly, as the deck perched high above the lake, gave her an excellent view of the fireworks illuminating the night sky. By the time the show ended with a large orange burst and a loud boom, the sky was completely dark, and most of the partygoers had returned to their libations and self-interested conversations.

"Well?" Simon asked. "What did you think?"

"You were right," Samantha replied. "It was a spectacular view. I'll have to admit, though, I like seeing the moonlight glistening off the water and dunes just as much."

"I never get tired of the lake," Simon nodded. "You know there's a legend about these dunes?"

"No," Samantha answered.

Simon smiled mischievously and said, "It's an old Indian tale, but it's a good one."

"I'm listening," Samantha replied.

"Black Lake," Simon began, "that's what Macatawa means, was on the border between the Ottawa and Potawatomi tribes before the Dutch came. The Ottawa were traders, and the Potawatomi, farmers. The Ottawa decided to build a village on the south side of Black Lake near the Great Lake so they could travel easily up and down the coast. After the first winter, the villagers got sick, and all but a few left the coast for the winter and traveled inland. When they returned in the spring, the village was gone...swallowed up by the sand dunes."

"That's not true?" Samantha sheepishly asked.

Simon laughed and said, "Probably not, but it makes a good story. They say you can go to the dunes in the moonlight and hear the moans from the lost village."

Samantha looked at him skeptically as Simon asked, "Do you want to see if it's true?"

Looking around at the party where she felt out of place, Samantha said, "Sure."

Simon took another drink of champagne and led her down the stairs to the sandy dunes. Almost all the people from town had headed back to town and the beach was nearly empty. A few hundred yards from the shore, Simon took Samantha by the hand and led her into the dunes.

Once they were isolated, Simon whispered, "Listen."

Samantha listened carefully but could hear nothing but the gentle shifting of sand in the light breeze. Without warning, Simon threw his arms around Samantha and kissed her roughly.

"What are you doing?" Samantha asked harshly, as she pushed him away.

Simon grinned impishly and replied, "That's the real legend of the dunes. You tell a pretty girl about the Indian legend and then she...well she's more likely to want to get close."

Simon lunged at Samantha again as his carefree persona changed. Simon grabbed her arm forcefully and pulled her to him.

"Stop it!" Samantha shouted. "You're drunk!"

Ignoring her, Simon gruffly wrestled with her causing her to fall on the soft sand ripping the sleeve of her dress.

Samantha righted herself immediately and screamed angrily, "You've torn my dress!"

Simon answered unemotionally, "I'll buy you another."

"Stop it!" Samantha shrieked again, as he grabbed her and pushed her back into the sand.

"What are you doing?" Samantha cried, as Simon grabbed her again.

Samantha screamed as loud as she could to attract the attention of the partygoers at the house, but the wind whistling through the sand dunes muffled her pleas. She managed to push Simon away again and tried to run in the thick sand. Samantha could hear the frightful sound of Simon's footsteps following close behind as he let out a strange, awful laugh.

"You local girls are all the same," Simon sneered. "Perfectly happy to drink my champagne, but then you won't play the game. You're just another tease."

A frightened Samantha ran futilely through the sand as she cried in terror. She looked back to see how close her attacker was, when a strong arm suddenly wrapped around her.

Samantha could see Simon Dupree several steps behind and was confused until she heard the angry voice of Isaac Vandaveer shout, "Whatever game you're playing...doesn't look fun."

"Mind your own business," Simon demanded as he tried to push by Isaac.

Isaac moved Samantha behind him and grabbed Simon by the collar. Simon, who was slightly intoxicated, tried to struggle but could not break the hold.

"Leave the girl be!" Isaac shouted in a tone of voice Samantha had never heard from the soft-spoken man.

Simon finally broke away from Isaac's hold and staggered back in the sand.

The agitated Simon squinted into the moonlight and scoffed, "You're that one-legged soda jerk. Get out of here. Don't you know who I am?"

"I do," Isaac confirmed, as Samantha cowered behind him, "but you're going to leave the girl alone."

Simon laughed casually before taking a swing. Isaac moved his head just enough to dodge the blow before savagely landing a right hand on the side of Simon Dupree's head. Simon was momentarily stunned and then angrily charged before Isaac landed another punch to his midsection causing Simon to crumple to the ground.

"Are you okay?" Isaac asked Samantha.

Samantha nodded as Isaac took her arm and led her out of the dunes. Isaac glanced back a couple of times to make sure Simon would not follow, but Isaac had taken the fight out of him. Samantha tried not to cry, but as it became clear she was out of danger, it was more difficult. Isaac did not stop and did not let go of her arm until he reached the car and put her inside.

Samantha could tell her employer was agitated as she said, "I'm sorry."

"You're not the one that needs to be sorry," Isaac replied. "I shouldn't have left you alone."

"It was my fault," Samantha said. "I met him last month and he seemed to be a nice guy."

"Simon Dupree is no 'nice guy,'" Isaac bluntly stated.

"I know that, now," Samantha answered, trying not to cry.

Isaac handed Samantha a handkerchief and sighed, "Here, use this to wipe your face."

Samantha wiped her tears and some of the sand from her face, while still shaking from the fright.

Isaac put the car in gear and drove away from the beach without questioning Samantha further.

"How did you find me?" Samantha finally asked.

"I decided I needed to make sure you got home," Isaac explained. "I drove you, so I felt responsible. When Margaret said you hadn't made it back from the beach, I was afraid you had gotten left behind. I just happened to be close enough to hear your scream."

"Thank you," Samantha said.

In a few minutes, Isaac Vandaveer delivered Samantha to the safety of the Kendall home. Samantha was able to sneak into her room without being questioned by Margaret Kendall. She quietly cleaned herself up and got to bed where she cried softly into her pillow. She thought of how terrified she had been of Simon Dupree and how much she wished to be back in Oklahoma. Beneath his veneer of chivalry, Simon Dupree was a beast. Samantha swore she would never make herself vulnerable again, even if that meant she never left the safety of her room.

CHAPTER 68

SAMANTHA AWOKE AT DAWN dreading work for the first time since she started her job. She almost convinced herself she was sick, but eventually dragged herself out of bed and made her way downstairs. Margaret Kendall busily prepared breakfast and seemed in high spirits, which made Samantha feel a little better. After delaying as long as possible, Samantha rode her bicycle to the alley behind the drugstore.

Isaac Vandaveer said hello, as he did every morning, and went about his work as if nothing had happened the night before. Samantha was quieter than normal and appreciated her boss's efforts to let her be alone that day. There was a delivery by the lake that afternoon, but Isaac made some excuse to drive his car and let Samantha stay in the store.

As the weeks went by, the incident faded into memory and Samantha went about her work. Isaac, knowing Samantha would be going to school in the fall, hired a young boy to make deliveries, which meant Samantha spent most of her time inside the safety of the pharmacy. It was a warm summer in 1917, but Samantha did not make any more trips to the beach and was content to stay in town away from the tourists.

Summer passed, and Samantha started school at Hope College, moving out of the Kendall house and into a dorm. Isaac Vandaveer let her work part-time, but most of her days were spent in class and reading in the evenings. Samantha took nursing courses that fall and joined the Women's Suffrage Association at Hope, but school quickly became routine for the freshman. Margaret Kendall fussed about Samantha moving on campus when her house was only blocks away, but Samantha felt it was time for her to make it on her own. Samantha saw Margaret regularly, however, and the older woman would fuss at Samantha's lack of social life. Samantha claimed her studies kept her busy, but in reality, there were not many young men left in town, and she was afraid to make herself vulnerable to most of the men she met.

As the days of autumn shortened, the massive trees of western Michigan turned into bright shades of yellow and red. Samantha had been accustomed to the short Cross Timber forest of Oklahoma where the trees turn to shades of brown, but the fall foliage of this northern forest was spectacular.

Autumn quickly turned to winter, and Samantha was not prepared for the first snow coming before Thanksgiving. Fortunately, Margaret Kendall came to the rescue to take Samantha shopping and made sure her young friend had warm winter clothing. Christmas was a hard time for Samantha. Isaac let her help with a gift display in the drugstore, which kept her busy, but the nights were long, and she began missing home—although she was not sure where home was any longer. It was Samantha's first Christmas without Papa, and as much as she tried to keep her mind occupied, memories of Papa and Jonathan Kendall made her glum. She had not heard from anyone in Oklahoma and did not even know where Jonathan was, but she missed the young man who had been more than a dear friend.

The Holland winter was long and hard with weather colder than Samantha had ever experienced. She longed for the warmth of spring, but the winter seemed to last forever. By the time April 1, 1918 arrived, Samantha had been in Holland a full year. There were many things she loved about her new home at Hope College, but the anniversary of leaving Oklahoma was bitter. She made dear friends in Margaret Kendall and Isaac Vandaveer, but as the days got longer, she found herself more and more wondering what her life might have been.

CHAPTER 69

JONATHAN KENDALL LOOKED OVER the rows of tents that comprised Camp Bowie and wondered if he would ever get to Europe to fight. Earlier conflicts between the Texas troops and the Oklahoma troops slowly vanished as Camp Bowie became the home of the 36th division of the American Expeditionary Force. The soldiers learned they had a common enemy at Camp Bowie, although they did not know in the early spring of 1918 if the enemy was the Germans or the United States Army.

Conditions had been brutal in the camp as thousands of soldiers became ill. Over a hundred died in camp from various diseases. Worse than the harsh living conditions and the sickness, which caused the camp to be quarantined, was the inability of the army to provide equipment for training. Morale finally improved once ten miles of trenches were dug for training and a rifle range was opened.

By March, troops engaged in realistic war games in addition to constant drills, hikes, rifle practices, and inspections. The practice fighting resulted in sprains, bruises, black eyes, and bloody noses as soldiers resorted to using rocks, fists, and slingshots during the skirmishes. The training tried to create realism with smoke bombs and explosions adding to the confusion. In May, ten men died when an errant mortar shell exploded in the trenches. The loss of comrades in training was a painful lesson in the realities of war. Training intensified as troops practiced all phases of modern warfare, including assaults with bayonets and fearsome-looking trench knives. Soldiers made the frantic charges shouting loudly, which must have sounded like the old rebel yell of Texas troops from fifty years earlier.

July 3, 1918, was the day for which Jonathan and the rest of the 36th Division had waited for nearly a year—the orders to break camp and head to Europe came with great celebration. Bugles blew and bands played, as trucks rumbled and troops marched to the trains for the five-day trip to New York City. The soldiers, many of whom had never seen a building over three stories tall, gawked in awe at the city's impressive skyline. The troops had no time to explore New York as they were quickly shipped to Camp Merritt in New Jersey to await transport ships.

Jonathan feared another long delay, but in two days, his company was herded onto a ship for the twelve-day journey. The ships were crowded with bunks stacked four-high, but Jonathan was in a cabin, which provided some privacy. Before the voyage to Europe, the mail caught up to Jonathan with a letter from Elizabeth Conklin. Jonathan found a quiet corner on the deck of the hectic ship before carefully opening the letter.

Jonathan looked at the letter with a feeling of melancholy. As much as he enjoyed Elizabeth's informative correspondence, the letters reminded him of Samantha Harvey. A year had passed since Jonathan had heard from the girl who wrote him so faithfully while he was in San Benito. As much as he tried to forget Samantha, it seemed she was still on his mind. Before opening the letter, Jonathan reached into his jacket pocket to retrieve a worn photograph of Samantha. Jonathan looked at the picture with thoughts of tossing it overboard, but after a few moments, he carefully placed it back in his pocket and began reading the letter.

Elizabeth Conklin promised a big surprise in the greeting, but began by detailing events happening in Chandler. The war dominated the community's attention, and the town was eager for any news about the boys from home. Jonathan grimaced at how unglamorous his service had been so far.

Turning the page, Jonathan gasped in surprise as Elizabeth wrote that Caroline was now married. Jonathan had heard Caroline met a man in Oklahoma City from earlier letters. Elizabeth wrote earlier that his younger sister was engaged, but the actual marriage shocked him. Elizabeth said Augusta had been the bridesmaid at the wedding held in the Presbyterian Church on Silk Stocking Row. The couple lived in Oklahoma City, where Caroline's husband managed some kind of business.

Jonathan put the letter in his lap and closed his eyes to visualize how his sister must have looked. After a few deep breaths, he realized he was once again imagining how Samantha would have appeared as his bride. Putting the letter away, Jonathan looked at a crescent moon and felt alone.

"We're finally going!" an excited Lee Gilstrap said enthusiastically, as he interrupted Jonathan's moment of solitude.

Lee Gilstrap was one of the men from the old Company B in Chandler for which Jonathan was still responsible. The seventeen-year-old Lee was always eager. Some of the company had been reassigned at Camp Bowie, and Captain Gilstrap had been promoted to Colonel, working as a staff officer at divisional headquarters.

"Yes, we are," Jonathan smiled. "What are you doing on deck?"

"I wanted to see the ocean," Lee answered.

"Why don't you take a walk around the ship to burn off some of your energy," Jonathan suggested. "It'll be a long trip, Try to sleep, and it'll go by faster."

Lee nodded in agreement and began marching around the gangplank as instructed. Jonathan wondered if the hyperactive Lee could survive on the ship without driving his bunkmates crazy. As

Lee disappeared, Jonathan peered over the ocean and looked up at the moon once again, wondering where his Samantha might be.

CHAPTER 70

"You seem distracted today," Isaac Vandaveer observed as a customer left the store.

Samantha Harvey had finished her first year of school and had come back to work at Mr. Vandaveer's drugstore for the summer. It was a slow day, so she cleaned the countertop at the soda fountain when Mr. Vandaveer had noticed her rubbing the same spot for an extended period.

"I'm fine," Samantha shrugged.

Isaac Vandaveer had worked with Samantha long enough to understand her tendency to daydream. Working at the store provided time for the two to know each other, and they had formed a strong friendship. When Samantha became lost in thought, it usually meant she was thinking about her past in Oklahoma. Isaac knew a lot about the young woman, but sometimes felt he really did not know anything. He decided this was one of the times that silence would be appreciated, so he did not press her further.

In a few minutes, the front door opened and a strikingly beautiful woman entered the pharmacy. The woman looked to be in her early twenties, but she had an air of sophistication that superseded her years. She was of medium height with rich brown hair and sharp brown eyes. Her face was delicate with thick red lips and high cheekbones. Samantha believed she might have had the most perfect complexion she had ever seen.

"Can I help you?" Isaac Vandaveer cheerfully offered as he clumsily got off his ladder and limped toward the attractive woman.

"I'm looking for Dioxogen," the woman smiled. "My fiancé scratched his hand, and he's such a baby."

"Sure," Mr. Vandaveer said, as he went behind the counter to retrieve a bottle.

Samantha noticed the elegant woman wore a large diamond on her left hand.

As the woman waited, she turned to Samantha and said, "I'll have a Coca Cola, too."

Samantha slipped behind the counter and proceeded to fill the order when the doorbell rang again. The crash of the glass on the hard tile floor echoed in the small store as Samantha quickly cowered behind the counter trying to hide.

"Did you find it?" the pleasant voice of Simon Dupree asked.

"Yes," the pretty woman replied. "He's getting it now."

The store became silent as Isaac Vandaveer came face-to-face with Simon Dupree. Although Samantha tried to be inconspicuous behind the counter, the arrogant man spotted her and glared in embarrassment.

"Hurry," Simon muttered in a flustered tone. "I'll be in the car."

Simon Dupree made a quick exit from the store leaving the woman behind. Mr. Vandaveer handed the woman the bottle of antiseptic, and Samantha began cleaning up the mess from the broken glass she had dropped.

Taking the bottle, the woman said, "I see my fiancé has been here before."

Looking at Samantha behind the counter, she added, "Yes, I suspect he has made a visit or two."

Samantha tried to avoid the woman's stare but eventually noticed the judgmental glare.

The woman turned to Mr. Vandaveer and said, "Charge it to the Dupree account."

Samantha continued to clean her spill when the woman said, "Don't worry about the Coca Cola, dear. You've done quite enough."

The woman left as Samantha and Isaac Vandaveer looked at each other.

Samantha dutifully swept up the glass and said, "I'm sorry. I seem to be all thumbs today."

Isaac Vandaveer looked at her and in a caring tone said, "Are you okay, Samantha?"

Samantha smiled artificially and said, "Fine."

Isaac Vandaveer looked worriedly at the young girl but did not press her to elaborate on her feeling at seeing Simon Dupree and his fiancé. Samantha was quiet during the rest of the workday and at five o'clock began to straighten things up so Mr. Vandaveer could lock up the store.

"Why don't I walk you home tonight?" Isaac asked as he shut the front door.

He had never offered to walk her home before, but with Simon Dupree back in town for his July vacation, Samantha appreciated the offer. Samantha had a short walk to Margaret Kendall's house, where she was staying for the summer. It would have been easy for Isaac to drive her, but it was a beautiful day and he seemed to want to walk.

With Isaac's limp, the two made slow progress down the street, as Samantha took the extra time to gaze in shop windows. Isaac took her by the arm, like he was protecting a little girl as they crossed the street to walk across the park toward the Kendall house.

"Do you want to talk about it?" Isaac finally asked as they strolled through the park.

"About what?" Samantha answered nervously.

"Simon Dupree," Isaac responded.

"There's nothing to talk about," Samantha claimed.

Isaac walked across the park without saying more, but as the two headed down the block to Samantha's home he said, "You haven't gone to the beach or anywhere since that night. You go to school, you come to work, but that's no life. You can't let a man like that make you afraid."

"I'm not afraid of him," Samantha boldly lied. "I've got a lot of things on my mind. My life has been complicated the past year, and things haven't turned out like I planned. It's hard to understand."

Isaac took a few more steps and said, "I think I might understand a little. I don't know what's happened in your past, but I know a little bit about life not turning out like it's supposed to. You're talking to a man that walks with the help of a tree stump."

"I'm sorry," Samantha said. "I know you've overcome so much, and I admire you...I really do. I'm just not so sure I'm as brave as I once thought I was."

Stopping for a minute, Isaac said, "Life is what we make it. It's like a stage, and we're the characters. What's done is done...you have to learn to live for today."

Samantha nodded as she kept walking.

"Did I ever tell you I was engaged," Isaac asked.

"No," Samantha said with a tone of surprise. "You haven't."

"I don't like to talk about it," Isaac said defiantly. "I thought she loved me...she said she did, but she couldn't deal with this."

Isaac pointed at the wooden leg.

"I don't think I could blame her," he continued. "It wasn't what she had bargained for, but I learned that I couldn't depend on anyone but myself to be happy. I think you'd do well to learn that too."

Samantha was taking Isaac's instructions seriously when she suddenly stopped three houses down from the Kendall house and gasped, "Oh, no!"

CHAPTER 71

SAMANTHA LOOKED AS IF she had seen a ghost, as Isaac watched her face turn pale. She stood motionless, as a strange man sat on the Kendall porch.

"Who's that?" Isaac asked, as he strained to get a better look.

Samantha kept her eyes fixed on John Kendall sitting casually on the porch and said, "You asked earlier what bothered me...most of it involves that man."

Apathetically Samantha trudged toward John Kendall with lethargic dread, while Isaac followed. John Kendall did not see her until Samantha stepped to the edge of the yard. He put down his paper and nodded a speechless greeting.

Turning to Isaac, Samantha said, "Thank you for walking me home...and for the advice. I'll see you tomorrow."

"Do I need to stay?" Isaac asked, sensing Samantha's reluctance to see the man on the porch.

Samantha shook her head and said, "No...I'll see you at the store tomorrow."

As Isaac limped back toward downtown, John Kendall smiled artificially at Samantha, as she walked to the porch and said, "What are you doing here?"

"I came to pay your tuition for next year," John Kendall informed. "You haven't asked for more money, but I promised to take care of things."

"I'm managing fine," Samantha coldly replied.

"I hear," John said. "That was a nifty trick you played getting my money to the Hellwigs to pay off the mortgage. It made me wonder why you didn't come back to Oklahoma once I couldn't foreclose?"

"There's nothing for me there," Samantha replied.

"My brother tells me you're doing well," John said.

"George and Margaret have been very kind," Samantha stated.

"And the man?" John asked nodding toward Isaac Vandaveer limping away. "Isn't he a little old for you?"

"He's my boss," Samantha snapped. "I have a job."

"Impressive," John said.

There was an awkward silence before John Kendall said, "I just came to pay tuition...and check on you."

"You mean check to make sure I'm staying away from Chandler?" Samantha surmised.

"Yes," John replied. "Something like that."

After another uncomfortable silence, Samantha finally asked hesitantly, "Have you heard from...Jonathan?"

John Kendall looked at his shoes for a moment and said, "Jonathan and I...we don't talk. He's...he's got a girl in town now."

Samantha swallowed hard at the news as John Kendall continued, "Elizabeth Conklin...she's a girl he knew...before you."

"He told me," Samantha said softly. "Jonathan still doesn't know...he doesn't know about us?"

John Kendall shook his head and said, "No...Jonathan doesn't know you're his half-sister."

"I see," Samantha sighed.

"Elizabeth writes him regularly," John Kendall said. "She keeps me informed. He left last week for Europe."

"Jonathan hasn't been over there?" Samantha asked.

"No," John Kendall answered. "He's been training in Texas."

Samantha had a strange range of emotions as she listened to John Kendall's sketchy information about Jonathan. She felt relief knowing he had been safe all these months she had been worrying, but she also felt sad thinking of the letters she had written and received when he had been in Texas previously.

"For all I know he's in France now," John Kendall concluded.

"But Jonathan's safe as far as you know?" Samantha asked anxiously.

John Kendall nodded and said, "As far as I know."

In a slightly different tone John Kendall said, "Caroline's married...just last month."

"Married?" Samantha asked in surprise. "Not to David Simpson, I'm guessing?"

John Kendall's face twisted slightly as he replied, "No...I haven't seen David since the day you left town."

"Good for Caroline," Samantha said bravely. "I hope she's happy."

"How about you?" John Kendall asked. "Margaret tells me you've had a few men stalking around including a rich fellow from Chicago?"

"I have no one," Samantha informed. "I have school and my job...you've taken everything else."

John Kendall took the mild scolding and said, "I guess I deserved that."

"No!" Samantha said in a strong whisper. "You don't deserve anything. Everything I've done I've done for Jonathan."

John Kendall stood up and said, "Is there anything you need?"

"No," Samantha said. "Thank you for paying the tuition...I'll try to put it to good use."

"I bet you will," John Kendall smiled as he stepped off the porch.

"Aren't you staying here?" Samantha asked.

Looking back at the house, John Kendall said, "I've said all I have to say to my brother. It doesn't take long for us to catch up. I'm leaving on the early train tomorrow, and I thought you'd feel more comfortable if I stayed in a hotel."

"I would," Samantha said bluntly.

John Kendall laughed half-heartedly and said, "You're as impertinent as Augusta. You're more like her than Caroline. Let me know if you need anything."

Samantha stoically watched as John Kendall made the short walk to the hotel. As soon as he turned the corner, Samantha sat on the porch weeping into the sleeve of her dress. After a moment, Samantha felt a hand on her shoulder and turned to see a sympathetic Margaret Kendall at her side.

"Let's get you inside, dear," Margaret gently suggested. "Things will look better in the morning."

CHAPTER 72

THE FIRST WEEK OF August 1918 found Jonathan Kendall on a troop ship looking over the bustling and utilitarian port of Brest on the coast of France. Smoke from scores of ships hung over the brackish water, presenting an overall depressing picture. It had been twelve long days on the transport ship, and Jonathan was ready to feel land.

Most of the Texas and Oklahoma soldiers had never seen a ship, much less been on one. The ocean crossing was a memorable experience, and many men claimed they got six meals a day—three going down and three more coming up. The soldiers left the ship the next day, and after recovering from being seasick, the 36th Division was itching to get in the fight. Most soldiers came from dirt poor farms, sprawling ranches, small towns, or rapidly growing cities in a part of the country that was frontier twenty years earlier. They were an independent and patriotic group ready to show their mettle.

Boarding trains, the soldiers were shuttled through Paris to camps near the front. Jonathan looked forward to seeing Paris, but the city seemed to be in chaos as the Germans had pushed to within 75 miles of the city only weeks earlier. Jonathan saw thousands of men missing arms and legs, as it seemed the train depot was an outdoor hospital. The French soldiers had a strange faraway stare making them look lifeless. Jonathan envisioned what war might be like during the months of training, but the sights in Paris were a sobering reality.

In Paris, the soldiers exited the train and took trucks to a shabby camp near the Marne River at a place called St. Dizier. The camp had a strange combination of confused normalcy. The newly arrived American soldiers were conspicuous with clean uniforms and polished boots. The new soldiers seemed out of place with the thousands of worn-looking men who took the chaos of the camp as routine. It had been a year since Company B from Chandler traveled to Camp Bowie. The Oklahoma 1st Infantry no longer existed, and Jonathan found Company B merged into the 142nd Infantry serving under Captain Taylor from Dallas, Texas. Captain Taylor had been in the army during the Pancho Villa raids and had a reputation as a stern but fair officer. Many men in the 142nd Infantry were from Jonathan's old National Guard unit, including the ever-energetic Lee Gilstrap, who served as bugle boy.

Jonathan could hear ominous artillery in the distance night and day, but the 36th Division was back to doing what it had done for the past year — drill, train, eat, and drill. Officers were busier than the enlisted men, but the mission for the 142nd and the rest of the 36th Division seemed to be undecided. General Pershing wanted the American Army to fight separately, but after several weeks, it was revealed that the 36th Division would be serving with the 3rd French Army under the direction of senior French officers. The rumors of the reinforcement role sifted through the camp with the expected complaining.

It was early October, and the French countryside already had a chill in the air when Jonathan got orders to move with the 142nd to the front. Jonathan's job of preparing the men demanded all his energy since landing in France, and he had thought of little else. The night before leaving for the front, however, Jonathan found a quiet spot to look at the picture of Samantha Harvey he carried.

"Your girl?" Captain Taylor asked in his Texas drawl as he looked over Jonathan's shoulder.

Captain Taylor was a man of few words, but he had dark, shifting eyes that always seemed to be searching. He was an average-looking man with the ability to project a commanding confidence.

Jonathan began to stand when Captain Taylor said, "Keep your seat."

The captain sat down as Jonathan said, "She used to be my girl."

"But not now?" Captain Taylor smiled.

Jonathan thought hard for a moment and said, "I guess in my memory she'll always be my girl."

Captain Taylor laughed and said, "For a soldier, that's as good as it gets sometimes."

Captain Taylor had obviously not come to talk about Jonathan's girl as he said, "You're headed to the front tomorrow."

"Yes, sir," Jonathan acknowledged, as he put Samantha's picture away.

In a calm and reassuring tone, Captain Taylor continued, "Everyone's told me you're a capable officer since I hooked up with the 36th and I've seen it through training."

"Thank you, sir."

"Tomorrow won't be training though," Captain Taylor stated. "Tomorrow will be the real deal. We've tried to prepare you as much as possible, but if I know anything about the military, it's that training isn't combat. I've been to the front, and it will be intense. If you've got an ounce of brains, and I know you do, you'll be scared out of your mind up there. What I need for you to do is not show it. Your men will be looking to you. There'll be a French interpreter to help you with the frontline officers, but the men will be looking to you…not so much what you say, but how you carry yourself."

"Yes, sir," Jonathan acknowledged.

"I have confidence in you, and your men need to have that confidence too," Captain Taylor explained. "The French should keep you boys in the trenches for a couple of days to let you get used to things. Keep your head down and watch the French. They've been going through this hell four years. They've had to have learned something. Make decisions and act sure...you're men will need that."

"Yes, sir," Jonathan nodded.

"Get some sleep," Captain Taylor suggested. "You'll need it."

Anticipation and anxiety filtered through the camp about the first trip to the front. The night before the move, soldiers gathered in small groups, and expectant whispers could be heard everywhere. Jonathan did not sleep well despite Captain Taylor's instructions. For the first time in a long time, Jonathan's mind was not preoccupied with memories of Samantha Harvey. Tonight his thoughts were on the combat to come.

CHAPTER 73

THE 142ND INFANTRY MARCHED to the front on October 4, 1918, on a cold, foggy morning. The well-worn path to the trenches was filled with ambulances and men staggering to the rear. The German offensive in the spring moved the front lines to within seventy-five miles of Paris, but the advancement had been stopped by the summer. Since the 36th Division had arrived in August, the Allies had been on the offensive, pushing the Germans back.

Jonathan's company arrived in the trenches around ten o'clock in the morning. Nothing in the training at Camp Bowie could have prepared the soldiers for what stood in front of them. Trenches roughly seven feet deep stretched for as far as the eye could see. The ditches were dirty, slimy protection from the loud bursts of gunfire and artillery in front of them. The smell was indescribable, and filthy men lounged in the mire as if they were on their front porches at home.

Looking over the battlefield, Jonathan could see a landscape of craters and scorched earth. In front of him, he saw clouds of rising smoke, as airplanes skimmed the horizon and observation balloons floated like giant sausages in the sky. The roar and crash of shells thundered nearby and killed two men less than one hundred yards away. Although the racket from machine guns and artillery was constant, one of the French officers assured Jonathan things were relatively quiet this morning. Jonathan's men found their place in the trenches, and he settled in for what he believed would be several days of observing and getting accustomed to the bedlam of battle.

The adjustment period did not last long. The next morning after a sleepless night, a French officer ordered Jonathan to prepare his men to move out the next day. Jonathan's request for clarification was met with a stream of what he believed was French cursing. The interpreter assured Jonathan the order was correct. Remembering the instructions from Captain Taylor, Jonathan calmly gave the men the orders and pretended he understood their mission.

On October 6, the 142nd Division moved to the crest of the trench, as a reserve unit for a frontal attack beginning at dawn. Jonathan felt the tension from the men around him as he struggled to display a calm demeanor. At dawn, a whistle blew, and thousands of soldiers scampered over the top of the trenches to an eruption of gunfire. In ten minutes, a frantic French officer screamed instructions at Jonathan. The interpreter assigned to him urgently replied that his platoon was to fill a gap on the right flank exposed to a German machine gun placement.

Jonathan nodded to the French officer before confidently shouting the order to move forward. Knowing he could not hesitate, Jonathan was the first soldier over the top. Fear made his legs temporarily numb, but as he began to move, the rugged terrain seemed to bounce in his imagination as he ran as hard as he could for nearly one hundred yards. A roar of gunfire from his right caused him to instinctively fall to the ground behind a shallow protrusion of earth barely eighteen inches high.

Next to Jonathan, a man fell limp with a bullet through his head. A machine gun's evil crackling pinned down the whole company. Jonathan raised his rifle without looking and fired intermittent shots at men he could not see. Artillery shells burst above, and even the inexperienced Jonathan knew the position would lead to certain slaughter. Jonathan peeked over the small embankment as the rest of the platoon clung to the bare earth for protection. Jonathan quickly ducked his head as the German machine guns flashed almost two hundred yards away. Looking to his left, Jonathan could tell the whole offensive was stalled by the flanking fire. If the machine gun position could not be taken, the surge would fail, and thousands would die.

Jonathan moved a few yards as machine gun fire pelted the dirt a few feet in front of him. Jonathan saw a series of deep craters and what he believed was an old trench about fifty yards ahead. The order to move would mean causalities, but Jonathan believed if they stayed in their current position, it would only be a matter of time before enemy artillery rained down death for them all. An uncertain Jonathan sent word to his sergeants to move on his command.

In a few moments, Jonathan and his men sprinted toward the abandoned trench. Jonathan felt a strange calm as he dashed toward what he thought was certain death. His legs pounded the uneven terrain, and he momentarily tripped over a low-hanging piece of barbed wire before quickly regaining his feet before diving into the trench through a hail of gunfire. Looking back, Jonathan saw men writhing in agony or lying lifeless in the field behind him — men he had ordered to their death.

Remembering Captain Taylor's advice, Jonathan presented a confident persona to the men making it to the trench. Jonathan watched artillery shells rock the earth behind them near their old position. The trench provided better protection from the machine gun still roaring in front of them, but Jonathan knew they had accomplished little and were no closer to taking out the menacing fire chewing through men along the offensive.

Jonathan reclined against the dirt embankment and closed his eyes briefly trying to think of something to do. He had not seen an officer of higher rank since his company went over the top. The machine gun position had to be taken, but it seemed an impossible task without losing his whole platoon.

As Jonathan calculated his options, he heard the thunder of horses galloping toward him as seven men rode behind his position toward the flank of the German machine gun bunker. It was a glorious sight as the men raced into the fray. Jonathan did not recognize the riders, but he saw a man wearing an American uniform clinging to the neck of a horse.

It seemed as if the heroic charge was not real, but Jonathan was witnessing it close enough to hear the pant of the horses. One of the French soldiers was shot in the head and then another in the leg. The five remaining riders spread out as the machine gunner took two more riders out. Jonathan's eyes focused on the man in the American uniform as he and the two other riders continued with reckless abandon. The American's horse went down as the machine gun flashed fanatically less than twenty yards from the position. However, as the gunner swung around to shoot at the two remaining riders, the American leaped to his feet and charged the position with a pistol in one hand and an evil-looking trench knife in the other.

As the machine gunner was engaged in fighting, the other men breached the bunker and Jonathan ordered his platoon to move. By the time they arrived, the machine gunners that had dispensed so much fear and misery were dead. Jonathan leaped into the bunker and quickly searched for the men who had made the wild charge. The three men looked glassy eyed, as dirt, smoke, and blood covered their uniforms while they seemed to shiver in feverish breathing.

Stepping to the American soldier, Jonathan shouted, "That was some fearsome riding!"

The man looked too stunned to talk, but eventually said, "I guess so."

"Where are you from?" Jonathan asked.

"Ponca City, Oklahoma," the man replied.

"Oklahoma!" Jonathan exclaimed. "Are you part of the 36th?"

"No, sir," the man replied. "I'm with the 11th Infantry. We've been assigned to the French."

"Jonathan Kendall," Jonathan introduced. "Chandler, Oklahoma."

The man spoke something in French to his fellow riders and then said, "Walt Johnson…good to see someone from home."

"We're with the 36th Division," Jonathan explained. "Most of us are from Oklahoma and Texas. If you're in the infantry, where'd you get the horses?"

Grinning, Walt Johnson said, "We kind of stole 'em. We were pinned down in the middle and saw these horses used with a supply wagon. We knew we had to cover ground quickly, so they asked who could ride, and I volunteered."

"You saved our bacon," Jonathan said.

"If I'd been thinking, I'd stayed put," Walt smiled.

Jonathan received orders to hold the position, and the men dug in for the night. Walt Johnson returned to his unit, and Jonathan determined he would try to find the heroic man from Ponca City when he got the chance. Sporadic rifle shots and artillery continued through the night, though Jonathan could tell the artillery was coming from further behind the lines. He could only surmise the day's action had some positive effect.

The next three days were a blur of fighting and madness for the men of the 142nd Infantry. The 36th Division suffered nearly three hundred casualties, but they helped push the Germans past the Hindenburg line. The troops fought intermittently, but nothing as intense as that first day. The Germans launched mustard gas on the company at a position near St. Etienne on October 8. Jonathan led a small reconnaissance squad, wearing uncomfortable gas masks, as they tried to locate the Germans who fought from defensive positions.

One of the soldiers Jonathan left behind in what he believed was relative safety was young, Lee Gilstrap. While Jonathan was gone, the 142nd endured heavy machine gun fire from a slope on their flank. The combination of mustard gas and machine gun fire was always a terrifying prospect. When several soldiers went down screaming in pain, the rash young bugler dropped his instrument and ran to rescue his fellow soldiers. The company's litter bearers had been killed, and the can-do young bugler made several more trips to carry the wounded out of the fire zone.

On his last trip, a sniper's bullet hit Lee in his backpack, knocking him to the ground. When Lee Gilstrap regained his feet, he aimed a rifle at the marksman who had tried to kill him. To Lee's surprise, the German soldier surrendered. Lee put the captured soldier to work helping him carry the wounded Allied soldiers to safety. As Lee aimed his rifle at the enemy soldier, he came across several more Germans cowering in shell holes and dugouts, having been trapped behind the advancing Allied line. Two of Lee's makeshift ambulance squad died by German gunfire, but in the end Lee used several prisoners to save many wounded from the mustard gas.

The fighting continued five days before the fatigued 142nd was relieved and sent to the relative safety of the rear area. Jonathan, who had been unable to sleep the first night in the trenches, found he could sleep in any mud hole after a few days of battle. As the 142nd Infantry marched to the rear encampment, fresh-faced troops in clean uniforms met them, reminding the soldiers of how they must have looked a week earlier. Jonathan Kendall collapsed into a cot in the officers' tent and stared blankly into the canvas ceiling. He had lost more men than he wanted to remember, and he wondered if he would ever be the same. He had not thought of Samantha Harvey during the combat, and Jonathan wondered if this would be the price he would have to pay to erase her from his memory.

CHAPTER 74

JONATHAN NEVER THOUGHT A cold bath and clean clothes could feel so good. He thought he might sleep for a week from exhaustion, but instead, Jonathan was up an hour before sunrise to enjoy the relative quiet of the camp.

"Lieutenant Kendall," Captain Taylor greeted in a concise tone. "Have a seat."

Jonathan sat on a canvas stool at the end of a simple wood table in a half-buried bunker the 36th Division used as headquarters.

Captain Taylor took a sip of coffee and said, "I've read the casualty report."

"Yes, sir," Jonathan said in a deflated tone.

"Leadership's a hard thing," Captain Taylor consoled. "There's no way the 142nd should've been put in that situation after one day on the line, but you boys proved yourselves. I talked to the colonel, and he says your unit overtook a machine gun position that had the whole line pinned down."

"It wasn't us, sir," Jonathan explained. "It was a fellow from the 11th and some French soldiers."

"I heard," Captain Taylor replied. "But I also heard your unit was in position and moved with audacity and courage in the face of danger."

"Thank you, sir," Jonathan said dispassionately.

Captain Taylor looked at his young officer a moment and said, "I know you feel responsible for the men we lost, but you kept a lot of soldiers alive and helped the offensive move forward. It had to be hell out there, but you made this unit proud."

Jonathan nodded in acknowledgement, but still did not feel he had done anything but survive.

Captain Taylor reached to grab a file and said with an uncomfortable smirk on his face, "I see the 36th has its first hero out of your platoon."

Jonathan tried to refrain from smiling as he replied, "Yes, sir. I guess some people just don't know when to keep their heads down."

"I've read the report," Captain Taylor said, "but I'd like to hear your version."

"I don't really have anything to add," Jonathan admitted. "I've only heard about the incident secondhand. I was upfront doing reconnaissance, and I guess Lee decided to capture the whole German army by himself."

"According to the report, Private Gilstrap helped carry twenty men to safety," Captain Taylor added. "Mostly using captured Germans to do the lifting."

"That's the story I've heard," Jonathan said.

"Is Private Gilstrap related to your old captain?" Captain Taylor asked.

"Yes, sir," Jonathan confirmed.

"And he's only seventeen?" the captain asked.

Jonathan's eyes shifted and he said, "If that. Lee's been one of those kids that hung around the guard back home. He's always into everything...kind of cocky some would say. He was too young to enlist, but his father wanted him to go with the hometown troops if he was going, so he's been the bugler since."

"Well," Captain Taylor sighed. "You'll need to find a new bugler. Private Gilstrap is being recommended for a medal...maybe the Distinguished Service Cross. The army's hungry for heroes, and your young private fits the bill."

"There'll be no one better for the role," Jonathan replied.

In a more serious tone, Captain Taylor said, "Our company's being replenished with what's left of the 11th Infantry."

Jonathan nodded.

"The bad news is, you're going back in the field in three days," Captain Taylor revealed.

Jonathan did not respond.

"The Germans are being pushed back, and the high command is determined to keep the momentum," Captain Taylor explained. "We don't want to let this thing revert back to a stalemate. The Americans are the fresh troops in the trenches, so it's up to us to keep up the pressure."

"Yes, sir," Jonathan acknowledged.

"Get your men hot meals," Captain Taylor instructed. "You'll head back to the front on Monday."

Jonathan saluted the captain and headed back into the cool October morning. Jonathan spent most of the day writing letters home to the families of the men who had lost their lives in the previous fighting. As he tried to relate how each man had served his country, Jonathan thought of what Captain Taylor might write if he were to become a casualty. Jonathan was not a superstitious man, but he had a bad feeling about returning to the front.

That evening, Jonathan walked around camp to get a feel of the men's morale. Soldiers clustered around covered fires in barrels to keep warm and share stories. Jonathan smirked at some of the brave tales he heard from men who had chewed earth to stay out of harm's way days earlier. Jonathan passed one circle of men from the 142nd retelling their experiences in a mixture of English and strange words he did not understand. He immediately recognized the soldiers, as some of the Choctaw Indians that had entertained the National Guard with their war dance at San Benito on the Mexican border. Jonathan nodded at the soldiers who flashed pleasant, broad smiles before returning to their conversation.

Jonathan continued strolling around the large camp, enjoying the clear cool evening in his clean uniform while looking for the man from Ponca City who had charged the machine gun on horseback. The 11th Infantry was being merged into the 142nd Infantry, so Jonathan felt he had a good chance of running into the man.

After a while, Jonathan spotted a group of soldiers talking in a familiar Oklahoma accent. Sitting opposite Jonathan was the soldier from Ponca City called Walt Johnson. Walt was a handsome young man with broad shoulders and sandy-blonde hair contrasting with dark smooth skin. He listened to other people retell the story of his heroics with an easy grin. Listening in on the conversation from the shadows, Jonathan could tell the men in the group were friends. He enjoyed their familiar banter and teasing.

About a dozen men were part of the jovial group. Jonathan could see all their battle tested faces by the firelight except the three men sitting with their backs to him. Sitting by Walt Johnson was a tall man named Tucker McMurry, who seemed to have many stories to tell. The conversation soon turned to girls from home. Tucker McMurry was taking considerable teasing from his friends about a girl named Rachel he promised to marry. He had been writing Rachel's best friend, Claire, and it was obvious Rachel knew nothing of the budding romance between Tucker and Claire. Walt Johnson suggested it might be better if the Germans captured Tucker before he had to go home and face both women.

Sitting on the other side of Walt was a quiet man named Lloyd Brooks from Pottawatomie County in Oklahoma. The timid Lloyd happened to be sitting by another soldier named Lloyd Wills from Shell Knob, Missouri. The man they called 'Oklahoma Lloyd' confessed he had his eye on a girl named Gwen, but revealed she did not know he carried a picture of her in his wallet. Walt Johnson admitted to leaving a girl named Lydie behind and said he had promised to marry her but would have to convince her father first. Jonathan remembered his picture of Samantha, as the men talked about their sweethearts.

Jonathan enjoyed warm memories of Samantha's letters from his time in San Benito, when his ears perked up at a familiar voice saying the word, "Caroline."

Jonathan walked quickly to the man whose back was to him, as Walt Johnson greeted casually, "How's it going, lieutenant?"

Jonathan did not acknowledge Walt and tapped the other man on the shoulder. As David Simpson turned around, Jonathan savagely lunged at his old friend, and the two tumbled in the dirt. Walt Johnson and Lloyd Brooks rushed to pull the two men apart as Jonathan landed a right hand firmly on David's eye.

"What's going on?" Captain Taylor barked at the fighting men.

As Jonathan was held back, Captain Taylor said in a stern voice, "Did you strike this man, Lieutenant Kendall?"

Before Jonathan could answer, David Simpson said, "No. I fell, and Lieutenant Kendall helped me up."

Ignoring David Simpson's explanation, Captain Taylor shouted at Jonathan, "Hitting an enlisted man will get you a court martial, mister!"

"I have no excuse –" Jonathan Kendall began to confess.

"Captain," David Simpson interrupted. "I've been drinking a little too much of this French wine, and Lieutenant Kendall was trying to help me keep my balance. You can ask any of these guys. They saw the whole thing."

David Simpson's buddies nodded in agreement to the fabricated tale, as Captain Taylor looked unconvinced.

"Why are these men holding Lieutenant Kendall then?" Captain Taylor questioned.

David Simpson looked at the two men corralling Jonathan Kendall and said with little hesitation, "I caused him to stumble, and they were helping him up."

Captain Taylor did not look happy, but without asking Jonathan to explain more, he said, "I hope Lieutenant Kendall understands he cannot strike an enlisted man under any circumstance."

"Yes, sir," Jonathan replied, as the captain continued his evening stroll.

David Simpson looked at Jonathan after Captain Taylor left and said, "Imagine meeting you here."

CHAPTER 75

THE MEN SURROUNDING DAVID Simpson did not know what to expect from Jonathan Kendall as his nostrils flared in anger at the man who had escorted Samantha Harvey out of Chandler and out of his life.

"Guys, this is my best friend, Jonathan—I'm sorry, Lieutenant Kendall from Chandler," David introduced.

Jonathan did not reply, but nodded.

"Lieutenant Kendall and I met," the affable Walt Johnson said, breaking the awkward silence.

"If you'll excuse us," David said to his friends, "Lieutenant Kendall and I have some things to discuss."

Jonathan waited until they were out of sight before he grabbed David by the collar.

"I see you're glad to see me," David joked.

"How could you take Samantha away from me?" Jonathan angrily charged.

David took a deep breath and in a serious tone said, "I didn't take her away from you."

"Lee Gilstrap told me he saw you on the train with Samantha," Jonathan said firmly.

David calmly replied, "That's true."

"You admit it!"

"To riding on the train with her, yes," David said. "But I didn't take her away—"

David stopped to think a moment before saying, "You don't know...do you?"

"Know what?"

"Why Samantha left...why I left."

Jonathan said meekly, "Not exactly, but I can put two and two together."

David sighed heavily and responded, "Two and two was not me and Samantha. She loved you, Jonathan...she still loves you."

"Why did she go away then?" Jonathan asked bluntly. "I haven't heard a word in over a year...I assumed you two—"

"I'm sorry for that," David stated. "We did leave on the same day, but not together. Your father sent her away...and she went."

"Why would she do that?" Jonathan inquired.

David hesitated as he looked around to make sure he and Jonathan were alone.

Stepping close to Jonathan, David said, "When I was working for your dad, I found out some things. He sent me to find out about a mortgage on a farm near Keokuk Falls owned by some people called Hellwig. Your father knew them from back in Warwick when he first came to Oklahoma. I heard enough people talk to figure out that your father had...a relationship with one of the Hellwig girls."

"What are you saying?" Jonathan interrupted.

"Jonathan," David said despondently. "Samantha's your half-sister. Your father is Samantha's father."

"That can't be," Jonathan muttered as the blood rushed out of his face. "It can't be."

"It can," David affirmed. "I've talked to a lot of people who know the Hellwigs. Your father was involved with Samantha's mother. When Samantha's mother found out your father was already married, she broke it off. She married old Mr. Harvey a few weeks later and went away. When she returned, she had Samantha with her. There's no way Mr. Harvey was Samantha's real father...I'm sorry."

Jonathan did not respond but stared blankly into the night.

"I had enough of doing your dad's dirty deeds," David explained. "When Caroline finally decided I wasn't worth waiting for, things became intolerable. I went to Tulsa to try a new start...until the army drafted me that is."

"Why didn't you tell me?" a shaken Jonathan asked.

David Simpson swallowed hard and confessed, "Your father paid me not to tell you. I felt bad about it, but I needed the money and figured he's the one that should tell you."

"He didn't," Jonathan responded.

"Samantha knew there would be a scandal when people found out you intended to marry your sister," David said sheepishly. "She thought she was protecting you by leaving. She begged me not to tell you...she was trying to protect you."

"Very noble of her," an embarrassed Jonathan responded.

"Jonathan—" David began.

"That'll be enough, private," an angry Jonathan Kendall said in a tone of authority. "You've explained things quite clearly."

"Jonathan," David said. "I'm sorry."

Ignoring his old friend's attempts to comfort him, Jonathan said, "Get back to your friends and get some rest. We'll be back at the front in a few days."

"Yes, sir," David replied weakly, as he followed the directive and headed back to the fire.

"David," Jonathan finally said after his friend had taken a few steps.

"Yes."

"I'd appreciate it if you didn't—tell anyone about this—" Jonathan requested. "It wouldn't be good for my men to—make jokes at my expense. These men need officers they can respect...even if those officers have been foolish."

"You don't have to ask," David assured. "I've never told anyone and never will. You don't have to worry about respect. According to Walt Johnson, you've already earned it."

David stepped back to Jonathan and said, "All this stuff doesn't matter to me, Jonathan. I am your friend."

When Jonathan did not respond, David walked slowly back to the fire.

In a few seconds, Jonathan said, "I know, David. Thank you and...be careful."

Jonathan turned and walked slowly back to his officers' tent while David Simpson returned to his friends—both men feeling the consequences of John Kendall's selfish transgressions. David felt sorry for his old friend, while Jonathan went back to his tent and did not feel anything.

CHAPTER 76

THE 142ND INFANTRY HEADED back to the front on October 14, 1918. Rumors abounded saying the Germans were close to the breaking point and the war would soon end. When the soldiers arrived back in the trenches, however, the rumors seemed like false hope. Although there had been numerous instances of mass surrenders, the German army was experienced, proud, and fighting from well-protected defensive positions. The Germans now bombed areas they controlled for over a year, and they were intimately familiar with the terrain. They also now fought with a dangerous degree of desperation.

The trenches, which had stalemated fighting during much of the Great War, served more as temporary shelters now, as the Allies constantly moved forward. The Germans possessed an uncanny ability to guess the Allied movements, however, and three supply depots had been destroyed by long-range artillery in the week since the 142nd returned to the front.

Jonathan had several additions to his company including David Simpson and several experienced soldiers from the 11th Infantry. David seemed to be good to his word of maintaining discipline by keeping Jonathan's secret, as the men quickly meshed with their new company and officers.

Jonathan sat in the mud of a trench eating cold, canned meat while on observation duty when a messenger ran to him and frantically shouted, "Lieutenant Kendall, Captain Taylor needs to see you right away."

Jonathan looked around and could not see any evidence of a crisis on the battlefield, but he put down his tasteless meal and followed the messenger to a bunker about a quarter of a mile behind the front line. As Jonathan entered the sheltered room lit by oil lamps, he noticed several American and French officers outranking Captain Taylor.

"Here he is," Captain Taylor noted as Jonathan entered the room.

Jonathan faced a serious-looking, older officer who was bent over a pile of detailed maps. Jonathan recognized the man as Colonel A. W. Bloor, commander of the 142nd Infantry.

"Lieutenant Kendall," Colonel Bloor asked pointedly. "I understand you have Indians in E company?"

"Several," Jonathan replied. "Mostly Choctaw, I believe."

"Full-bloods?" the colonel inquired.

"I don't know, sir," Jonathan answered, "but they're good soldiers. Is there a problem?"

Colonel Bloor ignored the question and asked, "Do they speak Choctaw?"

"Yes, sir," Jonathan replied. "At least I think it's Choctaw. It sounds like gibberish to me, but I've heard them talk among themselves many times."

Jonathan's answer caused a feverish discussion among the high-ranking officers as Captain Taylor said, "Wait outside…and don't go far."

A confused Jonathan obeyed and paced outside the bunker for a few minutes before Captain Taylor emerged.

"Let's walk," Captain Taylor suggested, as he moved away from the bunker and back toward the front.

"What's going on?" Jonathan asked, thinking some of the soldiers might have gotten into mischief.

"There'll be a big push in a few days," Captain Taylor confided. "You'll be briefed in a day or two, but the Germans are into our communication systems. The lines have been pushed back so far that we're using some of the old German telephone lines for communication. The Germans break our codes faster than we write them, and about one in three of our runners gets captured. We've sent several false messages over the lines the past days, and every time the German artillery rains down on the location. We need a coordinated attack and need the phone lines for quick communication."

"And you want to use the Choctaws to confuse the Germans," Jonathan concluded.

"Exactly," Captain Taylor replied. "Their language isn't written, and our code breakers think it will be darned hard if not impossible to decipher. I need you to round up as many of the men as possible that speak the language and bring them back here. The other units will be doing the same."

"Yes, sir," Jonathan said, as he continued walking to the front while Captain Taylor returned to headquarters.

By evening about eighteen Choctaw Indians had been recruited and sent to headquarters for an induction into military communication and terminology. Many of the soldiers were hesitant to put down their rifles, but it did not take much persuasion to convince them of the importance of the new assignment. One of the Choctaws said that Chief Pushmataha, who had died nearly a century earlier, had said the Choctaw war cry would be heard in faraway lands. The chief's prophecy was soon to be fulfilled.

Jonathan returned to the routine drudgery of life in the trenches, eating canned meat and wilted cabbage. Two days later, he was summoned again to headquarters for a briefing about the big offensive Captain Taylor had mentioned. Jonathan did not relish the idea of going back into combat, but he knew his soldiers were more experienced and better equipped than they had been during their first encounter. Jonathan slept in the rain-soaked trench the night before the advance with a tarp wrapped around him in an attempt to keep dry. No fires were allowed, and the Allied commanders in the sector were counting on their new, secret code to confuse the enemy. Jonathan Kendall prayed that the confusion would save the lives of the men under his charge.

CHAPTER 77

JONATHAN'S COMPANY WENT OVER the top of the trenches at dawn cued by a signal from one of the Choctaw interpreters. The code talkers had been stationed with each company in the 142nd and at central headquarters. Jonathan advanced with his men through the eerily quiet desolation of the war-torn terrain. Jonathan was close enough to hear a German soldier scream frantically before rifle shots began to crackle. The German's warning was too late, as the Allies quickly overtook the position, taking many prisoners.

Hope of a quick victory evaporated by mid-morning, however, as the Germans regrouped and inflicted heavy casualties with well-placed machine guns. The Germans then provided a steady barrage of artillery. By nightfall, the advance had moved only about a mile from the starting point. Heavy fighting continued the next three days until the Allies pushed to the southern bank of the Aisne River before stopping to resupply. The next two days involved mopping up stray units of the German army unable to retreat across the river. The 142nd lost 217 men in the fighting, and officers struggled to replenish their ranks.

The 142nd Infantry pushed across the Aisne River on a cloudy, blustery late October morning. After two days of fierce fighting, the

Allies secured a stronghold on the north side of the river. Soldiers occupied trenches and bunkers the Germans used days earlier. The fighting became more chaotic as the front line became indistinguishable. Remnants of earthworks and communication systems tangled as the armies pushed each other in a struggle for survival. Jonathan had not shaved or bathed in a week when he heard Captain Taylor call his name.

"How's your platoon holding out?" Captain Taylor asked as he looked around the tattered men lying in the muck of the old German positions.

"We're good, sir," Jonathan replied without much enthusiasm.

"The Germans have an artillery placement somewhere north of St. Mihiel that has the 2nd Division pinned down," Captain Taylor explained. "I need you to pick a small detachment to reconnoiter the area. They have it hidden, because the airplanes see nothing. We need to find that artillery. You'll leave tonight after dark. Be careful. If you meet resistance come back and report it."

"Yes, sir," Jonathan replied.

Captain Taylor gave a few more instructions before returning to a bunker near the river.

Jonathan returned to his men and put out the word to his sergeant to solicit volunteers to meet an hour before sunset. Jonathan leaned his back against the soft, moist earth and tried to sleep before the nighttime operations began.

"I hear you're leading this expedition," the jovial voice of David Simpson greeted, waking Jonathan from his nap.

Standing up, Jonathan saw David Simpson, Walt Johnson, Tucker McMurry, and Lloyd Wills.

"All of you volunteered?" Jonathan asked.

"Yes, sir," the group answered in unison.

"I've been volunteered, too," a dark skinned man with a drawling accent added. "Corporal Solomon Louis, from Hoochatown, Oklahoma."

"Code talker?" Jonathan asked.

The somber-faced Solomon Louis answered with a nod.

"We're heading east, southeast about three to five miles," Jonathan explained. "We're looking for a forward observation site or some evidence of an artillery unit. Hopefully we make it and return without being seen. We'll leave as soon as it's dark."

Jonathan dismissed the men until time to depart, but said, "Private Simpson, could I have a word?"

"Yes, sir," David replied, as the other soldiers went to find food before their evening hike.

Stepping closer to David, Jonathan said in a low voice without any military tone, "Why did you volunteer for this assignment?"

David sighed heavily and answered, "I heard you were leading the group tonight. I wanted to come."

"It might be dangerous," Jonathan informed.

Smiling David said, "Well then, you'll need someone to keep you out of trouble. When my buddies heard I was going, they volunteered too."

"Thanks," Jonathan said.

"For volunteering?" David quipped. "If it helps get the Germans out of France and me back to a clean dry bed, it's worth it."

"Not for volunteering," Jonathan said seriously. "Thanks for not making a joke out of me to the men."

David thought for a moment and said, "These men trust you...I trust you. Jonathan, I'm your friend. I thought you'd know that after all these years."

"I do," Jonathan replied. "I just need you to remind me sometimes."

David leaned toward Jonathan and said, "It's not your fault."

"What?"

"Samantha," David clarified. "It's not your fault, and it's not her fault either. You got to let things go. I hear the stories about how fearless you are. How you're out in front of your soldiers. It's not your fault, so quit trying to kill yourself."

"I'm not," Jonathan assured.

In a lighter tone of voice, David stepped back and said, "That's why I really volunteered tonight. I got to keep you safe. Who knows? I might be your brother-in-law someday."

The blood rushed out of Jonathan's face as he said, "Haven't you heard? Caroline's married."

Unfazed, the exultant David said, "I heard. I was talking about trying my luck with Samantha."

Jonathan smiled artificially at the humor as David slapped him on the back and went to find something to eat. Jonathan stood silently looking over the darkening landscape. He did not have time to think about his past. Jonathan's full attention was on the unknown landscape over the horizon and getting his soldiers back alive.

Jonathan led the men, including David Simpson, into the dark night, as the soldiers crawled out of the damp trenches and into the unknown. A fine mist made everything wet, but the moonless and very dark night meant protection for the small group. The battlefield was quiet with only the occasional clatter of gunfire in the distance and artillery shells launched by both sides to disturb sleeping soldiers.

The group moved silently over terrain that had been chewed up by years of shelling. The dark night offered protection but also made navigating slow. Jonathan stopped every few minutes to put his head under his overcoat to check the map with a flashlight. In the thick, dark night, it was impossible to make out any landmark, so Jonathan relied on his compass to keep them on direction.

After three hours, Jonathan estimated the group had moved less than two miles in the darkness. Seeing nothing, Jonathan signaled the men to spread out. In a few moments, the men could barely see the soldier next to them. About two hours before sunrise, Jonathan sent word down the line to halt. The reconnaissance had uncovered nothing, and Jonathan began to doubt his navigation.

As the order to halt spread down the line, Jonathan could faintly hear whispers when the ominous click of a rifle bolt caused him to stand perfectly still. A second after the sound, gunfire from the far right shattered the quiet of the night.

"Take cover!" Jonathan screamed as the men scrambled to find any piece of earth to shelter them from the fire.

Jonathan could not make out the terrain, but in a few minutes, a German flare illuminated the battlefield. As a machine gun began peppering the earth, Jonathan spotted a large crater twenty yards in front of him. With a few quick steps and a leap, he tumbled into the deep hole with three other men at nearly the same time.

"Where's that coming from?" one of the soldiers yelled.

"Everywhere," another soldier replied.

"Keep your head down," Jonathan ordered. "We've got cover here."

"What about our other guys?" the voice of Walt Johnson asked.

Jonathan waited until the flare had nearly drifted to the ground before he looked over the edge of the crater to assess the situation. The remainder of the men were scattered across the ground taking whatever cover they could. In less than ten seconds, German bullets sprayed the lip of the crater forcing Jonathan to duck as he screamed for the men to stay down.

"Who do we have in here?" Jonathan asked frantically.

"Johnson!"

"Wills!"

"Louis!"

Jonathan peered across the field again to see most of the fire was coming from the far left.

"Louis!" Jonathan called.

"Yes," Solomon Louis answered.

"Can you run in the dark?"

"Like a panther!" the man replied.

Jonathan looked at his map and quickly scribbled a note before handing it to Corporal Louis.

"Do you think you can find your way back to our lines?" Jonathan asked.

"I think so," Corporal Louis answered as he removed his ammunition belt and backpack to lighten his load.

Looking at the other two soldiers, Jonathan pointed into the trees and said, "As soon as this flare goes out, we're going to fire in that direction. Louis you make a run for our lines. Tell Captain Taylor we've engaged the enemy, and it's more than an observation post."

Corporal Louis nodded as the three other men prepared to open fire into the dark night. The gunfire was deafening as Jonathan, Walt Johnson, and Lloyd Wills opened fire on positions they could not see. After twenty seconds, Jonathan signaled to cease firing and turned around to see where the runner had gone. Jonathan was unable to see anything in the darkness, but heard a thud as two more soldiers dove into the relative safety of the crater. Jonathan peered into the dark night anxiously until another flare illuminated the field. Corporal Louis had disappeared to Jonathan's relief, and he believed the messenger could make it back.

"Who was on the far left?" Jonathan asked.

After some discussion among the five men in the crater, one of the soldiers said, "Simpson, I think."

Jonathan braved the incoming fire once again looking to the left. Even with the flare, he could see nothing. He crouched back in the crater, frustrated at the fog of war. In the next hour, three more men made it to the crater and reported that at least one soldier was dead.

No one had seen David, however, as dawn made its slow appearance.

As light began to appear, Jonathan could tell they had moved through a gap in the German lines. The crater was located in a stand of trees that provided some cover. Jonathan knew as the light improved, the Germans would launch artillery or mustard gas into the position. The reconnaissance team needed to retreat, but there was still one man missing—David Simpson.

"We've got to get out of here before it gets light," Jonathan forcefully instructed. "Crawl down that ditch and get to that small gully."

As the soldiers nodded, Jonathan began crawling out the opposite side of the crater.

"Where are you going, sir?" an urgent Walt Johnson asked.

"To find David," Jonathan replied.

"I'm coming, too," Walt stated.

"Me too," Lloyd Wills said.

"No," Jonathan commanded. "I've lost enough men for one night. Get back to the lines."

Without further elaboration, Jonathan crawled out of the crater and toward the left flank of the position. After fifty yards, Jonathan scampered into a thick cluster of leafless trees and was able to crouch as he moved quicker. Looking back in the dawn light, Jonathan could barely make out the squad moving to the safety of the small ravine and the friendly lines closer to the Aisne River.

Jonathan moved as quickly as he dared through the trees as leaves crunched menacingly under his feet. Kneeling at the edge of the tree row, Jonathan peered at an open field behind the camouflage of a berry bush. Pulling out binoculars, he scanned the field. His heart stopped as he spotted David Simpson tangled in barbed wire on the other side. The sky was lightening, and Jonathan knew he no longer enjoyed the cover of darkness. Without thinking, he sprinted across the field to help the wounded David.

Jonathan could not believe he was making the dash unmolested as he ceased zigzagging fifty yards from his target. As he approached David, however, an explosion of rifle fire pelted around him. Diving to the ground, Jonathan looked at his friend David draped helplessly on the barbed wire. The Germans had let David live to entice someone out in the open, and Jonathan took the bait. Jonathan continued crawling toward David when gunfire crackled behind him.

Looking back, Jonathan saw Walt Johnson and Lloyd Wills firing madly at the Germans who were shrouded in the trees ahead.

As the German fire moved to Wills and Johnson, Jonathan made it to his feet and to David Simpson.

"Can't you tell it's a trap?" David screamed as Jonathan slid beside him and desperately tugged at the barbed wire to pull David to the ground.

Jonathan groaned as he pulled hard on the wire, while David grimaced in pain. David had stumbled into an abandoned bunker surrounded by barbed wire. Three dead Germans lay nearby as a result of artillery. Jonathan ignored the morbid scene as he frantically tried to free David.

"It's no good!" David yelled. "Get out of here."

"Not without you," Jonathan insisted as the barbed wire gave way enough to allow Jonathan to lower David to the ground with bullets whistling by inches above.

David had been shot in the shoulder and leg as blood covered his muddy uniform.

"You're going to be okay," Jonathan tried to reassure, as David lay motionless on the ground.

Looking back at Walt Johnson and Lloyd Wills, Jonathan knew he had to get the badly wounded David across the field and to an ambulance or his friend would die.

CHAPTER 78

WALT JOHNSON FIRED RAPIDLY at a line of trees where he suspected the Germans were hiding.

"Are you sure this was a good idea?" Lloyd Wills asked as he too fired his rifle.

"I suspect Lieutenant Kendall would not approve," Walt dryly replied. "But David'd do the same for us."

Across the field, Jonathan made it to David Simpson and managed to get him untangled from the barbed wire. Walt Johnson watched Jonathan use David Simpson's rifle to return fire from his pinned-down position.

"Go get help!" Walt told Lloyd. "I'm going after them."

Lloyd tried to protest, but Walt Johnson removed his gear to make a dash to his comrades. Before Walt could remove his backpack, however, an evil ping was heard in the distance meaning gas canisters were incoming. In seconds, four canisters landed in the field between their position and Jonathan Kendall.

"Get your mask on!" Lloyd shouted, as Walt Johnson retrieved his equipment from the backpack he planned to abandon.

The morning air was still, as ominous, brownish smoke slowly spread across the field hindering the view. Walt Johnson moved to pick up his rifle when the whistling of artillery pierced the air.

"Get down!" Walt yelled, as the ground shook as shells pelted the open field.

Looking up, the smoke was clearing from the percussions when Lloyd asked, "Can you see them?"

"No!" Walt replied as he examined the catastrophic upheaval of earth in the distance. "I'm going."

Without giving Lloyd a chance to protest, Walt sprinted through the smoke toward the place he had last seen Lieutenant Kendall and David Simpson. Lloyd Wills watched as Walt disappeared into the haze. In a moment, he watched Walt stagger back to the trees.

"What did you see?" Lloyd asked anxiously.

"Let's get out of here," a despondent Walt replied.

Walt dropped everything, but his rifle and gas mask. The soldiers made their way through the trees and to the crater. It was almost full light when they navigated the ravine back toward the line.

"What did you see?" Lloyd asked again as they stopped to catch their breath.

Walt grimaced and said, "There was nothin' but a big hole and body parts everywhere. They're gone."

Lloyd did not press for details and could tell Walt wanted to get as far from the scene as possible. The two soldiers made it back to the lines in less than two hours without saying anything further. They made their report to Captain Taylor. The reconnaissance had uncovered a German unit that was preparing for a counterattack. Five companies from the 142nd Infantry were sent to the spot before the Germans could launch their attack, pushing the enemy almost back inside the borders of Germany.

After making the report to Captain Taylor, Walt Johnson returned to find a quiet place in the trenches. His hands shook wildly as he drank from his canteen before weeping uncontrollably at a sight he was afraid he could never forget.

CHAPTER 79

BY LATE OCTOBER 1918, the public's interest took a bizarre twist in western Michigan. The attention focused on the Great War in Europe shifted to the Spanish Flu infecting people across the country. Schools closed, and the governor threatened to ban all public gatherings, including church meetings. Hope College dismissed classes for the flu, and two days before Halloween, Samantha was back working every day in Isaac Vandaveer's pharmacy.

The drugstore buzzed with activity as fear and panic gripped the city. Many customers ordered by telephone, which Isaac Vandaveer had installed the previous summer. The steady stream of customers kept Samantha busy all day, and she was glad when the front door locked at five o'clock.

On her way out, Isaac said to Samantha, "Your aunt called about an hour ago."

"Wonder what she wanted?" Samantha shrugged.

"I don't know," Isaac apologized. "Sorry. We got busy, and I forgot to tell you."

"That's fine," Samantha assured as she pulled her scarf around her neck. "I'm heading there now."

A puzzled Samantha left Isaac Vandaveer's store for the short walk to her aunt's house. She had moved out of the Hope College dormitory two weeks ago to live with Margaret and George Kendall until the flu panic passed. She stepped quickly down Main Street and through the park. The afternoon was gray, and the streets were eerily vacant as Samantha hurried toward Aunt Margaret's house. The towering trees were two weeks past their peak of brilliant autumn coloring, and the landscape foreshadowed the stark winter to come. It was not yet cold, but a chilly breeze blew off the lake.

Samantha opened the front door and could immediately tell something was amiss. Margaret Kendall sat quietly in the front room and had not yet turned on any lights, as the sun began to hang low in the western sky.

"Hello," Samantha greeted in a worried tone. "I got your message at the store."

"Something's happened," Margaret Kendall said sadly.

Samantha's first thoughts were of the flu epidemic as she asked, "Is Uncle George feeling okay?"

"He's fine, dear," Margaret assured. "Have a seat."

Samantha complied as Margaret said, "I've got some bad news. We received a telegram today from John. It's about Jonathan."

Samantha was glad she had taken a seat, as the room began to spin and she felt faint. She nodded her head slightly to signal her aunt to continue.

"I don't know an easy way to say this," Margaret said. "Jonathan's been killed."

The words seemed unreal, as Samantha stared blankly at the wall of the darkening room.

Finally, Samantha asked, "What did the message say?"

Samantha listened, as Margaret said softly, "Not much. I'm sure the family's in shock. The telegram said he was killed by artillery near the Aisne River in France...His men saw the blast...the body was...Jonathan will rest in peace in France, dear."

Samantha wanted to believe it was all a big mistake. She wanted to tell her aunt that this was a cruel joke, but she had feared this day since she left Oklahoma, and Samantha knew the news was all too real.

"Is there anything I can do?" Margaret asked. "Anything at all dear?"

"No," Samantha whispered. "I'm...I think I'll take a walk...I'd like to be alone."

Margaret nodded.

George Kendall, who had stepped into the room when he heard Samantha enter, said, "We're very sorry, Samantha. I know this must be a shock."

"Thank you," Samantha replied lifelessly.

Samantha excused herself and headed out the door before Margaret said, "Take your coat, dear...it's getting chilly."

Samantha took the coat handed to her and stepped into a dreary landscape that seemed soundless and empty. Samantha did not know where she would walk but knew she wanted to be alone. She always felt alone since moving to Holland, but she had not endured the intensity of loneliness she now experienced. For some reason she always harbored some hope for happiness with Jonathan, but any hope left in her was now void.

The wind blew and the day grew dimmer as Samantha found herself in the dunes of Lake Michigan for the first time since her first summer. She did not know what she was chasing, but walking toward the fading sun seemed her only plan. Samantha thought about the letters she had shared with Jonathan—the hopes and dreams they had collectively planned for their future. Nothing seemed real, and everything seemed empty and hopeless.

Guilt's Echo

The pale yellow lighthouse that had brightened her day the first time she saw it, now looked faded and dim in the autumn sunset. The lake was still a magnificent sight, but the crashing waves on the beach seemed meaningless, and Samantha found herself wishing she were one of the grains of sand to be washed out and forgotten. Samantha knew life was more than one tragic event, but thinking of Jonathan dying alone in a faraway land was more than she could bear.

Although the wind whipped the waves high on the pier protecting the port from the ravages of the lake, Samantha was drawn to walk on the narrow wet pier to the far western end…the closest she could get to home and where she once found happiness with Jonathan. Waves crashed around her, and she moved far from the gentle beaches to the harsh conflict between the water and the rocks. As Samantha looked at the swirling water, dark thoughts slipped into her confused mind. One step—one stumble would send her tumbling into the violent, frigid water. It would be a tragic accident, but it would be an end.

As Samantha looked at the mesmerizing surf crashing about her, she heard a familiar voice call, "Samantha!"

Samantha turned to watch Isaac Vandaveer limp down the perilous walk toward her as the sun vanished behind the horizon.

"Samantha!" Isaac shouted again to insure he had her attention. "What are you doing out here?"

"I came for a walk," Samantha said lethargically, as she coughed in the face of the cold wind.

"It's freezing," Isaac said, as he slowly moved closer.

"I'm fine," Samantha said, as she felt her cold nose with her hand.

Isaac continued to walk cautiously toward her as he reached out and gently grabbed Samantha's arm to steady her.

"It's dangerous," Isaac explained. "If you fell in, I'd have a terrible time fishing you out."

Something inside Samantha let go at the sound of Isaac's caring voice...something that painfully reminded her of Jonathan. For the first time since hearing the news of Jonathan's death, she began to cry and could not stop the flow of tears as she buried her head into Isaac's shoulder. She did not know how long she cried, but when she finally stopped weeping, it was night, as the lighthouse nearly one hundred yards away provided a warm glow on the jagged rocks.

"Your aunt told me the news," Isaac explained. "She was worried when you were gone so long and asked me to look for you. Let's get you warm."

Samantha could not speak but nodded her head in agreement. Isaac put his strong arms around the girl and guided her down the treacherous walkway. There was something comforting about Isaac's attention, as he put her in the automobile and drove to the Kendall house.

Margaret Kendall was frantic at the sight of the windswept and weather-beaten girl. After some hot tea, Margaret helped Samantha to bed, while Isaac visited with George Kendall for a few moments. Isaac asked if there was anything else he could do, and then reluctantly left, knowing Samantha would be in good care.

Samantha lay silently in her soft bed, but sleep did not come soon. Surreal images of Jonathan filled her frightful dreams. She awoke several times thinking the news was her imagination, only to determine her nightmare was all too real. Although Jonathan had been out of her life for over a year, she could not believe he would now only live in her memory.

CHAPTER 80

"Do you believe in happy endings?" Samantha asked her aunt at breakfast the next morning.

Margaret Kendall put down her dishtowel and looked at the sad-eyed Samantha saying, "I don't know if there is such a thing as a happy ending, dear. Life's hard...sometimes for no reason at all. I'm an old woman and seen happiness, but I've seen plenty of heartache too. I tell you what I do believe in...I believe we're put on this earth to try and make it just a little bit better. I think you have to appreciate kindness where you can find it, and...you have to cherish your memories. In the end, that's really all you'll have."

Margaret believed her attempted encouragement inadequate, but Samantha smiled faintly at the advice.

Shutting the world out had a strange appeal to Samantha. Her night's rest left her tired and lethargic, but Samantha knew the pharmacy would be a madhouse, so she decided to dress and try to make it through the day. The prescription worked as she quickly began to feel less sorry for herself while helping the many people struggling with illness. The panic over the flu intensified as twenty people died in Holland in a week from the savage disease. Samantha had felt chilled and feverish from her walk the previous night, but she tried to convince herself it was just a cold.

Isaac Vandaveer noticed Samantha looking pale by the early afternoon. He ran everyone out of the store for a few minutes and drove Samantha home to rest. Samantha tried to assure her employer she was fine, but he insisted she rest and stay out of the store. Margaret Kendall was equally adamant about her getting rest, so she complied and went to bed.

A worried Isaac raced back to the pharmacy as people waited at the front door. Isaac was not able to close the store until after dark, as worried citizens clamored for remedies to protect them from the feared sickness. Isaac's calm demeanor helped defuse a near panic in the store, but he was anxious to check on Samantha after work.

Samantha was eating a bowl of warm soup when Isaac Vandaveer knocked on the door of the Kendall house. George Kendall invited him inside, and Isaac was pleased to see Samantha out of bed and feeling better. Although Samantha assured everyone she was fine, Isaac insisted she stay out of the pharmacy for the rest of the week. Margaret Kendall echoed Isaac's anxiety about Samantha being around so much sickness. Samantha did not argue and soon complied with their wishes — finding something reassuring in Isaac's attention.

Margaret Kendall was the first to notice Isaac Vandaveer's concern for Samantha went beyond that of an employer. Although Isaac was nearly a dozen years older than Samantha, he was seen in the community as a responsible and kind man. Margaret had not considered the match before, but she encouraged Isaac to check on Samantha, and soon the pharmacist was a regular visitor to the Kendall home.

Samantha still ached at the loss of Jonathan Kendall and even felt sorry for John Kendall, although she would never be able to forgive him for how he treated her mother. As weeks went by, fear about the flu began to subside, although many were still sick in the community.

The announcement of the armistice in the Great War in Europe was a bittersweet day for Samantha. Along with the entire nation, Samantha was happy the soldiers would soon return, but the day was a painful reminder that her beloved Jonathan was only days away from the safety of home when he was taken. Samantha had hoped someday she would be able to share with Jonathan their unique kinship and tell him how much he had meant to her. She imagined Jonathan would someday be happy with a family of his own and that she could be a part of his life as a loving sister, but now Jonathan was gone, and she believed his memory would always weigh heavily on her heart.

Part 5

The Homecoming

CHAPTER 81

Jonathan Kendall's eyes opened slowly, but nothing seemed real. A buzz of conversation rang in his ears, but none of the words made sense. Everything in the dimly lit room moved in a slow confusion, as he struggled to remember his name.

Jonathan Kendall, he thought to himself, from Chandler, Oklahoma. I'm in France, he remembered. I'm fighting a war. He struggled to remember, as the chaos of his surroundings started to focus. Remember, he said to himself, remember.

The dawn had been barely more than darkness when he crawled toward his friend David Simpson. Badly wounded and entrapped in the barbed wire of an abandoned bunker, Jonathan could remember David's screams, as he pulled him roughly to the ground and out of the line of fire. The two friends clung to the scant shelter of the hole with three dead German soldiers at their feet. Jonathan could only imagine David had surprised them before running into the wire.

Jonathan was frantically trying to get David to the trees where Walt Johnson and Lloyd Wills attempted to cover them with fire. He recalled the ominous clunk of the mustard gas canisters cutting them off from the shelter of the trees and remembered screaming in panic. Knowing artillery would soon follow, Jonathan did the unthinkable—he put David Simpson on his back and ran directly into the German lines. Jonathan felt the percussion of the blast more than he heard the explosion and then nothing. He lay painfully in a bed, not knowing where he was or what day it was.

"Goot-en targ," a tired looking man in a white coat said. "Vee gayt ess een-en."

"Huh?" the confused Jonathan replied.

The man repeated the phrase in a slower and louder tone, which did not help Jonathan's comprehension.

"He said, 'Good afternoon, how are you?'" a German soldier in a nearby bed said with a heavy accent.

"Where am I?" Jonathan muttered to the heavily bandaged man.

"Strasbourg," the man replied.

Jonathan looked baffled, and the man added, "Germany."

Before Jonathan could react, the man in the white coat spoke in a rapid combination of syllables that could not be understood.

"He wants to know if you are...if you have feeling in your left side," the bandaged man interpreted.

Jonathan now realized he was very sore as he slowly lifted his left arm, which caused shooting pain up to his neck. The man in the white coat, who Jonathan determined was a doctor, appeared satisfied and nodded before he went to the next bed. Jonathan could now see his left leg was raised and he had bandages on the side of his head.

"Am I a prisoner?" Jonathan whispered to the man beside him.

The man grunted strangely and said, "The war's over...as of last week. Why do you think the doctor's so concerned? You won."

"How long have I been here?" Jonathan asked.

"I don't know," the man said. "I've been here three days, and you were here then."

The man then said something in German to a tired-looking nurse, who dutifully walked to the man's bedside. The two spoke in German for a few minutes before the nurse left.

"She said you came from the front a couple of weeks ago," the man translated. "You've had a head wound and have been sleeping. That's why the doctor wanted to know if you had any feeling. They signed the armistice on November 11. The war's over."

The nurse came back and talked quickly in German to the man.

The man turned to Jonathan said, "She's telling you to get some rest. The American doctors will come in a day or two."

"How about my friend?" Jonathan asked.

The man looked somewhat annoyed at Jonathan's questioning, but he called the nurse once again and had a brief conversation.

"She said you came alone in the ambulance," the man explained. "She also said for you to rest."

Jonathan settled into his cot and tried to get comfortable. His mind rushed with concern about David's whereabouts and the status of the men he had led on the patrol. Jonathan felt totally in exile, as he listened to random phrases spoken in German that he did not understand. He still feared his enemies, so he tried to stay awake while keeping his eyes closed. Severe, unrelenting pain throbbed down his left side. Before long, Jonathan drifted into sleep. In a few days, the American doctor came and arranged his transfer to Paris for recovery.

Jonathan slowly healed and with the exception of a broken arm was able to maneuver around the army hospital. Jonathan learned David Simpson had not survived. Jonathan was saved from the mustard gas and the wounds he received from the blast by a brave German soldier who dragged him to the safety of the German trench. Walt Johnson, Lloyd Wills, and Tucker McMurry came to visit Jonathan. They all had fond memories and lively stories about their friend, David Simpson.

The soldiers of the 142nd Infantry were excited for the war to end, anticipating an early trip home. Spirits sank, however, as the rumors spread that the 36th Division would be part of the occupation army. Jonathan returned to his unit by April, just in time for the division to prepare for the journey home. The 142nd Infantry was located in a small town about 100 miles southeast of Paris. The troops had been entertaining themselves with football, basketball, and baseball games to pass the time.

Captain Taylor gave Jonathan a hearty salute at his return. The captain explained how he had agonized over the letter he had to send announcing Jonathan's supposed death, but how satisfied he was at having to admit his mistake in a second letter saying Jonathan was wounded and recovering.

Jonathan traveled with his company to Brest before sailing to New York and Camp Merritt. After a few days, the 142nd boarded a train that traveled through Pennsylvania, West Virginia, Ohio, and Missouri before traveling through Oklahoma, with stopovers in Enid, Oklahoma City, El Reno, and Chickasha for the locals to cheer their returning troops. The train finally reached its destination at Fort Worth at Camp Bowie where the 36th Division had been formed. After more fanfare in Fort Worth, the division was demobilized.

Jonathan stood on the train platform in Fort Worth dressed in his uniform with a ticket back to Chandler—even though Jonathan was not sure if Chandler would still be his home.

CHAPTER 82

THE NOVEMBER WIND BLEW cold as Samantha looked outside the pharmacy into a steel-blue sky. It looked as if it might snow for the first time this season, and there was an urgent excitement in the air. Hope College resumed classes, but the pharmacy had been so busy that Samantha decided to keep working. Isaac Vandaveer gave her and the town a scare when he became ill, but he recovered in a couple of days and luckily did not have to fight off the dreaded Spanish Flu still plaguing the region.

"Samantha!" Margaret Kendall shouted, as she opened the door of the drugstore to step out of the cold wind.

People in the store stared at the round-faced Margaret Kendall, as she breathed heavily with her red cheeks puffing.

"Aunt Margaret?" Samantha replied, as she looked at her frenzied aunt. "What are you doing out?"

"I have to see you!" Margaret said urgently.

"Sure," Samantha said, as she guided the woman to the back of the store and away from the inquisitive eyes of shoppers. "What do you need?"

"I have the most fantastic news," Margaret hurriedly answered. "I received a telegram not more than thirty minutes ago from Oklahoma—Jonathan's alive!"

"What!" Samantha exclaimed as she leaned against one of the shelves in the back room to steady herself.

"It's true!" Margaret bubbled.

"But how?" Samantha asked.

"I don't know the details, but they found him in a German hospital after the armistice," Margaret gleamed.

"Jonathan's alive!" Samantha shrieked in a voice loud enough to be heard throughout the store.

Isaac Vandaveer heard the commotion and quickly went to investigate.

"What's wrong?" he asked, as Samantha cried uncontrollably.

"They've found Jonathan," Margaret explained. "I had to come as soon as I could to tell Samantha."

"I can't believe it!" an overjoyed Samantha said, as she tried to wipe tears away. "Is he okay?"

"As far as I know," Margaret replied. "They've moved him to Paris, and I think they expect a full recovery."

"That's wonderful news," Isaac said in a pleasant but more rational tone than the women.

"Isn't it!" Samantha beamed. "I wish I could write him."

"I'll get the address," Margaret offered.

Samantha's tone suddenly changed, as she remembered the circumstance of her leaving Jonathan, and she said, "No…that'll be fine. I'll…I'll see him sometime. I don't need to bother him with a silly letter."

Margaret Kendall and Isaac Vandaveer looked at each other, but neither pressed her for more information.

"It's enough to know he's safe," Samantha smiled. "That's enough for me."

Without further rejoicing, Samantha returned to work. On the way home Margaret stopped to tell everyone she met the incredible story of Jonathan's resurrection. Isaac Vandaveer carefully watched his young employee throughout the afternoon, as she had a renewed energy and spirit that could not be mistaken. Isaac did not know how the news would affect his plans, but he was content to see Samantha happy.

CHAPTER 83

THE SNOWS COMING OFF the lake were heavy in early December, but Samantha Harvey had a warm glow to her spirit after learning Jonathan Kendall was alive. The epidemic of Spanish Flu disappeared nearly as quickly as it had appeared, but Samantha continued to work at the pharmacy. Isaac Vandaveer, who diligently watched out for Samantha during the fall, became a frequent visitor to the Kendall home. Samantha could not identify when the change happened, but Isaac had become more of a friend than an employer. In Isaac's mind, the relationship was moving past friendship, but he doubted the young woman could ever see him as more.

Margaret invited Isaac to Christmas at the Kendall home. Christmas for Margaret Kendall was the product of months of planning as her family came to the house to enjoy homemade decorations, a feast of a meal, and gifts she had carefully selected for her children and grandchildren. Although Margaret was always hospitable, Samantha felt somewhat out of place during these family events and was glad to have Isaac Vandaveer to talk with while the other family members spent time recalling their memories.

Samantha laughed, as Margaret's daughter Greta told a story about the stoic George Kendall being trapped in a dress shop in

Chicago, while the girls tried on a multitude of dresses for a reception they planned to attend. Margaret, unwilling to let her husband interfere with her shopping, would not let George complain, as he sat for hours in the store. By the time Margaret made her selections, the reception they planned to attend had already started, which caused George to take a scolding from his wife for not communicating.

The Kendall family in Holland was not a particularly outgoing family, but they had a subdued warmth and affection for each other Samantha admired. The stories, usually at George Kendall's expense, continued through the afternoon. George, despite his rather stern appearance, was very good-natured about the teasing. Samantha remembered her first impressions of George and her misjudgment about his character. George Kendall was as selfless with his family as John Kendall had been selfish.

By early evening, Isaac Vandaveer approached Samantha with a cup of Margaret's special cider, which the small children were not allowed to taste.

"I'm thinking about taking a walk and getting some fresh air," Isaac whispered. "Would you like to come?"

"In the snow?" Samantha asked, as she looked out the window at the four inches of snow blanketing the street.

"It's not that cold," Isaac replied.

Although the Kendall house was large, it was getting cramped with the extra company.

Samantha knew they would not be missed so she said, "Why not? Let me get a coat."

In a few minutes, Samantha stepped into the still night air and to magnificent winter silence, as all she could hear was the gentle crunching of the snow under foot.

"It's beautiful, isn't it?" Samantha gleefully noted, as she looked at the strange glow of the moonlight reflecting off the fresh snow.

"I always enjoy a Christmas snow," Isaac smiled. "The snow's not quite as magical in February."

Samantha laughed as they walked slowly down the empty street toward the park in the center of town. Samantha was in a cheerful mood, as they talked about unimportant observations and the sometimes-quirky Kendall family. Isaac's familiar limp, which Samantha rarely noticed any more, left an awkward and noticeable path as he trudged through the snow. The couple walked to the center of the park, where a fountain was frozen in a stunning snow sculpture when Isaac stopped to put his hands on Samantha's shoulder to gently turn her around. Moonlight glimmered off Samantha's rosy cheeks, and her smile radiated warmth that contrasted to the frigid surroundings.

Isaac did not say anything for a moment, as he looked into Samantha's eyes, but then he said in a shaky voice, "I'm glad you walked with me tonight."

Clearing his throat and talking in a more even tone he said, "I think you're an extraordinary girl. I've watched you this past year and how you handle things — I've — I've grown quite fond of you."

"I've enjoyed working with you," Samantha smiled.

Isaac looked around the empty park for a second before saying, "I'm not talking about work — I — I would like for us to be more."

Samantha looked at him seriously and said, "What are you trying to say?"

Isaac took a deep breath and replied, "Samantha, will you marry me?"

The air was eerily quiet, as Samantha stood speechless in the middle of the park looking at the fidgeting Isaac. The question shocked Samantha. She had spent a lot of time with Isaac the past year and even more the past month. Memories of Jonathan's proposal caused her to stare blankly at the helpless man in front of her.

"I think I know the answer," Isaac awkwardly sighed, as he took a half-step backwards.

"No," Samantha finally stammered. "I mean no you don't know the answer...you don't know everything about me or – "

"Or what?" Isaac patiently asked in response to Samantha's hesitation.

"I was engaged before," Samantha said.

"I didn't know," Isaac said as he watched her carefully.

Samantha paced away a few steps before walking back to Isaac to explain, "You're a good man Isaac, maybe too good for a girl like me. I've kept a lot of things to myself...and a lot of things from you."

For the next fifteen minutes, Samantha confessed the circumstances of her arrival in Holland. Isaac learned she was the illegitimate daughter of the man who was her fiancé's father. Samantha talked about her mother and the heartbreak she must have felt. She told him about her papa and the Hellwig family, which was her true legacy.

Isaac listened carefully with a sympathetic tilt to his head before saying, "Do you think any of that would matter to me?"

Holding out his arms as if demonstrating he was unarmed and defenseless, Isaac continued, "I'm a thirty-two year old, one-legged man with a face worthy of a sack and the social skills of a badger. I have no right to ask a girl like you to love a man like me, and for weeks, I've tried to do the right thing and remind myself that I shouldn't embarrass you with my foolishness...but I can't, Samantha. I love you...I don't care what you think of your past...I see your goodness now. More than anything I want to see you happy, and I'm willing to spend the rest of my life to make that happen."

Samantha was spellbound by Isaac's impassioned speech as he added, "I have a good business. I think you know that. I'm a fair man and will take care of you...protect you...and honor you. I know I have no right, but I'd like you to think about my proposal."

Looking meekly into the snow, Isaac said, "I'll understand if you say no, and I've prepared myself for that answer. I will always respect and love you no matter your decision. I would just ask...no beg you to at least consider me as more than a friend."

Samantha watched the white-knuckled man for a moment expecting him to say more, but after a brief moment she said, "I don't have to think about anything, Isaac. I'm honored and yes...I will be your wife."

A surprised Isaac was temporarily bewildered, as he stood looking at the beautiful young woman who agreed to be his wife. Awkwardly, he stepped toward Samantha to hold her for the first time. She embraced and kissed him with tears streaking down her cold cheeks.

The jovial Isaac took Samantha's hand, as they walked slowly back to the Kendall home. The couple talked about their future and what their lives could be. Samantha was happy, but her emotions were much different than her feelings for Jonathan Kendall had been. She had a strong affection for Isaac Vandaveer, but she had always harbored feelings of admiration more than passion. As Samantha stepped into the Kendall house, however, she was completely convinced she would be happy with Isaac.

The Kendall family was embroiled in another family squabble over the accuracy of one of the many tales they liked to tell. Margaret Kendall laughed heartily and smiled at Samantha as the young woman entered. Samantha grinned as she watched the family, dreaming she too might one day have a family of her own. Isaac excused himself after a few minutes, and Samantha followed him to the front porch for a kiss goodnight. Samantha stood on the porch and watched Isaac drive his car into the wintery night.

"Did you have a good walk?" Margaret Kendall asked, as the car disappeared.

"You knew, didn't you?" Samantha asked. "You knew he was going to ask me to marry him?"

Margaret put her arm around Samantha and said, "I've known he's had special feelings for you...I think longer than he's known. I didn't know he would ask you tonight, but I'm not surprised. I watched you when you came back in the house, and I knew."

"I sometimes think you know everything," Samantha smiled, as she leaned her head into Margaret's round shoulders.

"Are you happy?" Margaret asked.

"He's a good man," Samantha answered. "He'll make me very happy."

"That's not the question I asked, dear," Margaret replied. "Are you happy?"

Samantha thought for a moment and said, "Yes, I think I am."

CHAPTER 84

JONATHAN KENDALL SPENT AN extra day in Oklahoma City before traveling back to his hometown. Chandler hosted a big reception for their returning heroes, but Jonathan was tired of the parades and the cheers. He felt relieved to be free from the responsibility of leadership. Jonathan had seen too many things he feared would be hard to forget.

Jonathan was also not eager to see his father — the real reason he delayed his return to Chandler. His father had lied to his mother twenty years earlier, and he was still lying to Jonathan, thinking past transgressions could somehow be forgotten. Jonathan would return to Chandler and the house on Silk Stocking Row, but he was not sure what he might do when he confronted his father.

It was June of 1919, and the weather was already hot. After spending a cold autumn in the trenches of France, Jonathan swore he would never complain about the hot Oklahoma summers again. As he boarded the train, thunderheads boiled in the west promising tempestuous weather, which fit Jonathan's mood. He rode the train alone, which was welcomed after spending weeks on crowded troop ships and trains. He had missed the Chandler alumni celebration by a few weeks but did not mind. Jonathan was not anxious to relive the past.

A near-empty train depot greeted Jonathan's early afternoon arrival. He purposely gave the cotton gin a wide berth as he walked to David Simpson's home. Jonathan spent several hours with Mrs. Simpson retelling the circumstances of David's death and trying to comfort her. He left Mrs. Simpson and arrived at Eighth Street walking toward home. Jonathan walked quickly and inconspicuously past the Conklin house. Elizabeth Conklin had written him many letters, but he was not yet ready to see her. He had business at home, first.

The house looked as he remembered, if not a bit smaller. Jonathan gently opened the door to hear the pleasant and reassuring voice of his mother humming in the kitchen. As if sensing her son's arrival, Mrs. Kendall's humming stopped. She peeked around the corner and shrieked at the sight of her son's return.

"Jonathan!" she squealed, as she moved faster than Jonathan thought possible to throw her arms around her son.

"We thought we lost you," she cried, as she held her son tight while Jonathan smiled broadly.

"Jonathan!" a second shriek came from Augusta, as his tall, pretty sister scampered down the stairs in a not too lady-like fashion.

Augusta also threw her arms around Jonathan.

"Caroline?" Jonathan said, as Augusta and Mrs. Kendall continued to squeeze him. "I didn't expect to see you here."

Caroline stood in the background as if embarrassed in some way at Jonathan's arrival.

"I'm—" Caroline started to say something before smiling, "It's so good to see you Jonathan."

Caroline ran to Jonathan and wept uncontrollably as Augusta and Mrs. Kendall tried to console her. Caroline excused herself after a few moments and left the room still crying.

"What's wrong?" Jonathan asked.

Mrs. Kendall squirmed as Augusta blurted out, "Caroline's moved back home."

Jonathan raised an eyebrow and gave an inquisitive look as Mrs. Kendall finally said, "Caroline's had some problems, and she's come home for a time to sort things out."

Jonathan wanted to ask about Caroline, but he was instead bombarded by questions from Augusta and Mrs. Kendall about the war and his experience in Europe. Jonathan was polite but vague about the details of combat, and he told them stories about the countryside and cities to keep them entertained.

"Did you see David?" Caroline asked from the corner of the room when she returned.

Jonathan's demeanor turned more serious as he answered, "Yes."

"The telegram said he was with you when you were reported dead," Caroline said sadly. "Did you—"

Caroline stopped for a moment trying to compose herself before saying, "Did he suffer?"

Jonathan was chilled by the question, but lied, "No...I don't think so."

The answer seemed to relieve Caroline, as Jonathan stepped to her and said, "David was transferred into my unit, and I got to see him for a few weeks before. He was the same old David with more friends than a dog has fleas. Everyone loved David."

Caroline tried to maintain her composure, but thoughts of the deceased David caused her to once again cry and leave the room.

"Have you seen your father?" Mrs. Kendall asked.

"No," Jonathan coldly replied. "I don't intend to."

"Jonathan," his mother pleaded.

"I don't know how you can stand him," Jonathan said flatly, as Augusta stood by silently.

"That's enough, Jonathan!" his mother scolded.

"It's not enough," Jonathan stubbornly replied. "There will never be enough to make up for what he's done."

"Jonathan," Mrs. Kendall pleaded. "He's your father."

"Yes," Jonathan said. "He's my father and Samantha's father, and God only knows who else he's fathered. I'm going to find her…that I promise."

"Jonathan!" Mrs. Kendall shouted. "How dare you discuss this in front of Augusta!"

A flustered Mrs. Kendall said, "Augusta, go to your room please."

Jonathan was sorry he had lost his temper in front of his younger sister, as he watched the confused girl retreat to the back of the house.

"Why can't you let this go?" Mrs. Kendall asked.

"How can you let his deceit destroy this family?" Jonathan asked angrily.

Mrs. Kendall turned her back to Jonathan for a moment before saying, "I learned to deal with it for you and for Caroline and for Augusta. I learned to forgive your father for my children's sake! What happened was a long time ago. Don't you think your father's suffered enough?"

Jonathan's eyes flashed as he said, "That's the point. He doesn't suffer. It's everyone around him that suffers. You've had to suffer humiliation. Samantha's been treated like…like an illegitimate child her whole life. And now Caroline? Don't think I don't know what's going on. Caroline's separated from whoever she married in such a grand wedding that he orchestrated. Caroline loved David, and he threw him at Samantha rather than tell me the truth. In fact, he still hasn't told me the truth I had to find out from David…and poor David…he's blown to pieces, and Caroline can never know."

Mrs. Kendall waited for Jonathan to stop his rant before saying, "Things could have been handled differently, but that girl should never have come to Chandler. She's what's tore this family apart."

"She's about all the family that's important to me now," Jonathan replied. "I'm going to find her."

"Why?" Mrs. Kendall cried. "Why do you insist on digging up the past?"

"Because I need to," Jonathan snapped. "Where is she?'

"I don't know," Mrs. Kendall sobbed.

Jonathan looked suspiciously at his mother as she said, "I really don't know. Your father took care of things. I don't know, and I don't want to know."

"It doesn't matter," Jonathan reasoned. "She's out there, and I'm going to find her. Good-bye Mother."

"You're leaving?" Mrs. Kendall asked in surprise.

Jonathan nodded, "I'll be back after I find Samantha."

"Why?" Mrs. Kendall pleaded.

Jonathan thought for a moment and after a deep breath said in a kinder tone, "I have to know she's all right. Once I find she's okay, I can get on with my life."

Jonathan walked over to hug his crying mother, and then walked out of the house — unsure if or when he would return.

CHAPTER 85

Jonathan left the Kendall home conflicted. The disgust he felt for his father's deceptions tainted the joy of seeing his mother and sisters on his homecoming. Jonathan did not want to interact with anyone in his current mood, so he walked down the hill to the Statistical House located to the west of the Kendall home. The Statistical House was empty. It had been two years since the building had been occupied, and weeds had invaded the rock structure cloaking it in a natural camouflage. Jonathan had no business there, so he kept walking across the low field until he stopped at Oak Park Cemetery west of town.

Mr. Harvey's small grave marker faced Jonathan, as he remembered a spring day that seemed like another lifetime when he had asked Samantha Harvey to be his wife. Jonathan had seen terrible things in France, but none compared to the sadness he felt at the memory of this place. Turning back to look at the hometown of his youth, Jonathan used his hand to shield his eyes from the bright afternoon sun.

A surprised Jonathan then noticed something he believed must be a mirage or unlikely hallucination. Walking toward him, across the field separating the town from the cemetery, came a confident and determined young woman. Her lean figure and blowing strands of light colored hair were like a vision of a happier time. The wavy rays of heat radiated off the flat field making her look like a dream. Jonathan's heart raced, and a broad smile instinctively adorned his face as Samantha Harvey strode casually to him. It made perfect sense he reasoned. Of course, she would visit the grave.

Jonathan ran a few steps before stopping to look closely at the girl walking toward him. He was confused for a second. The girl was not Samantha; it was his sister Augusta, blossomed into a woman so much that he barely recognized her. Augusta continued to walk toward him with a poise reminding him so much of Samantha Harvey that it was painful.

"Hello, Jonathan," Augusta greeted as she approached.

"What are you doing here?" Jonathan asked.

"I came to find you," Augusta smiled. "I thought you might come here."

"I'm sorry about before," Jonathan apologized, remembering his outburst in front of his mother and Augusta.

Augusta looked pleasantly and innocently at her brother and said, "I'm not as clueless as people imagine. I've known about Samantha since the day she left. It didn't take much to figure it out, no matter how hard Daddy's tried."

"You know?"

Augusta nodded her head and looked around at the tall grass blowing lazily in the summer breeze.

"I know you have to find her," Augusta added. "I know you need to face her…to have some closure. She's our sister, after all."

"Do you know where she is?" Jonathan asked.

Augusta shook her head and said, "Father's kept that a secret. I guess Father keeps a great many secrets."

Jonathan could not believe the little girl he had known possessed such adult reasoning and maturity.

"She has family," Augusta added. "I watched her place one time when she went to visit. Their name is Hellwig...they live close to Keokuk Falls not far from here."

Augusta hesitated for a moment and said, "I heard Father talking one time when he didn't think I was listening. No one ever thinks I'm listening. He was upset because Samantha had sent them money. I think they may know...I think they may know where Samantha is."

Jonathan put both hands on his sister's cheeks before hugging her tightly.

"Let me walk you home," Jonathan offered. "Then I'll go find her."

Augusta smiled and said, "The last train leaves in less than an hour. You'd better run for it."

Jonathan smiled at his sensible and outspoken younger sister. Grabbing his backpack, he headed to town.

"Jonathan!" Augusta shouted.

Jonathan stopped and turned to his sister.

"Promise me you'll come home?" she asked.

"Someday," Jonathan waved. "Someday."

CHAPTER 86

FIVE O'CLOCK APPROACHED when Jonathan arrived at the small train station in Prague. After several inquiries, he found someone who knew the Hellwigs and got directions to their place. Jonathan rented a horse and saddle before riding south across the North Canadian River.

The horse panted heavily as Jonathan pulled up in front of a small farmhouse in need of paint. The place looked vacant, but he feverishly pounded on the door anyway. Quickly walking around the house, Jonathan could see no one. Jonathan looked around the desolate farm and could tell that the field had been worked recently, and the sparse furnishing inside the house suggested someone still lived there. As he searched the property, Jonathan noticed a trail through the woods barely wide enough for a wagon.

Jonathan let the horse rest and cautiously stepped into the thick woods. The thicket of forest was silent except for the screaming of grasshoppers surrounding him. The lonely woods were disconcerting to Jonathan. If it had not been for the humid heat, he would have thought the terrain looked like a battlefield in France. After less than a quarter-mile, the trail opened into a smaller field. A pathetic shack stood in the corner under a lone pecan tree.

Jonathan believed the dilapidated structure must have been abandoned, but as he approached, he could see through an open door that someone lived there.

"Hello!" Jonathan shouted to the echoes of silence.

"Is anyone here?" he shouted again.

Seeing no one, Jonathan cautiously stepped in the open door to see a cot, a rickety chair and a wood box that looked like it was used as a table. Jonathan froze as he spotted something he never expected to see in this broken-down place. Jonathan stepped further inside the one-room shack and picked up a picture to examine it carefully.

A puzzled Jonathan stared at the picture in confusion until the cocking of a gun behind him broke his trance.

"You the law?" a gruff voice asked sternly from behind him.

"No," Jonathan calmly replied, as he slowly turned around to face Marcus Lutz.

Marcus studied him for a minute trying to place the face, when he raised his shotgun more urgently and said, "You're that boy!"

Jonathan stood motionless with his hands instinctively held to his side.

"You're that Kendall boy!" the agitated Marcus shouted. "What are you doing here?"

"I came to see Mr. Hellwig," Jonathan explained. "Is he around?"

"No!" the man angrily informed. "He ain't around, and you don't have any business with him. Huck's paid off the place lock, stock, and barrel. I oughta shoot you now for even stepping on this place."

"Why do you have a picture of Samantha?" Jonathan pointedly asked, ignoring the threat.

Marcus looked puzzled before he spotted the photograph Jonathan held in his hand.

"Give me that!" Marcus demanded as he lowered the gun and grabbed the photograph from Jonathan's hand.

"Why do you have a picture of Samantha?" Jonathan asked again.

"Your daddy send you down here?" Marcus asked suspiciously.

"My father doesn't have anything to do with this," Jonathan replied.

"Your daddy has everything to do with this," Marcus claimed before saying in a more defeated voice. "If he was here, I'd likely already shot him dead."

Jonathan swallowed hard and looked at the sad man holding the picture frame carefully.

"I'm not my father," Jonathan said calmly. "And I don't think you want to shoot me. I didn't come for trouble, I just came for some information. Could you please tell me why you have a picture of Samantha Harvey?"

Marcus stared intently at Jonathan for a moment before looking again at the picture.

"It ain't Samantha," Marcus finally said softly. "It's her mother."

"I've seen pictures of Samantha's mother," Jonathan replied. "That's not her."

Marcus laughed half-heartedly and said, "You ain't ever seen a picture of Samantha's mother, cause this is the only one there is."

"I've seen it," Jonathan claimed, "at Samantha's house."

Marcus set the shotgun against the wall and said, "You saw a picture of Sarah."

Raising the picture to point at Jonathan, Marcus said, "This is Suzanne."

"Suzanne Hellwig?"

"Suzanne Lutz," Marcus said defiantly, as he lowered the picture and stepped outside.

Jonathan quickly followed the man and asked, "You're telling me Sarah Harvey is not Samantha's real mother?"

Marcus Lutz looked at his worn shoes for a moment, hesitating to respond.

Almost to himself, Jonathan asked, "My father can't be Samantha's father?"

Marcus Lutz moved faster than Jonathan thought possible and quickly used his forearm to pin Jonathan's neck to the weathered wall of the shack.

"What did you say?" Marcus angrily asked.

Jonathan was easily able to free himself from the man's grasp and replied, "John Kendall believes Samantha is his daughter."

Marcus Lutz looked as if he had been hit in the head, as he staggered back a few steps before letting a string of profanities ring through the empty countryside about John Kendall.

Jonathan listened to the angry rant, before Marcus took a deep breath and said assuredly, "Samantha's my daughter!"

Jonathan did not respond, but he watched the pained look on the face of Marcus Lutz.

"I was married to Suzanne," Marcus explained. "John Kendall was sweet on Sarah and took her places...spent money on her. Sarah was nearly twenty-five years old and was happy to have a man pay attention to her...until she found out he had family. Sarah was humiliated by the whole affair. John Kendall didn't have no respect for the Hellwigs then and helped the bank foreclose on the place. Sarah had worked with Mr. Harvey at the school, and they had been writing letters back and forth so they married soon after. Sarah didn't want to be a burden to her family anymore."

"Suzanne and I were married," Marcus continued. "She was only eighteen and living with her sister, but we was married and no one can say different. I got the papers to prove it. Suzanne's brother Lawrence wanted me to go into town to straighten things out with

John Kendall one day, so I went. We'd been drinking, and when Lawrence couldn't find him, he decided robbin' the bank would help get the farm back. I's so drunk I don't remember much, but Lawrence got shot, and they sent me to prison. I was nineteen at the time and knew I'd be an old man before they let me out. I found out Suzanne was with child when I was in prison. I begged her to divorce me and find someone to raise our baby, but she died during the birth. Sarah took the child, and Mr. Harvey adopted her. I never told nobody, 'cause what kind man wants his baby girl to have a convict for a father."

"Better a convict than John Kendall," Jonathan muttered.

"I see you've got to know your father pretty well," Marcus Lutz sneered. "John Kendall's taken everything from me...but he can't claim my daughter, too."

"Do you know where Samantha is?" Jonathan asked.

Marcus shook his head and said, "It's better she don't know 'bout me."

"But where is she now?" Jonathan pressed.

Marcus looked at the eager young man and said, "I don't know, but she wired some money to Huck awhile back. I think he said it came from someplace in Michigan."

"Thanks," Jonathan said as he started to walk away.

"You ain't goin' to tell her?" Marcus asked.

Jonathan stopped and walked back toward the worn, broken man and said, "I have to. Mr. Harvey will always be her papa, but believe me she'll want to know...she'll want to know about you."

Jonathan then surprised the haggard man by hugging him and saying, "Believe me, she'll want to know."

CHAPTER 87

THE STABLE MANAGER IN Prague was not happy when Jonathan returned the ragged horse after a hard ride back from Keokuk Falls. The trains had already quit running for the evening, as Jonathan frantically hunted for a ride to Chandler. No one was making a direct trip, but he caught a ride to Meeker before finding a truck heading north to Chandler.

It was nine o'clock at night when Jonathan passed the courthouse in Chandler and headed down Silk Stocking Row to confront his father.

"Jonathan?" a soft voice from the porch of the Conklin house called.

Elizabeth Conklin had heard Jonathan was back in town and had been waiting to see him for most of the afternoon.

Jonathan wanted to walk by the house but decided he needed to stop after taking two more steps.

"Hello, Elizabeth," he greeted.

"I heard you were back in town," Elizabeth said sweetly. "I thought maybe you'd come see me."

"I've been busy," Jonathan explained.

"Oh," Elizabeth sighed. "Did you get the letters I sent? We were all so happy to find out you had survived."

"Yes," Jonathan said. "I very much appreciate the letters, and I'm glad to be alive too."

Elizabeth smiled strangely, as she could sense the reunion was nothing more than friendly.

"I've got to go," Jonathan said apologetically.

"Will you come by later?" Elizabeth asked.

"I don't think I'll have time," Jonathan replied. "I'm heading to Michigan...probably tomorrow."

"So soon?" Elizabeth pouted.

Jonathan nodded and said, "Again, thanks for the letters...I've got to go."

Jonathan felt uncomfortable at the awkward conversation, but he had to see his father and find out Samantha's location. Elizabeth had been a sweet girl, but their relationship had always been nothing more than friendly. Samantha Harvey was somewhere in Michigan living her life under a cloud of deceit. Jonathan knew he could make things right, but he felt the need to find Samantha as soon as possible.

The Kendall house was illuminated, and Jonathan did not bother knocking, as he barged in the front door to find his father sitting in the front room.

"Jonathan?" a surprised Mr. Kendall said as he looked at his son.

Jonathan did not respond for a moment, but then demanded, "Where is she? Where is Samantha?"

John Kendall groaned and began to say, "You have to —"

"I don't have to do anything but find Samantha," Jonathan interrupted.

"You don't know the situation," Mr. Kendall responded.

"I don't know about you telling Samantha she was your daughter?" Jonathan hotly replied.

Mr. Kendall's face turned ashen, as he hurriedly said, "Keep your voice down...I know you're upset."

Jonathan laughed insincerely and said, "Keep quiet so your reputation stays intact? I'm beyond upset...I'm amazed at the extent you'll let your past indiscretions ruin the lives of everyone around you!"

"I don't regret my life or what I've done for my family," Mr. Kendall hotly defended.

Jonathan shook his head and said, "That's the problem. You never regret anything. You rationalized in your mind that nothing's your fault and that every single thing revolves around how people see you."

"I won't fret my life away with guilt for something done more than two decades ago!" Mr. Kendall shouted.

Jonathan looked sternly at his father and said, "You don't live with guilt. Everyone around you carries the burden of your guilt because you've never let your manufactured reputation admit to anything! I've lived with your guilt. Mother's lived with your guilt. Even poor Caroline lives with your guilt, and Samantha...Samantha was an innocent girl that you've destroyed because of your vain pride. You may not acknowledge your guilt—but your guilt echoes like an endless tragedy for everyone around you."

John Kendall looked angrily at his son but did not make a defense.

"I'm going now," Jonathan proclaimed. "I'm going for Samantha."

"You can't!" John Kendall shouted. "She's your sister...Okay I'll admit it. Does that make you happy?"

Jonathan stepped close to his father and said, "You fool! All you had to do was admit your mistake. Samantha's not your daughter! She's not even the daughter of Sarah Harvey. Samantha was adopted when Suzanne Lutz died. Does that name ring a bell with you? If you'd ever gotten over the conceit that drove you to continue your selfish deception, you would have known that!"

John Kendall looked dazed and confused as he said, "That's not possible."

"It's more than possible," Jonathan declared. "I've talked to Marcus Lutz today, and Huck Hellwig confirms it. Marcus Lutz is Samantha's father, and Suzanne Lutz was her mother. Why did you think Mr. Harvey approved of my relationship to Samantha?"

"I—I," John Kendall stammered.

"If you'd ever got past your self-importance, you would have known the truth twenty years ago and been a real father to your family," Jonathan preached.

John Kendall made no reply, as he contemplated the truth behind his denial.

"Where is she?" Jonathan demanded.

A defeated John Kendall muttered, "She's in Michigan. A town called Holland on the coast. I sent her to stay with my brother."

Jonathan looked at his pathetic father with no remorse, as he left the house and planned to catch the first train out of town to find Samantha.

CHAPTER 88

JONATHAN KENDALL HAD REHEARSED his reunion with Samantha on the long train trip a hundred times. He admired the tall forest that surrounded the landscape of western Michigan, but his mind focused on Samantha. Every fifteen minutes he found himself taking her tattered photograph out of his pocket to see her bright eyes and sly smile beckoning him.

A baggage handler at the train depot pointed Jonathan in the direction of George and Margaret Kendall's house. Jonathan walked quickly through the quaint town and then sprinted across the park in the center of the city before slowing down to a modest trot as he approached the Kendall house.

Voices from the backyard caught Jonathan's attention, as he immediately recognized the subdued laugh of Samantha. Hurrying around the side of the strange house, Jonathan stopped to see an older, heavy-set woman talking to Samantha who was sitting in the afternoon sun. Jonathan could see Samantha's profile and admired her for a moment while the older woman stopped talking to stare at the stranger in her yard. Samantha, noticing her distraction, turned gracefully to see Jonathan standing less than twenty steps from her.

Samantha looked at her aunt before standing to say, "Jonathan?"

Samantha ran to him and threw her arms around Jonathan's neck to squeeze him.

"I thought you were dead!" she cried with joy at seeing him.

"I'm here," Jonathan beamed. "I came for you."

Jonathan kissed Samantha and held her so tightly she could barely breathe. The joy overwhelming Samantha evaporated with the kiss. Mr. Kendall had convinced her Jonathan must never know the truth of their unlikely kinship, but now that he was here, Samantha's mind spun in a surreal maze of uncertainly. Separating herself from Jonathan, Samantha stepped back as if to get a better look at him.

In a more demure tone, Samantha said, "It's so good to see you, but you shouldn't have come."

"So you're Jonathan," Margaret Kendall interrupted, as she maneuvered to hug the nephew she had not seen in so many years. "I'm your Aunt Margaret. I haven't seen you since you were a toddler."

"Nice to meet you," Jonathan politely replied before turning his attention back to Samantha. "I've come for you, Samantha. I've come to take you home."

"Home?" Samantha replied weakly. "Jonathan...you don't understand—"

"I understand everything," Jonathan smiled. "I've come for you."

"Jonathan," Samantha sighed.

"Let's sit down," Jonathan offered.

"I've got to check on George," Margaret said in a serious tone. "I'll leave you two alone."

After Margaret left, Samantha collapsed in the wooden lawn chair and shook her head while saying, "You shouldn't have come."

With a gleaming smile, Jonathan said, "You don't understand. Samantha, you left town believing an evil, malicious lie. I know my father told you that he was your father."

"You know?" Samantha asked. "I'm so relieved. I've worried so much about it. Then I got word you had been killed in the war —"

"Samantha," Jonathan interrupted. "I'm not your brother...That's what I've come to tell you. We're not related...we've never been related. It was all a huge lie."

"That's not possible," Samantha muttered. "Why would your father...Could he really hate me that much?"

"He didn't know," Jonathan explained. "He couldn't see beyond his own self-centered world. I went to Keokuk Falls and found Marcus Lutz. Marcus and your Aunt Suzanne were married, but your real mother died in the delivery. You were adopted by your aunt...your real aunt...it's confusing, but I talked to Marcus Lutz, and he told me that he was your real father...he even showed me the birth certificate in your mother's things. Suzanne Lutz was your mother."

Samantha stared blankly at the news as if she were looking right through the excited Jonathan. She had never considered the possibility she had been adopted. Her parents had never mentioned it.

"Papa wouldn't have," Samantha whispered to herself.

"What?" Jonathan asked.

Samantha did not answer but started to cry, as Jonathan leaned over to hold her in his arms for comfort.

"It's okay," Jonathan said. "I'm here now. Everything will be okay."

Samantha struggled to regain her composure and said, "You shouldn't have come, Jonathan. It seems everything I do hurts you."

"What do you mean?" Jonathan replied. "You could never hurt me."

Samantha looked pathetically at Jonathan and said, "I'm married."

A flabbergasted Jonathan leaned back and said in a baffled tone, "To who?"

"To me," Isaac Vandaveer answered, as he stepped behind Jonathan. "She's married to me."

Jonathan watched the plain-looking man limp across the yard to stand by his wife.

"Isaac, this is Jonathan...Jonathan Kendall," Samantha sadly introduced.

Ignoring the introduction, Jonathan asked Samantha in a demanding tone, "How long?"

Samantha looked at Isaac and said, "Since May...about six weeks."

Samantha reached up to touch Isaac's hand that was resting on her shoulder to say, "Isaac, could you go inside and see Margaret...Jonathan and I have some things to discuss."

Isaac was reluctant but complied with his wife's request. The backyard was uncomfortably silent as the squeaking of the screen door signaled Isaac was inside.

"Married?" Jonathan said in disbelief. "To him?"

Samantha nodded and said, "He's a good man."

Jonathan, struggling to contain his temper, said, "How could you?"

"I thought you were my brother!" she whispered as loudly as she could without being heard by anyone but Jonathan. "Then I thought you were dead! I...I needed someone, and Isaac was there for me."

"But I love you," Jonathan said. "I tried to get you out of my mind for over a year...then I found out Marcus Lutz was your father. We were meant to be together! Can't you see that?"

Samantha, who typically was poised and confident, now looked unsure and confused as she said dejectedly, "I'm married to Isaac, now."

"Samantha," Jonathan pleaded. "You didn't know the truth. I know you still love me. I know you still have feelings for me. I see it in your eyes."

"Character's more than the look in a person's eye," Samantha replied. "I'm married now."

Grabbing her gently by the shoulders Jonathan said, "Get out of it! There's not a judge in the land that wouldn't grant you a divorce or even an annulment. It wasn't your fault."

"It wasn't Isaac's fault, either," Samantha said. "What would your life be like with a divorced woman? Do you think your father would accept me any better?"

"I don't care wit about my father!" Jonathan exclaimed angrily. "I care about you!"

Samantha buried her head in her hands and roughly rubbed her forehead and eyes as if to see if this were but another of her bad dreams. She looked at Jonathan and remembered so vividly why she had fallen in love with him—why she was sure she would always love him.

After Samantha's silence, Jonathan said, "Come back with me."

"I can't," Samantha sobbed.

"Please," Jonathan begged.

Samantha wiped her eyes and replied kindly, "Please leave, Jonathan. Forget me and get on with your life. I have."

"You can't mean that?" Jonathan pleaded.

"I do," Samantha nervously replied.

Jonathan stared at her and said defiantly, "I'm going to the train station, now, but I'll always love you, Samantha. If you change your mind—when you change your mind, I'll have you as my wife. If you don't come, you've broken me. I'll wait at the station for your answer."

Jonathan wanted to say things better, but his beloved Samantha was distraught and unhappy — that he could not bear. Looking at the house, he saw Isaac Vandaveer standing in the doorway, respecting his wife's wishes to be alone. Without saying more, Jonathan picked up his bag and headed to the train station.

CHAPTER 89

"WHAT WILL YOU DO?" Isaac asked gently, as his wife wept quietly in the backyard of Margaret Kendall's house.

"It's all so much," she cried.

"I know," Isaac consoled softly. "I know."

Samantha sat silently in the still of the backyard, her mind a mass of confused emotions. As much as Isaac would have liked to help his wife's pain, he knew he was powerless.

"I overheard enough to know he's not your brother," Isaac said softly.

Samantha nodded, continuing to stare into the green grass as if it might hold some answers or at least some comfort for her.

After the long silence Isaac finally said, "I won't stand in the way of your happiness — you know that."

Samantha fought back tears and said, "I know, Isaac."

Isaac carefully and lovingly watched Samantha. He was still getting to know his wife, but he knew Samantha well enough to know what he needed to do.

"You have to go to him," Isaac finally said.

"I know," Samantha replied.

Samantha rose slowly and kissed Isaac on the forehead before making the walk to the train depot. She walked slowly at first before thinking there might be an early train and she might miss Jonathan. Walking faster across the park, she practically ran through the empty downtown to the train station on the other side. Stopping at the entrance, she spotted Jonathan standing alone leaning against the corner of the depot.

Spotting Samantha walking toward him, Jonathan said, "You came!"

Samantha nodded, "I had to. I couldn't let you go like this."

"You're not leaving him are you?" Jonathan said in a wistful tone.

Samantha smiled, "Did you think I could?"

"No."

Jonathan could not say more. His emotions made his throat contract, and his eyes were moist, as he was content to look at Samantha as he had imagined her for over a year.

"I couldn't let you leave without letting you know I love you, Jonathan," Samantha explained. "I loved you then, and I love you now. You need to know that."

"But you won't leave with me?" Jonathan sniffled bravely.

"I'm married," Samantha smiled. "For better or worse, richer or poorer...Isaac's a good man. If I would break his heart, I wouldn't be worth having. I think you understand that."

Jonathan nodded, as he wiped tears from his cheeks.

Samantha stepped close to help him and said, "You're not like your father, Jonathan. I hope you understand that. You're a good man, and I know you'll do great things because you have greatness in you. I've seen it."

Samantha now crying said, "Find a good girl and love her like I know you loved me."

The two embraced, as Jonathan choked up and could barely breathe.

Stepping back, Samantha asked, "Are you going to come back to the house and visit your aunt and uncle?"

Shaking his head, Jonathan said, "Naw...I've already got a ticket on the evening train to Chicago."

Samantha nodded and asked, "Will you go back to Oklahoma?"

Jonathan looked around and replied, "I really don't know. My life's kind of brand new right now."

Samantha smiled through her tears.

Jonathan said, "There's a guy waiting for you over there."

Samantha turned around to see Isaac standing patiently at the far end of the train platform.

"I know," Samantha said, as she gave Jonathan one more hug before walking slowly back to her husband.

Stopping after a few steps, Samantha turned to say, "I'll always remember."

"Remember what?"

"You," Samantha smiled. "Our first talks, our letters, our plans, your nights on my front porch, your talks with Papa. I'll remember the joy I felt knowing you were alive. I'll remember you as you are right now...I'll remember you always."

With a pained expression, Samantha continued, "I'm happy, Jonathan...I want you to be happy, too."

Before Jonathan could reply, Samantha turned quickly back to Isaac. Jonathan watched her make the long walk and relished every second of her graciousness. As much as he wanted her, he knew he had to let her go. As Isaac and Samantha Vandaveer strolled back to their home, Jonathan stood alone in the train station knowing his life would never be the same.

CHAPTER 90

Jonathan Kendall returned to Oklahoma, but not immediately to Chandler. He never forgave his father for the deceit and selfishness that nearly destroyed Samantha and took her away from him. Jonathan never spoke to his father again. He moved to Oklahoma City and prospered in several business ventures while maintaining his involvement as an officer in the National Guard. Elizabeth Conklin married a few months later and left Chandler. Jonathan knew it was for the best.

Caroline, another victim of John Kendall's deception, divorced soon after the war ended and moved back to the Kendall house. Augusta did not marry until she was nearly twenty-five years old, and after several years as a teacher, she became a preacher's wife. Augusta ended up with six rowdy boys, and Jonathan took every opportunity to spend time with his nephews. Lou Berta Cassidy ended up marrying a young dentist that moved to Chandler and never left her hometown.

John Kendall passed away in 1925, and Jonathan finally returned to Chandler to attend the funeral. Jonathan moved back to Chandler to help take care of his mother, but she died a few months later. Jonathan managed the land holdings his father had acquired through the years and moved in with Caroline temporarily, but the living arrangement eventually became permanent. Jonathan built a house on the eastern edge of Chandler overlooking the old Harvey place north of Indian Springs and sold the Kendall House on Silk Stocking Row.

Jonathan Kendall possessed the character his father had tried to manufacture. He managed the family business efficiently and sold portions of the land to the farmers that worked it. Jonathan was generous and benevolent in the community. When Huck Helwig sold his place to move to the oil town of Cromwell, Jonathan hired Marcus Lutz to work in Chandler as a carpenter, and he turned out to be handy with tools. Marcus Lutz prospered with Jonathan's help, and when Samantha's father passed away, the former convict was buried in Oak Park Cemetery close to Mr. Harvey. Jonathan felt an unusual kinship with Marcus Lutz, since they had both lost the women they loved.

For a time, Jonathan was considered the most eligible bachelor in Chandler — some would say the county. Jonathan, however, believed there was only one, true final love for him, and she belonged to someone else. The Great War taught Jonathan that happy endings were a fable and character manifests itself in overcoming the obstacles of life no matter how bitter. He had seen Samantha do it, and he tried to demonstrate it in his own life. Caroline attempted to match him with eager and attractive young women for years, but she finally found the endeavor fruitless.

Caroline reconnected with the Kendall family back in Michigan, but Jonathan knew he could never go there. Jonathan was far from a hermit but lived in one room in his house, allowing Caroline to keep the rest of the place as she liked. His bedroom was simple in appearance with plain furnishings and a military neatness. The only decoration was the old photograph of Samantha discreetly placed on the corner of his night table. The photograph was old and faded. Jonathan felt guilty every time he looked at it, but the picture comforted and haunted him in a strange way he could not understand. Jonathan sometimes studied it for hours memorizing every detail.

Jonathan traveled often, hunting up former soldiers from the 142nd Infantry to relive old times and to remember their fallen comrades. He became active in many civic organizations and was always willing to lend a hand to a good cause. The Great Depression caused hard times in Lincoln County, but the frugal and shrewd Jonathan managed to hold on to his properties through the worst of it. As the Second World War started, Jonathan manned the front lines, selling bonds and running scrap iron drives to help the boys overseas. After the war, his scant social life revolved around supper with his sister, the old picture of Samantha, and a local homecoming event called the Chandler Alumni Banquet.

Chandler's alumni weekend presented a bittersweet slice of nostalgia for Jonathan. He enjoyed seeing people revisit their hometown and visit with old classmates, but he also remembered David Simpson during these times and never went to a banquet without classmates recalling the deeds and misadventures of his friend. Alumni weekend also reminded him of his first meeting with the enchanting young girl he had planned to marry, but now kept only in his memory and a faded photograph.

"Are you ready yet?" Caroline barked from downstairs as Jonathan struggled with a necktie.

"In a minute," he shouted back curtly.

He and Caroline had lived together for many years, and she had long taken over the job of helping Jonathan organize his life.

"Banquet's starting soon!" Caroline reminded.

"I've got a watch," Jonathan whispered to himself. He shouted back to his sister, "Why are you in such a hurry tonight?"

In ten minutes, Jonathan came down the stairs to the tapping foot of his impatient sister.

"How do I look?" Jonathan asked, as he turned around for Caroline to inspect his attire.

Jonathan was fifty-three years old by the 1947 alumni banquet, but he did not appear so old. He stood tall and had the erect posture he had learned in the military. His graying temples were becoming silver, but he hunted regularly with friends from around the state and started playing golf with Lou Berta's husband on the course where the old National Guard campgrounds once stood.

Caroline smiled at her brother and said in a disapproving tone, "You look like it's 1925 again. You'd think a man of your means could buy a new suit a least once a decade."

"What's wrong with it?" Jonathan asked as he held up his arms for closer inspection.

Shaking her head, Caroline replied, "You look fine, as always...let's go."

Stepping into the warm May evening, Caroline looked at Jonathan's shiny Cadillac parked in the drive and said, "How can a man buy a new car every year and never buy a decent suit?"

Nudging his sister along, Jonathan said, "Because the suit won't take you anywhere. The car takes me where I want to go. Why are you so concerned with my appearance?"

"Never mind," Caroline said in a tone of frustration. "It's not like you'd change on my account."

Caroline slid into the car for the short ride to the American Legion and the reunion. Jonathan never looked forward to social events, but he always seemed comfortable at them, as he was able to converse about a wide range of subjects with everyone from old classmates to former soldiers.

Alumni weekend reminded Caroline of a happier, simpler time. Caroline was active in planning the event, and people relied on her, as they had during her high school days. Tonight, however, Caroline stood inconspicuously in the corner observing things.

Jonathan viewed social gatherings as a tiresome obligation. He would rather stay home to read a book or listen to the radio instead of playing the frustrating game identifying classmates that aged almost beyond recognition. Tonight was no different. Caroline watched her brother but also waited anxiously to see who might come this night.

Caroline recognized the woman standing at the door before anyone else. The slender woman lingered, deciding if she would step inside. Caroline quickly glanced at her brother, but he had not seen the woman. Jonathan Kendall seemed to sense her presence, however, and looked up to see Samantha Vandaveer standing in the doorway. Samantha's sandy hair was shorter, with touches of gray. Her face was not quite as smooth as the photograph embedded in Jonathan's memory, but he could never mistake the pleasant smile, delicate cheekbones, and soulful, hazel eyes.

"What's the matter?" a friend asked, as Jonathan stopped talking mid-sentence to see if his eyes were playing a cruel trick on him.

"Excuse me," Jonathan replied blankly, as his eyes stayed focused on the woman.

Jonathan moved toward her. There were a few wrinkles in the folds of her eyes and cheeks when she smiled, but Jonathan would have recognized her anywhere. After he took a few steps, Samantha spotted Jonathan and flashed a blushing smile, as he stopped and stood speechless for a moment.

Samantha finally said, "Hello, Jonathan."

"Samantha?" Jonathan declared in an unsure voice. "What are you doing here?"

Appearing slightly confused, Samantha replied, "I came for the reunion. Didn't Caroline tell you?"

Jonathan looked to see his sister standing across the room watching them.

"I had no idea," Jonathan said.

An uncomfortable silence seemed like an eternity before, Samantha said, "I thought Caroline would have told you. She insisted I come."

Turning to look at Caroline again, Jonathan said, "She did?"

Samantha nodded and said, "I hope that's all right. I don't want to be awkward."

"Of course not," Jonathan quickly assured. "It's great to see you."

"It's great to see you, too," Samantha smiled.

Caroline kept her distance, although Samantha would have liked for her to have helped with the cumbersome conversation.

"Did you come in today?" Jonathan asked.

"Yes," Samantha said. "This afternoon."

"Very good," Jonathan smiled uncomfortably. "Well—I guess there's lots of people you want to see. I won't take up your time."

Samantha did not speak, but looked shyly at her polished shoes.

Jonathan started to step away when she said, "You're really the person I want to see the most, Jonathan."

Jonathan stopped to smile kindly.

"Caroline really didn't tell you I was coming?" Samantha asked again.

Jonathan turned around to signal Caroline to join the conversation, but his sister had disappeared.

"No," Jonathan replied. "She didn't."

"Caroline talked me into coming," Samantha explained. "She said I ought to come to the reunion. I—I assumed you wanted to—I thought you knew."

"No," Jonathan smiled. "But I'm glad Caroline invited you."

Jonathan stood in the doorway with Samantha as people gently nudged them out of the way to enter. A buzz of conversation crackled inside the crowded room, but Jonathan focused on his reunion with Samantha.

"Would you like to step outside for some air?" Jonathan suggested. "Maybe see the town...it's awful noisy in here."

Samantha smiled and said, "I'd love that."

CHAPTER 91

Jonathan led Samantha out the door and asked clumsily, "What would you like to see?"

"I would like to see Papa's grave," Samantha replied.

"Of course," Jonathan said. "I'm parked around the corner. I'll be glad to drive you."

"Thank you. That would be nice."

Jonathan walked around the corner with Samantha before he worked up the courage to ask, "Did your husband...did Isaac come with you?"

Samantha walked a few steps before saying, "Isaac passed away last year. I would have thought Caroline told you?"

"I'm so sorry," Jonathan said.

Stepping to his car, Jonathan hurried to open the door for Samantha.

Once inside, Jonathan asked, "Why do you keep thinking Caroline has told me about you?"

"Caroline's the one that talked me into coming," Samantha explained. "She came to Michigan when Aunt Margaret passed away last winter. She suggested I come, and she's even written me reminders."

"I didn't know," Jonathan muttered.

"Would you mind driving by Silk Stocking Row?" Samantha smiled. "I'd love to see it once more."

"Of course," Jonathan said, as he wheeled the big car toward Eighth Street.

Samantha sat quietly and peered out the window as Jonathan drove by the houses on Silk Stocking Row.

"The Conklin house could use some paint," Samantha observed.

"These big houses are hard to maintain," Jonathan replied.

"Do you still live in the big house on the edge of the hill?" Samantha asked, as the car approached the road leading down the hill and toward the cemetery.

"No," Jonathan answered. "I sold it after mother died. Caroline and I live across town overlooking Indian Springs."

Samantha smiled and asked, "Do the raccoons keep you up at night?"

"Not so much," Jonathan smiled. "But I keep the pistol handy just in case."

"You never married, Jonathan?" Samantha asked.

"No," Jonathan replied. "I'd have been pretty hard to live with. Caroline would attest to that. Do you have children?"

"Two sons," Samantha beamed. "Al turned twenty-seven this past February. He was in the Navy during the war and runs the pharmacy for me now. Isaac was sick for several years, and I had to run the store during the war. I was happy to turn things over to Al."

"You became a pharmacist," Jonathan smiled. "I remember you telling me you wanted to do that years ago. I shouldn't be surprised."

Samantha shook her head and said, "It just worked out that way...mainly out of necessity. Isaac's been ill for several years and had a hard time working every day."

"How 'bout your other son?" he asked.

"Jonathan's twenty-five," Samantha replied. "He was wounded in Normandy during the war but made it home safe."

Jonathan did not say anything for a moment before asking, "Your son's name is Jonathan?"

"Yes," Samantha affirmed. "I wanted to name him after someone I admired."

"Isaac didn't mind?" Jonathan asked.

"Isaac was an extraordinary man," Samantha replied. "He was comfortable with who he was and didn't have a jealous bone in his body."

"I worried about my boys so much during the war," Samantha confessed. "It reminded me of times I worried about you when you were being a hero."

"I was no hero," Jonathan refuted.

"You always were to me," Samantha replied seriously. "You had the courage—the decency to stay away when I married. That made my life easier. I always thought it heroic."

Jonathan looked straight ahead and said, "It never seemed heroic to me—it—it just seemed—I don't know what it seemed like, so I got on with life."

Trying to change the subject, Samantha said, "My Jonathan is moving to Bartlesville and is married to a wonderful girl."

"Did he go to work for Phillips Petroleum?" Jonathan asked.

"Yes," Samantha replied. "How'd you know?"

"I didn't," Jonathan said. "I just know they're a big outfit always hiring smart people."

"My son Jonathan was an engineer before he was wounded," Samantha added. "I'm stopping in Bartlesville tomorrow to help find a place for him to live."

"You're leaving so soon?" a deflated Jonathan asked.

"I'm afraid so," Samantha replied. "The train leaves in the morning."

Disappointment flooded Jonathan's thoughts, as he had wanted to have more time to catch up on Samantha's life. They arrived at the cemetery with about an hour of daylight left, and Jonathan knew their few hours together were precious.

Samantha knelt at the grave of her father a few moments before looking around and saying, "It's so well kept."

"They do a nice job," Jonathan said, as he looked around at surrounding graves that were not as carefully mowed.

"You don't have to be so humble," Samantha smiled. "Caroline's told me how you come here and keep the grave up…I…I appreciate it."

"Caroline's talked a lot," Jonathan mused. "I admired your father."

"Papa thought a lot of you," Samantha replied.

Samantha looked around at the other markers before staring at Marcus Lutz's grave.

"It was a decent thing you did for him," Samantha said quietly. "I—Uncle Huck told me you gave him a job and helped take care of him."

"I figured I owed it to him," Jonathan replied. "He was a good worker…I learned he was a good man. We—"

Jonathan stopped talking and made Samantha asked, "What?"

"We talked about you quite a bit," Jonathan sheepishly admitted. "I guess that's something we both had in common—we both lost you."

The two old friends stood on the hill overlooking Chandler until the last rays of sunlight clung to the twilight sky. They talked about their lives and memories they shared from years before. After the initial awkwardness of their conversation, the two talked like old times—as if the years and the tragedy they shared had never happened.

After their long reunion, Jonathan said, "It was so good to see you again—I—I can't describe how good it's been for me—a surprise greater than I could have ever imagined!"

"You can thank Caroline," Samantha said. "I wouldn't have had the courage to come without her insistence. I wasn't sure you would want to see me after all these years. I'm—I'm glad I came."

"I can't get over how much you look like I remember," Jonathan said. "I've...I'm embarrassed to say, I've kept your photograph through the years...I...I was always afraid I might lose you in my memory like I—"

Jonathan stopped talking and Samantha sighed, "Like you lost me."

"Yes," Jonathan confessed.

Samantha watched the shadows of the evening fade into darkness as the lights from the houses on Silk Stocking Row twinkled like bright stars on the hillside before turning to Jonathan and saying, "You never...lost me. There was nothing you could have done, I believed a lie and married Isaac. He was a good man—"

"You don't need to explain," Jonathan interrupted. "You did the honorable thing. You were right that day at the train station—I wouldn't have expected anything different from you."

Samantha's forehead wrinkled as if she were in deep thought as she finally said, "The day you came to Holland—the day you walked into Margaret's backyard. I was telling her I had just found out I was pregnant...Isaac didn't even know."

"My timing must have been—terrible for you," Jonathan sighed.

"It wasn't your fault, Jonathan," Samantha assured. "It was never your fault."

Wanting to change the awkward conversation, Jonathan said, "Things have gone well for you though? I'm not surprised."

"They have," Samantha answered. "And you? I understand you've done quite well for yourself—and helped a lot of folks in doing it."

"I've done all right," Jonathan blushed. "I guess I figured it was time for a Kendall to give back for a change."

In a more serious tone, Samantha asked, "Why didn't you ever marry, Jonathan? I know you must have had opportunities."

Jonathan shrugged and said, "My standards were awfully high."

Samantha was quiet and looked like she would have liked to explore the subject further, but instead she leaned back and breathed in the warm air, as moonlight now replaced the twilight.

Watching Samantha, Jonathan said, "You look just like you did that night on the Conklin's roof...do you remember?"

"Some things you never forget," Samantha laughed, "but your eyes must be getting weak if you think I look anything like I did back then. I remember Woody ran off with Lou Berta and you got stuck with me. In fact, it was Caroline who talked me into coming to that party just like she did tonight."

"Caroline's always taking care of me," Jonathan smiled.

"And you take care of Caroline?" Samantha said. "That's what she's told me."

"Caroline and I take care of each other," Jonathan replied. "It's hard for a divorced woman. Caroline's better off than with that snake she married, but—that's in the past. It took Caroline a long time to get over David. Caroline's been seeing a widow man the past year—in fact it's Woody Carlson."

"Woody!" Samantha shrieked. "Does he still live in Chandler?"

"Still lives on Silk Stocking Row," Jonathan said. "Caroline tells me they're just friends, but...Woody's pretty spry, and I think there's something going on there, but Caroline would never admit to it."

The wrinkles of time were invisible to Jonathan as he continued to look into Samantha's eyes as if trying to conjure up the right thing to say.

In an uneven tone, he finally said, "I can't tell you how special it's been to spend this time with you tonight...after all these years. I...I've wanted to keep up with you but...I didn't think it would be appropriate."

Samantha quivered slightly as she replied, "You've never been anything but gallant, Jonathan. There are some people in your life that you feel lucky to have known—and you're one of those people to me."

"You must know you've been that person to me, too," Jonathan said.

Samantha smiled at Jonathan's gracious attention and said, "There's something I've wanted to give you."

"What is it?" Jonathan asked, as Samantha fumbled through her purse.

Handing Jonathan a piece of paper, Samantha said, "It's an address—mine. I thought—Well, Caroline thought you might want to write sometime."

Jonathan carefully took the piece of paper and studied the address before placing it carefully in his wallet.

Conjuring up fond memories of the letters they shared so many years before, Jonathan leaned over to hug Samantha gently and said with a tear in his eye, "There's nothing I would like more."

CHAPTER 92

THROUGH THE YEARS, JONATHAN realized it had not been the indiscretions of his father that ripped apart the Kendall family, but John Kendall's inability to admit to his mistakes. The guilt John Kendall tried to hide echoed through the years, hurting the family he had tried to protect with deceptions to guard his character.

Jonathan wrote Samantha for a time, but after a few months, he knew letters were not enough so he drove Route 66 through Chicago and to Michigan to see her. He worried Samantha would not be the woman he had conjured in his memory, but after the initial awkwardness of getting reacquainted, he knew Samantha had always been his true love. Jonathan never believed in happy endings, but his marriage to Samantha the following year proved that the ending of a story is never written, and life is what you choose to make of it.

Jonathan moved to Michigan to live with Samantha. He had believed as a young man that he would grow old with Samantha, but he was content to start their life together with the gray in their hair already visible. Jonathan missed Oklahoma, but he felt he had the most important part of his home with him—Samantha.

Jonathan and Samantha traveled back to their home state often to visit her son and grandchildren in Bartlesville. Augusta's husband had also moved to Bartlesville to work at a small college starting there in an old oil mansion. Jonathan always relished getting to see his nephews and his sister Augusta in Bartlesville, but he especially enjoyed watching his wife with her grandchildren.

Caroline married Woody Carlson after many years of friendship and moved into the house next door to where she was raised. Jonathan and Samantha came to stay with Caroline every May for alumni weekend to see friends and remember the past. They would visit the graves in Oak Hill Cemetery and spend time reflecting on the things that were and might have been. Jonathan and Samantha especially enjoyed long walks around the hill on the western edge of Chandler looking at the stately homes around the corner from the courthouse—remembering their lives from years ago on Silk Stocking Row.

THE END

Fact from Fiction

Guilt's Echo is a fictional story based on some real-life events around the time of World War 1.

Fiction

All major characters and personal events surrounding the characters are fictional as well as many of the places in the story.

Fact

Chandler, Oklahoma served as the training base for the Oklahoma National Guard before World War 1. Roy Hoffman, the highest-ranking officer in the National Guard, was instrumental in having an annual encampment at his one-time hometown. The Statistical House still stands in the town and remnants of the rifle range can still be seen west of Chandler.

Legendary lawman Bill Tilghman once lived in Chandler, Oklahoma and did have a house in the section of town known as Silk Stocking Row. James B. A. Robertson was another Chandler resident, who moved to Oklahoma City and became Oklahoma's 4th Governor. Roy Hoffman, Bill Tilghman, and James B. A. Robertson are all buried in the Oak Park Cemetery in Chandler.

Lee Gilstrap served as bugler and soldier for the 1st Oklahoma Infantry, which later became part of the 142nd Infantry of the 36th Division in Europe during World War 1. Lee Gilstrap captured several German prisoners and rescued scores of men from enemy fire and mustard gas by using his prisoners as litter bearers. Lee Gilstrap was award the Distinguished Service Cross for his actions.

Although not officially citizens and serving without the right to vote until 1924, over 10,000 Native Americans served in the United States military during World War 1. The 142nd Infantry used Choctaw soldiers primarily from Oklahoma as code talkers in the later stages of the war. According to tribal documents, there were 19 Choctaw code talkers: Tobias Frazier, Victor Brown, Joseph Oklahombi, Otis Leader, Ben Hampton, Albert Billy, Walter Veach, Ben Carterby, James Edwards, Solomon Louis, Peter Maytubby, Mitchell Bobb, Calvin Wilson, Jeff Nelson, Joseph Davenport, George Davenport, Noel Johnson, Billy Schlicht, and Robert Taylor.

According to Choctaw historians, Pushmataha, a Choctaw chief who died in 1827, predicted the "Choctaw war cry" would be heard in foreign lands. Pushmataha had no idea how right he would be.

If you like this Bob Perry story, look for:

The Broken Statue

Mimosa Lane

Brothers of the Cross Timber

The Nephilim Code

Non-Fiction books include:

Dynamic Thinking:
   Models for Organizational Leadership

Spiritual Renewal:
   Transforming the Mind

www.bobp.biz

Made in the USA
Charleston, SC
20 July 2010